JED THOUGHT HE WOULD NEVER FORGET LOUISA . . . UNTIL HE MET THE ARIKARA INDIAN MAIDEN . . .

"You are haughty," Sunblossom whispered, feeling herself in a dream. How did he come to be so close to her?

"So I have been told." Jed's voice was powerful, proud. "I answer that I have paid the price—and I have earned what I will enjoy."

Before Sunblossom could utter a sound, let alone a scream, Jed gathered her in his arms and kissed her. His lips thrilled her, just as his embrace set her pulse racing. She nearly relented, but something inside her screamed, *No! I am Arikara!*

She was fast, but Jed's response was faster. His hand snapped out, almost too quick to see, freezing her own in midair, as the knife she held flashed silver in the moonlight, shiny death.

"I said my life was no easy prize to take," he breathed, still holding her close. "But I give it to you."

Deliberately, he let go of her hand. The princess slowly brought the blade up to his throat. She used the flat of it to raise his chin, guiding his head first one way and then the other. His handsome face held no fear or worry. She could not stop the half-smile that grew in her heart and on her lips as Jed stood there so brave and somber, ready to pay the penalty for the stolen kiss.

JED SMITH

FREEDOM RIVER

Fred Lawrence

A Dell/Standish Book

Published by
Miles Standish Press, Inc.
37 West Avenue
Wayne, Pennsylvania 19087

Dell ® TM 681510, Dell Publishing Co., Inc.

ISBN: 0-440-04214-3

Printed in the United States of America

First printing—July 1981

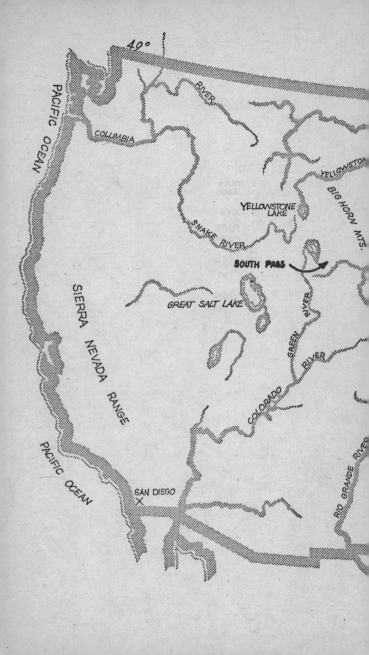

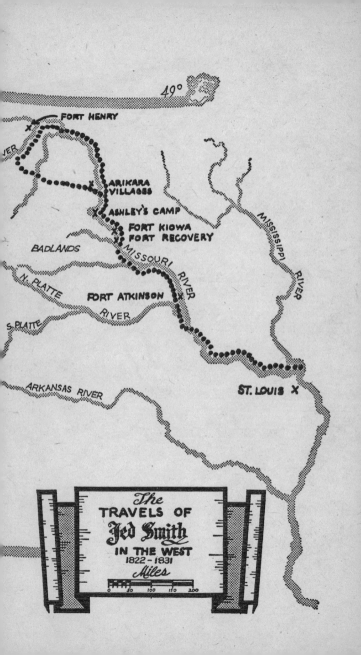

49°

FORT HENRY

ARIKARA
VILLAGES

ASHLEY'S CAMP

FORT KIOWA
FORT RECOVERY

BADLANDS

MISSOURI RIVER

MISSISSIPPI RIVER

N. PLATTE

FORT ATKINSON

RIVER

S. PLATTE

ARKANSAS RIVER

ST. LOUIS X

The
TRAVELS OF
Jed Smith
IN THE WEST
1822 - 1831
Miles

0   50   100   150   200

FOR

Stephen Ostrow
  Who has their spirit

PART ONE

THE RIVER

Chapter 1

The stag froze. A moment before, it had been unconcernedly browsing the pale green, tender shoots at the base of a cottonwood. Now the stag had become a statue, a motionless, red-brown form five feet high at the shoulder, its antlers thrusting into the air like the branches of a tree.

There was only one tiny movement: the quivering of its nostrils as it searched the breeze for some scent to explain the faint *click* it had heard. The hazy glow that was the stag's consciousness did not have the power of distinction, but a man might have wondered if the sound had been made by a woodpecker, or a twig snapped by a wild hog, or something *metallic*—

The stag never heard the explosion. The half-ounce lead slug smashed into its neck, killing it instantly. The stag crashed to the ground, its nerve-dead hind legs gave one last feeble kick, and then all was again still.

"You'll go nowhere," the tall, black-haired, blue-eyed young man said, and bent to the job of reloading his Hawkens rifle. Two single-shot pistols hung from his belt, but wiser, more experienced hands had long ago drilled into the mind of twenty-three-year-old Jedediah Strong Smith that a fellow who wanted to live never went anywhere without a loaded Hawkens. Its big punch was the only thing likely to stop an angry grizzly with killing on its mind.

Rifle at the ready, Jed stepped from his place of concealment in the wild grapevines. He swore softly as his black, greasy, fringed buckskin shirt caught on a nettle.

Christ's blood! This land was so different from the tranquil woods back East. Back home. On either side of the river, tangled brush with spurs and thorns as keen as a scalping blade waited to tear at a man's clothing and skin as he scrambled to climb across fallen trees piled as high as his chest.

And the heat! Jed shook his head, then rubbed the stinging sweat from his eyes. Here it was only early May, and already he began and ended the day bathed in his own wet stickiness that bound the woodticks and swarming mosquitos to his flesh.

Jed pulled out his Bowie knife and began to prepare the stag's carcass. As he worked he stopped often to look and listen, in case the smell of spilled blood attracted some predator.

But there was only the crash and roar of the Missouri River, and the squeal of the huge driftwood logs as the current ground them down to splinters on their long journey to the sea. Jed had grown to like the river's sounds during his long days and nights alone along its banks. Other hands had said that the water's thunder and the flotsam's groans had brought them shuddering memories of the recent war with the British. Jed had been too young to take part in that conflict; perhaps that was why the river's night sounds held no terror for him. He slept to its noise the way a babe sleeps to his mother's lullaby.

In any event, Jed thought, as he continued his

work over the stag, the life song of the big Missouri, winding just out of sight through the grove of cotton-woods was far preferable to the stink and racket of St. Louis.

Just a few months shy of a year ago, Jed had arrived to tread the narrow, muddy streets of St. Louis's waterfront, looking for something still vague and undefined in his mind—for an *opportunity*.

He had taken a room in a shabby boarding house where a witch of a landlady had warned him against liquor or women in the room on pain of eviction. The prohibitions did not worry him. He never drank, and a woman . . . well, even had he desired one, which he hadn't, the experience would have been far too painful a reminder of what he had left behind at home, just this side of the New York border, in Erie County, Pennsylvania.

He had spent a week wandering the bustling city perched upon a hillside, just a few miles below where the Mississippi joined the Missouri River. Merchants, dandies, bankers and ladies in silks and velvets shared the streets with rugged mountain men dressed in leather. Gangs of keelboat men, exhausted from their tasks of poling the barges laden with furs and supplies on the waterway of this frontier center of the pelt trade, strolled four abreast along the boardwalks. Drunk, giddy with relief that their work was momentarily done, the boatmen would knock any man from their path, sending them into the mud along the elevated walkway.

Jed had heard shots as he explored the waterfront and had seen men staggering, with blood flowing from between their fingers as they clutched at bullet and knife wounds. He'd seen whores scream with laughter as one of their own was flung from a second-story window by a drunken trapper. He'd been amazed to see

black men who spoke French instead of English, and
homes in the more genteel section on the hill above
made entirely out of red brick, but most of all, to see
so many young men like himself, looking for a new life
"out West," and so many employers willing to give it
to them.

The fur trade, it seemed, had room for everyone.

It was the February 16, 1822 edition of the *St.
Louis Trumpet* that turned out to hold the key to Jed's
fate.

He had spent the morning listening to the offers of
the various men trying to put together trapping expeditions to the upper waters of the Missouri. Tempting as
the offers were, Jed felt he should hold out for more
than a mere wage. To his thinking, the trappers were
the lifeblood of any such endeavor. It was their hard
work which would garner the pelts, their lives that
would be lost due to attack from wild animals and Indians.

To a few prospective employers Jed had tenta-
tively mumbled his ideas about "a partnership." All
had laughed and immediately shown him to the door.

Young Jed Smith was feeling failure as he wandered the streets, eventually finding himself back at the
waterfront. As usual, the docks were crowded with
laughing and swearing men loading and unloading
food, lumber, hardware, ammunition, cloth, and of
course, the precious resource on which the economy
was based, bales of furs. All the activity just made Jed
feel more alone. The garbage floating in the water
around the dock's pilings depressed him even more.
How he longed to be out in the new country, where all
was fresh and clean! In the new country to the West a
man could have ideas as tall as the mountains, as wide
and clear as the sky—

"No, please!"

Jed could hardly see the slight, middle-aged man dressed in an ill-cut, impractical flannel merchant's suit squeezed between three broad-shouldered, muscular men.

"My hat! Damn you, you bullies!"

"Bullies! Aye, lads! Did you hear him!" The largest of the three laughed as he took several paces back and flung the little man's hat to one of his companions, who caught it and kept the game going. The little man ran helplessly among them, squawking like an outraged bantam rooster.

The three men, dressed in the style of riverboat men, wore collarless, long-sleeved shirts, short, baggy trousers held up by suspenders, and heavy, thick-soled, laced boots. The largest of the trio, obviously the ringleader, had a pistol tucked into his waistband. One of the riverboat men stuck out his foot, and the little merchant tripped and fell to the ground, his shouts of outrage turning to a cry of pain.

"Here now," Jed heard himself say. "Leave him alone."

All three turned to face Jed while the merchant sat cradling his shin. The largest now held the little man's hat. A broken-toothed grin spread across his face, which was burnished mahogany by the years spent in the sun on the river. Slowly he closed his huge ham of a fist around the hat, then tossed the crumpled mass of felt into the water.

"All right then. It's over," said one of the three, a balding, blond man who clearly had no stomach for further teasing of the little merchant.

"It's over when I says so," the leader growled. He ran his hand over his slicked-back, dark hair, and took a menacing step toward Jed.

"Careful now, Mike," called the last of the three, a man with a burn scar running down one cheek, along his neck, and down out of sight beneath his shirt. "It's the slammer for sure if the constable nabs us again."

Mike, it seemed, was taking no notice of the warning for he advanced upon Jed. Mike was slightly taller than Jed, who stood at six-feet two-inches, and seemed about twenty-five pounds heavier than Jed's own one hundred and eighty. But a lot of that weight advantage seemed to be centered in the lout's big belly.

Jed was confident that he could give the bully a good fight. What worried him was the remark about the constable. During his week in the city, he had seen ample examples of the efficiency of St. Louis's law enforcement organization. Time in jail for brawling was not likely to impress any prospective employer.

"All right," Jed smiled. "It looks like neither of us needs the trouble."

"Is that right now, boy? It strikes me you should have thought of that before you butted in." Out of the corner of his eye Mike saw the little merchant climb to his feet and try to run away. "Grab that wee dandy!" he ordered his cronies. "After I bust this lad's face, I intend to toss that little varmint into the drink!"

Mike moved in fast, his big hands held out in front of him like the grappling hooks the dockhands used to snag keelboats.

Jed bounced lightly on the balls of his feet. His mind was clear, ready for the charge. Now the only worry he had was for his linen pants and shirt. They were the only decent clothes he had in which to meet prospective employers.

Jed tried to deflect his opponent's arms, but the man's incredible strength washed over him like a wave. Before Jed knew quite what had happened, he was high in the air, the breath being forced out of his lungs by Mike's powerful bear hug squeezing his ribs.

Jed had had more than his share of scrapes back

home. As his vision began to grow dark, he reached down, grabbed his opponent's ears and twisted with all his might.

The big man howled and dropped Jed to the ground. But large as he was, he was also fast. Before Jed could twist away, Mike's big hands were scuttling like wharf rats up around Jed's neck.

As Mike's fingers closed around his throat, Jed brought his elbows up, then down, smashing into the riverboat man's forearms and breaking his grip. The big man's look of amazement turned into a grimace of anguish as Jed's right fist drove deep into his belly, while his left crossed over to connect with the tip of the man's jaw.

Jed stepped back as his opponent fell to his knees, huffing and shaking his head like a poleaxed steer.

"Finish the brute!" called the merchant.

Jed glanced over to where the little man was being held captive by the two other riverboat men. Each had one of the merchant's scrawny arms in his grip. The little fellow was between them, his patent-leather shod feet barely grazing the ground.

"Let him go," Jed said wearily.

"I'll kill you!" Mike roared as he launched himself at Jed.

Mike's cronies gulped as Jed's knee slammed up against their leader's chin. The sharp crack of his lower jaw driven against his upper sounded like ice breaking up during the river's spring thaw.

Jed stepped aside as Mike plowed past him to come to rest on his stomach. A moan came from the big man as he lay there.

"Now I said let him go," Jed muttered, turning toward the other two.

The man with the burn scar suddenly shouted, "Oh God, Mike! No!"

Jed whirled.

His opponent had flipped over onto his back and propped himself up on one elbow. The pistol that had been in his belt was now out and pointed at Jed, its hammer snapped back into firing position.

Jed dove to one side as the pistol roared, its sharp report echoing off the high wooden walls of the warehouses surrounding them.

"Oh Lord! I'm murdered!" screeched the merchant. His two captors stared in horror at the man sagging between them. The right shoulder of his flannel suit was now stained a dark, wet crimson.

A small crowd had gathered to watch the fist fight, but all activity had stopped at the sound of the shot. As Jed looked around, he found himself in the center of an ever increasing mob. Thankfully, all were pointing their fingers toward the man with the gun, who sprang to his feet and bolted away to lose himself in the crowd. At their leader's cue, the other two riverboat men dashed away, letting the merchant slump to the ground.

Jed went to the wounded man and gently folded back the blood-soaked lapel of his coat. The pistol ball had entered high, missing the fellow's collarbone. Considering what could have been, Jed counted the hapless merchant lucky.

"You'll be all right," he soothed. "It's a minor wound."

"What happened?" asked a low, calm voice.

Jed looked up from his kneeling position to take in the blue trousers and tunic, and finally, the whiskered face of a constable. For the first time since coming to the merchant's rescue Jed's heart began to pound in fear. Taking a deep breath, he told his story to the police officer. The merchant and several onlookers confirmed everything.

"Can this one walk?" the constable asked, looking at Jed but gesturing at the wounded merchant.

"Yes I can," the little man huffed. "And I can talk as well."

"Come along then," the constable sighed. "We'll get you to a doctor."

The officer helped the wounded man to his feet. When the fellow suddenly sagged, the constable called for volunteers to help carry him to a nearby doctor. A couple of dock workers stepped forward and slipped the man onto a long, wide board which became a makeshift stretcher.

All around the crowd dispersed. Jed watched the man being carried away, the constable walking alongside the stretcher.

"He never even thanked me," Jed muttered to himself, and then he began to laugh. "Almost get myself killed and the little twerp . . ."

He stopped. The bold headlines of the folded newspaper lying on the ground where the man had fallen caught his eye. Must have fallen out of his pocket, Jed thought. He picked the paper up and read the story. Nodding to himself, Jed then set out at a determined pace, leaving behind him the cries and curses of the men moving their heavy burdens along the wharf.

General William H. Ashley, retired leader of the territorial militia, present lieutenant governor of the great state of Missouri, stared across the expanse of his polished oak desk at the young man standing self-consciously before him. He looked about ready to burst out of his old but clean linen suit. Long ago Ashley had learned that being poor was no crime.

"I'm sorry if my clothes are a bit dirty, sir," Jed

began, as if he had read the other man's mind. "You see, at the docks I—"

"Don't mind a boy being poor," the General cut him off sharply. "It's those who don't want to work to change their station in life who turn my stomach, Mr. . . . uh, Strong, is it?"

"No, sir. It's Smith. My name is Jedediah Strong Smith," Jed corrected, and then added another "sir," for good measure, hoping it didn't sound too obviously like the afterthought it was.

The thin, gray-haired, hawk-nosed man leaned back in his chair, nodding and smiling, as if somebody had just whispered something amusing in his ear. Jed figured General Ashley to be in his fifties, but he wasn't sure. The general's salt and pepper goatee could be adding false years to his age. Certainly the General's bright green eyes testified to Ashley's vigor, and his thick, ropey forearms, visible beneath his rolled-up sleeves, along with his gnarled hands, made it quite clear that the man had not spent his entire life behind his expensive desk.

"How'd you find out about our little business undertaking?" Ashley inquired suddenly, snapping forward in his chair and fixing Jed with a stare. "Who talked, eh? Come on lad, *someone* had to spill the beans."

"No, sir," Jed stuttered. "I—"

"Then how'd you find out? We've not had the time to hire the criers to announce the expedition—"

"I read about it, sir."

Ashley stopped in his tracks. "Read? You can *read*, boy?"

"Yes." Jed tugged the rolled-up newspaper out of his back pocket. "I read all about you and Mr. Henry in the *Trumpet*."

"I don't believe it," Ashley remarked simply.

"Read for me now. From that fish wrapper you've got there."

Jed stared at the man behind the desk, then cleared his throat and began. " 'Latest Entry In Fur Trade Race. The *Trumpet* has learned that the renowned General Ashley—' " Jed stopped and looked up, blushing.

"Panderers," Ashley said mildly. "Well, go on, boy. You're doing fine. Skip all that about me, and get to the meat of it."

" '—along with the retired Major Andrew Henry, intends to mount a fur trapping expedition to ascend the Missouri River to its source. Over one hundred men will be hired, to remain in the employ of Ashley-Henry for one to three years. One problem marring the bright future of the endeavor is the question of where to find the men. Never has St. Louis seen such a brisk competition for qualified men to brave an uncivilized region said to possess wealth not seen by mortals since the days of the fabled Incan empire . . .' "

"Stop!" Ashley commanded. "Lord above! What confounded drivel they're printing these days. . . ." He trailed off to gaze at Jed. "But you can *read*, boy. How'd you come by it?"

"And I can write, as well," Jed beamed. "And do my higher sums, such as multiplication and division. And I also know my history. For example," he tapped the newspaper and continued to ramble on, "the Incas were a magical race who lived in Peru . . ."

"Enough, boy!" Ashley thundered. "I'm not here to garner your entrance to Harvard!"

"No, sir," Jed mumbled, now quite embarrassed. "Of course not, sir. You've asked how I was taught. It was by a friend of my father. A kind and fine old doctor who lived near my family in Pennsylvania, which is where I grew up. My father was a farmer, but I didn't take to that calling."

"Did your father mind your leaving home?" Ashley asked.

"No, sir, he had my brothers." Jed smiled shyly. "My father always said that he'd never seen a lad cut out for two such dissimilar pursuits as hunting and book learning. I left with his blessings and his hopes that I accomplish big things."

"I agree with your father that the ability to read and write is a rare thing in a lad of your build," Ashley nodded. "There are many with such skills in St. Louis, but they're all pale, sickly specimens. They've no aptitude for the rigorous life. The river would break them. But you're quite strong enough. And your skills of the mind impress me. You say you're a good shot as well?"

"I never miss," Jed proudly announced. "Just give me a try on that point is all I ask."

Ashley looked him up and down for a long minute, and then remarked shrewdly, "Well then. Tell me this boy, why is it you've not been snapped up by my competitors? They've all been recruiting for weeks."

Jed looked down at his boots. The old fox had trapped him! He'd wanted to make his pitch his own way, but now he'd have to come out with it.

"Well?" Ashley scowled. "I'm waiting."

"It's like this, sir," Jed began, mumbling.

"Speak up!" Ashley ordered, his fingers tapping the top of his desk impatiently. "I've not got all day."

"It's like this, sir," Jed began again in a clear, loud voice. "I won't work for a wage. I've got a plan, and if you'll hear me out, I believe you'll see that it's the way to get the drop on all your rivals. You'll have recruited the cream of the crop of qualified men." Jed took a deep breath and stumbled on, not daring to look the General in the eye, but taking his silence as a sign of permission to continue. "My plan goes like this. You hire the clerks and boatmen you need in the usual way, pay the likes of them a fit and usual wage. But your hunters and trappers, sir, they're to get no wage, but only what it costs to outfit them with weapons, equipment and supplies for the expedition. At the end of the trapping season each year the men who actually gathered the pelts should be paid one half the profits their individual contribution of furs brings here in St. Louis."

"I see," Ashley said. "If you garnered a thousand dollars' worth of skins, you'd get five hundred when the time came to reckon up. Your companion might have brought in two thousand dollars' worth, so he'd get one thousand."

"Yes, sir," Jed agreed, daring to look up, at last. To his amazement, the General seemed to be calmly pondering his suggestion.

"But without paying a regular wage, I'd have no control over my men. No hold with which to make them follow orders. . . ."

"Begging your pardon, sir," Jed said. "But you can't buy a man's courage or bravery, or even obedience, once the going gets rough. My proposal would have men flocking to your door. You could pick the wheat and discard the chaff. A good man would struggle hard for you, because at the same time he'd be struggling to protect his share."

"This will cost the expedition much more, young fellow—"

"Begging your pardon, sir," Jed interrupted, "but the expedition will get more."

"Of course the expedition will have to take its costs off the top of the profits," Ashley murmured, keeping his eyes on Jed's. Amazing, Ashley thought.

The boy had started out staring at the floor, but now his clear, blue eyes were fixed with determination.

"That would have to be negotiated, sir," Jed advised respectfully.

"Why you impertinent young pup!" Ashley began, but he couldn't keep the ruse going. He found himself laughing. "Aye! And I know just who'd be doing the negotiating for the rest of the hunter-trappers, all of whom think a book's only good for kindling to start a fire, that writing paper's useful for blowing their noses, and a pen's main function is to clean out their ears! Aye, lad! Skin me alive for being a fool, but I like it! I like your plan. It'll make the other companies see red at first, but later they'll turn green when all the old hands line up at the Ashley-Henry door." The General was silent a moment as he regarded Jed. "All right, then!" He slammed his palm down on the desk. "We'll do it! And may I trust that you'll be the first man hired under such an arrangement?"

"Thank you, sir!" Jed crowed exultantly. "You won't regret your decision!" He stepped forward to shake Ashley's hand.

"There's just one final point to be settled," the General muttered, glowering at Jed. "You've no crimes in your past, have you, boy? You didn't leave your Pennsylvania one step ahead of the law, now, did you?" Ashley's glare bored into Jed.

"Why, no sir."

"Once we leave St. Louis we leave the law behind, but I want no criminals on this expedition. A little roughhousing is one thing, but evil acts of criminals are entirely another!"

"Sir, I left Pennsylvania for . . . personal, intimate reasons." Jed blushed.

Ashley thought that over and then smiled, his features softening. "A girl? Is that it, eh?"

"Sir," Jed blushed, feeling the blood course hot and strong beneath his cheeks. "Please, I'd rather not. . ."

"All right, then," Ashley replied gruffly. "I don't want to pry. I was young once too." He chuckled, then returned to business. "Now then, Jed, I've yet to get my clerks, and there's some men out back sleeping in my yard who mean to sign on as experienced keelboat men as well as apprentice trappers. Their knowledge of the former more than makes up for their ignorance about the latter. I mean to send them downriver immediately to see about the condition of a keelboat I've located. If you would, I'd like you to write down their particulars and get them off on their journey."

"Yes, sir."

"By the way," Ashley gestured complacently, "since clerkly duties are above and beyond what your normal duties would normally be, I feel obliged to pay you a bit right now."

"Thank you again, General," Jed grinned. "I've about run through my initial stake, so the money will come in handy."

"Thought so," Ashley remarked. "Here's my account book and a pen. Go see to those fellows, fill in your own particulars, and then come see me when you're through."

Jed left the room and headed down a flight of stairs, through the kitchen, and out the back door into the spacious yard of the General's residence. As he went, he let his mind fill with exuberant visions of a rich, fabulous future. He'd someday be as important as General Ashley. This was an omen! But unlike the General, he'd never plant himself behind an oaken desk. He meant to be a mountain man whose empire would stretch from one horizon of the wilderness to the other.

Jed stopped short, all visions of the future flying from his head like pheasants from a blind when the hunter's first shot is fired. There, lazing about the General's yard, were the three bullies Jed had just done battle with that morning!

"Oh no!" cried the one with the burn mark. "Mikey! We're doomed!"

Mike leapt to his feet, his long, tanned face paling as if he were seeing a ghost. "What be you doin' here?"

"I work for General Ashley," Jed explained, not without a certain amount of gleeful malice. "He asked me to fill in the particulars about you gents." Jed held out the account book. "But looks like I've got plenty to tell him before you even open your mouths."

"Billy was right then," moaned the balding blond one. "Now we'll rot in prison!"

"Hold quiet a moment, lads," Mike ordered. He approached Jed slowly, his big hands held out in supplication. "If you rat on us, uh . . . what be your name?"

"Jed."

"Jed, if you rat on us—"

"Make that Mr. Smith."

"Mr. Smith, then," the big man corrected himself, breathing deeply to keep control. "If you tell the General about our, uh, misadventure, this morning, we'll be locked up for sure."

"You shot an innocent man this morning," Jed broke in. "While you were aiming at me, I might add."

"Aye, and it was a foolish thing to have done, I admit that. I swear we only meant to have some fun with the little monkey, and it got a wee bit out of hand, that's all. But nobody got kilt, right? Right?" He waited for Jed to agree.

"Yes. By the way, where is that pistol of yours?" Jed asked, examining the man's empty belt.

"I tossed it into the drink," he replied sheepishly. "Guns and me don't seem to get along."

"Please, sir," Bill, the burn-marked one chimed in. "We'll never do it again. Don't rat on us, we only want to make a fresh start of it, in the wilderness."

"And in that way, stay out of jail," Jed pointedly added.

"And what's wrong with that," Mike argued, the pleading note gone from his voice. "Lad, have you ever been in a cell? Do you know what it's like to never see the sun or the blue sky? To sit in your own filth in the dark, with the four walls crowding in on ye? To be taunted by guards, bitten by fleas, tormented by rats and by the unbearable loss of your most precious possession—your personal freedom?"

Jed turned away, his brow knit in confusion as he pondered what Mike had said. Mike, his grey eyes glinting, winked at his two companions.

Ashley had said roughhousing was acceptable, Jed mused. Perhaps that's all these men were: rogues out to have a good time who occasionally got a bit carried away. But the one named Mike shot at you. True, but he's thrown his pistol away, and he seems truly sorry. The bottom line of it was that Jed, who longed for the wide open spaces and freedom of the wilderness, simply didn't have the heart to condemn any man to the nightmare horrors of a prison cell. It just wasn't the kind of thing a wilderness man—or one who longed to be one—did to a fellow.

"All right, then," Jed began sternly. "We'll let bygones be bygones. Now give me your particulars and then get the hell out of St. Louis on your commission for the General, before the constables catch up with you and we all have hell to pay."

"Aye, lad," Mike laughed. "We'll never forget you for this."

"Never mind," Jed blushed. "You," he said, pointing at the scarred man, "what's your name?"

"Bill Carpenter," he answered promptly.

"And you," Jed asked, pointing to the balding man.

"Tom Talbot."

Before Jed could ask, the big man burst into speech. "And you, Jed Smith, have earned the lasting friendship and eternal gratitude of Mike Fink, half horse, half alligator and king of the riverboat men!"

Having finished butchering the stag's carcass, Jed loaded the haunches of meat onto his back, stuck his rifle through his belt, and labored through the underbrush to the bank of the river. It was here that Ashley's keelboat, the *Yellowstone Packet*, would pick him up.

As Jed waited he listened to the music of the birds, felt the honest ache of hard-used muscles. He'd put on ten pounds since leaving St. Louis on the expedition, and none of those pounds was fat.

He looked out at the swiftly moving, mud-yellow waters, and up to the trees and the sky. Yellow water, bright green foliage, clear blue sky—all colors seemed preternaturally brilliant out here in the clean air untainted by the myriad woodfires of cities and towns like St. Louis.

In all, Jed had never in his life been happier than he was now. He was a trapper for the Ashley-Henry expedition. He was born to this land, and the land beyond—he knew that now. Before he had only dreamed as much.

Only one thing marred his happiness, darkened his exuberance the way a cloud cutting across the sun darkens the day. It was an innocent enough looking sheet of stationery, folded in quarters, wrapped in the thinnest doeskin and tucked beneath his shirt, against his heart.

It was this letter that had set him on the path which had led to General Ashley's door, and the wilderness. He knew that he would tug the scrap of paper out and read it again and again, that even if he didn't he would relive the letter at night, in his dreams.

The hollow pain suddenly returned. It was a surging, overwhelming agony, as intense as it had been a year ago, when he'd been handed the letter. Of all the things the Lord had put in the world, things of fur and tooth and claw, of all the bad men and bad lands, nothing terrified Jedediah as much as that lingering pain, and the knowledge that though he was a full-grown, strong, young man, he was helpless to heal his own broken heart.

Frowning, Jed banished the nagging, dismal thoughts from his mind as the *Yellowstone Packet*, the first of Ashley's two craft, rounded a bend in the river and came into view. He held one of his pistols high in the air and fired a signal blast. An answering shot from the deck of the low, squat keelboat clapped and echoed across the water.

His many days of being a solitary hunter were over for now, Jed guessed. In a few days they would reach Fort Atkinson, the last outpost of military authority. Soon after that, they would be in hostile Indian territory.

Chapter 2

Dawn broke blue-grey, and the pastel-banded sky slowly grew lighter, to the accompaniment of the ever-present sounds of rushing water, and the sudden, cheerful greeting of the new day by the birds that made the timber stands on either riverbank their home. Jed watched the sun climb, filtered to a small, pink rosette by the morning mists.

The keelboat crew, led by Mike Fink, was already at work. But Jed and the rest of the hunter-trappers, who had no part to play in the daily routine of the ship, stayed wrapped in their warm Hudson's Bay Point blankets long into the morning. Most of the hunter-trappers had slept outside, on the roof of the seventy-five-foot-long, twenty-foot-wide craft, which looked like nothing more than a barge with an enclosed, rectangular box of almost the same dimensions plopped on top of it. The keelboat crew, known as voyageurs, made their beds in the dank, stale, but sheltered-from-the-elements confines of the boat's hold and cargo box interior.

"Damn you, you river scum!" Mike Fink shouted as he stalked the width of the boat's front platform. "Raise your poles! I'll not tell you all again!"

Jed watched the twenty voyageurs, the crew hired to navigate the keelboat, ten on each side of the boat, scurry from the vessel's stern to its bow, along the narrow, cleated catwalks which stretched along each side. The voyageurs positioned themselves to thrust their long, ash-hewn poles into the river bottom. At Fink's command of "Lower the poles!" they did just that, groaning and wheezing as they pushed down hard and walked in place as the craft passed along under their feet. In this way, the boat was literally levered up the river. When the front man reached the stern, Fink yelled "Raise the poles!" and the crewmen scurried forward to repeat their arduous task.

"Damn! A man can't get no proper rest on this rats' nest, I reckon," a hoarse voice grumbled.

Jed looked over at what seemed to be a one-man tepee of blankets, complete with a firehole from which wafted a plume of sour-smelling pipe tobacco smoke. Hiram Angus poked his head out of the blanket heap, his corncob pipe clenched in his teeth.

"Watch 'em, Jed!" Hiram crackled, his brown, leathery face splitting into a grin. "Fink runs 'em like a cat runs mice."

Jed smiled to himself from his comfortable vantage point. His blankets were warm, and his bed, formed from artfully arranged bolts of cloth, was soft and relaxing. Tough as the life of a hunter-trapper was, it struck Jed as infinitely preferable to the slave labor endured by the keelboat voyageurs. It was a view shared by all the trappers, and, like Hiram, they all enjoyed mocking the boatmen. Jed didn't see the point of taunting men breaking their backs for the expedition, but it was important that he fit in with experienced mountain men like Hiram Angus, and so he kept his opinions to himself.

Hiram looked as old as the mountains he'd conquered when Jed was just a baby. He was a small man, and the years had bent and twisted him the way the wind off the prairie shapes a cottonwood, but every ounce of his diminutive frame was wiry muscle. He had a bald, walnut-brown dome of a skull fringed with white, woolly hair, a nose that had been smashed flat in some long-forgotten tavern melee, and eyes of the palest blue, still sharp enough to spy what younger men would invariably miss.

"Whenh!" Hiram's goose honk filled the air as he loudly blew his nose into his fingers and kicked himself free of his blankets. "Hell, boy—wait 'til we trade these rags and doodads for buffalo robes," he said, his gesture taking in the holds of the keelboat. "Then we'll sleep like we're back in our blessed mama's arms. For sure!"

The bolts of calico and flannel cloth, colored blue and scarlet, the blankets, pots and pans, hand mirrors, trinkets of cheap metals and beads, needles and thread, knives for skinning and butchering, and assorted odds and ends, would all be traded to the Indians of the Missouri Territory for horses and buffalo robes. The robes were accepted only to sweeten the deal for the chiefs, since the men of the expedition could take all the buffalo, or "pte," they wanted once they reached the herds' grazing land.

The trade goods, the currency of the expedition, were all stored in the hold of the keelboat, with the exception of the blankets and cloth, which the men were temporarily using for bedding. The supplies for the men, the powder and ball, spare weapons, beaver traps, and foodstuffs—sugar, coffee, salt and flour—were kept in the drier cargo box, upon which Jed, Hiram and the other trappers were now lying.

"Raise the poles!" Mike Fink repeated in his

endless litany of commands. "Watch it now, lads. We're coming to some shoals."

General Ashley had made Fink the captain—or in keelboat lingo, the "patron"—of the *Yellowstone Packet*, and had privately expressed to Jed that he wished he could have found a good patron for his second boat, the *Rocky Mountains*, trailing a dozen yards behind. Jed's scheme of splitting the profits had indeed supplied Ashley with the best of the available hunter-trappers, but keelboat men were in short supply due to the competition among the fur companies. Ashley had been forced to scour the grog shops and whorehouses of St. Louis to make up two full crews. As it was, the patron of the *Rocky Mountains* was a broken-down old sailor who followed Fink's directives shouted across the water.

"Here, boy," Hiram tossed a chunk of roasted venison—the remains of last night's supper—to Jed as the smell of coffee being brewed filled the air. As Hiram chewed on his breakfast, he squinted up at the late September sky. "This hoss does hope Henry's boys has built us a nice enough lean-to for the winter."

Major Henry, Ashley's partner in the expedition, had left St. Louis a month earlier with a complement of sixty men. The plan was for them to build a combination post and fort at the mouth of the Yellowstone River, up where, by all accounts, the mountains began.

"If he hasn't, won't one of the other fur companies with posts along the Missouri give us shelter?" Jed asked.

"Hell, boy! You've got the makings of a mountain man, but a lot to learn about human nature," Hiram laughed, shaking his head. "They'd give us shelter for sure, but not as Ashley-Henry men. Ya see, the Missouri Fur Company has got a place called Fort Recovery up yonder on the Freedom River," he continued, using the wilderness man's name for the Missouri. "Fella named Pilcher, a good hoss, is their chief. Fault is, Pilcher needs boys like us hisself. Same goes for a mean old cuss goes by the name of Cayewa. He's a Frenchie, heads up the Frenchie Fur Company, and they's got a fort on the Freedom as well. Young Cayewa now, he'd just as soon gut-shoot us as let us get to the beaver afore he does."

"So they'd both offer us shelter, but we'd have to sign on with them," Jed said slowly. "Desert the General."

"That's it, Jed," Hiram agreed. "And a lot of these boys would go if that was the only way they could keep from being frozen come the snow." He puffed on his pipe to get it going as he held a glowing ember from one of the cook-fires to the bowl. "I heard the Brits are trying to reach the beavers by a different route. They're traveling the Mississippi to the St. Peters river."

"Christ! We can't let the foreigners beat us to it," Jed scowled.

"Right, boy. The Missouri Fur Company is American, but they ain't got the men to put up a fight. It's up to us two-hundred-odd boys that Mr. Henry and Mr. Ashley has got. These United States are dependin' on us fetching the beaver pelts from the upper waters before any damned foreigners!"

It was around noon that calamity struck. Jed and the others were watching as the keelboat crews cordelled. The boats had several means of propulsion, but each depended on an exacting set of circumstances. Each boat had a sail to use when the wind was right, which was almost never on this twisting river. Also, there were six pairs of oars which poked from the forward section of the cargo box, but to use them required deeper water than they now had. Then there was the dreaded method of poling, and there was the most common method of cordelling.

The cordelle was a long, stout rope that ran from the keelboat to voyageurs grouped on the riverbank. The men simply towed the boat upstream, scrabbling through the muck and marsh, gaining inches at the expense of their backs. For all that, the voyageurs much preferred cordelling to poling. Fink had been forced to order poling through most of that morning because the shoreline was too tangled with brush and too muddy to give his men proper footing.

Now the voyageurs were straining, but happy. They sang filthy verses to familiar songs as they towed their boats. Fink was ashore as well, often waist deep in the cold rushing water as he cajoled and coddled his men to heave ho.

Jed was just climbing up to the low roof of the cargo box to take over as sentinel. General Ashley had ordered a trapper, armed with his Hawkens rifle, to be posted as a lookout. The lookout's job was to protect the voyageurs on the riverbank from grizzly bears. To Jed, who during his youth in Pennsylvania had spotted only the occasional black bear, the number of grizzlies inhabiting the timber stands along the Freedom River was incredible. On some days as many as twenty of the evil-tempered monsters had been spotted. Fortunately, this portion of the river seemed to be free of them.

The scream from the riverbank brought the sentinel on duty, Bill Sublette, instantly alert. Before the sound had tapered off, Bill had his rifle to his shoulder, and its hammer back ready to fire. The tall, gaunt, Kentucky-born woodsman moved his rifle back and forth in a slow, steady arc, his keen, brown eyes squinting for a sign of movement in the brush. But no huge, shaggy form rose up to fill the Hawkens' sights.

The scream had been replaced by shouts as the voyageurs converged upon their fallen comrade.

"It's one of the boys pulling the *Rocky Mountains*," Bill muttered.

"What happened? Did you see?" Jed asked. He craned his neck to look back at the boat behind their own. "Look, it's out of control!"

Mike Fink was wading through the water toward the *Rocky*'s crew. "Damn fools!" he bellowed. "Hold onto that cordelle!"

But Jed saw that the line had gone slack as the crew gathered about the fallen man. There were shouts from the trappers on board the *Rocky Mountains* as the boat turned sideways and began to roll sharply in the current as the Missouri pushed it backward.

Fink had rallied the crew, but the momentum of the river was too much for them. One by one, kicking and swearing, they became tangled in the cordelle and dragged across the sharp rocks and splintered driftwood as the *Rocky Mountains* bobbed and turned, a seventy-five-foot-long toy captured by the river's steady rush.

"She's gonna hit that shoal, for sure!" Bill gasped. His hatchet face paled as he pointed one long, bony finger at the helpless keelboat.

There was the screech of tortured wood, cries from the men on board, and then the *Rocky Mountains* tilted sharply, showing the roof of its cargo box to Jed as its keel was rolled onto a sand bar by the Missouri's mighty current. Several trappers were thrown into the yellow water by the impact, their moccasin-clad feet dancing along the tilted decks, and then dancing in thin air, their arms pinwheeling in space, until the splash.

General Ashley was pacing back and forth across the stern of the now-anchored *Yellowstone Packet*. His body was one long, corded muscle of rage as he shouted orders until his voice broke in hoarseness.

It was pandemonium aboard the *Rocky*. Galvanized into action by the plight of their fellow trappers, those safe on board hurled lines to the men treading water. Others were trying to salvage the cargo and supplies, the cooking equipment and weapons that had been spread across the roof of the craft while the trappers lazed in the sun. Much of that cargo was now strewn on the shoal, bobbing downriver, or else sunk out of sight beneath the flowing yellow water.

Immediately, two skiffs were lowered from the *Yellowstone Packet*. One went to retrieve the fallen voyageur whose scream had started it all. Jed watched as Mike Fink effortlessly lifted the unconscious crewman into his arms and waded out to meet the skiff.

General Ashley had taken the other skiff to survey the damage done to the *Rocky*. By the time he was preparing to come back, an angry Mike Fink was aboard the *Yellowstone Packet* with the injured voyageur.

Jed was on the cargo box, now on duty and on the lookout for grizzlies. A conference between Fink and Ashley took place on the forward deck of the *Yellowstone* directly beneath Jed's position.

"What happened to your man?" Ashley demanded before he was even finished scrambling up the deck.

"Snakebite, sir," Fink replied. "He'll be all right. His mate nearest him on the cordelle slit and starred the wound, sucked out most of the poison."

"Well, that couldn't be avoided, I suppose." Ashley took a deep breath to calm himself. "Thank the Lord, there's no damage to the *Rocky*. We'll use the *Packet*'s crew along with the *Rocky*'s to tow the boat off that shoal. Then we'll—"

"Begging your pardon, sir," Mike interrupted. "In addition to the man snakebitten, I've got two others that belong to the *Rocky* who've had their backs twisted. They'll not be able to work for at least a day."

"We've no time to waste, Mr. Fink," Ashley glowered. "We must be on our way as soon as possible. My competition is too close."

Mike shrugged, and spat into the water. "I need some replacements. Will your trappers lend a hand?"

"I can only ask, Mr. Fink," Ashley muttered, shaking his head.

Above them, Jed thought over the predicament Ashley was in. The General had no hold over the trappers since he wasn't yet paying them. In a sense, they were like junior partners rather than employees. At their best, wilderness men, a rowdy bunch, could usually be talked into doing what their leader wanted. At their worst, they could flatly rebel, secure in knowing that a position was waiting for them at competing fur companies along the Freedom River. But one thing was crystal clear to both Jed and Ashley: Wilderness men drew the line at doing the work of voyageurs. It was very likely that they might chalk off the Ashley-Henry expedition as "gone beaver" and desert. That would mean the General would lose everything salvageable to his creditors, and Jed would lose his chance of becoming rich, as well as becoming a wilderness man.

"I'll help cordelle, sir," Jed called down.

Both Ashley and Fink stared up at him.

"Well now," Fink grinned. "I'd say that lad is equal to two men. I have reason to know that for a fact."

"Thank you, Jed," stated Ashley solemnly. "I'll remember—"

Only one trapper, Hiram Angus, offered to join Jed on the cordelle. At first Mike Fink laughed at the small, thin old man, but when Angus grabbed Mike's hand in his own and squeezed, the patron's eyes widened with surprise, and his taunting scorn abruptly stopped.

"I'm too old to have the fool notions those other hosses have," Angus snorted in answer to Jed's query as to why he agreed to help. "Besides, this old boy intends to make this his last hunt." He winked at Jed. "Too many young greenhorns like yourself is coming along. Makes me realize that I've had my time in the woods. It belongs to the likes of you all now. Anyway, if the General goes under, that means my retirement stake goes gone beaver with him. I reckon I got a bigger interest in the General being a success than the younger children on this here expedition." Angus lay back in the skiff drawing near the *Rocky*, closing his eyes and letting the sun bask his face and bald head. Suddenly one pale blue eye came open, peering at Jed the way a robin eyes its juicy warm dinner. "Excepting," he drawled.

"Excepting what?" Jed asked suspiciously.

"Come along, boy!" Angus said. "Excepting *you*, Jed. The General has got his eye on you for a real comer. And it's the other way around, as well, I bet."

His wink and chuckle made Jed blush. Was his ambition so plain to everyone?

Any embarrassment Jed might have felt was soon forgotten in the hellish labor of dragging the stranded keelboat off the shoal. Two cordelles had been cast from its deck. On one, Angus labored along with the crew of the *Packet*. Both Jed and Mike Fink joined the line manned by the injury-diminished crew of the *Rocky Mountains*.

Jed was stripped to the waist, the sweat pouring off his torso as he hauled with the others to Fink's bawled command.

"Pull!"

The skin of Jed's fingers and palms was rubbed raw by the friction of the rough hemp, which cut through the leather strips wound about his hands.

"Pull!"

Insects attracted by the wet, salty coating of his body darted into his eyes, nose and mouth, stung his back and chest. Their breeding and feeding grounds disturbed by the cordelling crews, the insects rose to become a single dark, buzzing cloud, whirring around the heads of the increasingly miserable voyageurs.

"Pull!"

Each step forward was a muscle-tearing struggle as Jed's feet sank into the ooze, and the thorns and thistles bit through his leggings and into the flesh of his thighs, buttocks and groin. Each second seemed a minute, each minute became an hour, and the hours of effort translated into mere inches of movement as the shoal held stubbornly to the keel of the *Rocky*.

Ahead of Jed, a man stumbled and began to fall to the ground. Mike Fink, just a few feet away, grabbed the fellow by the scruff of his neck and gave him a backhand slap across the face. The slacking voyageur shook off the blow and returned to his labors, pulling and huffing, his head nodding in dreamy exhaustion, a dumb beast of burden.

Jed let his mind take him away from the physical agony of the cordelle. The man ahead of him was the ox they'd used to pull the plow through the waves of rich, moist soil back home in Pennsylvania. Jed, named after his father, could see the elder Jedediah, a smaller, more worn version of his own adult self, shaking his head in mock anger, dismissing the twelve-year-old Jed each Sunday evening for his week with Doc Simons.

"Let him go, papa," his elder brother Ralph

would laugh. "He could only sow corn if the how-to of it was written on the ground." But when the two boys were alone, Ralph would whisper to Jed, "Learn all you can. You're the smart one of us. Learn and don't look back."

And Jed wanted to learn. The world of books and pens and print was as challenging to him as the world of timber, spoor and rifles. It was his father who had cultivated the seeds of learning in him. He saw Jed peering and pawing over the pages of the family Bible, squinting at the lines of print on the worn, gilt-edged pages, the firelight reflecting off his furrowed brow.

"What do the words mean, papa? How do you say them? There's meaning here, but how is it taken?" Jed would look up at his father, who could only shake his head, for the family Bible was an heirloom, a talisman rather than a book; none of the Smith family could read.

On one such night, while Jed and Ralph lay wrapped in blankets on pallets downstairs, his parents lay awake on the straw mattress laid across the attic loft's floor. A single candle burned, throwing shadows on the rough planks that buttressed the cabin's roof.

Jed's mother asked, "Have you decided?"

"It's been arranged," his father replied. "I've talked to Ralph about it as well. He's a good boy, a smart lad himself for being only fourteen. More like me." The elder Jedediah now smiled at his wife. "He's agreed to take on the extra chores for his brother, but Jed is not to know this. He'd feel too guilty."

Jed's mother burrowed in close to her husband, pulling his arm around her. "This is a gift Jed must be tricked into accepting," she agreed.

The next day, the elder Jedediah called his youngest son to his side. "Jed, you've wandered past Doc Simons' place, haven't you?"

"Yes, papa."

"Well, he's got no sons of his own, just a daughter named Louisa. About your age I reckon. The poor man was complaining to me about the lack of helpful male hands about the place. I've arranged that for a wage paid to me, you'll do chores for the doctor. You'll start there today. Come home on weekends."

"But papa," Jed stared up at his father's lined face, his tired eyes. "I'm needed here. To help you."

The elder Jedediah rested his big, calloused hand on his son's shoulder. "Ralph will do some extra, boy. For we need the money Doc Simons will pay. And never fear, Jed." The man's voice was soft. "I'll have some things for you to do when you come home."

"If that's what you want, papa," Jed murmured, clutching the small bundle of clothes his father had handed him.

"Aye, boy. It's what I want. Go now!" The elder Jedediah watched his namesake scamper off. And as the boy disappeared down the road, he whispered a fervent prayer that he had, indeed, sent his youngest son running off into a better future.

"Pull, damn your miserable hide!"

Mike Fink was back at the man he had slapped a few moments ago. But now, no amount of fear-instilling violence could goad the exhausted man on. The voyageur hung suspended from the cordelle; the whites of his eyes were showing, and his feet were like those of a scarecrow's as he was dragged along through the tangled brush.

"Mike, take him away," Jed begged. "Let him rest or you'll kill him for sure." His own voice sounded like a broken old man's as it came from his parched throat. "I'll take his slack around my waist," Jed said fiercely. "Let him rest!"

Mike's face was a mask as he helped to wrap the excess line around Jed's waist, but his voice was uncommonly kind as he muttered, "Not much longer 'til she's floating free, lad." He placed one hamlike hand on Jed's shoulder and then the patron was gone, his snarling whip of a voice receding down the line as he demanded more and more from his exhausted crew.

The kindly touch of Mike's hamlike hand on Jed's shoulder felt like Doc Simons' when he first greeted the shy, young boy standing in the doorway of his study. "Well, come in then," the tall, stoop-shouldered Doctor Titus Gorden Vespasian Simons smiled. "I don't bite, you know."

"No sir." Jed stumbled in, his bare feet sliding on the polished parquet floors. Sunlight was streaming in through the big bay windows, bringing out the rich hues of the red, blue and brown leather bindings of the books which lined the room on shelves of mahogany.

"You don't mind if I call you Jed, do you Mr. Smith?" Doc Simons asked as he polished his spectacles on the points of his satin vest.

"What?" Jed mumbled, staring at the books.

Behind Jed, a girl about his own age giggled, only to be hushed by the fat, grey-haired housekeeper who had let Jed in through the back door. The girl was pretty, with long, raven-black hair plaited into a single braid down her back. She was dressed in a pink, lacy dress which Jed was sure could belong only to a princess.

"I asked if you minded my calling you Jed," the doctor repeated.

"No sir," the boy replied, still not able to tear his eyes away from the walls of leather and paper.

Simons followed Jed's gaze, read full well the message in the barefoot boy's yearning eyes. "Well now, Mrs. Harris will show you to your bed in the alcove behind the kitchen. Mr. Harris, my yardsman, will start you on your chores once you've settled in. Mostly you'll be chopping wood and caring for my horses. Does that suit you?"

"Oh yes, sir," Jed replied, finally shifting his gaze to the face of the man he would now be working for. The doctor was clean-shaven, with thin, brown hair combed straight back. His brown eyes were magnified by the gold-rimmed spectacles perched on the bridge of his long, thin, slightly hooked nose. In all, they gave Doc Simons the look of a not particularly fierce eagle.

The doctor was known to Jed by reputation. As a physician his devotion to the sick of the neighboring counties was legendary. There were no patients so poor that they couldn't count on Doc Simons hitching up his buggy in the dead of night to come treat them or their children. The doctor would take payment in a bushel of apples or a couple of chickens if need be, for he had enough wealthy patients to keep him financially secure.

"Did your father explain all to you?" Simons asked Jed.

"Yes sir. I'm to stay here through the week in exchange for wages paid to my father."

"That is correct, Jed." Simons smiled to himself. No money was actually to change hands. Jed's father had come asking if he would tutor the boy in exchange for work around his home. He had been glad to oblige. He was not a religious man, except to say that he worshipped science and knowledge, and so considered it a sacred duty to pass education along to the scant few who desired it. It had taken only a moment for him to see that Jed was such a rare individual. The boy positively radiated a thirst to learn. Beside that, if the truth be known, the doctor envied Mr. Smith his two sons.

His own wife Eve had died giving birth to their only child, Louisa. It would be fine to have a young man around the house, to hear the boy's voice echoing in the hall, even if that boy was here only on loan.

"You may go now, Jed," Simons said. "Get settled in and then go to work." He turned to address the housekeeper. "Mrs. Harris, see that the boy is fed before he begins."

"Of course, sir," Mrs. Harris huffed. "I've already laid out a nice slice of pie and some milk. What do you take me for—"

"Quite right, Mrs. Harris," Simons cut her off with a resigned wave of his long, slender hand.

Jed was being steered out of the room by the woman when the doctor called to him.

"By the way, Jed. You'll have one other duty here," Simons began, careful to keep any inflection out of his voice that might give away the game. "Each afternoon I instruct my daughter Louisa in reading and writing and so on. I'll require you to be here to help my daughter learn by keeping her company. Of course, while you're sitting with us, you might as well take part in the lessons, I suppose."

"Yes, sir," Jed whispered, petrified that the trembling in his voice would make him seem too selfishly eager, perhaps even causing the doctor to think twice and change his mind. *He was going to learn to read*!

Doc Simons nodded. "Then we'll begin that part of your job today at . . ." he pulled a gold pocket watch from his vest ". . . at four o'clock. Mrs. Harris will fetch you when it's time. Until then, Jed," he held out his hand.

Jed thought about what was required for a moment and then stepped forward, taking Simons' hand. "Until then, sir. Um, thank you, sir."

Mrs. Harris took Jed's hand and led him from the

study. As they strolled toward the kitchen they passed
the dining room. Jed stared at the cabinets which
housed the formal china and crystal. The light leapt
like liquid fire from the etched designs and facets of the
goblets and cordial glasses. The tumblers shimmered so
that the boy could only think—

"Pardon, Mrs. Harris, ma'am?" he chirped, tugging at her apron.

"What is it, boy?"

"Those, ma'am," he asked, pointing at the
glassware. "Are those diamonds?"

Behind him he heard Louisa's gay, tinkling laughter, like sweet bells filling the air, slowly fading as the
little princess scampered up the palace's hallway
stairs, to rooms filled with such wonders as Jed could
scarcely imagine.

"She's free!" Mike Fink yelled. "She's floating
free!"

The voyageurs cheered even as they fell exhausted where just a moment before they'd been
crawling, looking for a hand or foothold in the boggy
mess of the riverbank.

Jed turned with the voyageurs to see the *Rocky
Mountains* wobble, slide, then rock in the water, newly
launched off the shoal.

"Tie her down, now!" Mike Fink shouted. "Else
she'll float right damn back on that mud bar!" The
keelboat patron danced a jig as he slapped the men on
their aching backs.

As the others still cheered, giddy with fatigue,
Jed's keen ears picked up another sound. It was a regularly spaced, rasping, breathing noise coming up behind him, growing louder as it approached. He whirled
around, caught in the cordelle still wound about his
waist. His feet became tangled and he fell on his back,

staring in fear in the direction of the hoarse, rhythmic grunting, knowing what it had to be. . . .

The grizzly crashed through the nettled thicket, its bewilderment at the noise all around it quickly changing to fury as it regarded the prone thing twisting and writhing on the ground. The bear rose up on its hind legs. Now it was seven-feet-tall, seven feet of golden, shaggy death as it roared its challenge, advancing on Jed, its hind legs jerking it along in a nightmare parody of a human gait.

Jed screamed, knowing even as he did that it was too late. Like everyone else, the sentinels posted on board the *Packet* would be distracted, watching the *Rocky Mountains* floating free. He had no weapons. He couldn't run. He was a dead man.

The grizzly was close enough to fall upon him now. Other screams had joined Jed's, and far away he heard the report of a rifle. Thick, ropey strands of saliva flew from the grizzly's jaws as it was rocked by the impact of the bullet. But the sentinel's ball had struck too high, burying itself in the brute's meaty shoulder.

Now, made angrier, the bear's eyes glowed cold with malignant hate. It would do its job. The animal was close enough for Jed to see the dried, rotten meat encrusting its claws, and the swarm of ticks that crawled about its thighs and awful groin. The lumbering grizzly's stink engulfed him now. He could feel its body heat.

Jed closed his eyes and opened his mouth, but this time, instead of a scream, he roared his defiance, and there came to his lips the only name that could distract and comfort him as he prepared for the pain of the grizzly's teeth and claws.

Jed's cry was overridden by Mike Fink's, who flew through the air to wrap his big arms around the monster's neck and firmly locked himself onto the bear's back. Jed watched as Fink shoved the blade of his Bowie knife into the bear's throat. And as he tore the blade outward, out came the grizzly's throat. The animal moaned as its blood pumped up out of the torn throat tubes, a crimson fountain spewing onto Jed.

Two more shots came, and both half-ounce lead balls plowed into the grizzly's barrel chest, smashing its massive heart. Mike jumped clear as the beast fell sideways to the ground. As the grizzly shuddered to its death, Mike cut an ashen-faced Jed free from the tangles of the cordelle.

Before Jed could find the breath to speak, Mike said, "No thanks needed, lad. I owed you since you saved me from the constable way back in St. Louis." As he helped Jed to his feet, the keelboat man began to chuckle. "Aren't you glad now, lad, that you let me talk you out of turning me in?"

Fink threw back his big head, matted with several weeks growth of beard and fresh bear's blood, and let loose an ear-splitting roar of laughter.

"Thank you, Mike. I'll never forget this," Jed finally managed.

"Aye, lad," Mike agreed, wiping the tears of laughter from his eyes. "Don't worry. I won't let you. By the way, who was that you shouted for?"

Jed shrugged. "No one."

"I mean just before that beast was about to eat you up. Come now, lad, who is she?" Mike persisted.

"No one, I said," Jed muttered and walked away.

"No one, eh?" he muttered slyly. "Why she must be quite a woman, this Louisa. . . ."

Chapter 3

"Damn, Jed! Come on down!" Hiram Angus stared up through the gathering dusk at the second-floor window. Uttering a string of cuss words that would do justice to any wilderness man, he slammed through the door of the barracks. The door, haphazardly hung on leather hinges cut from an old pair of boots, moaned in protest. He pushed his way up the rickety set of stairs, past a Sioux squaw who lay sprawled across the landing. She was a whore, one of the many at Fort Atkinson who serviced for pennies the visiting expeditions of fur trappers. Now she bared her breasts for Hiram in an automatic response devoid of any emotion. Not that the red people had feelings like white folk, Hiram thought. "Go on, woman," the old trapper remarked tiredly. "Had enough of that last night and this morning. Tonight's for drinkin'." He continued on up the wooden stairway, into the big room where he found Jed lying across one of the bunks, his nose buried in a book, as usual.

"Jed! Didn't you hear me howling for you?" Hiram scolded. "What you spending your time reading for anyway? A soul would think we hit Atkinson every day by the likes of you."

Jed grinned at Hiram and closed the volume.

"What's the name of that book—" Hiram stopped in mid-sentence as he pondered the worn leather cover with its gold embossed cross. "You readin' the Bible with whores banging down the door?" He shook his head in mock dismay.

"It's my family's Bible," Jed told him. "My folks gave it to me before I left home for the West."

"Well, boy," Hiram said slowly, evidently giving the matter serious thought. "This hoss reckons you've given the Lord his due for tonight. Now let's go get drunk!"

Jed tucked the book back in his possibles sack, the small, leather bag a wilderness man used to keep together his personal odds and ends. He tucked his brace of pistols and sheathed Bowie blade into his belt, and followed Hiram down the stairs and out into the cool night air.

The evening's activities were just beginning. The muzzle flashes of pistols fired by rowdy, drunken trappers having themselves a "mountain's good time" illuminated the fort's back alleys and dead ends. The explosions bounced off the stockade's whitewashed outer walls, temporarily drowning out the hand-clapping, knee-stomping music issuing from a dozen beckoning grog-shop doorways.

"This way, Jed. The best tavern's over yonder." Hiram led through the muddy maze of walkways. The four walls of Fort Atkinson enclosed a huge area divided into narrow, winding paths by the blocks of buildings devoted to supplying the fur trade with goods and supplying the traders themselves with a purse-emptying good time. Atkinson's motley bazaar of eating and drinking establishments, whorehouses, gunsmiths, dry goods vendors and fur trading establishments—both the Missouri and French Fur Companies had major posts

here to consolidate the pelts their men brought in—
were all open twenty-four hours a day.

Located forty miles above the mouth of the Platte
River, Fort Atkinson was the final, extreme boundary
of the power and authority of the United States. The
fort was the high watermark of the military expedition
of 1818-19, which had been designed to establish a
military presence at the mouth of the Yellowstone.
This was as far as the military's grandly thought-out
campaign had reached. Nevertheless, the fort was an
impressive place for the men who had traveled the wilderness between here and St. Louis.

One-quarter of the fort was occupied by the heavily armed Sixth Infantry garrison, led by Colonel
Henry Leavenworth. The rest of Atkinson was given
over to commerce and entertainment. Once an expedition left its gates, the last vestige of civilization in the
West was left behind as well. Beyond Atkinson, the
world was ruled by animal, Indian and fur trapper.

Hiram kicked open a set of swinging doors and
pulled Jed down a short flight of stairs into a cellar
aptly named, in Jed's opinion, "Boudines." Boudines
was wilderness argot for an elk's, buffalo's, or any
edible animal's intestines. When lightly broiled, boudines were considered a great delicacy.

The low-ceilinged tavern was filled with tobacco
smoke and the raucous noise of men having themselves
a spree. Various buckskin-fringed white men stood
shoulder to shoulder with blanket-wrapped Sioux
braves, who spent the coins their women brought in on
cups of "skull varnish," a potent mix of corn mash al-
cohol, tobacco, red peppers and river water.

"Lookit them Indians," Hiram whispered in Jed's
ear. "Drink themselves blind, they will."

"I thought it wasn't allowed," Jed said.

"These here are Sioux," Hiram shrugged. "Old

Manuel Lisa, a trapper who makes even me look like a young rooster, taught 'em to like the sound of coined money. Now the Sioux are merchants more than marauders. They got to spend their money on something. Now the Rees upriver, they're a mean group of braves. Ain't housebroke yet. They carry quite a few trappers' scalps. No hard drink for them. Any mountain man dumb or plain evil enough to bring hostile Indians hard drink deserves what he gets: a bullet from any man, white or red, who can manage to put one where it belongs." Shaking his head, Hiram continued, "But we's got time enough to worry about the Rees when we gets there. Now let's go join our boys over at that table."

Through the room's blue haze, Jed could see Bill Sublette, John Clyman and some of the others, including Mike Fink, sitting around a wobbly, greasy table formed out of two sawhorses and three planks laid side by side. All had their pistols lying on the table beside their cups of skull varnish. Jed went to their table while Hiram fetched two drinks.

"Hy'ar," Clyman said by way of a greeting. He removed his wide-brimmed, blue felt hat from the bench to make room for Jed. As Jed slid in, Hiram put a cup of skull varnish in front of him.

Although Jed didn't drink or smoke—he'd already seen too many men made clumsy by drink commit fatal mistakes in the wilderness—he'd learned enough about wilderness manners not to refuse the tin cup. He'd simply leave the drink where it was and, sooner or later, Angus, Clyman, Fink, or one of the others would drain their own ration and reach over for his. When the time came, abstainer or not, Jed would be expected to buy his round for the boys, not withstanding the short supply of money for the wageless men of the Ashley-Henry expedition.

"Well now," Mike remarked in exasperation as Hiram crammed himself into a corner, "we've left no room for Louisa."

The table erupted in laughter. In bragging about how he had saved Jed's life from the grizzly a few days before, Mike had made sure to spread the story of Jed's final, panic-stricken cry. Already the men had begun betting next season's pelt profits on carefully considered opinions on whether Louisa was Jed's mother, his sister, or the wife, or girlfriend left behind.

Staring down at his untouched drink, Jed endured the merriment at his expense. Just the day before he had complained about it in private to Hiram, only to be sternly reminded that such ribbing was a way of life here.

"This hoss still reckons she's his sweetheart, pinin' her heart out for him," Bill Sublette speculated, his long face growing thoughtful beneath its thatch of sandy blond hair. "Yep. . . . Her heart is just pounding away beneath her two pink little breasts."

"Two pink, heap-big breasts!" John Clyman revised, his bushy brown beard hiding any trace of his smile.

"Enough!" Jed roared. His high cheekbones were flushed red, and his blue eyes were bright and spoiling for a fight. While the table roared its delight, both Clyman and Sublette, the two men who had fired the shots that finally brought down the grizzly, gave Jed two claps on his back that rocked him forward.

"Well, women will be the deaths of us all," Hiram advised the group. He himself had been married three times to three different squaws. The first, a Sioux, had taken ill and died while in childbirth, back when Hiram was Jed's age. The baby was stillborn. The second, a Crow woman, lived with him for fifteen years, but one day up and disappeared, taking with her a pack of

eighty prime beaver pelts and his best Hawkens gun.
Ever since then one of Hiram's favorite sayings was
that "The Crows 'ud never hurt a white man cause
then who'd they have to steal from?" For his last wife,
he went back to the Sioux. She was a good one, but
again, it seemed that the Sioux's proximity to the white
race had made them a sickly people. This squaw took
fever and died one night in her sleep. After that,
Hiram figured that three tries were enough for any
hoss and devoted himself to the solitary life of the fur
trapper.

He puffed on his pipe until it was going good and
hot, and then offered, "So Jed's in love, eh? Well,
that's what comes from good looks. A broken heart."

"Hell, Mike," John Clyman winked. "Maybe you
shoulda let that there grizz put the poor boy out of his
misery." He managed to hide his eyes from Jed by
twisting around to examine the beadwork on his brand
new buckskin shirt. He'd gotten it just that day, in
trade for his old one and a broken-bladed Bowie, from
an old squaw who sewed for her living.

"Well," Bill joined in. "Jed is a mighty fine-
lookin' figure of a man. Maybe we should've let that
grizz take the shine off him some."

"Grizz woulda scraped it off for sure," somebody
else agreed.

"For sure," Hiram echoed, and spat out a mouth-
ful of pipe juice onto the floor.

Once again the men broke out in laughter, but
this time Jed joined in. As Hiram had pointed out after
the incident, there's nothing in the whole wide world
funnier than a dead grizzly. The attack had happened.
It was now over. And Jed was still alive. In the wilderness, bad things survived became funny.

One of the men, Jimmy Beck, went for another
round as Mike suggested, "You know, maybe this

Louisa isn't a woman at all. Maybe she's Jed's old coon hound."

As Jed stared down into his lap, pretending not to hear, Hiram silently shook his head at Mike, who good-naturedly shrugged and began to spin a different yarn. "Well, it wasn't a woman who chased me out here. I ain't a wilderness man but I'm hankering after the woods and wide-open spaces, a welcome change after me years on the rivers of this here United States. I guess I gotta say I'm not doin' too bad. Here I already kilt me a grizz with just my knife. Throat-cut the brute, just like Davy Crockett was supposed to have done." He ran his thick fingers through his slicked-back, black hair, preening for his audience. "Course, we ain't seen Davy Crockett, but you all saw me—"

"Speakin' of women," Jimmy Beck interrupted, returning to the table with his burden of filled tin cups, "this here boy has got the story to beat all. It's about old Natty Smyth—"

"Hang onto your skivvies, boys! Old Jimmy is tellin' himself a whopper!" Bill Sublette broke in.

Jimmy Beck drew himself up to his full five-feet five-inch height. "That the way your stick floats, Billy?" he glared, his freckled face matching the color of his mass of curly red hair. "Well then, here's your drink!" He poured the cup into the amused Sublette's lap, who calmly reached across and helped himself to Jed's skull varnish.

"Well then," Bill drawled, pointing down at his groin. "Here's the booze, Jimmy. Why don'tcha git down on your knees and lap it up?"

This time the group's laughter was cut short abruptly as a long, grey shape, big as a male wolf, made its way beneath the swinging doors and snaked down the stairs into the tavern. It was a dog, but one straight from hell, Jed thought. It stood three feet high at the shoulder, had the rough, curly coat of a rat-eating terrier, the yellow eyes of a panther, and the jutting, fang-filled underjaw of a mastiff. Its nails clicked across the floor as it made its way about the tavern, all the while giving throat to one long, continuous growl.

"Here's damp powder and no fire to dry it," Sublette murmured.

"What's going on?" Jed demanded. His voice was loud and the dog, attracted by it, began to stalk toward the table, its fur rising high along its spine, its yellow eyes unwavering.

"Steady now, Jed," Hiram cautioned. "The worst is about to come."

Jed turned at the sound of the swinging doors. A huge figure began its descent down the stairs. The flickering light from the candles and oil lamps scattered about the windowless tavern only added to the man's awesome appearance. His long, dark hair reached down to his full beard, and both were matted with grease and dirt. He wore a sleeveless, buckskin shirt drawn tight about his ample belly by a wide belt from which hung three Bowie knives. He did not wear white man's trousers, but instead, an Indian loincloth, and rawhide leggings. He carried no pistols, but a British-made fusil, a sawed-off shotgun normally used to hunt buffalo from horseback, hung from his right shoulder, suspended by a leather thong.

"He must be over six-and-a-half feet tall," Jed murmured. He'd thought himself a big man at six feet two, until he'd come West and met men like Mike Fink, but this giant even dwarfed the keelboat patron.

The newcomer snarled something in French at the dog, which immediately retreated behind him. The man slowly surveyed the entire room, his gaze falling finally on the table occupied by the Ashley-Henry men.

Jed stared into the man's tiny, gleaming eyes, and

at once was reminded of the grizzly's eyes. Here was the same malevolence, but this time that evil was backed up with a keen, calculating intelligence. Jed felt himself shudder and quickly looked at the other men at the table.

They were all gaping at the stranger in mesmerized fascination, the way a bird stares when locked in the cool, reptilian food-leer of a hungry snake.

The huge stranger approached their table, his big dog weaving around him. "Hiram Angus," he spoke in his thick accent, his eyes locking on the old trapper. "Of all, I should have thought you would know better."

"Well now, this hoss doesn't get your drift," Angus muttered nervously. "Not a'tall," he gulped, "Cabanne."

The grey wolfhound uttered a sudden, low growl, seemingly in objection to the sound of its master's name on Hiram's lips.

Cabanne pulled a coin from a pouch around his neck. He tossed it at Jimmy Beck. "You, Jimmy, go fetch this group a round of drinks. Clearly there is not enough loot at this table to satisfy the thirsts of trappers." He stared at Beck, who was still staring. "Fetch the drinks now, Jimmy," he ordered.

As Jimmy scurried to do his bidding, Bill Sublette scowled and invited with a sigh, "Mighty friendly of you, Cabanne. Why don't ya set yourself down and join us for a round?"

The distaste in Sublette's voice was obvious, but the Frenchman evidently chose to ignore it. His big arm reached for a chair from a neighboring table. It was occupied, but the fellow in it quickly got up when he saw who wanted it.

"I have business to discuss with you men," Cabanne began. "My own employer, Joseph Brazeau, known to you as 'Young Cayewa,' has need of trappers. A fair wage will be paid." Beck returned with the round of drinks and Cabanne drained his tin cup in one long gulp. An ugly smile came to his lips. "Hiram, old friend. You first, I think. . . . All is agreed then?"

"Well, uh . . ." Hiram looked about him at the others at the table.

"You do not refuse?" Cabanne's voice was little more than a whisper, but there was menace in his tone, the way there is warning in a serpent's hiss. "The French Company needs engagés. You are not challenging Cayewa?"

"We're Ashley-Henry men," Jed spoke up. "We're not for sale."

"Who is this cub?" Cabanne sneered.

"My name is Jed Smith." His pistols were on the table. He had never killed a man, but at this moment, Jed was wondering what this confrontation was going to come to.

"Jed Smith, do you wish to become meat for my dog?"

"Here now, Cabanne," Bill Sublette soothed. "Easy there. We do work for General Ashley. That's all there is to it."

"Work for what?" Cabanne spat. "You are not paid wages like the other fur men. You are paid promises. Promises that Ashley and Henry will bring you to the places where the pelts can be taken. But the French have claimed these places for the future."

"We heard you were working the Grand Detour, by Kiowa outpost," John Clyman interjected. "You can't claim it all, Cabanne. Not you, not even Cayewa himself."

"Do not tell me what I or my employer can do," Cabanne grinned. "If you do not work for the French, then you are the enemies of the French. Now, all of you. Do you wish to have coin in your pouches, and Cayewa's protection? Or do you wish to be dead?"

"We're working now, as you've been told," Jed replied. "We're—" Jed thought about it a moment. "We're free trappers, that's what we are," he triumphantly decided. "I don't know about the others, but I don't take kindly to threats."

"Easy now, boy," Hiram Angus whispered as the tavern grew quiet.

"Free trappers," Bill Sublette said slowly, savoring the words. "Yep, this hoss likes the sound of that. Hear it, Cabanne? Free trappers. That's what we are."

Cabanne surveyed the table, wondering how such a young greenhorn could win the loyalty of experienced men. Then he shrugged and offered Jed a sly smile. "It seems I was mistaken. There are no trappers in need of employment at this table. Jed Smith, we will shake hands so that there will be no hard feelings, yes?"

Jed pondered the Frenchman's face. He didn't trust Cabanne for a moment, but what could he do? To refuse to shake the man's hand was unthinkable.

Cabanne extended his own hand. "Jed Smith," he spoke softly, "I am waiting."

Slowly, Jed lifted his right hand from its place between his pistols. He was aware of the other men's eyes upon him as he stretched it across the expanse of planks toward Cabanne's.

A howl of victory came from Cabanne as his own right hand locked about Jed's wrist. He slammed Jed's hand to the table, palm up, while almost too fast to be seen, Cabanne's left hand suddenly held a Bowie knife. Now his eyes glittered as he pressed the razor edge of the blade into the soft spot where Jed's twitching fingers joined his palm.

"Jed Smith," Cabanne taunted. "Shall I have your fingers? Will you be a trapper with your right hand a useless clump? Do you not take kindly to this threat, Jed Smith?"

"Here now, Frenchie," Mike Fink growled. "I ain't no wilderness man either, but I'll kill you if you harm that boy." As the keelboat man slammed his own chair back and rose to his feet, the grey wolfhound sprang at him. Fink fell to the tavern floor crying out in alarm as the dog's jaws clamped about his throat.

"Hold, Tooth!" Cabanne commanded, never taking his eyes from Jed's pale, sweating face. "Lie still boat man and Tooth will spare you. I think he waits hungrily for the boy's tender fingers. What do you think, Jed Smith?"

Jed flicked his gaze down to his hand pinned to the table under Cabanne's grimy fingers. His wrist had gone numb. Cabanne's strength was appalling, Jed felt as if his wrist had been locked between the steel teeth of a beaver trap. When he didn't answer the huge man, Cabanne pressed more firmly on the blade of his Bowie. Jed winced as his blood welled up around the gleaming edge of the knife.

My fingers!—Jed fought down the panic welling up in him, ready to spew forth like vomit. *Think!* No one here can interfere. The wilderness man's code doesn't allow for siding with a "greenhorn." *You've got to save yourself!*

Cabanne laughed at him, clearly enjoying Jed's fear. "Will you beg for your fingers, boy?"

Without two hands a man was helpless to load a gun or chop wood, to skin a pelt or do anything. *Without his fingers all would be ruined.* The plea for mercy was a whimper about to rise in his throat, when another spoke first.

"Hey, now, Cabanne," Hiram Angus said quietly. "The lad here is a—well, he's like a son to me, I reckon. I sure would take it kindly now if you spared him." The old trapper waited for a response, and when none came from Cabanne, he continued. "Well, I might even see my way clear to sign on with you and Cayewa. If you spare Jed's fingers."

The note of wistful sadness in Hiram's voice felt like a slap to Jed. Once again he was being saved. Hiram couldn't forcibly save him, so he was doing it by sacrificing his retirement, mortgaging away *his* future for a slave wage, merely to save Jed's *own* future.

"Maybe you work for nothing for this lad," Cabanne taunted, a look of raw, cruel pleasure suffusing his ugly face.

At that moment Jed's fear for himself turned into blind animal rage. As the gloating Cabanne, unable to resist seeing Hiram's suffering, shifted his eyes for an instant, Jed's foot beneath the table shot forward to drive his moccasined heel deep into Cabanne's groin.

The Frenchman wheezed in pain and his knife hand lifted a fraction of an inch in reflex.

In that split second Jed's own left hand shot forward, and in a flash he had the snout of his pistol jammed into Cabanne's face. The click of it being cocked filled the silent tavern.

Cabanne released Jed's right hand and let his bloodied Bowie knife clatter to the table.

"Now," Jed began in a shaky voice, though he took care to keep his pistol steady. "I've never killed anyone, Frenchie, but I swear the good Lord would smile down on me if I splattered your evil brains all across the floor."

Cabanne closed his eyes. "Do not shoot."

"Don't do it, Jed," Hiram warned. "You shoot 'im and it'll be a trappers' war between us and them." The urgency in his voice turned to glee as he looked at Cabanne. "Didn't I tell you this young hoss was like a son to me, eh?"

Jed pressed the gun a little harder against Cabanne's forehead. He watched a droplet of the man's sweat lazily trickle a zigzag course along the furrows of his brow, to bead on the metal flange of his pistol's sighting blade. "Get that dog of yours away from Mike," he ordered.

"Yes, all right," Cabanne said quietly. "Tooth, here."

"Away from us!" Jed quickly said.

"Tooth! Behind me!" Cabanne snarled, amending his order. The hound reluctantly crept behind its master, but the low growl never stopped humming from its throat.

Mike Fink got to his feet, wiping away the drool the dog had left around his neck. "Shoot the hellhound, Jed. For me, do it!"

"No!" came a deep, commanding voice from the stairway of the tavern. It, too, was accented French.

"Who is it?" Jed demanded. He kept the barrel of the pistol on Cabanne, knowing that his own safety still depended on keeping Cabanne at bay. Just as the others at the table couldn't interfere between Cabanne and himself, their code of ethics would keep anyone else out of the fight. "Come out of the shadows so that I can see you."

A deerskin-garbed man slowly approached the table. He was totally bald; his shaved skull glistened ivory-yellow in the dim candlelight. He was of average height, but strongly built, with thick, muscled arms and a barrel chest. A pistol hung from his belt, but the man took care to hold both hands in the air.

"My name is Joseph Brazeau," the man began as he took in the scene at the table. "Here I am known as Young Cayewa. And you are?"

"Jed Smith." He pressed forward his pistol. Cabanne's head rocked back until there was an audible crick from the man's neck and he was almost staring straight up at the ceiling. "So this vermin works for you, does he?"

Cayewa flinched at the insult, but his voice was calm as he nodded. "Yes, I regret to say. So, Cabanne. The young man has managed to get the drop on you. Now I must wonder, who at this table is the greenhorn and who is the wilderness man?"

It's a stand-off, Jed mused. *He deserves it but I can't murder him, not like this. In cold blood. But now how do I let go?*

"Mr. Jed Smith," Cayewa addressed him. "If I gave you license to take this fool's life, would you join my company, at twice his wages?"

Jed shook his head. "I'm a free trapper. An Ashley-Henry man."

"A pity," Cayewa replied. "Then I must ask you to spare my man's life. I need him on the trapping lines."

Jed didn't answer, but kept the pistol pressed against Cabanne's forehead as he considered what to do. He could hear his own pulse throbbing in his ears as he flicked his eyes to Hiram's face.

"Let him go, Jed," Hiram urged.

Jed gave it another moment, for show, but finally drawled, "My arm is getting a mite sore." He slowly lowered his gun.

Heaving a great sigh of relief, Cabanne collapsed into his chair. "Get out of here," Cayewa told his man in disgust.

Cabanne stared at Jed for a second, then, without a word, got up and quickly stalked out of the tavern, his dog trotting along behind him.

"I thank you for his life, Jed Smith," Cayewa said. "But I must say to you—to you all—my men spend their wages, here, today! You men have nothing but dreams. Dreams are for children." Again his eyes linked with Jed's. "And children do not long survive in the wilderness. We shall meet again, perhaps. On the river." He turned on his heel and made his way across the floor, up the stairs and out of the tavern.

There was a long moment of silence at the table.. Then Jed remarked, "This hoss reckons you boys all need a drink."

Angus, Sublette and the others all laughed until the tears streamed from their eyes. Then Clyman, mimicking Jed's shaky voice, said, "My arm's a mite sore," and the laughter began anew. Strangers in the tavern joined in as well, and soon the noise level inside the place was back to normal.

Jed tossed a coin onto the table. "Mike, would you get the round? My legs are a wee bit wobbly."

"Aye, lad," Fink laughed, and snatching up the money, went to the bar.

Jed's heart was still pounding, but now from exhilaration. His gaze swept the table, everyone was nodding his approval. *I've done it*, he thought joyously. *I beat the brute at his own game. But what if I'd had to shoot? I've never killed a man. Could I have done it?*

Jed let the rich laughter and lightened mood of the table wash the nagging doubts away. *I'll do what I must*, he decided. *But this time, not killing was the braver choice.*

"Angus, why is Cayewa's head shaved like that?" Jed asked.

"Years ago, when he and his boys was up in Ree country, it was the custom to shine up your scalp so that the heathens would pass it by. No brave wants to hang a naked flap of skin from his belt. He wants it full of long hair. I guess the style still sets well with Cayewa. But a real man takes his chances. You won't see me soapin' up my skull come our entrance into Ree territory."

"That man you faced down, Cabanne," Sublette broke in. "He's killed more men than are sittin' here at this table. And that cur of his, Tooth, it's killed just as many at its master's command. It follows Cabanne like the devil's own."

"Cabanne and Cayewa," Clyman muttered, shaking his head. "Keep your nose open, Jed. This hoss thinks you made yourself two bad enemies, for sure."

"I can handle them," Jed replied.

"Listen, boy," Hiram scolded. "Don't get cocky. My heart was purely crying for them fingers of yours."

Jed glanced at the cuts on his right hand. They were shallow and had stopped bleeding. "I got the drop on him, didn't I, Hiram?"

"Hell, readin' your Bible early this evenin' musta done you some good," the old trapper grumbled. "Cause you sure had the good Lord on your side this time, but let me give you some counsel. Out here, the hawks usually eat the larks, and not the other side 'round. That's nature's way."

"I understand that," Jed said impatiently.

"Then understand this, boy. Best not to trust in God concerning Hisself with what He's done given over into Mother Nature's province."

"Dead right. For sure," Bill Sublette agreed with a nod. "For that's the wilderness man's way."

Chapter 4

Henry Leavenworth automatically sucked in his belly as he stood up from behind his desk. Surreptitiously tugging at the front of his blue, rough-woven wool tunic, the commander of the military forces garrisoned at Fort Atkinson strode to the map of the upper Missouri hanging from his office wall. Just entering his late middle age, Leavenworth had taken to wearing his hair long, down past his collar, in the wilderness man's style. The long hair, in combination with his handlebar moustache, gave him what he hoped was a rakish Indian-fighter look.

Standing at the map he was acutely conscious of his bulging stomach. It was, he had long ago realized, the product of too much food and drink, of too much time on the hands of an old soldier unfairly exiled to this overgrown red-light district on the edge of nowhere. Leavenworth glanced at his two guests, but neither General Ashley nor the fellow jotting down the notes of the meeting seemed to have noticed his profile-saving subterfuge. Or if they had, Leavenworth reconsidered, perhaps they were simply too respectful of his office to exchange ridiculing glances. They were Americans, after all, and not those damned French.

He stared at the map in the sunlight streaming through the open door of his roughhewn, modest office, glinting on his gold buttons and shoulder braid. The Missouri River climbed ever upward through what Leavenworth secretly dreamed of as untamed wilds as strange and alien as the unreachable surface of the moon, up to the point called the Grand Detour.

Leavenworth pointed at the loop. "Here, gentlemen, you'll find the river taking you thirty miles around to make a distance of, say, five miles."

About a mile and a half according to Hiram, Jed thought, but he said nothing to contradict the pudgy officer. The Colonel obviously knew little about the lands beyond his fort.

"I expected a bit more detail," Ashley commented sardonically.

Jed stifled a laugh as he lay back in his armchair. The poor map the Colonel was poking at was almost blank. The Missouri was a thin blue vein winding along a barren, beige background. Here and there, tepees and grizzly bears had been painstakingly painted in to represent where some greenhorn of a cartographer thought the Indians and wildlife were. The map maker was strong on art, but weak on his geographic knowledge. Jed had learned more about the region in Doc Simons' library.

Jed put down his pen. Ashley caught his eye and nodded once, clearly in agreement that no useful information was to be garnered in this meeting.

"Both the French and the Missouri Fur Companies have outposts somewhere around there," Leavenworth said, his voice vague, his finger wavering as it traced the first part of the Grand Detour. "The Missouri Company has only a skeleton crew keeping their post going. There's Josh Pilcher, a few trappers and a lot of clerks. You'll reach their Fort Recovery first.

About ten miles up the Detour you'll come upon Brazeau's Fort Kiowa. He's pretty well staffed. It's his French Company that reigns supreme."

"And why is that?" Ashley demanded. "It would seem to me that we ought to have the upper hand."

Jed had to smile. Ever since word of last night's confrontation with Cabanne and Cayewa had reached Ashley, the General had been furious.

"This Cayewa fellow tried to steal my men," Ashley said. "Lucky for me they stood up for themselves. Especially Jed here." Ashley smiled. "Now, I'm not saying I need you to protect the interests of the United States, which the Ashley-Henry expedition represents, but it seems to me that you at least ought to uphold the law in these parts."

"There *is* no law in these parts," Leavenworth shot back.

"And that's your fault!" Ashley glowered, jumping to his feet. "The French obviously have no respect for your authority. They act like your fort belongs to them."

Leavenworth regarded the General. With his bulging green eyes and goatee, he looked like a mad billy goat. Running his hand along his moustache to hide his smile, Leavenworth said, "Please, General. Sit down. Let me explain the reality of the situation to you. It's been a long time since I've had such distinguished company as your own."

Jed watched as Ashley, mollified by Leavenworth's tone, returned to his chair.

"General Ashley," Leavenworth began, "it's my understanding that you made your fortune during the war with the British. In munitions, wasn't it?"

"Yes. I and my partner," Ashley replied. "But what has this got to do with—"

"And did you see any action during the now-christened War of 1812? With your militia unit, I mean to say."

"Somewhat," Ashley sniffed.

"Somewhat, eh?" Leavenworth smiled. "I was at the battles of Chippewa and Niagra. I rose in rank during those confrontations, somewhat north and east of these damned parts. Those battles were ten years ago, I grant you. And I was ten years younger." Here the Colonel smiled sadly. "And thinner, I grant you, but I was a good soldier then, and I'm a good one now. While you were making your money and this young fellow Jed Smith was holding on to his mother's apron, I was saving the Union from the British!"

As Jed listened, the years seemed to drop away from Leavenworth. Suddenly the fat, weary-looking officer didn't seem foolish at all. Jed got a sense of the force and power the man had once possessed and given to his country during those hard winters against the British.

Leavenworth's dignity and hidden strength had clearly impressed Ashley as well. The expedition leader's voice had lost its rage, and was now quite humble as he said, "My dear Colonel Leavenworth, please accept my apologies."

"Never mind," Leavenworth dismissed the entire matter with a wave of his hand. "I brought up all that ancient history to point out to you that despite present circumstances, I am not the buffoon you take me for." He left the map and returned to his desk. Pulling open a drawer he removed a sheaf of crumpled papers and tossed them into Ashley's lap. "Those are copies of requests I've sent to Washington. Each takes months to get there, and more months for its reply to get back to me. Each urgently informs my superiors of the state of affairs concerning the French and the Arikaras Indians—the Rees, as you trappers call them." Leavenworth paused, and his forceful manner drained away. He retrieved the pile of papers from Ashley and returned them to his desk. Then he collapsed heavily into his own chair, his puffy face staring at his two visitors.

"May I ask what Washington's position is on these matters?" Ashley's tone of voice made Jed think the General already knew the answer to his question.

"As to the Indians?" Leavenworth shrugged. "They are not to be engaged in battle without proof of their hostility. Now, I do not pretend to be an expert on Indian affairs, but it strikes me as unreasonable to expect Grey Eyes, one of the warrior chiefs of the Ree villages, to allow a survivor to come back downriver and tell me about an attack. Trappers go up the Freedom. Some return and some don't. Washington wants no costly war against the savages unless there is solid proof to rally the public to the cause. So I sit and wait."

"Upriver the Rees have never even seen a soldier," Jed interjected. It occurred to him that he probably ought to have asked Ashley for permission to speak, but when he glanced at his employer, nothing seemed to be amiss. "Hiram Angus says that the Rees don't even believe Fort Atkinson exists. They don't even believe there's such a thing as the United States. They figure that all white men are trappers, and that all the Rees have seen is all there are of us." Jed was now wonderfully aware of the full attention of the other two.

"Why shouldn't they believe as much, or as little, I should say," Leavenworth winced. "All of this," he gestured beyond the walls of his office, "all my infantry, my cannon, the very might of this nation, has been made impotent by a spineless Eastern bureaucracy."

Ashley started to speak, but Leavenworth held up his hand. "And that brings me to the French. No doubt you are aware that your good President, my esteemed Commander-in-Chief, Mr. James Monroe, has quite a long history of friendship with the French."

"I detect some note of sarcasm in your voice," Ashley smiled.

"So have others," Leavenworth replied. "Perhaps that's why I'm posted here. I've made no secret of my feeling that our country should concern itself with certain priorities, and let the foreign nations beware—" He stopped and shrugged. "Although I do admit the possibility that the larger view of things that Washington has could be dissimilar to, and take precedence over, our reality here."

"I personally agree with your point of view regarding the situation," Ashley grumbled. "President Monroe's time spent in Europe, representing Mr. Madison's previous administration, has made his perspective more international than I'd like."

"Well, Monroe made his national reputation through his skill in negotiating the Louisiana Purchase. I give him that," Leavenworth shrugged. "But during the presidential campaign he ran on a promise of peace, claiming that his international experience in diplomacy would keep us out of anything so unpopular as the War of 1812."

Jed nodded. "I remember how everyone used to call it 'Mr. Madison's War.'"

"Ah, young man," Leavenworth sighed. "You make me feel my age."

"So Monroe doesn't want to follow Madison down the path of unpopular presidents," Jed thought out loud. "But then, that means the French can do any damned thing they please out *here*—"

"Just so long as all the voting city-folk back East think kindly of him over their imported teas and wines," Leavenworth finished for him.

"But there has to come a time to stand up for your rights," Jed exclaimed passionately. "The President is taking the easy, short view over the long range one!"

Leavenworth smiled. "You'll find the short view the one most usually taken by those who already have something to lose." For a moment a wistful expression passed over Leavenworth's features. "At least those who put themselves before the greater good . . ."

"Come now," Ashley chided the officer.

"In any event, I think you've got the right spirit, Jed," Leavenworth said briskly. "I see now how you got the best of Cabanne." The officer winked. "Oh yes, I heard all about it. It's the talk of the fort. Cabanne and Cayewa left for their outpost right after that incident. Didn't want to take the ribbing, I suppose." His laugh was deep. It seemed long overdue.

"It's never seemed to me to be smart to talk about one's victories," Jed shrugged. "Unless one is sure that the enemy can't retaliate. I . . ." he glanced at Ashley and then corrected himself, "*we* can't be sure of that at all, can we?"

Leavenworth's chuckles trailed off. "Jed, the political situation has tied my hands. My very position here as the representative of the United States has weakened me. I can't even insult Brazeau, let alone take action against him. He is in touch with his country's diplomats and they lobby the President directly. You are right to look out for yourself, because here, I'm sorry to say, the only justice you'll come across is that which a man can win with his own two hands."

The three men wrapped up their meeting on Leavenworth's words of caution, the Colonel and the trapper clearly having earned each other's profound respect.

* * *

Jed wandered through the maze of the fort, carrying out Ashley's orders to round up the men and get them packing in order to continue the journey upriver. Ashley had confided to Jed that since Cayewa had left so abruptly, it figured that the Ashley-Henry expedition had better get going after them. The men weren't going to find any beaver pelts in the taverns. The weather was also pressing them on. It was just early fall, but already the sky had begun to take on the dull lead-grey look of winter.

If Jed had been a different sort of man, he might have been taken with the fact that the men readily obeyed his commands, that such deference to an untested man was quite unusual, that even if Jed wasn't yet a bonafide "hoss," he, for sure, was no longer a greenhorn. But Jed's mind was not on the impression he was making on his fellows. He was mulling over something that Leavenworth had said in passing. The soldier's remark had struck a deep chord in the young man: *You'll find the short view the one most usually taken by those who already have something to lose* . . .

It revived a deep memory.

"But why should you ever want to risk your life out West?" Doctor Simons asked, his voice perplexed, his brown eyes earnest behind the gold-rimmed spectacles. They were at the dinner table in the room Jed had marveled at not so many years before.

"Sir, there's room for a man to stretch and grow out West. Why, there's no foolish laws telling a soul what he can and can't do, there's no limitations, no restrictions. A man—" and here he blushed, "—a man who has nothing could make himself rich as a king!" Jed found his heart was pounding and his throat was dry from the passion he felt. He lifted his wine glass, stared at it. It was one of the very glasses he had

thought were precious jewels when he had first come to
this house. As he brought the glass to his lips his eyes
locked with Louisa's, who sat across from him at the
damask-covered table.

She was twenty years old now. The impish, laughing, little girl with the plaited, black braid had grown
up to be a beautiful young woman with a full, shapely
figure, and ravishing, raven hair cascading around her
shoulders. Her eyes were as brown as her father's, but
where his were warm and wise, hers were young, impetuous, full of fire and spirit.

During the years Jed had spent growing up in the
Simons household, Louisa and he had been insepara-
ble. All through their adolescence she'd been a sparkling, mischievous sprite keeping him company or
teasing him as he did his chores, encouraging and wor-
shipping him during their lessons with her father, for it
had turned out that Jed was the quicker student.

"Is that what you think, Jed? That you have nothing?" Doctor Simons quietly asked as Mrs. Harris went
around the table, serving the roast.

"No, sir, of course not!" Jed quickly said. "I have
the love of my family, and I'm so very grateful for all
that you've done for me." Nothing could be more true
than that, Jed mused. Here he was, sitting in a fine
wool suit, with boots on his feet and an expensive gold
pocketwatch in his vest. They were things bought with
the salary Doctor Simons had been paying him since he
was eighteen for looking after the doctor's various
businesses and properties. "I've no head for figures,
Jed," Simons had complained, "but you know how to
do things right, or else get others to do them."

Jed had brought in his older brother Ralph to
help, as well. Both divided their time between the Simons estate and their own family's much more modest
farm. Even though Ralph was uneducated, he had the

same sort of business canniness. Both Smith brothers were common sights in and around the Simons household, but because of his years as a youth spent with them, Jed felt like—and was considered—one of the family.

Indeed, Jed had suffered much guilt during those years. How dismal and narrow was his family's world compared to that of the Simons! Each weekend had stretched like an eternity as he waited for it to be Sunday evening, the time when he could gracefully take leave of his own family, and the drudgery of plow and ox, to escape into the world of books.

And to Louisa's company.

She was his heart's other half, his soul, his joy. She filled his days with bliss and encompassed his dreams the way the bright blue sky hugs the earth. Oh, Louisa was his beloved—he had told her so, and at long last, one blustery cold winter day, she had given him a cool, sweet kiss which sent his pulse soaring and told him she felt the same.

Not very long after that, Jed very seriously asked to speak to Doctor Simons in the library, where the young man asked for Louisa's hand in marriage. The elder Simons was very pleased and formally offered Jed the position he'd actually held for the last couple of years: superintendent and manager of all the family holdings and businesses.

Though Jed was polite and properly grateful, he didn't accept the offer outright, telling Doc Simons that he wanted to think a bit more about what kind of career he wanted for himself. Simons nodded, but his thoughts were troubled as he watched Jed leave the room.

It had been obvious to the doctor for a long time that Jed and Louisa's friendship had blossomed into something deeper, more passionate. The doctor had long taken it for granted that the boy he had treated as a son would one day actually become his son-in-law. Indeed, Louisa, who had grown up with the benefit of a contemporary and complete education provided by her physician-father in such matters as biology, but without the benefit of a mother's genteel, restraining influence, had been quite forthright and frank with her old papa.

The conversation, unbeknownst to Jed, had taken place the day before he had so anxiously asked to speak with Simons. Louisa, her eyes bright with a newly awakened sense of womanhood, had pulled her father into that very library to explain all about how she was going to marry Jed, move to the city for a while to live in the Simons' townhouse in Philadelphia, help manage the family holdings with her new husband, and eventually return to the country house to raise their family.

"You know that makes me happy, child," her father had smiled. "You have my sincerest blessings. I only hope I don't have to wait too long to see some grandchildren about the place."

"Is that what you want, papa?" Louisa had asked, hugging him.

"A grandson, Louisa?" He'd beamed like a small boy, but then his bright smile had faded. "But what does Jed have to say about this life plan?"

Louisa's confident depiction of the future slowed for a moment. "Oh, Daddy!" she'd laughed, her eyes sparkling and her cheeks flushing a delicate pink. "Jed wants to marry me. Don't worry. As for the rest," she'd confided to her father as if he was her best friend, "it's only sensible. Jed loves you as much as I do. Why would he ever want to leave our home?"

So fervent was the elder Simons' hope that the blissful things his daughter had predicted would come to pass that he'd brushed away the worrisome thoughts troubling him, the way he'd lately been brushing away the physical symptoms he knew were old age coming to call at long last.

"Louisa, you know I give you my blessings." He hugged his daughter tightly. She had grown up having her own way. She was strong-willed, intelligent, the match of any man.

But the doctor also knew that Jedediah Strong Smith was not just any man. Now he merely stared at the food on his plate, his appetite gone. It had become clear that his wishes for Louisa would go unfulfilled, for Jed wanted to move to the West, and most likely take Louisa with him. Either way, Doc Simons knew he would lose something precious. Jed would be away a long time, either alone, or with his only child, his beloved Louisa. And time was precious. It was one thing the wealthy physician didn't have.

He'd not told Louisa of the diagnosis he'd made on himself just a month ago, when the pains coursing through his body had become almost too much to bear. Now he couldn't tell her, or Jed.

"There's land just for the taking, sir," Jed informed him between mouthfuls of roast beef. "There's plenty of timber and water—"

"And savages," Louisa broke in, pouting. "And horrid animals!"

"Come on, Louisa!" Jed laughed. "You're not afraid. I've taught you to hunt as well as I can."

"But you think it'll be a lark. It won't be, Jed." She glanced at her father. How pale he looked! Clearly all this nonsense was upsetting him. "Let's not talk about it anymore."

"It isn't the Garden of Eden out there, I know that." Jed's voice was calm, level, but there was the strength of steel beneath his polite, dinner-table tone.

"But the West is wide open, young. It's, well, it's the way I am. I think it's the only place big enough for me. It's what I want—"

"Is it *all* you want?" Louisa demanded, pushing back her chair and jumping to her feet. "Please excuse me, papa. But Jed has quite ruined my appetite and I find the conversation too childish, too dreary, too boring, and too damned stupid for words!"

Mrs. Harris, who had entered the room unnoticed, trailed by a tall figure dressed in work clothes, hopped out of Louisa's way so that the angry young woman ran smack into the arms of Ralph, Jed's older brother.

"Oh, excuse me," Louisa stuttered. She glanced up into his face. Except for his dark blond hair and hazel eyes, and a few inches added height, he greatly resembled Jed. It was in their personalities that the two young men truly differed. Although a year older than Jed, Ralph had always been shier, the less confident of the two. But Ralph's physical strength, his self-taught, practical knowledge of the farm and its related businesses, and his common sense, made him just as respected by all. And if he didn't have his brother's spirit and education, Ralph did have the knowledge to coax a crop out of soil that Jed would have considered worthless and the patience to dicker a good price for the miller's services when Jed would have thrown up his hands and impulsively alienated the man by issuing a "take it or leave it" ultimatum.

"It's all right, Louisa," Ralph managed. Though his hands were hard and calloused, the tips of his fingers were quite sensitive. Where they touched Louisa's silk-covered upper arms, they felt as if they were on fire. Then suddenly she was past him and gone from the room.

"Mr. Ralph," Mrs. Harris announced, albeit

somewhat belatedly. "Sit, young man, and I'll fetch you a plate." She waddled out of the room, grumbling about Louisa's mouth and a bar of soap.

"Seems she's a bit riled with you, eh, Jed?" Ralph grinned as he plopped himself down in a chair. It was one of his rare attempts at joking, but unfortunately, neither Jed nor Doc Simons seemed to be in a light mood. "Uh, I can stay only a little while. Got to get back out. I reckon that cow is going to birth herself a fine calf. . . ." He waited for the two men to remark on the news, but both seemed wrapped in their own thoughts. "Yep. A fine calf," Ralph repeated for his own satisfaction and began to devour the heaping portion of roast beef and potatoes Mrs. Harris had just placed before him.

"If you'll excuse me, sir, I'll turn in. It's been a long day," Jed said. He got up and made his way around the table to where Ralph sat. "Want me to come spell you at the barn?" he asked, smiling, his arm resting on his brother's shoulder.

"No, thanks, Jed," Ralph sighed. "You're no good waitin' on a cow. I reckon I better tough it out. Not that I mind, 'cause I don't. It's nice and peaceful . . . ah, I reckon I just like bein' there when it happens."

"A born mid-wife to heifers," Jed teased.

"Go on," Ralph laughed back. "Get outta here before I getcha suit all messed up."

"Good night, Jed," Doc Simons sighed. "Don't worry about Louisa. She'll calm down by morning."

"Yes, sir." As he left the room he heard Ralph say, "There's a few matters concerning the back acreage we ought to talk about, sir."

"Yes, of course, Ralph," Simons responded absently. "Oh! Where are my manners! I haven't even offered you wine. . . ."

Their voices trailed off as Jed made his way to the winding front staircase. Though Ralph seemed content with his life, Jed often wondered if Ralph resented what their father had done for him. Ralph, after all, was the first-born, and it seemed odd to Jed that Ralph had not been the one chosen to learn to read and write. He wondered, guiltily, if Ralph envied his fine suit of clothes, or his fancy, expensive gold watch and chain. He wondered if Ralph yearned to have a woman like Louisa, for as far as Jed knew, the land was Ralph's only mistress. The couple of times Jed had tried to talk to Ralph about it, Ralph had always cut their conversations short with something he had heard in church: "To every thing there is a season, and a time to every purpose under heaven." Ralph, his brother, was a man who could barely write his own name, yet who understood the ways of the world and mankind far more intimately than Jed. A man who possessed more wisdom than Jed had knowledge.

His mind now whirring with heavy thoughts, Jed took in the plush red and blue carpet running up the stairs, the velvety finish of the expensive wallpaper. His fingers slid along the smooth, hand-rubbed, walnut banister. Perhaps he had misjudged Louisa. Perhaps all of these fineries—the superb furniture, exquisite crystal and china, the laces and silks—were not just luxuries, but necessities to her.

He tiptoed past Louisa's closed bedroom door. Light was coming from beneath it; she was still awake. He didn't want her to hear him. Occasionally in the past she had called out to him in such situations, bidding him to come into her room and talk. At first the requests had horrified him, and he'd always refused in deference to her father. But as Jed matured, he'd come to realize that Louisa's trilled invitations were merely the product of the vixen side of her nature. She knew he'd never accept, and so took great pleasure in acting lewd.

But he was in no mood for games tonight. He'd drunk too much wine at dinner, he feared. His head was light, and his mind was in a state of confusion. Louisa, he knew, was quite up to the rigors of emigrating West. She could ride and shoot, cook and sew. But what if she really didn't want to go? This would be the first time that she and Jed had set themselves a battle of wills. There had to be a way to convince her! Jed knew he was destined to thrive out West as a land baron. But he also knew one other thing—he loved Louisa. He loved her totally, completely, and he had to have her by his side.

His own room was down the hall, far from Louisa's. Doc slept downstairs in a wing of the house, so Jed had no fear of waking the man as he moved about. Jed struck a match and lit the candle on the dresser by the door. He shrugged off his jacket, peeled off both his vest and shirt in a single motion, and dropped the garments on a nearby straight-backed chair.

Suddenly another match flared. Another candle was lit, this time on the nightstand beside his bed. "Whatever you do," Louisa implored him in a whisper, "keep your voice down."

Jed was speechless. He couldn't tear his eyes away from Louisa, who sat cross-legged on his bed, wrapped in a white silk dressing gown. The moon's luminescence streaming in through the window bathed her in silver light. She looked so lovely, more exquisite even than she'd appeared in his dreams. "Louisa, please," he begged, his voice grown husky with emotion at the very sight of her. "This is wrong."

"Not wrong," she said. "Just—wanton." She patted the bed. "Come sit beside me—"

"What? Louisa, no!"

"Well, suit yourself," she smiled wickedly. "Curl up on that nasty old chair and go to sleep then. But I warn you, I'm not leaving until we kiss and make up. I hate to quarrel with you. Let's not do it anymore. Look, Jed! I brought us some wine." She held up a small carafe, shimmering red in the candlelight. "But only one glass. It was all I could manage. I thought I heard Mrs. Harris plodding in, and I panicked. I hid in the pantry until she was finished getting Ralph's dinner. Then I came up here." Louisa smiled again and poured a full glass of wine. "We can share this glass." She took a sensuous sip and extended the glass to Jed. "Well? Are you going to stand there like an ox all night? Or are you going to come sit beside me and apologize for being so silly at dinner?"

"Oh, Louisa," Jed sighed. He stayed where he was, feeling as if his feet had taken root in the floor.

"Is it you're afraid to sit next to me? Oh my, and I thought my Jed wasn't afraid of anything."

He took a wavering step toward the bed.

"Oh, men!" Louisa set the glass down on the nightstand and jumped off the bed to face him with her hands on her hips. "Are you coming, or do I have to drag you?" She impatiently shifted her bare foot, and as she did so, the front of her white gown momentarily parted. Jed caught a glimpse of her knee and the front of her thigh. Her skin looked silken in the shimmering light.

"But the way you're dressed. It isn't proper." Jed shook his head, even as he approached her.

"What? My gown? Well, then, I'll just take it off." She shrugged her shoulders and the white silk wafted to the floor like a snowflake. "Do you like me, Jed?" she breathed. "Oh, I hope you do. I've always hoped you wouldn't be . . . well . . . disappointed. . . ."

"You're lovely. And I do love you," Jed whispered. And then he was running his hands over the curves of her body. His fingers trembled across the lush softness of her full, upturned breasts, as her nipples grew taut beneath his touch. He watched the pink flush of excitement color her cheeks and quicken her breathing as she pressed her lips to his.

Her kiss was moist and sweet. It was a thousand times more intense than it had ever been before. Louisa's fingers unbuckled his trousers. Her hands were like fans on glowing embers as she slid them across his bared buttocks, down along the thick, corded muscles of his thighs. His devastation was total. As Louisa fell back on the bed, she pulled Jed down upon her. Her fingers curled about his manhood, and drew him into her. She cried out softly, but only once, and her gasp was more of a song than of pain.

The perspiration glistened on their bodies as they rocked together. Jed stared into her eyes and thought, *We're each being born again. Seeing each other for the first time—*

And then all thought was gone and there was only the touch and scent of Louisa. Groaning, she drew him even deeper, until he was lost in the tides and waves of her body.

Joined in flesh, their moans came in unison, soft gasps blown into each other's soul as their mouths locked in an endless kiss.

Minutes later, Louisa gave him a warm look as she tangled her fingers in his shiny black, tousled hair. "You see now," she whispered, her lips pressing against his ear. "You don't need to go anywhere. To explore wild country. I'll be your wilderness. I'll be all you need. We'll have our children right here!"

Jed's movements jarred the nightstand. The nearly full glass fell to the floor, shattering in a tiny, bell-like crash. The wine spotted her pure white crumpled gown crimson.

Chapter 5

Fort Atkinson's dock was swarming with merchants, either haggling to unload their merchandise, or else watching the activities of the keelboat men preparing the *Yellowstone Packet* and *Rocky Mountains* for the continuation of their voyage. General Ashley had decided at the last moment to take on some extra supplies of trading goods to replace the few boxes of cargo lost during the accident on the river. Word of a potential buyer had spread around the fort like a prairie fire. The shopkeepers resembled the black birds that swooped and hovered above the swirling river, looking for any scrap tossed off by the expedition.

The General paced the worn, cracked boards of the old wharf, dickering with the few merchants he hadn't already talked to, and muttering to one in particular about interminable delays, and just where was that river rat of a keelboat patron, Mike Fink, anyway?

"Find him?" the General asked as Jed approached. His question had been more like a warning.

"I've looked everywhere," Jed told him. "Every whorehouse and tavern in the fort. I can track a deer by sense of smell alone. Tell the spoors of a hundred different animals. But I've got to say, looks like Mike Fink's vanished."

Ashley seemed speechless with helpless rage. He began to gesticulate wildly at Jed, his mouth opened and closed soundlessly and all the while his long, thin face grew progressively redder. Finally he stalked off to meet with a general store owner who had lugged a box full of glass beads down to the pier.

All around the two boats, squaw whores moaned and cried. The women waved little squares of calico to signal their lovers. The boatmen loading their vessels ignored the whores, while most of the trappers slept off their hangovers on the roofs of the keelboats. The men's lack of appreciation for their performance, however, didn't stop the women's wailing and keening, nor did it stop the fluttering of their handkerchiefs, like flags in the wind. Would they truly miss the men, or merely the coins the men put in their pouches? Jed thought wryly.

He almost tripped over Hiram Angus, sleeping curled up like a buckskin-brown old hound on some sacks of flour destined for the *Yellowstone*'s hold. The trapper coughed and grumbled in his sleep. Jed waited for him to come to life.

"What are you botherin' me for, boy?" Hiram managed. "Lord, stop those whores from screechin' so! A man needs his rest. They sound like kitties in the grip of heat."

"Hiram, where's Mike Fink and his boys? Do you know?"

"My head!" Hiram groaned, putting his hands over his ears. His eyes finally opened and they were as red as twin sunsets on the Freedom River. "Oh, shut 'em up," he wailed, almost, but not quite, drowning out the whores. "Somebody tell 'em they won't go thirsty for long. By the by, another boat will be here for 'em. There's always another."

"I reckon," Jed agreed. "For women there always is. But Hiram, I'm looking for Mike so that we can shove off."

"Mike, eh?" Hiram thought about it. "Now, reckon I last saw 'em at Angie's."

"What's that?" Jed demanded. "Where is it?"

"It's a whorehouse, what else?" Hiram scowled.

"Well, I didn't know about it."

"Course you didn't!" Hiram laughed. "You don't go, so how you gonna know? Oh, my head!"

"Where?" Jed asked.

"Settin' right on top of that there tavern where you faced down Cabanne. Now let this old hoss get some sleep."

Angie's turned out to be all of one smallish room, run by a wrinkled old crone who went by that name. The fact that the old hag was white lent the place some distinction, even if the actual whores were all Sioux squaws, just like everywhere else.

The room smelled like an outhouse. How could men find satisfaction in such a place, Jed wondered? There weren't even curtains for privacy between the rickety cots—their straw mattresses torn, their grey sheets foul with stains—crammed into every available foot of the space.

Angie herself was sitting in a rocking chair sewing together some ragged cloth for sheets when Jed climbed the stairs and stood in the doorway. She offered him a grin, exposing a mouth half-filled with green, rotting teeth. "You want a girl?" she croaked, her voice rattling like pebbles down a tin chute. "We'll fix you up, right fine."

Across the room, one of the whores separated herself from a small circle huddled around a keg of skull varnish. As she approached she stared at Jed with dull eyes. Her face was expressionless, an Indian mask carved from wood. She opened the buffalo robe draped across her shoulders, showing him her squat, shapeless body with sagging breasts.

The whore's gesture more than her nude form brought back the memory of Louisa. It snapped and bit briefly into his heart like the tip of a whip.

Jed turned away. "I'm looking for three men," he told the witch in the rocking chair. "One's a big man, with black hair. One of his friends has a burn scar down one cheek. Their names are Fink, Carpenter, Talbot. Were they here?"

"Threw 'em out," the ancient woman spat as the whore picked up her robe and went back to the others and their keg. "Two of 'em was fightin' over one of me girls. No fightin' allowed here. Threw 'em out." With that she went back to her sewing.

Back in the fresh air and sunlight, Jed took deep breaths to clear the stench from his nostrils. His own dark memories, combined with this last encounter upstairs, had poisoned the fort for him. Now, everywhere he looked, all he saw was the foul garbage of too many men in one place. What devilish thing was it in the human race that caused the sum of so many people together to be so much worse than the parts that were just individuals? How he longed to be on the river! To be exploring its banks as a solitary hunter! When he was in the open country he would just be, just concern himself with the business of living, without the haunting memories of what once was, and what might have been.

He heard a groan coming from behind the building.

Rounding the corner into the shadowed, reeking alley, he saw Fink leaning against a rear-entrance wall,

a jug of skull varnish tilted to his lips. Carpenter, his
burn scar a livid red against the pale white of his
cheek, was slumped nearby. To the unmarked side of
his face, he held a blue scrap of cloth, the kind the
whores at the dock waved. An anxious Talbot stood
over him.

It was Carpenter's groan Jed had heard. He went
to the man and gently pulled away the cloth. "Oh
Christ," Jed muttered. Carpenter's cheek had been
sliced down the middle. Jed could see the man's teeth
poking through the jagged slash. "How'd it happen?"
Jed looked up at Talbot.

"None of your business," Fink slurred, his face
against the wall. Then he said, "I cut him." He held up
his Bowie knife. It was the same one he had used
against the bear when he'd saved Jed's life. "I did it
with this. The bastard took my woman last night. Before I was finished with her."

Tom Talbot took a few menacing steps toward
Fink, but then faltered as he eyed the long, sharp
Bowie. "I told him, Jed," he blurted. "I said, 'It's hell
to cut your friend for a whore.' I told him!"

"And I told you," Fink returned sullenly, "she
was mine. My whore."

"Come on, Billy." Talbot helped the bleeding
Carpenter to his feet. "I'll get him sewn up and to the
boats," he told Jed as he led Bill from the alley.

"Sew him up good!" Mike shouted. His laugh was
bitter, heavy. It faded abruptly to a choking laugh.

"Come on, Mike," Jed prompted. "We've got to
set out. You're needed at the boats."

"Right." Mike drained the last drop from the jug,
tossed it away and fell into step behind Jed.

Once they were out of the alley Jed observed
Fink. The man's eyes were half-closed, his big face

sagging from the effects of drink. "Damn, Mike," Jed shook his head. "Carpenter was your friend."

"My friends do what I tell 'em," Mike growled. He sounded like a man half asleep, but there was no mistaking the brutal meanness in his drunken voice.

The stinking sum of the blessed parts, Jed thought, and pulled away to walk alone.

Alone—

Louisa, Jed thought, did you finally lose or gain what it was you wanted?

He willed away her image as he made for the boats. Soon he'd be past the Grand Detour, past the Ree villages, finally in the uncharted wilderness.

Only then would he let himself decide if his emigration had been worthwhile. Only then would he know what it was he himself had lost, or gained.

PART TWO

SUNBLOSSOM

Chapter 6

The mouse, a tiny grey oval, scurried along the molding's edge. When it came to the corner formed by the two paneled walls of the room, it stopped and sniffed the air; its tiny saucer ears rolling and twitching. The mouse's body trembled as its feet picked up a vibration from the hardwood floor. It was about to make its heart-stopping dash directly across the room, to the safety of its hole in the far wall, when the top of the Bowie knife burst through its body, pinning it to the wood beneath.

Cabanne bent and carefully tugged the knife out of the plank so that the dead mouse stayed firmly skewered.

Nearby, Tooth sat, every muscle of its body quivering, as if in gigantic parody of the mouse. Saliva dripped from the grizzled hound's slack jaws. Already a dark pool had formed between the dog's front paws. Only Tooth's yellow eyes betrayed any sense of intelligence or purpose. They tracked Cabanne's every movement. The twin black pupils were like miniature, inky mirrors reflecting the glinting steel blade that had something furry and wet atop it.

Cabanne watched in satisfaction as his pet's head

dipped and swooned with the strain of remembering the command of "Hold!" The Frenchman had trained Tooth to sit stock still like that all day, until he gave the animal an order releasing it.

Bored with the game, Cabanne finally gave one soft whistle. Tooth launched itself at its master to come up short at the man's feet. The dog's limbs were jerking steel springs as it balanced itself on powerful hind legs and opened its jaws, resembling a fledging bird awaiting food from its parent. Laughing, Cabanne whipped down the knife. The bloody morsel slid off the blade to fall into Tooth's gaping maw.

The dog swallowed the mouse without chewing. Its tongue, rough as sandpaper, flicked out and around its lips to snatch any last droplet of blood, and then, with a little sigh of contentment, the huge dog padded away to curl up in a corner, its eyes still on its master.

"They come, Cabanne." Joseph Brazeau peered out through the wide-open window on the river side of Fort Kiowa's watchtower. The window was without glass, but had shutters pierced with gun slits for fending off Indian attacks. But for as long as anyone could remember, the shutters had been thrown back and secured to the whitewashed walls by leather thongs wrapped around wooden pegs.

The fort was perched on a high promontory which jutted out from an elbow-like bend the Freedom made as it meandered along the thirty-mile loop known as the Grand Detour. As usual, rays of sunlight reflecting off the river brightened the watchtower's room, which was bare except for two hard-backed chairs and a table, upon which sat a tall, slender, brown bottle, and two small glasses.

"There! Cabanne. It is the Americans." Brazeau muttered a curse beneath his breath as he watched Ashley's two keelboats travel the stretch of river one hundred yards below. The boats had their big, square, white sails unfurled, this part of the Missouri being favored with a shoal-free, gentle current, and a steady, upriver breeze.

Although Brazeau could see figures on the two keelboats, he could not make out who they were. He watched until the two boats had passed Kiowa, and then shifted his gaze to take in the rough cliffs opposite the fort, and, beyond them, the stands of willow and cottonwood with their leaves turning yellow-red in the first fall chill. On this portion of the Missouri the thick forests had thinned out to mere fringes of trees, beyond which, Brazeau knew, were great prairies dotted with dark seas of bison, herds of elk, antelope and deer, along with the ubiquitous black bear, and its warrior cousin, the grizzly.

How he loved this land! Brazeau had always considered the Detour to be paradise on earth, the Garden of Eden as the Lord meant it to be. But now a serpent had slithered into Brazeau's paradise.

"The Americans have passed us now." There was irony in his voice as he turned from the window to take the chair across from Cabanne, who was lounging in his own chair, tilted back, his feet propped up on the table.

"Then it is now clear for us to proceed against Joshua Pilcher's Fort Recovery," the bearded Frenchman said.

"It is clear," Brazeau nodded. Serpents? Why, the Americans were a nest of snakes! Pilcher's Missouri Fur Company's threat to the French would be effectively blunted by Cabanne's ploy, but now the Ashley-Henry expedition was making its way to the upper waters. . . .

All of Cayewa's men were busy working the fertile beaver waters of the Detour. That made Pilcher's outpost, located a dozen miles downriver, their immediate competitor. But Brazeau knew that the fur company that controlled the upper waters, and which had the best relations with the Rees, would one day control the entire fur trade of this region.

"It must be us," Brazeau said out loud.

Cabanne heard him and nodded, not needing to ask what his employer meant.

Both men viewed the situation between themselves and the Americans as a state of war. An undeclared war perhaps, but a violent, murderous one, for all of its covertness. This land and its riches had always belonged to the French. God Himself had willed it so. Hadn't it been His hand that had guided the French explorer-priests Marquette and Joliet to the mighty Missouri during their voyage down the gentle Mississippi River? They had brought the French flag to this land of plenty almost one hundred and fifty years ago. And hadn't LaSalle picked up where they had left off? Hadn't he, exhausted and tortured by the rigors of his journey, but constantly buoyed and comforted by God's guiding light, laid claim to the vast Mississippi basin, all the way to the mighty Rocky Mountains, in the name of Louis the Fourteenth?

"The Americans foolishly believe," Brazeau fumed, "that because their puny nation has so far lasted the breadth of a day on this continent, it all belongs to them!"

The anger and hostility in his voice was so evident that Tooth—still lying curled in his corner—raised his head to offer an ominous growl.

"They are children," Brazeau raged on, unmindful as his silent audience, Cabanne, lazed and yawned. "They are children pompously playing 'King of the Hill,' not realizing that at any moment real men will come along to topple them, to box their ears and send them tumbling into the mud."

Cabanne nodded, his eyes on the brown bottle on the table.

"Their continent!" Brazeau laughed bitterly. "They think the world is so large. . . ." He shook his head, unable to go on. He sighed, and when he spoke again, his voice sounded almost regretful. "They are too naïve, these Americans, even to understand what might lie behind the cultured voices of our polished diplomats, cooing like pigeons into their cowardly President's ear."

This time Cabanne laughed. He had no grasp of history, of international politics, of affairs of state. But he knew quite well what lay behind the diplomats' "cultured voices": *he* did, and men like him, who were the foot soldiers in France's war to preserve what it had claimed.

Not that Cabanne felt much personal loyalty to France. Joseph Brazeau's father, Louis Brazeau, known as "Old Cayewa," had brought his family to St. Louis forty years ago. The son, Young Cayewa, had often lectured Cabanne on how the Brazeau family had been licensed to trade the Missouri River by the French government, how the Brazeau family could trace its lineage back for hundreds of years. He himself had even journeyed back East once, to Washington, in order to dine with the French ambassador and to "discuss strategy." Cabanne preferred to implement rather than discuss strategy.

Cabanne had no idea who his father was, and neither did his mother, a Parisian whore. As a child, his world had been the gutters and back alleys of Paris; his playmates the urchins of whores, and derelicts. He'd lived on spoiled food found in piles of reeking garbage, or else snatched fresh food from the displays of shopkeepers, outrunning the gendarmes.

When he was ten years old, he crept upon a sleeping drunk and slit his throat with a jagged shard from a broken wine bottle, just to see what it felt like. That was when Cabanne first realized nothing pleased him more than an act that would cause another pain. The boy kept the secret of his joy to himself. No one would rob him of this pleasure, so much better than rutting with whores.

When he was thirteen, and quite big for his age, he himself fathered a child which he promptly drowned in a bucket of water while his fifteen-year-old child-bride screamed in horror. Cabanne then wrapped his grimy fingers around the little whore's throat. She was a slut, like his mother! She deserved to die! He'd squeezed that little throat until the screams stopped, but to his lasting regret, he hadn't squeezed quite long enough. The still, thin body he walked away from, assuming it was dead, was still alive. The girl recovered to accuse him of infanticide. The story of his drowning his own offspring was trumpeted throughout the city. Soon, even the criminal denizens of the underworld joined in his pursuit. They'd have taken his head for sure, if they had caught him.

Cabanne was able to reach the wharfs. He became a stowaway on a merchant ship bound for the Americas. He was fortunate to be discovered by the cabinboy. The lad was sixteen if he was a day, but he whimpered like a newborn babe when Cabanne's hands reached out for his throat.

Cabanne cracked the boy's neck and threw him overboard. His luck held, for when he met the captain, he saw that the man was a scoundrel like himself who cared little about who did a job as long as it got done. Cabanne became the new cabinboy, and managed to last out the voyage peacefully. He jumped ship once their destination was reached, linked up with the French fur traders plying their trade, and eventually came into Brazeau's employ.

Brazeau considered himself a general in the war between the French fur companies and the Americans. Cabanne saw himself as an infantry soldier. He was an indifferent fur trapper, for he had little patience for sitting and waiting, but he was invaluable in a trappers' war because that meant there were men to be killed. And killing was what he did best.

"Tell me again," Brazeau suddenly said. "Tell me how Pilcher's outpost will be no more."

"Skull varnish will do it," Cabanne smiled. "Skull varnish will wash the Pilcher fort away. It took me and my men months to smuggle enough of the brew out of Atkinson. Nobody saw us. Nobody knows we have it. The Ree war party is camped in the timber, between us and Pilcher's fort."

"Which village are they from?" Brazeau asked. He reached out and tilted the brown bottle on the table so that the light from the window revealed the level of its contents.

"They're from Bear's village," Cabanne mumbled. He was staring at the bottle in Brazeau's hand, staring at it while his mouth watered and saliva flowed so it wet the black whiskers of his beard. In that bottle was cognac, the finest of French brandy! Brazeau had it sent to him from the East. It had been so long since Cabanne had been given a taste!

"Yes? From Bear's village?" Brazeau coaxed, tilting the bottle this way and that.

"Please, Cayewa. A drink—"

"Finish telling me first."

Cabanne moaned, but did as he was told. "They are a group of braves unhappy with the coming marriage of Bear's daughter to Grey Eyes, 'guvner' of the other village. The marriage is to unite forever the two villages, but the war party from Bear's village is composed mainly of young men. They are braves who have not yet seasoned themselves in battle, and they wish this honor. Bear, as you know, has forbade all bloodshed in honor of his daughter's betrothal."

"So you will bring them the skull varnish, and once it has given them courage, you will send them to Pilcher's Fort Recovery, where they can count coup, earning themselves battle-hardened-braves' feathers for their headbands, at last. . . ." Brazeau smiled in appreciation of the plan as he poured them both a measure of the cognac. He watched as Cabanne became oblivious to all else but the small glass of brownish-gold liquid. "You are like your dog begging for its mouse," Brazeau chuckled. "Go on then. Drink."

Cabanne snatched up the glass and poured its contents into his mouth. His cheeks bellowed out as he swirled the liquor about, savoring its fine burn on his tongue. Then he swallowed.

Brazeau took pity on him and poured him another glassful without making him beg for it. "There will be enough of the skull varnish left?" he asked.

"There will be plenty, Cayewa. It will not take more than a keg to rile the war party, and I have cached away ten times that amount." Cabanne roared a deep laugh, partly fueled by the cognac, partly by his joyous anticipation of the coming attack on the Americans. "I myself will lead them, Cayewa. I will show them how to crack the defenses of the outpost. Pilcher's company, small as it is, will be no more."

Brazeau poured him a third glass. He himself had not yet touched his first, but now he lifted it in a toast. "Then it will be time to deal with the Ashley-Henry men."

"I must have Jed Smith's scalp on my belt, Cayewa," Cabanne growled. "Its place will be here," he touched the spot between two of his sheathed Bowies. "Jed Smith's scalp belongs to me, yes Master Cayewa?"

"So you beg for another scrap, do you?" Brazeau smiled. "Take any scalp you can, Cabanne. I care little about individuals. My concern is with the Ashley-Henry expedition. By the time we've finished with Pilcher, they will just be reaching the Ree villages."

Cabanne shrugged. "There will be plenty of skull varnish left. There will be plenty of braves looking for a fight. As soon as I am able, I will leave for the villages. I will need only a few men. We will travel overland. There will be no chance of Ashley's party spotting us." Now he grinned, hungrily. "No chance of Jed Smith spotting me. Until it is too late."

"That is your own personal affair," Brazeau repeated as they touched glasses and drank.

Chapter 7

The birds flocking overhead were the first sign Jed noticed that the expedition was nearing the Ree villages. Larks the color of old gold, purple finchs, ruby crossbills, satiny orioles in bright yellow vests, and bright bluejays appeared to play around the keelboats' masts, while ravens black as night swooped and dived, cawing their greeting. To Jed, it was as if a rainbow had shattered itself into myriad, musical pieces in order to welcome the men. He considered the birds a good omen.

"Prettier than a maiden's red lips, ain't they?" Hiram questioned. "Them birds found themselves a good home when they happened on the Rees. These heathens keep farms. The women do most of the work, while the men hunt buffalo. The birds come to eat up all that good corn, squash and pumpkins. Course, it's a mite late in the season for growin' things," Hiram added, "but birds is stupid critters. These here will hang around 'til the snow's about ready to fall."

"When will that be?"

Hiram looked up at the sky as if to see the winter coming. He nodded sagely at Jed. "Another few months, I reckon."

It was now more than a month since the expedition had left Fort Atkinson. Jed had spent the time learning the rudiments of the Ree language from the expedition's interpreter, Eddie Rose. Eddie, a middle-aged man with the sharply pointed features of a ferret, had spent some early years living with the Arikara tribe, and indeed, legend had it that Eddie had a squaw wife in almost every tribe on the Missouri but the Rees, as well as a spouse in Crow country, up around the Musselshell. A ferocious fighter who had done in many braves in hand-to-hand combat, Eddie had found himself inducted into various Indian families simply because the Indians found it easier than killing him.

"If they can't break your back, they make you an honorary 'guvner,'" Eddie had once told Jed. "Jest like white folks will do."

At first the experienced interpreter had been skeptical when Jed approached with an offer of a fine powder horn in exchange for lessons in the Ree tongue. But Jed's years of studying with Doc Simons paid off once again. He knew how to approach a language. What Eddie had called the "bones" of the Ree language Jed considered the extremely uncomplicated rules of grammar. What Eddie had referred to as the language's "blood," Jed defined as the limited vocabulary. Approaching Eddie's helter-skelter output of knowledge systematically, the way Doc Simons had drilled into him, allowed Jed to amaze the wilderness man by mastering a working knowledge of the tongue in a very short time.

"Eddie, you still have a wife of the Ree nation?" Jed had once asked during one of their lessons in which they spoke nothing but Arikara.

"No," Eddie sounded wistful. "She died a while back, when I was just a young man, like yourself. You

see, the Rees used to be part of the Pawnee nation, but
they split themselves off and founded their villages a
long time ago. You shoulda seen it then. What we are
coming upon is just two villages, because that is all
that is left. But back when I was a young man, there
were thirty-two such villages. It was a city, it was.
Greater than St. Louis, I'll tell you that much." Eddie
spat over the side of the boat into the yellow waters of
the river. "Cleaner than St. Louis, too."

"Eddie, what happens?" Jed asked, staring up at
the clouds, white tufts of finest gun wool against the
bright blue sky.

" 'What happened?' is how you say it, boy. Pay
attention to what you are doing. How am I going to
take that fine old powder horn from you if I cannot
graduate you on account of your laziness? Anyway, the
pox is what *happened*, Jed. I guess the early French
and Spanish brought it with them. It went through the
Ree nation like a Hawkens buffalo round. Of course,
that was way before my time. But it seems as though
the pox still comes around every once in a while, just
like the seasons. My squaw died during one of those
times."

"Hiram told me to keep my guns nearby once we
reach the villages. He says the Rees are nasty." Jed
tried to keep his voice calm, mature, even though the
thought of some action both thrilled and frightened
him. "Reckon we'll see some action?" he asked, lapsing
into English.

"Well now, I don't rightly know, Jed. I'll say this
much though, the Rees have never been the white
man's friends." Eddie sat up, speaking English as well,
his face dark and serious. "Some will say they fear
nothin' but the Crows. Others will swear it's the Black-
foot that give 'em the night creepies. But I know that
the Rees teach their young from the beginning to hate

the white race. It's on account of the pox. The Rees figure that if they killed white men from now 'til the end
of the world, they wouldn't be more than half evened
up for what the pox did to their nation."

"But that was the French and Spanish, right?"
Jed's heart went out to the Rees as he imagined their
terror and sorrow. There was nothing in their religion
to explain such unimaginable devastation.

Eddie just laughed. "Hell, Jed. They'd never been
exposed to white men's sickness, so we coulda brought
it on 'em just as well as the French or Spanish. The
foreigners just happened to git there first, is all. Anyway, the Rees don't care what a varmint calls hisself.
White is white. That's somethin' else you gotta learn
boy," he winked at Jed. "To a savage, all us white boys
looks alike."

The story of the Ree devastation had saddened
Jed, and had occupied his thoughts for several days.
But now that dark history was replaced by excitement
as the first keelboat man to spot the Ree villages let
out a shout.

"Right now, boys! Haul in the sails. Look lively!"
Mike Fink shouted. "You boys! Get the poles and
brace us. We'll be in their damned front yards we don't
watch out!"

Jed rushed past Fink to station himself at the very
prow of the boat. He strained his eyes for the first
glimpse of the villages, while his ears filled with the tu-
multuous barking and howling of the Rees' dogs.

General Ashley came up behind him to confer
with Fink. "Anchor in mid-channel, patron," he ordered. "These savages are risky business."

"Aye, sir," Mike grumbled. "But I don't like this.
Look there, General!"

Both Jed and Ashley saw what Fink was worried
about. The two villages were about three hundred

yards apart, dug into the right bank of the river. They were on high ground, situated on the top of a wide, sandy beach sloping gently up from the water. All along the ridge, just before the start of the towns, there was a long, thick stockade fashioned out of driftwood and brambles. Several entrances had been hacked into this barricade, and moccasined feet had trudged ragged, winding paths up the incline over the years. But, on the whole, the site seemed to be one solid citadel from which the Rees could fire down on the expedition with little risk to themselves.

"And look there, General," Fink pointed to a swirl of water in the middle of the river between the two villages.

"A whirlpool?" Ashley stammered, his tone incredulous. "How can that be?"

Fink laughed bitterly. "Aye, a whirlpool, but a man-made one—if you can call those savages men. They're clever, General. They've sunk driftwood down to the bottom. That's the current running around it."

"Anyway we could sail around that, eh patron?" Ashley began hopefully.

Fink shook his head vigorously. "No sir, the boats don't handle that accurately under sail-power. The passages on either side of that there whirlpool are too narrow. We can't cordelle either." Fink's thick arm stretched out, his finger directing their gaze along the left bank of the river. There the ground was also high, but studded with rocks and boulders. "The boys can't tow no boats at that angle, General."

"But that terrain certainly could give the Rees cover," Jed mused.

"Yes, it could," Ashley quietly agreed. "I gather poling is our only way out of this?" he asked Fink.

"Aye, sir. It is if you want to continue on upstream, that is. Going downstream, all we'd have to do is raise anchor," Fink said hopefully. "The current would float us back the way we came in a flash."

"Thought you wanted to become a trapper, Mike," Jed teased.

"I do, boy," Fink scowled. "But I'd rather keep me hair on me head while I'm doin' it."

"Well, we aren't going downstream just yet, patron," Ashley observed dryly.

"And we can't pass them by, Mike," Jed added. "We need horses."

"What?" Fink turned around.

"The General's partner, Major Henry, is expecting enough steeds to outfit our trapping party," Jed explained. "Without them, there won't be any way to pack down our pelts to a point where we can transfer them to the keelboats. There was no way we could have brought the horses all this distance and beyond from St. Louis, and there's no way we can buy them upriver. Word is the Crows cherish their horseflesh. Anyway, they get them from the Rees, as well."

"Ain't there nobody else we can trade with for nags, General?" Fink asked fretfully.

"Well, the only other herd in the vicinity belongs to the French Fur Company," Ashley answered. "And somehow I don't expect our friends," he paused, as a sardonic grin crept across his face, "I should say, *Jed's* friends, will sell them to us."

"If they did, like as not they'd be lame," Jed laughed.

"Aye," Ashley chuckled. "Now then, patron. Anchor us in mid-channel. I intend to take a skiff to shore and begin to parley with the Rees."

Mike bawled out an order to his first and second mates, and headed toward the stern of the boat to relay the orders to the patron and crew of the *Rocky Mountains* drifting behind the *Packet*. The first and second mates were new men, over from the other keelboat. Talbot and Carpenter had previously held the jobs, but they'd transferred to the *Rocky Mountains*. Ever since the incident in which Fink had attacked Carpenter, the two keelboat men wanted to stay as far as possible from their ex-friend.

"General, I've got an idea," Jed began once the two were alone. "I've been doing a lot of thinking about how the Rees feel about white men, and it seems to me the last thing we ought to do is slink up to them like whipped dogs. If we act guilty, they'll feel bound to punish us, and this hoss don't reckon that's the way to start a parley."

Jed was interrupted by Ashley's laughter. "You certainly are starting to sound like a wilderness man, even if you haven't yet set your eyes on a peak," the General joked.

Jed half smiled at Ashley's remark. "Anyway, sir. I think we ought to establish a landing party. Pretty as you please, right there on the beach. We're going to have to eventually anyway."

Hiram Angus and Bill Sublette came up behind them. "Don't sound bad, General," Hiram interjected. "Indians usually are only as brave as their foes is cowardly."

"Yep, General," Bill Sublette offered. "March right up to their front door, give 'em a big smile and say we's here for a visit and what you mean you hasn't baked a cake? It jest might work."

"I'll consider it, but for now I just want a small landing party," Ashley decided. "It's a good idea, Jed. And we'll try it if all goes well. But I can't risk the lives of so many men on such a gamble."

"Aye, sir," Jed nodded, trying to hide his disappointment. He'd been trying hard to become Ashley's right-hand man, figuring that the time was ripe, the

General's partner being upriver and all. Having a trapper's share of the profits was fine, but having a partner's share would be better still. He had come to see that running a trapping company was just as challenging as trapping the beavers. And the challenge, any challenge, was what brought Jed out West.

"I'll tell you what, though, Jed," Ashley continued. "Since you've become handy with the Ree lingo, come along with me and Eddie Rose." He turned to Angus and Sublette. "You two boys want to take a ride, too?"

"Reckon so, General," Angus answered for the both of them.

As Sublette turned to gather his gear, he slapped Jed on the back, gave him a big grin, and said, "Rees supposedly got right handsome women. Maybe you'll forget all about that there Louisa of yourn, eh boy?"

Chapter 8

The Arikara people tell it like this: On the morning that the Grandfather Of All Things sent their future up the Stream of Life, he that was the Nation's Guardian felt the push of the white men's two big boats hours before the birds swarmed to cry in misery and the dogs raced to the Wall to howl in mourning.

But that is how they told it to white men, or rather, how the white men "saw" what the Arikaras had "heard." The white men's interpretation presumes hindsight and foresight, and so their interpretation is inaccurate. The Arikara people do not have expectation or regret. To the Arikara people, the white men's capacity to expect what will be, or regret what has gone before, matches their folly in thinking they can own a piece of Grandfather's good earth.

He that was the Nation's Guardian was sitting cross-legged in his lodge, staring into the embers of his dying fire, lit the night before. Crumpled behind him were his sleep robes of finest buffalo skin, to his right, his war lance, bow, quiver and war shield, to his left, his rifle and bullet pouch. He that was the Nation's Guardian was not thinking of past or future, but was searching inside his belly for the sound and feeling of the *present,* to which he could fix his mind to start the day.

The present was everywhere, always, but often, like the Stream of Life in winter, when its waters were icy and the color of ripe corn, it was difficult to jump into. That all Arikara men were to live listening to the sound of the present in honor of Grandfather's mysteries was Law, but the Nation's Guardian knew that men were like dogs and horses: Some were strong, courageous, serious and loyal, others were weak, cowardly, silly, and flighty as a squaw before she's known a man. The Law was to be heard, but the Law could not be enforced, for how could you change a man's thinking? It was the Nation's Guardian's duty to set an example. If he were worthy of the honor, all right-thinking men would heed.

Today the Nation's Guardian had much to think about. He wanted to confront it with a clear head and heart anchored to Grandfather's music, but stalking that clarity was not easy, for his male emotions and the adventures of his soul at night, while he slept, constantly betrayed him. These two things washed away the spoor of *now,* the way the rain washed away the spoor of the deer.

Ah Grandfather, he thought. *What a trickster You are to put so much pain in the World!*

He looked up, watching the smoke from the fire spiral toward the hole in the lodge's stick, grass and mud ceiling. He sent a prayer to ride the smoke up to where it could catch Grandfather's attention like a fragile little mosquito buzzing the ear: *Please, the Arikara nation needs this marriage—*

His marriage was the first step on the long trail away from the poison the white men had brought. The last time the sickness had visited his people he was just a boy of ten winters. He had watched his father and

brother die, but one night, while the people hid in
their lodges so that the poison could not find them, and
while the moans and death songs from the families the
poison had found wafted through the village like cold,
clammy fog, he'd had a dream.

In the dream, his soul had looked into the fire.
Now, all right-thinking people know that in the fire
many things can be seen if one's eyes are open. The
flames had talked to his soul that night. The flames had
said:

> *"Grey Eyes! You will not die, for your heart
>   loves your people;*
>
> *"Grey Eyes! Your heart burns pure with that love
>   so that the poison fears you like it fears us;*
>
> *"Grey Eyes! See how beautiful we are! Where will
>   our beauty be tomorrow?*
>
> *"Grey Eyes! Burn this way! That way! Light the
>   way for your people!*

The next day, the little boy of ten winters had
been much relieved to know he would not die of the
poison, but more important, he realized that the Law
had settled on him to burn bright, the way the flames
settle on dry wood. He realized that one day the elders
would make him the Nation's Guardian.

As he grew to manhood he kept his vision to himself, but used it as a guiding example in all endeavors.
As the flame flickered fast, he became quick in all
forms of combat. His knife, arrows and bullets flew
straight and true, and had bit into twenty-seven Sioux
braves by the time his twenty-first birthday had come.
The twenty-seven scalps hung at this very moment
from his coup pole, propped in the corner of his lodge.
When the breezes blew through the chinks in the mud
plaster, the inky black strands of hair rose and fell.

But he had not considered himself ready to become the Nation's Guardian until he had killed a white

man. The Law said such killing was all right to do, and needed no reason, for the white men were not human, like all the people in the varied nations of the World. If the whites were human, where were their white women, for example? Where were their white children? Clearly Grandfather turned his face away from such an imperfect race.

When his twenty-fifth birthday had passed, three white trappers, foul-smelling and greasy, with long, ugly face beards hanging down like extra scalps, had entered his village. He was Ranking Brave at that time, the Second in Command to his Nation's Guardian, who was an old man who no longer thought of adding to his own coup pole. The whites must have sensed that— they were beings always looking for a fight, it seemed—for instead of paying for the horses they wanted, they stole them.

Now, it is the custom among the Arikara people that when some injustice is done to them, it is the Ranking Brave's duty to put matters right. Should such an injustice be done today, it would be Little Soldier who would be sent to avenge the matter, for the Nation's Guardian must stay and watch over his people.

But back then, it was he, Grey Eyes, who was the Ranking Brave, and so it was he who was sent to bring back the horses. He tracked the three white men for two days and nights, finally closing in on them. The night was as black as dreamless sleep, with long, grey clouds cutting like knife blades across a thin sliver of moon. The whites had built a big campfire, and as Grey Eyes spied on them from his hiding place in the brush, he knew it would be all right. The campfire was a good omen. Fire was his dream friend.

He waited patiently, still as a rock, until the two trappers went to sleep, and the one on watch duty began to nod his head with weariness. The whites must have thought that because the Nation's Guardian was old and toothless, the nation itself had no teeth, for they were careless in the manner in which they camped.

Grey Eyes left his gun and bullet pouch in the brush, took up his skinning knife, and crept up to the sentry. He moved slowly at first—measured step after measured step—the way the wolf begins its trot after the deer, but soon he had his rhythm in tune with that of *now,* and knew that he and the world were *one,* and so would make no noise.

He came up behind the sentry and cut his throat. The white's life was gone without a sound. The two other trappers slept on. Grey Eyes cut the first's throat without even waking the man, but it was while he was kneeling over the third and last that a serious thing happened. Even as he cut the red death smile into the man's throat, the white's eyes opened and his hands clutched Grey Eye's hand in supplication. At once Grey Eyes knew the Law was terribly *wrong,* for he had seen it in the dying white's eyes. Despite his color and his foul smell, Grey Eyes saw the Spirit of Life— the Human Soul—leave the white man's ever dimming eyes. White men *were* human.

But he did what he was sent to do. He left the whites' bodies for the flies after taking their scalps, and led the horses they had so foolishly stolen back to his village. What he had learned about the whites' humanness he kept to himself. No one would understand. He was not sure *he* did. *The Law was wrong. . . .*

Soon after that, his nation elected him Guardian. Now, at thirty winters, he still proudly wore in his headband the white feathers which signify his rank. And today, as he sat in his lodge, staring into the embers of his dying fire, he was moving closer to his ultimate goal.

The nation was small, and to make matters worse, divided by bitterness. Blame the white men's poison for this as well, for twenty winters before, when the heat of the summer had brought the poison back that last time, and he was only a small boy of ten dreaming his fire dream, a young man named Bear, who was then Ranking Brave, defied the Guardian (who was, it must be told, half-dead of the poison) by saying: "Let half the people follow me to begin a new village. No exchange will take place between the new town and the old, and so the white men's poison will not find the people who follow me."

It turned out that the poison could *not* cross the distance between the old, lower village, and the new, upper one. As the curse raged through his own village, Grey Eyes saw the people grow angry and envious of those who had followed Bear to safety. As far as Bear's people were concerned, the fact that they were spared meant that Grandfather must favor *them,* and as fortunate people will do, they cruelly taunted the suffering people of the lower village, saying that their death songs, the sacred tunes that souls rode like fast horses to heaven, sounded like the thin screams of rabbits just before the owl plucks them from the earth.

The people of the upper village chose Bear as their Guardian, and he refused to care for the lower village. Even as a boy of ten, Grey Eyes knew that this was wrong, that the Law was helpless and weak when the people were scattered. But he could say nothing. Who would listen to a boy when Bear was as big and strong as his animal namesake?

There was a knock at the wooden door of Grey Eyes' lodge. "Enter," he ordered.

Little Soldier glided into the lodge, scarcely having to duck his head to do so. Only five feet tall, Little Soldier had proven himself in so many battles with the

Arikara's eternal enemies, the Sioux, that he had become Ranking Brave of the village. "Boats come. The white men will soon reach us, Guardian." His voice was deferential and his manner hesitant. He was a right-thinking brave and had no wish to disturb his leader's time of quiet. But he felt that the white men's impending arrival was important enough to merit such an interruption. "They will wish to enter the village, Guardian. What is to be done?"

Grey Eyes seemed not to hear him. His face, usually calm, handsome, the face of the soaring eagle which sees all things, was dark, and his eyes were turned inward. "I had a dream last night, Second."

Little Soldier stiffened to attention. The Guardian's use of his rank as opposed to his given name meant that matters of great importance were to be discussed. He sat down, cross-legged, next to Grey Eyes. He did not look at his Guardian, but instead, stared straight ahead, as was the custom at such times, so that his ears would not miss a single word.

"My soul went wandering in the dream world, and it came upon a fire," Grey Eyes began.

Little Soldier began to relax. "The fire is your friend, Guardian."

Grey Eyes sorrowfully shook his head. "No, I saw the fire through eyes misted with rage. And the fire this time was no friend of mine. It spoke in a harsh voice, the voice of the people of the upper town long ago, when they watched this village's agony. The flames said, 'Grey Eyes! Your heart is no longer pure. It burns with quite a different flame. What can a man own? The more he desires the less he has. . . . Grey Eyes! We, the flames that sustained you, will now eat you up! As your inner flame reduces you to ash, the smoke will rise up to sting Grandfather's eye. The eye will cry for your people, for the flames of the real world will have your nation—' " He stopped, willing away the emotion he felt. Emotion was his enemy now. It contradicted the Law. That was the message of the flames, that, and . . .

"Second, the dream tells of my death. . . ." He looked at Little Soldier. "It tells of the death of our nation."

"But the nation will be mended by your marriage, Guardian," Little Soldier protested. He felt fear such as he'd never before known, not even the time he was alone and surrounded by a Sioux war party. His mind raced in desperation to offer a different interpretation of what his leader had just recounted to him. "You've not understood it, Guardian! Listen to me! The dream means only that things will be different once you marry Bear's daughter. Bear himself has changed! Once he was strong and thick, now he is old and tired and wants only to smoke his pipe in peace. He wants to re-unite the two villages as much as you do! He's offered his daughter, his princess, to you so that as man and woman are joined together in marriage and lovemaking, so will be the lower and upper villages. Have we not already built the long wall protecting us all from whatever comes up the river? Soon the space between the two villages will be filled with the lodges of new-born people, and our two towns will become one large city the way it used to be. The way it is supposed to be! The nation will once again grow, just as your own family will grow when the princess gives you children. Don't you *see*, Guardian?" Little Soldier was sweating with effort, so hard was he straining to find the truth. "The fire is . . . The fire, well . . . Just as fire marches through the forest, so will our nation, *changed in size*, march along the river." Here Little Soldier stopped to nudge Grey Eyes in the ribs. "And as for you, it means that you will indeed burn up, in the arms of the princess! *You,* who for so long have refused any woman as a sacrament to this blessed union! *Those* sustaining flames of celibacy, *those* are the flames that will change once you lay with the princess! Those are indeed flames that will eat you up!" Little Soldier began to laugh with relief. The Law said that there were many realities. He had just woven one, and he silently swore to himself that he would make this one happen. His Guardian had been strong for so long for all his people! If Grey Eyes' eyes had grown tired, then he, Little Soldier would be his eyes. "Guardian, all this is what your vision means."

Grey Eyes smiled at his Second, his comrade, and did not contradict him. Perhaps what Little Soldier said was true. "The whites. Allow them to enter the village peaceably. Do nothing to provoke them. The princess visits me today, along with her father. I wish all to be serene. Her visit will make me so. Leave me now. I will compose myself for today's two confrontations."

As Little Soldier slipped from the lodge, Grey Eyes once again listened for the music of the world, the music of *now.* He would balance his mind on the edge of a stretched-taut string: So balanced, he would greet the whites, those strange beings with no fixed tribe and no women of their own race. The whites had no Guardians, but only Ranking Braves who ruled by brute strength, like the wolves ruled the jackals. The whites did not honor the search for inner wisdom.

All this the Nation's Guardian perceived as a righteous punishment brought down upon the whites for what they themselves had brought down upon the Arikara nation. Grandfather could be stern, as when he brought the winter winds and droughts and floods. All the tribes—the Mandans and Crow and even the Sioux—no matter how they felt about each other, universally pitied the whites, for they had no homeland,

and could only wander alone, or in small groups, foolishly chasing after the skins of beaver and buffalo, paying the various tribes with marvelous things like guns
and ammunition to help them stockpile the pelts, many
more than so few whites could ever need, for what purpose Grey Eyes couldn't imagine.

Of course, there was still too much hatred in the
hearts of the Arikara people to actually pity the whites.
But there was no way the deaths of so few whites could
ever make up for the loss of so many of the nation. So
why bother to kill them at all, unless, of course, they
became a nuisance, in which case, they would be
stamped out like the vermin they were?

In the past Grey Eyes had earned the affection of
his people by giving to those particular women whose
families had lost the most members to the whites' poison the occasional trapper who came to the village and
was foolish enough to be disrespectful. The squaws
would stake their victim down and start by plucking
out his eyes. The screams of the tortured trapper
would bring much laughter to all the lodges within ear-
shot. After all, as the Law pointed out, it was not as if
the whites were *human,* like the people of the nation. . . . *But they are,* Grey Eyes would think at
those times, remembering the eyes of that dying trapper. But Grey Eyes was the Nation's Guardian; he
would represent the Law. . . .

Today, however, his mind would be balanced on
that taut string of hospitality over a pool of violence. It
would take some onerous act on the part of the whites
to push him off that string into the pool he'd fill with
their own blood.

Thus he would honor the coming visit of the
princess, his bride-to-be. Her beauty and grace
represented what he wanted for his nation. She symbol-
ized through her virginal, womanly ways, the healing

powers of the world. Grey Eyes had grown to desire her as much as he'd always loved his nation. In many ways, the princess and the nation had become the same thing in his mind. He would treat the whites well, if possible, to show his people, and his bride-to-be, that there was gentleness and kindness born of strength in the World, as well as violence and death.

If only last night's dream didn't trouble him so! He had a vague feeling the whites who had today arrived fitted in somehow. . . . But how exactly?

He rose and ducked through the doorway of his lodge. Outside, he blinked in the sunlight. It was a warm, soft day. He shrugged off the hide vest he was wearing and tossed it back into the lodge. One of the braves who served him would later put it in its proper place. Bare-chested, wearing only his loincloth and deerskin leggings, the Nation's Guardian strode toward the wall, from which he could watch the approach of the whites' landing party.

Little Soldier took up his position behind Grey Eyes. As they walked, the Ranking Brave asked his quiet question. "Guardian, did your vision indeed have to do with your coming marriage? Do you think what I told you is right?"

Grey Eyes smiled. He thought: *Let your interpretation indeed come true, Second, for all our sakes.* "It had nothing to do with the princess," he said. "Or everything."

Chapter 9

"Damned quiet," Jed remarked. The village seemed deserted. Except for the cries of the birds overhead, the only sound that reached the landing party was the rough scraping of their own little boat as it ran aground on the pebbly shore.

"You'd think they'd be a bit curious," General Ashley muttered in agreement. He anxiously scanned the long, shadowy barricade running along the ridge.

"They see us jest fine, General," Hiram Angus allowed tolerantly. "As far as curiosity goes, they've had their fill o' white men, I reckon." He laughed grimly. "More than their fill."

"We'll be all right. Jest keep yer noses open," Eddie Rose told them all as they climbed out of the skiff. "Jest don't do nothin' to git them riled. They might get a bit close, and git to pickin' at yer clothes and all, but don't pay it no mind. They's like a hive of bees, the Rees is. A bee don't give a damn if you don't like the fact he's buzzin' around yer nose, just don't swat him unless'n' you want a sting. The Rees is as mindless a bunch of savages as them thar bees—"

"Oh come on, Eddie," Jed broke in impatiently. "They're people, is all. . . ."

"Boy!" Eddie snapped sharply, stung by what he took as a note of disrespect in Jed's voice. "You jest let me do all the talkin' up there amongst them! Ain't no time for you to be showin' off yer studies!"

Jed shrugged.

"Hear me, boy?" Now Eddie's tone was low, ominous. There was violence in it. *I've a short temper, boy,* he thought. *Don't git on the wrong side of Eddie Rose*—"Hear me?"

Jed waited until the last possible moment, and then replied, "Hear you, Eddie," but in a voice that clearly indicated that "hearing" and "obeying" were two different things.

Eddie's eyes tried to find Jed's in a contest of wills. *He can take me,* Eddie thought, and at once was immensely saddened, as all men of action are when their own mortality is pointed out to them by someone younger. He glanced around him for support from the other men, but Bill Sublette was busy tugging the skiff up onto dry land, the General was scrutinizing the wall that protected the villages, and Hiram Angus was only laughing at him for being a fool. Eddie gave it up.

"Old gives way to the new," Hiram philosophized. "But this hoss knows one thing, Jed. Them Rees got respect for their elders, right Eddie?" he winked.

"Damn straight," Eddie moped.

Jed took Hiram's rebuke to heart. He was not a bully and had no wish to hurt Eddie Rose. Besides, Jed knew that the interpreter had learned his lesson, and would never again attempt to issue an order to him. "Eddie? Do you think a fellow ought to stay with the boat, just in case?" Jed asked, in an attempt to make it up with the elder trapper.

"No, Jed. Them Rees is honest." Eddie was happy to accept the peace offer. "And if they think we're suspicious of them, they might take it as an insult."

Bill Sublette handed them all their rifles. "Let's quit this jawin' and git on up thar," he groused.

The climb up the ridge took only a few minutes, but when they passed through the gate cut into the barricade of driftwood and thorns, it was like entering another world as far as Jed was concerned. They were met by a party of thirty braves. Some were armed with fusils and rifles, but most carried only lances. The braves seemed to be surprised by the small number of men in the landing party.

Eddie Rose cackled with pleasure as the braves surrounded the five whites. "They's embarrassed themselves by over-reacting. Looks like you was right to bring only a few of us, General Ashley." He gave Jed a big, innocent smile, the kind a cat offers after it's eaten the canary.

"Go on now," Ashley mildly shooed away a young Rees brave who had boldly stepped up to him to finger his goatee. "Childish heathens, ain't they?" He reached into his possibles bag for a handful of the small, round mirrors he'd brought along as an introductory gift, but the young brave's fingers clamped about the General's wrist as he dug into his sack.

"Hold on, now, sir!" Eddie Rose warned. "Don't go spookin' 'em. Let me say my piece afore you give 'em anything." In Ree tongue he said, "Greetings to the Arikara nation. The Ashley-Henry family brings friendship gifts to join in peace with the proud Arikaras." In English he said, "You can give 'em that junk now, sir."

Ashley distributed the mirrors to the pleasure of the braves. One of the Rees stepped up to Jed and tried to take his rifle. Jed shook his head and said in his best Ree, "Not for you, Arikara soldier, but better gifts will be offered."

The brave laughed in delight at his speech, and backed off from his attempt to disarm Jed. The other braves laughed as well.

Eddie Rose grinned. "You may not know it, but you just told yer first joke in Ree tongue. He was goin to try and take all our guns, most likely, but by yer actin'—or *bein'* innocent—you talked him out of it without actually defyin' him. Remember that, Jed. You ever want to say no to a Ree, pretend you don't know what's he's talkin' about."

The braves motioned with their lances and rifles toward the village, and began to lead the surrounded landing party that way.

"We'll be all right for now," Eddie told his comrades. "We've given 'em stuff, Jed's made 'em laugh and we're outnumbered as hell, anyways. They can't touch us right now without a loss of face. Might as well relax, there's nothin' to worry about 'til we met their Guvner."

"Chief, you mean," corrected Ashley.

"Mean what I said," Eddie nodded. "Ain't got no chiefs out here in the real world, General. Got guvners. I'll explain later."

As they ambled toward the village Jed took the time to examine the physical features of the Arikara men all around him. On the average, they were under six feet tall. They looked hard and fit, but their builds were long and slender. Their arms, for example, were thin and sinewy instead of rounded and thick like white men's arms. All the same, they looked as if they'd be tough customers in a fight. Jed thought about how a little housecat, skinny as nothing, could get steel hard with muscle when the time came to whip a big old dog.

They were dressed in loincloths and hide leggings. Some wore sleeveless leather vests, but most, due to the balmy weather, went bare-chested. They wore no ornaments except for headbands from which protruded varying numbers of feathers of different colors. He supposed the head-dresses signified rank.

The braves all had shoulder-length hair in shades of auburn to black. Jed was shocked to see several pairs of hazel eyes scattered among the predominate brown. In all, these slender, graceful, light-skinned men were a far cry from the picture-book representations of howling, drum-thumping Indians he'd pored over in Doc Simons' library. But as Eddie Rose had pointed out, this was the real world. . . .

His first view of the village stunned him. He'd been expecting anthill-like mounds of dirt surrounded by filth. What he saw was row upon row of log cabins, progressing in an orderly fashion for about a half mile toward the plains. Narrow, but hard-packed dirt streets separated the blocks of cabins, which Eddie called "lodges." On both sides of the streets, wood-lined gutters sloped down toward the ridge to drain off rainwater.

"Iffen they want, they can reverse the pitch of them gutters so that the water goes into their growin' plots in back of these blocks of lodges," Eddie explained, pointing. "The horse corrals and shelters is off to the side there."

The streets were filled with Arikaras making a great show of going about their business while they took what they probably imagined were surreptitious glances at their visitors. The braves who had greeted the trappers were now proudly displaying their mirrors to the others.

Jed saw that all the women wore ankle-length

deerskin dresses decorated with ornate beadwork. Most of them carried crudely made hoes, reminding Jed that it was the females who did most of the farm work. The children who tagged along behind the women were naked. Eddie had said that a boy didn't take on a loin-cloth until he was old enough to join in a hunt.

A tall, bare-chested brave detached himself from the crowd and approached Jed and the other trappers. He had only white feathers in his headband, and from the way the other Arikaras solemnly made way for him, Jed guessed that he must be some sort of official, maybe even the chief.

"That there is Grey Eyes, the Guvner of this here village," Eddie hissed to the others.

General Ashley reached into his possibles bag for a mirror.

"No!" Eddie said frantically. "Don't give him nothin', General! It'd be an insult to the Guvner. He takes things only for the Arikara nation. Nothin' for hisself."

"He *is* the leader? Not the medicine man or anything?" Ashley asked, looking perplexed.

"No sir," Eddie shook his head, devoutly wishing that Ashley's more experienced partner, Major Henry, was around to help him babysit for this bunch of greenhorns. "Grey Eyes is the chief, all right, but don't go gettin' confused about what that means. He's sorta combination priest and military leader, get it? He's their *flag*, General. He's their interpreter of their sacred Law. Listen up, you others. Don't even breathe while he's talkin' to us. You get outta line, yer scalps will be hangin' from his coup pole afore sundown."

As Grey Eyes spoke, Jed moved slightly away from where Eddie Rose was whispering his translation to the General, Hiram Angus and Bill Sublette. He

wanted to sharpen his own skills with the Ree tongue
by translating for himself.

"—that by coming to the Arikara nation today,
the whites will be treated as honored guests, as good
omens," Jed heard the Guvner say in a deep, rich
voice which carried to the edge of the surrounding
crows. "They will join in the pte hunt and feasting in
honor of the—" and here there were several words Jed
couldn't make out, "—ceremony for the honored visitors from the upper village. To preserve the peace in-
augurated by Guvner Bear of the upper village,
harmonious trade will commence between the Arikara
people and the whites, who are welcome to establish
their campfires on the beach."

Grey Eyes turned and strode away, as Eddie Rose
let forth with a jubilant "Ya-hoo! We done lucked out,
General! The old boy's got marriage on his mind instead of fightin'. Bear, the Guvner of the upper village,
and a mean cuss in his day, although I reckon old age
has mellowed him some, is comin' today with his
daughter. She's for Grey Eyes, she is. All we gots to do
is sit back and be entertained until the time comes for
horse tradin'!"

"When will that be, Eddie?" Ashley frowned.
"Major Henry is far enough north that the snows
will be hitting him very soon."

"A couple of days, I reckon, General," Eddie
shrugged. "They's in a good mood, sir. I wouldn't try
to rush 'em."

"This hoss reckons Eddie's right," Hiram added.
He patted Ashley on the back in a fatherly way. "Let's
us just set up our camp and settle in fer a little buffler
huntin'. Hey, Jed! You ever taste pte? Sweet meat,
boy. Sweet meat! The best thar is, next to beaver tail,
of course. . . ."

*   *   *

The procession left at dawn the next day. It was a colorful sight. The Ree hunters wore ceremonial shirts splashed purple, pink and yellow by natural dyes their women had wrung from various barks and leaves. All around them, old men, women and children pranced and waved lances from which flew lovely pennants honoring pte. No small wonder, for the majestic plains bison supplied literally everything that the Rees could not grow.

It was pte, the buffalo, that supplied fresh meat, and flesh that was dried and savored during the barren winter months. Pte's skin supplied thick, furry robes to keep the Rees warm in winter. In summer, they stayed cool and comfortable in clothing made from pte hides scraped thin and bare. Pte's rib bones formed runners for the Ree's dogsleds; the other parts of his skeleton formed the raw material for tools and implements. Even the hooves of pte had their use: They were boiled down for a glue to cement arrowheads and feathers to arrows. Knife sheaths, quivers, needles, thread, spoons, pillows, shields, decorations—pte supplied them all. The horns at the tip of his head might become a pair of ladles, the lining of his stomach was the Ree's water bucket, the long tail was the only sensible thing to use as a fly swatter.

The Rees called the creator of all things Grandfather. The buffalo, which supplied all things to the nation, was called "Uncle." At the head of the procession danced a long figure dressed in a buffalo hide to which the animal's head was still attached. His song told of the love and gratitude offered today by the Ree nation to the pte about to be slain.

The procession stretched for miles as it slowly made its way to the hunting plains. There were one hundred Ree hunters, fifty from each village, and each brave had vied long and hard through many games and contests for this honor. Not only was this a hunt in celebration of the coming marriage which would reunite their two villages, but this was also the last chance of the season for kills on a massive scale. The breeding season of pte was in the summer, from June until late September. As spring came each year, the males and females which wandered in smaller groupings during the winter joined together in vast, countless rolling herds. The bulls would bellow their challenges to each other as they fought to rut with the cows. Their earth-shaking, savage tumult would continue until winter hinted its arrival, whereupon the herds would drift away, southward, not to be seen again in such numbers until spring's green kiss came once again to the northern plains.

There were three hundred pack horses along to be used to transport the butchered kills back to the villages. Dog-drawn litters would cart what was left over.

Forty trappers had also come along on the hunt. Very early, before the sun had risen, Hiram and Eddie had led the party of forty interested in taking part in the hunt from their small camp on the riverbank back to the village. There they were outfitted with Ree horses they would later barter for. Ashley had stayed behind to supervise the activities on the riverbank, saying that he'd no desire to learn the art of buffalo hunting from horseback, adding that you, "can't teach an old dog new tricks——." But how envious would the General have been, had he seen all these superb horses!

Jed had learned to ride in Pennsylvania. His own family had not owned any steeds, but Doc Simons had several suitable for riding, in addition to the drays which pulled his wagons and carriages. By the time Jed was in his mid-teens, he was quite an accomplished rider.

Listening carefully, Jed could hear a vague rumbling, even over the noise of the procession and the yapping of the dogs. A strong, musky odor began to fill the air.

"We must be close, eh Hiram?"

Just ahead, Hiram swiveled around in his saddle to face Jed. "Relax boy. They's still a good fifteen miles away."

The trappers were riding in a group just behind the Ree hunters, which placed them in the first quarter of the procession. Grey Eyes was somewhere up ahead, riding with Bear, the Guvner of the upper village, and Bear's daughter. Bear was a big old fellow, and probably had been a tough cuss in his day, Jed had thought, though he was now bent over with age. There was loose, flappy skin where there once must have been strong, thick muscles. Jed hadn't really been able to catch a good look at the princess. She was draped in a shawl of fine, bright calico which covered her head as well. Jed caught only a glimpse as the sun glinted off the beadwork of her frock, and then she was past him, to take up her position in the lead.

They rode on. It was about noon when the procession began to spread across a ridge.

"We're here, Jed!" Hiram said as he goaded his own horse up the hill.

The excitement in Hiram's voice was evident to Jed, and the reason why hit home full force when his own horse had climbed the ridge. The expressions of awe from even the most seasoned trappers reached his ears, but Jed was struck speechless by the sight. The herd of buffalo, huge and black, stretched across the prairie for as far as the eye could see.

"A man could ride all day, Jed," Hiram said, "and he'd never find the outer edge of them."

After a dizzying moment, Jed managed to ask, "How many? How many are there?"

Hiram shrugged. "A million? Thirty million? Who can count that high? One thing's for sure, boy. There's more pte than a man could ever need. There's pte to last forever!"

As Jed watched, Rees, acting as drivers rode down the crest to cut away a portion of the herd for the hunt to concentrate on. The Rees rode through the mass of bison, slicing through it like a knife. A small group of the animals, numbering perhaps a thousand, were separated from the rest. To Jed, the process was more like whittling: The thousand bison amounted to no more than a shaving of wood off of a tree trunk.

"Everyone but the hunters will stay up here, where it'll be safe," Hiram said. "Remember what I told you, Jed. Them brutes will run you down iffen you let 'em." He cocked his rifle. "Here we go, boy."

The hundred and forty Ree and trapper hunters eased their horses along in a slow trot down the ridge. They'd formed themselves into one long, unbroken line, a wall of horses and riders to keep partitioned off the pool of pte from the sea of the herd.

Gradually, rhythmically, the line gained speed and momentum. Hiram rode up and down the breadth of the trappers' section of the charge, it being a matter of pride to him to see that the white men kept the same straight-edge that the Rees did.

Suddenly the Indians let loose with a blood-chilling howl that broke the tension. Their fine line shattered into its separate pieces.

"Ya-hoo! Let's go, boys!" Hiram's shout was primordial, exultant. His behavior was more like that of

the Rees than a white man as he wheeled his pinto
pony hard around and galloped at full speed toward a
clot of boffalo.

Although the sky was bright blue and cloudless,
thunder filled the air. Although the prairie grass was
bright green and full of life, the lumbering black mass
seemed like hell's swarm set loose upon the earth.

Jed rode at full speed, just behind Hiram. His
own horse, a roan gelding, seemed to know what to do
with little coaxing from him. At one moment the horse
was barreling toward the dark herd of pte, dim-witted,
foul-tempered brutes standing six feet high at the
shoulder, the smallest measuring ten feet from nose to
tail. At the next instant, Jed's mount was galloping
parallel to a bull, angling in so close that Jed could
reach out to ruffle the shaggy fur on its big hump, or
grasp the foot-long horns thrusting out from the
beast's massive, lowered head.

The noise had grown unbelievably loud. First
there was one shot, and then another, and then another, until soon the gunfire from the individual
hunters had rattled along into one continuous blast.
The gunfire, the thundering hooves and sonorous bel-
lowing of the stampeding buffalo echoed in the ear until the sense of hearing faded into a blessed state of
oblivious numbness.

Jed leaned over to shove the barrel of his rifle
hard into the back of the buffalo's head. The booming
report of his gun was lost in the great general roar all
around him. The only way he knew the rifle had fired
was from its recoil. As the buffalo faltered, Jed's horse
veered clear of the beast. Jed looked back to see blood
streaming from both wide, black nostrils of the bull as
it slid forward for twenty more yards, carried along by
its own momentum, before lying still and dead in the
dust.

Reining in his mount, Jed slowed to a stop in order to reload his rifle. Pistol balls were useless against the buffaloes. The only charges strong enough to drop the brutes were the half-ounce rifle slugs, or the awesome blasts of shot from the short barreled fusils. The latter was the Arikaras' main weapon in the hunt, but Jed had to admire how many of the braves were bringing down pte with just a well-placed arrow.

Reloaded, Jed kneed his horse into a canter. He saw Bill Sublette fire and bring down a buffalo, reload while his mount was still running at full speed, and fire again, killing another of the animals.

The experienced pte hunter's method was to carry several rifle balls in his mouth, so that his spittle would moisten the lead and made them stick to the gun powder. When the time came to reload, the hunter would cradle his gun in the crook of his arm, pour the powder down the barrel while giving the weapon a shake to distribute the explosive evenly, and then pop the moistened bullet down the way the powder went, where it would stick without benefit of a rifle patch.

The order of the herd had completely broken down in the noise and confusion. A buffalo was careering toward Jed. The animal's eyesight was weak at best. During a hunt, when the scent of death was all around, a terrified buffalo simply ran blindly in the direction of least resistance, counting on its two-thousand-pound bulk to smash through any obstacle foolish enough to get in its way.

Jed took aim and fired. The buffalo tumbled onto its snout and then over on its back, blood gouting from its punctured heart as it quivered to its death.

Jed reloaded his rifle and coaxed his mount into an easy trot. The initial fury of the hunt seemed to be abating. At least four hundred of the animals lay dead on ground now turned to crimson mud. Despite the immensity of the slaughter, Jed was a trifle sorry that this most magnificent experience was coming to an end. After all, it wasn't as if any part of the beasts killed was going to go to waste. Even as he watched, both braves and trappers were slitting the throats of the fallen animals, to drink long and deep of thick red blood which supposedly had the taste of warm milk.

Hiram rode over. "How many you get, Jed?" He was grinning from ear to ear, and blood was splattered across his buckskin shirt.

"Two, so far."

"Two! Waugh! Why, I kilt eleven, Jed! Two?" he repeated, muttering to himself as he began to ride away. "Look, boy!" He reined in his horse, and pointed back toward the ridge from which they'd come.

Jed turned to see a horrifying sight. Two Ree hunters were driving a small group of twenty or so bison toward the ridge, so that they could be slaughtered at leisure in an area convenient to the women and old men who would be doing the skinning and butchering. But something was wrong, for the herd suddenly began to stampede. One Ree had a chance to fire his fusil into the charging beasts before his rearing horse was disemboweled by the lead bull. The Ree disappeared in a swirl of dust and hooves.

The other Ree brave had wheeled his horse around and was riding hard for the base of the ridge, where the princess herself had ridden down with two other women in order to begin work on the very herd which now threatened her life.

"What the hell is she doin' down here!" Hiram exclaimed. "Them pte is gonna stomp her for sure! Lookit! The brave's tryin' to beat 'em to her first!"

But Jed was already riding hard toward the scene.

He could see that the brave had not gotten enough of a lead on the raging herd. The Ree must have shouted something, for the three women looked up, and seeing what was coming toward them, made for their horses while the brave, in a last, desperate suicidal ploy, swerved his horse directly across the path of the bison. About a third of the stampeding number stopped short to mill in confusion, but the rest pounded right over the courageous Ree. Now there was nothing between the rushing animals and the women.

They've made it! Jed thought as he watched the three swing up onto their mounts and ride for their lives up the ridge. But his relief was short-lived. The princess' horse stumbled on some loose rocks. As the other two women rode off without looking back, the princess, still in her calico shawl, was thrown from her horse as it slipped back down the slope, tumbling over itself and then regaining its feet to trot off. There was no way in hell she could outrun those bison on foot. Jed whipped his already racing steed into a full, flatout run. There was nobody as close as he was. The princess's life was in his hands.

He reached the spot where the second brave had sacrificed himself. The bloody body of the man was a momentary flicker as Jed twisted half out of the saddle to scoop up the dead man's fusil. The Ree hadn't fired his gun, and Jed prayed that was because he hadn't had the chance, not because it wasn't loaded. He'd need more than one shot to turn the herd, and he wouldn't have time to stop and reload his own rifle.

He was at the rear of the herd now. Digging his heels into his horse's flanks to get some last bit of speed, he rose up in the saddle, his own rifle extended toward the lead bulls. It would be a difficult shot at this angle, but there was little choice. He was now at the halfway mark of the herd. The princess was scrabbling up the ridge, but its very slope was slowing her down.

Jed fired. One of the bulls went down in a spray of blood, but still the herd raced toward the ridge.

He was now at the front of the lumbering mass of fear-crazed bison. He reined his horse into the path of the lead brutes, as the Ree had done, but Jed had no intention of dying: His goal was to ride a razor-line angle of direction to turn the path of the beasts. One inch too little and his efforts would be useless, one inch too much and his life would belong to the buffaloes' hoofs and horns.

He was parallel with the remaining lead bull now, no more than thirty yards from the princess who had stopped her futile attempt to escape and had now turned to face her death. Jed jammed the short, squat barrel of the fusil into the last, lead bull's ear, and said a final prayer as he pulled the trigger. He'd not had time to check the little shotgun's load.

The fusil gave a tremendous kick, and the bull's head literally dissolved, its blood and brains and bits of skull went flying back onto the bison behind. They bellowed in fear as the blood of their own kind soaked their faces. Panicked, leaderless, they began to turn.

But their turning had not come soon enough. Their momentum would take them to the princess before the maneuver was completed.

There was no time to think, to plan, to figure one's chances of survival. Jed uttered one defiant roar as he rammed his horse across the path of the stumbling herd. As he reached down to sweep the princess up into the crook of his right arm, his wild-eyed horse screamed in pain and terror as a bison's horn hooked up to draw a wet, red, jagged line across its trembling, sweat-matted haunch. The very breath of the buffaloes seemed to scald his body as Jed clutched the princess and rode for their lives. It seemed their moment of death had come now, and as Jed peered into the face of the woman he was going to die for, he had time to see a mass of incongruously golden hair, an angel's face, and a pair of lovely brown eyes, that, incredibly, seemed more exhilarated by their predicament than afraid. Then they were past the path of the charging herd, out of it entirely. They'd made it!

Jed reined in his horse and began to speak to her. But the princess slipped from his grasp and ran to her father and Grey Eyes, just pulling their own mounts to a stop.

Looking around, Jed realized that the two Ree Guvners, and Hiram and Eddie Rose had been just behind all the while. But he'd been the one to reach the princess first! He'd been the one to save her!

"Damn crazy youngens," Hiram fumed as his horse reared and bucked to a stop. "Old Bear over there oughta blister his daughter's bare bottom for that dumb stunt of hers in comin' down offa the ridge! And I oughta do the same to you, Jed Smith. Hell, boy! Them pte had gotten you, there wouldn't a been enough left to bury!"

Jed just laughed as he soothed his own horse. His mind was on the princess, the feel of her in his arms.

Grey Eyes and Bear rode over. "We wish to thank the white for saving the life of my daughter," Bear said to Eddie. "Tell him that his brave act will be immortalized in song around the Arikara campfires."

Eddie turned to Jed. "He said—"

Jed cut him off. "I heard him for myself." Speaking in the Ree tongue, Jed said "My act of courage was made possible by this fine horse, property of the Arikara nation. Such horses have brought my expedition to your nation. If we have been of service to the Arikara nation, we are grateful."

Bear laughed and nodded, well-satisfied with the right-thinking of such a humble response from a white. Only Grey Eyes seemed to be in an ill-humor over the turn of events.

"He looks like he's sorry we made it," Jed whispered to the two other trappers as the princess, now mounted on a new pony, rode up to stop beside her betrothed.

"Hell, boy, you just don't understand the Ree way of thinkin'," Eddie remarked. "In savin' her you had to put your white man's hands on her."

"But she's alive," Jed stuttered. "Would he'd a rather I let her be killed?"

Eddie shrugged. "Reckon he's still thinkin' that one over."

Jed felt the princess's gaze upon him. He looked up at her, but too quickly had to avert his eyes from her loveliness. "Lordy! She's a beauty!" he found himself laughing out loud. He was giddy, and wondered if it was because of the rescue, or if his excitement had another cause. . . . She was still looking at him, and so he couldn't resist saying in Ree, "What man would not risk his life to save a woman of such beauty?"

"Oh Jesus," Eddie moaned as Grey Eyes' expression darkened with anger. The Ree sat tall in the saddle, and his right hand strayed toward the knife hanging from his belt as the princess urgently whispered something in his ear. Eddie watched the Guvner's hand. If he pulled that knife, he'd have to follow through on his attempt to kill Jed, or else suffer a loss of face. At that moment Eddie decided that if Grey Eyes pulled his knife, he himself would shoot Jed in the back. He couldn't allow the life of one young, foolish would-be wilderness man to jeopardize the lives of the other thirty-nine trappers at this moment surrounded by heavily armed Rees, and thereby jeopardize the success of the Ashley-Henry expedition. He glanced over at Hiram, who nodded once to Eddie. The old boy understood.

But the princess was still murmuring into Grey Eyes' ear. She laughed softly, and, to Eddie's immense relief, the Ree Guvner smiled himself, and his hand moved away from his knife.

Jed had missed all of it. His attention had been on the princess. At first she'd seemed startled to hear him speak in the Arikara language, then she'd seemed offended that Jed had referred to her at all. He wondered what it was she was saying to Grey Eyes, why she'd laughed, and the Guvner had smiled. Then she gave him a haughty glare and a toss of her glimmering mass of hair, but just before she wheeled her pony around, Jed was sure he caught her ghost of a smile. It made his heart begin to pound.

"The Arikara nation accepts what you said as a compliment," Grey Eyes sternly told Jed. "Never again refer to the princess, white. Or your tongue will lie in the dirt, food for flies." He rode off in the direction the princess had taken. Bear just looked at Jed, and then followed.

"Reckon you two are now even," Eddie remarked dryly. "You saved her life before, and now she just saved yours."

"Don't go makin' eyes at a Ree princess like she's some damned Sioux whore," Hiram scolded.

"How beautiful she is, Eddie!" Jed laughed. "And she's got blonde hair. How can that be?"

"Well now, I thought you knew everything, Jed," Eddie said sarcastically.

"How *did* they come by their light hair and light eyes, Eddie?" Jed asked.

"Well, boy. These here Rees have been on the river for hundreds of years. And all kinds of folk have come up the Freedom meetin' and greetin' 'em. Reckon they's just ended up with all kinds of blood floatin' around in their veins. And they's a light-skinned people anyways. Grey Eyes hisself got his name cause a his light-colored peepers. Reckon they's got the white and the black blood all mixed up inside 'em, is all."

"What's her name?" Jed asked, wondering when he would see her again. At the feast tomorrow, most likely. . . .

"Now you jest forget about that there little minx, Jed Smith!" Eddie exploded. "Why, do you know I almost hadda—"

"Eddie!" Hiram said sharply. "No need. . . ." he glared at the interpreter.

"Her name, eh?" Eddie muttered to himself, scowling back at Hiram. "Well now, it's like this, Jed. She's royalty, and Ree royalty got long names. . . . The Indians call the Lord Above the Great Mystery. But sometimes, when they wants to get personal, they calls Him Grandfather. They figures that the sun above is Grandfather's eye, and that the light from it bathes all livin' things in His goodness."

"Eddie? Her name?" Jed repeated softly.

"I'm a comin' on it, I'm a comin' on it," Eddie assured him. "Well now, so ya got Grandfather, and his light comes down, and uh . . ." he shrugged. "Hell, boy, closest thing we gots to it in our language is Sunblossom."

"Sunblossom!" Jed laughed delightedly. "Hear that, Hiram? Sunblossom! All right! Cause when she looked at me, boys, this hoss felt warm all over! Lord above! Sunblossom!"

Eddie and Hiram exchanged looks of long-suffering patience. "Come on, boy," Hiram sighed. "Iffen we wants to keep our hair—"

"Them's that got hair," Eddie said significantly, glancing at Hiram's bald dome.

"We's got some explainin' of the facts of life ta do to you," Hiram concluded. "Falls for a Ree princess. Lord above is right!"

Chapter 10

The Arikara feast began the day after the hunt, at mid-morning, and would continue, Jed was told, until the wee hours of dawn. Wisely, Grey Eyes, the host, had designated as the feasting area the stretch of land between the upper and lower villages. All day the cookfires had been burning, and by sunset, the bright, warm flames had combined with the delicious smells of roasting food and the joyous cries of the children to turn what had previously been a barren no-man's land into a place of great comfort, and good will. There were about thirty-five hundred people in both villages combined, Eddie Rose told Ashley, Jed, and all the trappers from both boats, none of whom would ever have dreamed of missing such an extravagant meal.

There were the choicest parts of the buffalo: the roast tenderloins and the steaks sizzled in the hump fat of the beasts, along with golden plump mushrooms. As their contribution to the feast, the trappers had brought along several sacks of flour and sugar. The former was mixed with minced tenderloin and bone marrow and fried to become what the trappers called french dumplings. The latter was sprinkled on wild berries, or, to the delight of the children, licked from their fingers, straight from the sack.

Buffalo was not the only meat cooking. The Rees had stockpiled hams from deer, elk, and antelope. Wild geese, smeared with a thick coating of mud, feathers and all, were thrust into the fire and covered with coals. The mud slowly fired into clay, and when it glowed red hot, the cooks pulled the vessel from the fire. Once it cooled, a swing of an axe cracked the coating, and it was peeled away from the cooked bird, taking with it the skin and feathers, leaving the flesh clean and done to perfection.

There was catfish boiled into a hearty, thick soup. Boiled squashes and sweet corn basted with the plentiful bison bone marrow. As Eddie Rose said, "Pte marrow could fool a dairy farmer into thinking it was butter. . . ."

There was corn hominy, slowly simmered greens, crisp crusty breads, and to wash it all down, huge vats of hot, herbal teas, and buckets of achingly cold water drawn from a near-by spring. Some of the trappers wanted to bring along kegs of skull varnish for themselves, but Ashley had expressly forbidden it. "Only a fool could believe that the Rees would not catch on and demand their share," he had said, adding that "even fools knew that Indians and the hard stuff don't mix."

"Yep," Eddie Rose pontificated, lulled by the warmth of the fires and his full belly, "thirty-five hundred Rees, and I reckon that every last one of 'em is queuing up for his or her share of vittles."

"Fink and his boys is damn fools for missin' this spread, for sure," John Clyman said, rubbing his stomach.

Jed could only agree. The riverboat men, led by Fink, had steadfastly refused to have anything to do with "the heathens" as they put it, and had even refused to step off their crafts to stretch their legs down along the bank.

The trappers were sprawled about in groups of ten or so, separated from the Rees by mutual inclination, although both red and white men had been getting along, much to General Ashley's satisfaction. Jed was lying with his feet toward the fire and his head pillowed on his possibles sack, staring up at the stars and the full, golden, autumn moon. Ashley, Rose, Hiram Angus, Bill Sublette, John Clyman, Jimmy Beckworth and a few others who had slowly become Jed's group of closest friends all sat or lounged nearby. Off in the distance, they could see Grey Eyes and Bear dutifully accepting what appeared to be congratulations from virtually every adult Ree from both villages. Ashley, craning his neck to watch the goings on around Grey Eyes and Bear, asked, "How many fighting men do you think they have, Eddie?"

"Reckon about six hundred warrior braves, Sir."

"Hell, that's a drop in the bucket," John Clyman scoffed, wiping the grease from his beard with a handful of leaves.

"Waugh! This hoss seen fewer Rees do in five times that many Sioux," Jimmy Beckworth offered. "Nobody beats them for tough customers in a fight," he nodded vigorously, his mass of red hair glimmering like copper in the firelight.

"Hear that, Jed?" Hiram Angus whispered. "You stay away from that there princess, or Grey Eyes will eat you for breakfast."

"You're getting old, Hiram," Jed drawled. "This here hoss hankers after that girl." He stifled his laugh as he waited for Hiram's explosion. He didn't have to wait long.

"Old! Old am I! Waugh, boy! Would you like this

old man's fist against your mouth?" Jed's laughter soothed him, though, for then he said, "Just funnin' me, eh?" Hiram laughed himself. "That's fine, then, but Jed, iffen you likes the look of Ree girls, why you could buy any one of 'em with jest one of yer pistols there."

"I don't want just any Ree girl. I want Sunblossom." It was a flat statement. "Eddie!" Jed shouted across the fire. "When's the wedding supposed to take place?"

"Reckon about a month from now. They's got some kinda Ree holiday comin' up. That's what they's waitin' for."

"It's just not like you, Jed Smith," Hiram grieved. "Not like you atall to wanta take another man's woman?" The old trapper wore a crafty look as he stole a glance at his protege, convinced that the boy's guilt on that score would overwhelm his passion. But never in a hundred years would Hiram have expected Jed's reply.

"Why not?" Jed's tone was bitter, cold. "It happens all the time, Hiram. All the time."

Hiram peered at him. "What is it boy?" he asked softly. "You got some burr under yer saddle. Talk it out, Jed. Yer among friends."

Jed looked around him. He thought he could confide in Hiram, but not the others. "All right, Hiram," Jed said. "I'm telling you, and only you. Get it? Let's take a walk."

Both men rose and slowly ambled toward a shallow, narrow tributary next to the growing fields while Jed told this story:

Jed and Louisa had grown close, so close, in fact, that practically every night Jed stayed at the Simons' household, he simply waited in his bed, thick and heady with passion, for his bedroom door to open, and

Louisa's sylph-like form to flit through the darkness. Never on those nights did she cajole. Never did she even mention their future, or where it would be spent. She was simply an enchantress who kept him on her isle through her womanly charms.

But one night, Jed could no longer keep concealed from their small paradise what he most feared. "If you love me," he said with apprehension, "you must come with me. My future waits for me out there."

Louisa rolled on top of him, so that her breasts pressed against his chest, and his fingers moved lovingly to the swell and curve of her buttocks. "And if your future out West should not include me?"

When Jed answered, he spoke slowly and carefully, wanting her to hear every word, not wanting to go through the agony of saying it a second time. "Louisa, you are my life, my love. You owned my heart from the first day I saw you, when I came here as just a boy. But now my future is waiting for me. If I have to journey to meet it without you, then I'll journey as a cripple, for my heart will forever be where *you* are. That's all one person can give another, Louisa . . . that's all. . . . Everything else is dross. If I have to meet my future a half-man, I will. But I intend to meet my future, woman. . . ." He cried, and his own tears surprised him.

Louisa smiled, and shook her head. "I fear I've become entangled in my own web," she murmured, and began to kiss him. "Yes, I'll go with you."

They agreed that they should marry as soon as possible, and that Louisa should tell her father of their plans the next day. Giddy with happiness, Louisa agreed—if Jed agreed to come back to Pennsylvania once a year so her father could see his beautiful grandchildren. Jed solemnly promised. They kissed. And as soon as the sky grew light with the dawn, Louisa slipped on her nightgown and tip-toed from Jed's chambers.

Early the next morning, Louisa, eager to begin a new life, went in search of her father. Mrs. Harris said that he had risen early and was out of the house. Ignoring Mrs. Harris's protests, Louisa went into her father's small, stuffy office to wait to break the good news to him. Waiting, Louisa looked around the familiar old office, touching the examining table and studying the half-empty medicine bottles, recalling childhood memories of playing there. Soon bored with waiting, Louisa began to idly open the desk drawers. Inevitably, she found the book—her father's diary, and, mischievously, began to read. . . .

Two days later when Jed returned to the Simons' house from business, he immediately sensed something was wrong. Death came to mind first. Whose, he was not sure. The fact that the house was dark, save for the burning porch lantern, seemed to confirm his suspicion.

The front door was unlocked. He tore through the empty first floor of the house shouting for somebody to come and meet him. As Jed entered the dining room, Mrs. Harris stepped from the shadowy hallway. Her eyes were red-rimmed from weeping and her face broken with misery.

"What's happened?" Jed asked, his voice low and soft, expecting to hear the worst.

"The Doctor. Ask the Doctor," Mrs. Harris shook her head. "He's in his office, where he's been all yesterday, and all last night, and all today. He won't take food. Just sits at his desk and stares at her letter. It's no good, Jed. Tell him it's no good killing himself—"

Jed went straight to the old physician's office. He knocked once, called, "It's Jed."

Simons' hoarse, raspy voice told him to come in.

Jed was appalled. The man seemed to have aged overnight. The faint pool of light cast by the candle on the desk highlighted Simons' sunken cheeks, and his ghost-pale complexion. The physician, sitting at his desk with his hands folded on the blotter, stared at Jed for a moment and then said, "Son, she's gone."

She'd left two letters, one for her father and one for Jed. After Jed read his, the doctor simply said, "I'm so sorry for you, son. . . ."

"I don't believe it," Jed said, his sorrow slowly replaced by rage and bitterness. "She wanted to come with me. She told me so. She was going to tell you about our going."

"Are you sure of that, son?" No sooner had Doc Simons said that than his face suddenly filled with anguish. He moaned—the sound like wind in the trees—and pressed a shaking hand to his chest.

"Sir! You're sick!"

Doc Simons feebly pointed to a bottle of brandy on a side board littered with yellowed medical treatises and ancient bills. Quickly, Jed poured them each a glass and held one out to Simons.

The physician reached out blindly for it, with trembling, claw-like fingers. Perplexed, Jed folded the man's hand around the glass, but then stared in horror as Simons let it slip. The glass bounced off the desk, and splashed the liquid across the blotter.

"What can I do, sir?" Jed asked helplessly.

Simons waved him off. He leaned back in his chair and closed his eyes. "It's nothing," the physician muttered. "Pour me another brandy."

Jed did as he was told. But when Simons reached across for the glass, he found his hand trapped inside Jed's own. "You treated me like a son," Jed said, feeling how cold Simons' hand was, dry and cold as death itself. "I've loved you like a father. Tell me what's wrong."

Simons began to cry. "Curse me for being a foolish old man," he muttered, and then was silent for a moment. "It's my heart," he said at last. "It's a chronic heart. I've had it for years, and will most likely have it for years to come. But, nobody knew it, and nobody's to know now."

"Yes, sir," Jed vowed. "Does Louisa know about your health?"

"I believe she does not. And you must not tell her."

Jed nodded, and looked back at the letter. As he stared at it the merciful numbness of shock receded, and the first pangs of the ache he knew he'd carry inside him forever began to gnaw. He could not understand how she had left him. But far more incomprehensible was how she had chosen his own brother, Ralph. Why? Why? His mind whirled.

"What are you going to do?" Simons whispered.

Jed considered the question. "Still go," he said. "I was going to be a farmer, a landowner. I was ready to build something for my family. But there's other ways of living out there." His look was fierce, determined. "There's men in the West who live alone, see no one except for their own kind. They take everything they need from the wilderness, and from the mountains." Jed nodded once, his bargain with himself sealed. "Everything they need. . . ."

"Don't go." The pain in the old man's voice was simple, stark.

"I can't stay," Jed said quickly. "Not here. Not to see them together. I've got to go. Now. As soon as I can."

Simons wept. He leaned back in his chair and closed his eyes. After a bit Simons whispered, "I love you." He'd gathered himself for it, as if it'd been a chasm he'd had to leap. He and Jed sat silently all through the night, sat with each other in the dim candlelight. The doctor fell asleep, and that was when Jed found the old man's diary. Jed read until he fell asleep.

When Jed jerked awake in his chair early the next morning, he found Simons slumped in his chair. Simons didn't respond to Jed's gentle taps. The doctor had quietly passed away sometime during the night.

That day, Jed built the coffin, and dug the grave all by himself. Mrs. Harris wanted to send word to Louisa in Philadelphia, and Jed let her, knowing that he'd be gone by the time she would receive the message and could possibly make the return journey.

The minister came to say his words, and Jed waited patiently for all that had to be done. When it was over, he picked up the shovel and filled in the grave. There were many people at the funeral, but to Jed it was as if there was nobody there at all except himself and the spirit of his "father." Jed's own parents, now aging and greying, were there. Jed loved them, but all the same, he knew who it was he was putting into the ground.

When it was all finished, Mrs. Harris, her old husband standing bashfully behind, asked Jed if he would stay on to watch over things.

Jed shook his head. "My brother, the new master of the house, will take care of it."

His brother, of course, had taken care of much more than just the Simons' homestead, as Mrs. Harris later confirmed.

A time to seek, and a time to lose. . . .

Jed wasn't truly convinced of how or why, but Ralph and Louisa had found each other. It had been Jed's turn to lose all he loved and seek a new life.

A time to love, and a time to hate. . . .

Jed's time for love was over. And now hate festered in him like a burning ulcer. But whom could he blame? Whom could he hate? His own brother, who stole the only woman he had ever loved? Or Louisa herself? Or himself, for naively seeing only the short view of his life?

A time to keep silent, and a time to speak. . . .

Jed had nothing to say to anyone. There was nothing for him to do but leave quietly, not argue with anyone over what had happened. Louisa had her reasons, which Jed would never understand, nor care to know.

A time to laugh, and a time to weep. . . .

Still, he could not forget the happy times they had had, filled with an all-consuming love. And he would never ever forget what he had seen written in Doc Simons' office: "Forgive me, Jed." Even now, it brought hot tears to his eyes.

"And that was a year ago," Jed muttered thickly to Hiram. "I've had a lot of time to think about it, and I still don't know for sure why. If she—or Ralph—had only said something. If there'd been the smallest whisper. There was no clue, no warning. Suddenly they were gone. . . ."

"Surely, lad . . ." Hiram's voice was hoarse with unaccustomed sympathy. "Surely, in all your thinkin' on it, this past year and some, ye've got an idea o' some sort."

Jed looked at the older man gratefully, thankful for the degree of understanding in Hiram's voice. In the telling, he'd thought the story might bring forth ridicule.

"Yes," he nodded, "perhaps there is an explanation, though I've told no-one. That night, sitting by Doc Simons, I saw his desk was open, and someone had been reading his diary. While he slept, I opened the pages. He'd known what was coming. He'd known he was bound to die, and it was all told on those pages. Then I saw the tear-stains. She'd tried to brush them away. I know they were Louisa's tears, not his. He was much too brave to cry over his own fate. Hiram . . ." Jed's voice cracked, and he had to take a deep breath to regain his composure. "Hiram, I think she planned to go with me right up to the minute she read those pages. I think she sat there at his desk, thinkin', and all alone with her grief for him, and she thought of him dying there while she traveled faraways, never to see him again." Jed shook his head. "She couldn't do it, Hiram. She couldn't go along, but she couldn't face me, either. And I suspect that's when she wrote, 'Forgive me, Jed.' Forgive her!" Jed had to take another breath, and he couldn't look at Hiram anymore. "And there was Ralph, waiting there for her." Jed shook his head. "Strange fate, that her choice should have struck her father down."

Jed and Hiram had walked far. Hiram had maintained a respectful silence, but somehow Jed wanted the man to say something, anything to break the tension. Finally, Hiram spat into the dry leaves and uttered a short, impertinent, "Waugh!"

"I'm sorry, Hiram. I didn't mean to. . . ."

"Hell," the old man cut in. "That's one b'ar of a story you've got there. That's why I allus say, boy, give me a squaw-wife any time."

"Maybe she's happy," Jed shrugged. "I'm sure she is."

"Why not, boy?" Hiram said, watching him. "Hell, the thing of it is, you're here now. Put her behind you, boy."

"That's what I'm doing, Hiram."

"But not by gettin' yourself scalped by Grey Eyes! The princess don't want nothin' to do with you—"

"Eddie Rose has married squaws. He's told me how mountain men can get adopted into tribes by marriage, and they don't have to live with them. She and I could leave here. I could set her up right nice in a cabin—"

"You're talkin' foolish, boy," Hiram warned.

"If she takes a liking to my courting, we've got nobody to answer to but ourselves, Hiram," Jed explained. "I'm not looking for trouble, but I'm not afraid to try for what I want. If that's arrogance, so be it. I've already paid dearly for the trait. I reckon I oughta get my use out of it."

"You're either gonna be a great wilderness man, or you're gonna be dead," Hiram smiled, shaking his head.

"I reckon so," Jed grinned back.

Hiram clapped him on his back. "I'm goin' back to the boys before the Rees miss us and wonder what we're up to. Take your time."

Sitting on the bank of the small stream, Jed wondered if Hiram's fear of Grey Eyes was born of old age, or experience, or both. Jed wished the savage no harm, but he himself was an American, born of stock that had whipped the British and those savages who had sided with them twice, once during the Revolution, and again during the War of 1812. The wilderness was part of the United States. Just because the Rees and the Crows and the Blackfeet and all the rest didn't know it didn't change that fact. From what he'd heard, the Sioux hadn't known it for a while, but they sure as hell learned fast enough when they'd had to. The Rees deserved their share as citizens, but they had to realize that they were no longer in charge.

Over to his left along the banks, Jed heard someone moving. He strained to listen. Behind, the raucous sounds of the feast had faded, to be replaced by the chirping symphony of the crickets, and the occasional call of an owl overhead.

Jed moved in the direction of the sound, stepping lightly, the balls of his moccasined feet making nary a sound, even when they fell upon dry leaves. This was the time that Jed loved, the moment when he could stop thinking and let his impulses and instincts take charge. He needed an outer environment that matched his inner one at such times. This is what the wilderness had to offer him. This was its siren call.

Enough moonlight filtered through the trees for him to make out a figure on which he was closing. It was a woman, and the glint of her hair when she turned to glance back told him it was the princess.

Jed dropped back into the shadows of the trees. He smiled as he watched her peer back, searching for a sign of him. She was good, aware of the world. He could tell that about her, for he knew from experience that most *men* could not tell when he was on their trail.

She watched for another moment, and then, seemingly reassured, continued along the stream. What was it *she* wanted to ponder with only the night and its music for company? Was she trying to come to terms with the memory of his touch, as he was trying to come to terms with the memory of hers?

He paced her as she walked, now making some noise as he approached so as not to frighten her.

She turned toward him as he stepped off of the path and into a clearing. The stream was a beautiful silver ribbon in the moonlight. Its gurgling rush a lullaby. And the princess was even more beautiful to Jed. She stood tall and proud as she watched him, and not the least bit afraid. The cloak she wore against the night's chill flowed to just above her ankles. She gathered it tighter about herself as she drew closer—it was just the hint of a protective movement, but that slightest sign of her vulnerability made Jed's heart beat faster.

He stopped a few paces short of her, and held up both hands in a gesture of benevolent intent. He smiled, and said in Ree, "I was tracking you, woman."

Their eyes met, and Jed could see the twinkle in hers, giving lie to her mouth's thin line of disapproval.

He took another step forward. "Yes, woman, I am on your trail." He saw her hand dip beneath her cloak, and he hesitated, not wanting to spoil the magic of the meeting by pushing her into flight, or a misguided attempt to defend herself.

"Who are you?" she asked. Her voice was low, throaty, sensuous.

"I am your enemy," Jed teased.

The princess mockingly brought her hand to her mouth. "But you saved my life. . . ."

"Then I am not your enemy," Jed said softly, taking another step closer. "Though some would say I am. But you know different, do you not?"

"But you are not human. . . ."

Jed's laugh was warm and hearty. "I had you in my arms for a moment, and you were holding on to me. Did I not feel like a human to you then, woman?"

Now it was the princess's turn to laugh. When he'd swept her up out of the path of the raging pte, they'd ridden together for just a few moments. But during that time she'd felt his muscles, curved and hard, like the carved bones of the antelope and elk, but yet, not like bone, which is cold and dead. He was warm and alive. She'd felt his vibrant maleness come to attention as she pressed against him. . . . She'd heard the music of his emotions, quivering like bow strings in response to her nearness. . . . She shook away these thoughts. Remember who you are, the daughter of

Bear, Guardian of the Nation, betrothed to Grey Eyes, our union to represent the renewed harmony of our nation. Betrothed—!

She turned to escape, but Jed said quickly, "I know your name. In my language it is *Sunblossom*. In my language it means "the beautiful flower of the sun up above. Please! Do not leave!"

She hesitated. "In your language it is . . . ?"

"Sunblossom," Jed slowly repeated.

"Sun—blos—som" she drawled, wrapping her mouth around it.

"Good enough," Jed smiled. He pointed to himself. "I am called Jed."

The princess nodded quickly, and then looked past him toward the path, and the trees. "Jed, it would mean your death if my people find you here with me."

"Have I not already risked my life for you?" he whispered. "And I would do so again and again to be with you. And my life will not be an easy prize for your people to take should it come to that, Sunblossom, darling."

"Dar—ling?" she repeated, making what Jed considered to be quite an endearing mess of the pronunciation.

"It means loved one? Love? Damn," he muttered. According to Eddie Rose, there was no Ree word that quite translated into what men and women meant when they referred to amorous love. "The average Ree gets hitched up to whatever squaw he can afford in terms of payin' off her old man," Eddie had explained. "The royalty gets hitched up out of a feelin' of duty toward the nation. Their danged social standing means more to 'em than passion."

But Jed no longer believed that. He could no longer imagine this woman cold, without passion and longing, not when he was standing so close that he could feel her heat. "Darling means what a man feels for his wife," he said.

She laughed. "You are a funny thing, talking of me in such a manner," she blushed. "I am promised to Grey Eyes. Wife, indeed! You talk like a young brave before his first battle! Be careful, young brave, or Grey Eyes will give you your first fight. And your last."

"You don't sound like a woman pleased with her wedding," Jed said.

Now her eyes flashed with real anger. "I am Daughter of Bear, Arikara Guardian—"

Jed cut her off. "Out here, under the moon and the stars, by the mountains, names and titles do not seem to mean very much. I see us as a man and a woman, and I am telling you now that I mean to have you, princess or no. If you do not like that you can tell Grey Eyes, and me and him will have it out. But I think you will not tell him, will you?"

She ignored the question, and said instead, "And what of *your* Guvner, with the face of a goat?"

"Ashley? General Ashley," Jed laughed.

"He wishes to trade for horses from the Arikara nation."

"That is true. You could cause trouble there, Sunblossom. Please do not." Jed looked into her eyes. "For me?"

"You are haughty. . . ." she whispered, feeling herself in a dream. How did he come to be so close to her?

"Someone else just told me that a few moments ago." Jed's voice was powerful, proud. "And I answered that I have paid the price and so might as well enjoy it."

Before she could utter a sound, let alone a scream, Jed gathered her in his arms and kissed her. His lips thrilled her, just as his embrace set her pulse racing. She nearly relented, but something inside her screamed, *No! I am Arikara!*

She was fast, but Jed's response was faster. His hand snapped out, almost too fast to see, freezing her own in mid-air, as the knife she held flashed silver in the moonlight, shiny death.

"I said my life was no easy prize to take," he breathed, still holding her close. "But I give it to you." Letting her go, Jed took a step back. Holding her eyes with his own, he waited. She was a Ree, and she had the knife, but she was also a woman whose touch just now had betrayed her inner feelings.

The princess slowly brought the blade up to his throat. She used the flat of it to raise his chin, guiding his head first one way and then the other. His handsome face held no fear or worry. She could not stop the half-smile that grew in her heart and on her lips as he stood there so brave and somber, ready to pay the penalty for the stolen kiss.

"You *are* a funny thing," she murmured, letting the blade fall to her side. "Since you so little value your life, it is a meaningless gift," she smiled. "Accordingly, it is not fit for me. I shall not take it."

"I have another gift for you then." Beneath his shirt, Jed wore a small cross. He now removed it from around his neck. "This was given to me by my mother. It means much. Wear it?"

The princess now looked genuinely confused. "You have a mother?" she asked. "There are no women of your kind—"

Jed laughed. "Just because you have not seen them does not mean they do not exist. There is much you have never dreamed of, my Sunblossom."

"And there are things you have not seen," she replied in playful tones.

"Will you wear this cross, woman?" Jed asked formally.

The princess plucked it from his fingers and turned to run. "To take is not to give, the Arikara nation understands this," she called over her shoulder. "Warn your Guvner!" And then she was gone down the path.

Jed stood where he was, rubbing his chin, and wondering what she meant by her last remark. What the princess had mentioned before came back to him: Ashley's horsetrading parley did depend on peaceful relations between the Rees and the expedition. In his newly felt passion for the princess, he might very well have jeopardized everything. He resolved to be more careful, to bide his time until Ashley had what he needed from the Rees.

But her taste was still on his lips. . . . Whatever happened, he couldn't let her go through with her marriage to the Guvner Grey Eyes. She didn't want to marry him, Jed could tell. As he started back along the path, he swore to himself that he wouldn't lose this woman. *Nothing would make him lose his woman a second time.*

He'd not taken more than ten paces along the path when he froze. The hairs on the back of his neck began to rise as his ears picked up the faint, dry sound of leaves crackling. Jed gauged the rhythm of the sounds: They were being made by a creature on four legs, not two.

Jed sniffed the air for the animal's scent. He stood stock still, his neck craned, and his nostrils flared. A wilderness man's life depended on his own alertness and familiarity with his surroundings. It was said that Eddie Rose could tell whether it was a party of Sioux, Crow, Ree or Blackfeet that had passed, just by sniffing the ground they'd tread upon. Hiram had claimed the same skills when he was a young man, and his senses were still fresh. Jed had discovered that he possessed the same talent back in Pennsylvania. Even when just a boy, aptitude and concentration had allowed him to hone this talent until he could catch the scent of quail faster than his dogs.

During the last year he'd increased his catalog of scents, so that he could now distinguish between deer, antelope and elk, between black bear and the grizzly. He could pick up a wolf pack while it was still miles upwind, and yet—

And yet this particular scent was confusing. *Jackal,* he thought. *Wolf-jackal-fox-human . . .* , it was all those rolled into one, but over all, blurring the impression, hung the stale, sour odor of violent death. The thing out there in the darkness smelled of all the creatures it had killed to fill its belly. The scents of its victims attended it like ghosts haunting a house.

From somewhere in the shadows came the huff of heavy breathing, a rasping sound that all but shredded Jed's already taut nerves.

He strained his eyes but saw nothing as he slid his pistols from his belt and cocked them. A breeze brought the scent to him full force in a suffocating wave. The thing was very, very near. Jed waited, not daring to move, for the sound of his own body would rob his ears of the precious moment of warning as the creature charged.

An owl hooted and like magic the scent was gone. Jed lowered his pistols, their butts slippery with his perspiration.

So lightly armed, Jed had no desire to go into the brush in order to track the thing, but its scent had been as tantalizing as a half-remembered nightmare. He vowed never to forget it.

Chapter 11

His long, low form snaked through the brush, and wherever he roamed and until he had passed, every night thing that lived on the ground stopped its breathing in an ironic parody of its ultimate future. The rodents gnawing bark or stalking insects, the moles, and even the polecats and foxes that were themselves predators, all froze to await their fate as the huge, grey death-maker padded by.

But Tooth had already fed. The sweet, sticky taste of warm blood still hung in the back of his throat, the gnawing in his sloping belly had not yet again begun. As he loped along, his yellow eyes saw little, for a canine's vision, quick to spot movement, is slow to see detail. His nose and ears led him along through a dim, but richly populated world of smells.

He moved in a large circle, like a pencil on a string, and where the long, invisible string began there sat his god. As Tooth traveled, the juices of his killer's brain simmered and steamed. He had been within striking distance of the thing his master hated, the thing that had made his master-god exude a fear-smell so intense it had driven Tooth into a protective frenzy.

The hound would never forget that enemy scent.

He had been stalking the female thing as she ran along
the path, but the enemy scent had turned him in mid-
stride. The grizzled fur on his hackles had risen as he'd
approached the enemy, bent on doing bloody violence.

But there was another instinct warring for Tooth's
attention as he strained and pointed toward the enemy.
There was a rabid fear, born from the instinct he had
for this enemy that had bested his god-master. Even as
Tooth willed himself to attack, the best he could manage was a jolting, false start. So it was with joyous relief that he bounded into retreat in answer to his
god-master's call.

Tooth was indeed the lord of all hounds, and saw
the world only as the sum of so many sweet things to
kill. But he was still a dog, and answered always and
only to his master-god.

Cabanne knew there was no need to again make
the hootowl call, that Tooth, as always, would obey the
first. He leaned back against the tree trunk and waited
for his dog to return. As he did so, he pondered on
how best to use the advantage the impetuous Jed Smith
had offered him.

It had been Cabanne's great good fortune to have
been prowling about the perimeter of the two villages
in order to witness the return of the upper village's war
party of young braves. He'd watched them slip into the
bustle of Grey Eyes' feast without attracting attention
to themselves. They'd stowed their weapons, along with
their grisly trophies. Bear had seemed to disapprove of
their presence, but Grey Eyes had taken no notice of
them at all. Both Guvners would be surprised when the
news of Pilcher's fort reached here, and both would
have to act pleased, or else lose face before the nation.
Young Cayewa would be pleased to hear that all had
gone well. As Cabanne had carefully planned, Fort
Recovery was no more.

He had been about to make his way back to the comforts of the small camp his men had set up deep in the woods when he'd heard a voice call out. Investigating, he'd been able to spy and eavesdrop on the exchange between Jed Smith and the princess.

Tooth bounded through a hedge to collapse into a reclining position at Cabanne's feet. The big, bearded Frenchman absently stroked his pet's massive head as he murmured his thoughts out loud. "Grey Eyes will be very interested in knowing what his lady's been up to, I think. And that should keep Ashley from getting his horses quickly."

Tooth grinned up at him slavishly, his yellow eyes adoring. Responding to Cabanne's affectionate tones, the hound thumped its tail against the ground.

"The princess is a sweet-looking woman, my pet," the trapper softly laughed. "I think I see a way to have her myself, and at the same time halt the Ashley-Henry progress. When I am done with her, you may have her heart, Tooth."

The hound licked his hand.

"Her golden scalp we will make a present of to Jed Smith. No doubt he will wail to know his love is in the land of the dead, but never fear Tooth, we will dispatch him to join her. Cabanne will see to it that the two lovers are united again, in their graves."

He hoisted himself to his feet, and as Tooth danced and capered about his legs, slowly made his way back to his makeshift camp. There was much to plan, much to tell his men. Cabanne's mind was filled with pleasurable musings. He had plenty of the kind of work that he did best to do.

Jed was surprised to see that all of the trappers had left the feast, which was still going strong as far as the Rees were concerned. They were still singing and dancing, which Jed used to his advantage in sneaking past the villages and down to the camp on the beach. He had no desire to remain alone among the Rees, especially since there was always the chance that he had misjudged Sunblossom, insofar as her keeping their meeting a secret.

He was shocked to encounter a very nervous sentry as he approached the small grouping of Ashley's tents. Rifles were pointed his way until he had identified himself.

An agitated Hiram Angus rushed up to him, saying, "Thank the Lord, boy! This here hoss figured you'd met with foul play!"

"What's happened, Hiram?"

General Ashley said to bring you to him as soon as you was rounded up," Hiram informed him as he tugged Jed along. "Those damned heathens up there! They thought all their dirty work was secret, but they didn't reckon on anybody passin' by the scene for some time to come. Thank the Good Lord for Charbonneau—"

Jed stopped the old trapper as they reached Ashley's tent. "That you, Jed?" the General bawled. "Get in here!"

"Hiram, stop babbling, and tell me what's gone on?" Jed hissed.

Hiram returned his exasperated look. "If you'd stick around you'd know, boy. Ree war party outta Bear's village attacked Josh Pilcher's Fort Recovery, down along the Grand Detour. There weren't but fifteen good old boys defendin' it, and all fifteen lost their scalps!"

'*To take is not to give, the Arikara nation understands this*,' Sunblossom had called over her shoulder. '*Warn your Guvner . . .*' And now fifteen Missouri Fur Company trappers were dead. *She'd known about the war party all along!* Jed hung his head in misery. When they'd kissed, hatred between the red race and the white had seemed so far away—"You're sure it was Rees that did it?" he asked in a wretched voice.

"Aye, boy," Hiram scowled. The light from Ashley's tent cast an amber glow on the scene as the old trapper danced a jig-in-place, a lock-step of excitement and anger.

All around, trappers were grumbling among themselves, or else standing and glaring up at the Ree barricade, shaking their fists in the direction of the Indians who had so recently been their hosts.

"Look to yer powder and ball, and sharpen yer blade," Hiram said as Jed made his way into the General's tent. "Looks like we may have ourselves an old-fashioned trappers war against them Rees after all!"

PART THREE

BLOOD IN THE RIVER

Chapter 12

He looked about sixty to Jed. He was a tall, stooped man whose bemused expression and sparse, grey-blond hair and beard gave him the diffident appearance of a merchant. He'd stared into the tin cup of coffee he'd cradled in both hands as if he could read the future in it, only looking up to smile when General Ashley had said, "Jedediah Strong Smith, meet Toussaint Charbonneau."

Charbonneau! The famed interpreter for Lewis and Clark, and husband of the squaw Sacajawea, who herself did so much to make the explorer team's journey to the Pacific a success! Jed took a seat beside the smiling Frenchman.

"Charbonneau has signed on with us," Ashley continued. "He's brought us sad news concerning Josh Pilcher's Fort Recovery. It seems a Ree war party has wiped out all fifteen of the men stationed there."

"Pardon, sir," Jed spoke up. "Hiram just told me. I remember that the French Fur Company's Fort Kiowa is between the Rees and Pilcher's fort." Jed glanced uneasily at Charbonneau. "Excuse me for mentioning it, but it strikes me powerful strange that a bunch of Rees looking for action should go out of their way to confront Americans when a nice, juicy French outpost is sitting just about under their noses."

"Jed Smith," Charbonneau began in a heavily accented voice. "None of us are fools here. Your General mourns for his fellow Americans now dead, but perhaps he does not mourn so much for the deaths of his competitors, eh? Young Cayewa is my fellow countryman, and I have served him for many years. Today I have decided to offer my services to the Ashley-Henry expedition. I will say no more about the actions of my countrymen than to warn that he is your sworn enemy. Today I perhaps disapprove of his actions. Tomorrow I may return to his employ." He nodded to Ashley. "That is all about the French in my presence, if you please."

"I meant no disrespect," Jed stuttered.

"And I heard none, my boy," Charbonneau assured him. "I have found that it is the personal allegiances to country and loved ones that are among the more difficult aspects of life for a man to manage." Here he smiled. "My old adversary, and often-times friend, Hiram Angus, has made mention of certain traits we may share concerning this subject."

"What's he talking about?" Ashley demanded.

Jed shrugged. "Sir?" He wondered how evident was his blush.

Ashley took a moment to glare suspiciously around the tent before continuing on. "Eddie, what's your reading of the situation? Why the hell have they been so hospitable to us if they've got scalping on their minds?"

Eddie's dark brow furrowed. In the flickering candle light he looked as if he were wearing a sad clown's mask as he sipped his coffee. "General, I don't think they know what's happened," he finally offered. "Grey Eyes and Bear put a stop to all fightin' in honor of the weddin'. Trouble is, fightin' is the only way a young man can advance in the tribe. I suspect it was a renegade war party. That it went out lookin' for blood without Bear's or Grey Eyes' say-so."

"Agreed," Hiram said, his initial fury subsiding. "Rees don't lie, General. No way in hell they gonna give a party like tonight's iffen they knows they have warriors out."

"I also agree," Charbonneau added. "And I would wager that the war party came from Bear's village. He is old, and has no clear-cut second-in-command. Grey Eyes is young and strong, and has as his Ranking Brave, a young fellow named Little Soldier. No group of young, hot-blooded braves would dare defy such a strong Guvner and Second."

"Gotta be Bear's boys who'd figure they could get away with it," Eddie Rose nodded.

"What's got you all troubled, Jed?" Ashley suddenly said. "You've been sitting there, your face all screwed up and dark as storm clouds. Speak your peace, boy!"

Jed glanced past the General to Hiram, who shook his head. Obviously this was not the time for him to confess to a romance between himself and the princess promised to Grey Eyes. . . . "I've been thinking that these Rees are strange birds, sir. It doesn't much matter who the war party belonged to, only that they got away with it. From what I've picked up so far, it figures that both Guvners have got to commend their boys. They don't figure white men as humans, sir. No way they're gonna punish Ree warrior-braves for scalping whites. It'd be well, they sorta translate it as 'a loss of face.' It's got to do with their honor, sir. . . ." he trailed off.

"Jed's right," Eddie Rose said. "Iffen the Guvners don't know about it tonight, they'll pick up on the war party's boasts by dawn. When that happens, Bear will tell Grey Eyes he was in on it all along. That'd be much less humiliatin' to the old boy than confessin' it's all news to him."

"Do the Rees know you're with us?" Hiram asked Charbonneau between puffs of his pipe.

"No, Hiram. Only Young Cayewa knows I've journeyed this way. . . ." He seemed about to say more, but instead, he only nodded and got up to fill his cup from the coffee pot.

"Then the Rees don't know that we know about the massacre," Ashley said. "All right, boys. Here's how it goes. We play it innocent. We need those horses. If the Rees don't suspect we're wise to their dirty doings, they'll maybe continue on being friendly to us. As far as I'm concerned, the attack on Pilcher's never happened."

Charbonneau's amused chuckle was soft, but the cynicism behind it was unmistakable.

"They were our countrymen," Ashley acknowledged. "But they were also our competitors. If I ever have the chance to avenge them, I will, but right now, my responsibility is to my creditors, and my partner." Ashley looked Charbonneau in the eye. "And to my men."

The French guide's bemused expression had returned. He acquiesced with a wave of his hand. "As I mentioned, personal allegiances are often difficult to manage," he said politely.

Jed had taken the time during the exchange to evaluate the newcomer. Charbonneau's history was already well known to him. Indeed, Doc Simons had given Jed the published journal of Lewis and Clark as soon as the boy had mastered the fundamentals of reading. But it was one thing to read of a famous figure's officially recorded exploits, quite another to meet the famous figure in the flesh. Jed was impressed with the old guide's way of seeing things not in black and white, but in shades of grey. As soon as the immediate crisis was over, and Ashley had their horses safely in hand, Jed resolved to talk to Charbonneau about his own situation concerning Sunblossom. Surely the husband of Sacajawea would understand Jed's desires!

"All right," Ashley announced. "Jed, you'll be in charge of the landing party on the beach. Hiram, you'll be Jed's second in this, for I'll want him with me and Eddie when we go up to the villages to begin our parley. I reckon I'll need both fellows up there to interpret once the going gets hot and heavy."

"What about the keelboat crews?" Jed asked.

"You got yerself trouble there, General," Hiram advised. "Never shoulda stood for that there Mike Fink refusin' to come ashore. Pardon me for sayin' so, but when you let Fink get away with that, it was like makin' him yer equal in command."

"Your criticism is well leveled and well taken," Ashley sadly agreed. "I tell you now what I confided to Jed awhile back. Getting decent boat crews was near impossible. I had to settle for some disreputable fellows. Falstaff's Battalion was genteel in comparison."

"Falstaff, eh?" Hiram repeated dubiously. "Don't reckon I heard of that hoss. . . ."

"English cuss," Jed chimed in, keeping a straight face. He was conscious of Charbonneau's eyes upon him as he heard the Frenchman's soft laugh.

"The point is," Ashley chuckled. "I'm not sure we can count on them to back us up should it come down to a fight between us and the Rees.

"That don't shine too good, General," Eddie muttered.

"It makes for a powerful lot of heathens against

not too many trappers," Hiram commented as he exhaled a cloud of blue tobacco smoke.

"I want none of the other trappers to know what's happened to Pilcher's boys, and above all absolutely *none* of the keelboat men are to know," Ashley told them all.

"No problem there, General," Jed said.

"Jed, I want you to row out to the boats tomorrow and let the boat men know that we've begun our parley," Ashley said. "You get along with Fink as well as any of us. Charbonneau, I think you had better lie low for a bit. I don't want either the Rees or the keelboat men to get a whiff of you." He stood up and stretched. "That's it, boys. Might as well turn in and get some rest. We've got a couple of busy days ahead of us. Hiram? Eddie? Do you think we need sentries?"

"We've got 'em whether we need 'em or not," Hiram chuckled. "But don't worry, General. Them Rees ain't about to come chargin' down on us while their bellies is all filled with pte meat."

"I'd like to wake up with my hair," Ashley joked.

The men laughed and began to file out of the tent.

"Jed," the General called. "When you can, write up the results of our meeting tonight in the log. Good night, boys."

Jed pulled on the oars of the skiff, sending the little boat cutting through the yellow, rushing current of the river. Halfway to the keelboats, he took a moment to pull in his oars in order to peel off his shirt. His glistening chest and arms had grown thick. He figured that he must have put on at least twenty pounds, all muscle. Sweat ran down his back. While most wilderness men grew their hair long, past their shoulders, and wore it braided up and tucked beneath their hats, Jed had hacked his off with his Bowie knife, so that it just reached the nape of his neck. (Wouldn't his dear mother peg him for a roughneck now!) Jed was also one of the few men in this part of the world who still shaved regularly. And each time he stared into the mirror and scraped his cheeks, a gaunt-cheeked, steely-eyed hoss stared back. Nobody's greenhorn, for sure.

Jed rowed along in the four-man skiff. There were two others: one that could hold twenty men and supplies, and another that was half that size. He had to exert great force just to control the boat made clumsy by the river's natural turbulence and the whirlpool blockade constructed by the Rees. He wished he'd had a hand or two more to help him. But rowing was not a trapper's job. And Eddie Rose was busy with the General, and Hiram, Jed thought, was just too old to handle the oar. Sweating and cursing as he rowed across the water toward the distant keelboats, he vowed to himself that should he ever head up an expedition the men would damn well know who was boss.

The sunlight shuttered by swiftly scudding clouds, winked and flared against the water as Jed closed in on the two big keelboats. They had been tied together, side by side, to create one big, floating home base.

It was bad, Jed thought. The Rees could wait until dark and then, unseen, slip their tiny, two-man bullboats—circular, floating "bath tubs" made out of sapling branches and dried pte skins—into the river to swarm around the hobbled-together keelboats like flies around a butchered carcass. He wondered if Ashley knew about this, if Ashley had even taken the time to notice at all what was going on concerning their only means of transportation.

At least Ashley was right in trying his best to keep the peace between his expedition and the Rees. Better to turn the other cheek than to bring the wrath of six hundred braves down upon a handful of unorganized trappers and untamed river men.

Jed scanned the deck of the boat nearest him, the *Yellowstone Packet*. Fink had no sentries posted. Jed literally had to shout to get the attention of the lazing crewmen. Finally, one fellow deigned to dangle a pole his way. Jed grabbed it and hauled his skiff alongside. He tossed a rope up to the crewman and the little boat was made fast against the mother craft.

There was no ladder offered, so Jed stretched his arms until his fingers found the cleated edge of the catwalk deck. He hoisted himself up, and then over the top. The crewmen had just stood up and watched; evidently, the idea of giving Jed a hand had never crossed his mind.

"Where's Fink?" Jed demanded.

The crewman shrugged and turned to return to his business. Jed was in no mood for insolence. A wilderness man took no guff from anyone. He spun the crewman around and grabbed him by the front of his collarless shirt. The crewman was as big as Jed, but he suddenly found himself slammed against the side of the cargo box and lifted up, so that his clumsy, thick-soled boots were dancing on air.

Jed repeated each word slowly, while the man stared at him with the startled, skittish eyes of a frightened steed. "Where is Fink, boatman?"

"I dunno," the man stammered. "Lemme down, I say. Fink's—"

"Right here!" Mike laughed as he rounded the corner. "Now let my boy go, Jed Smith! You're on *my* territory now!"

Jed let the frightened crewman slump to the deck as he turned to face the keelboat patron. The man's eyes were bloodshot with drink, and his blue-black hair was grease-matted. *Drunk as a skunk,* Jed thought as Fink tottered closer. He'd said, '*My territory. . . .*'

"Come with me, boy. We'll have a drink."

Jed let himself be led to the other side of the boat. Planks had been laid across the parallel decks of the two boats so that a large, wide platform had been created. Upon this, the crews of the two boats lounged and gambled among themselves, while below the river coursed along.

Fink pulled Jed down beside him and offered a half-empty jug of skull varnish. Shrugging at Jed's refusal, the patron tipped the jug to his lips and gulped down great swallows of the potent stuff, chugging away at it like it was a container of purest spring water.

Just beside them, a fight had broken out between two men who had been playing a game of "hand." Jed considered it a foolish children's game. One fellow held a rock, coin or whatever behind his back, and then extended his two fists. The other player had to guess in which fist the object was held. But there was nothing childish at all about the intensity of the play, and the possible size of the stakes. Men had lost their wives, horses, guns, scalps, and often enough, their very lives in playing this game. It could go on for hours, the crowd watching dividing up into teams, and almost always, the end result was violence from the loser.

One of the struggling players had pulled a knife, but before he could stab his opponent, Fink reached over, and plucked the blade from his fingers. Then, in an almost languid movement, he slammed their two heads together so that they collapsed into a heap of arms and legs.

"Boys is gettin' rowdy, Jed," he said by way of explanation. "Tired of hanging around these heathen Rees." His words were slurred, and the reek of the skull varnish hung in the air all about him. "We maybe are gettin' ready to shove off. You boys oughta think about comin' along."

Jed told him what had been agreed upon about the horses in Ashley's tent last night, leaving out all mention of the Pilcher massacre and Charbonneau's arrival.

"Tell yer damn General to hurry it up, then," Fink warned. "I tell ya we're ready to move on. Gots to see the mountains, boy! They's waitin' for us, right boy?"

"These boats belong to General Ashley, Mike," Jed said evenly.

Fink's eyes narrowed into slits for a moment, but then his expression softened. He slapped Jed on the back, and, eyeing his bare chest, said, "You've filled out a mite, boy."

"As I remember it, I took you well enough when I was still a soft greenhorn," Jed bantered back.

"Aye, that you did," Fink laughed in agreement and fond memory. "That you did. . . . Jed, listen to me now. Me boys is a rowdy bunch, and while I'm head bull around here that's only until the boys get it into their head to gang up on me. Then it'll be like a pack of dogs against a grizzly. Ya know? Sooner or later, them dogs wear the big beast down. I tell ya true, boy, the General's got a weak link in a chain floatin' out here—" Mike paused. "What do you want?" he snarled as Bill Carpenter crawled out of the hold.

The jagged slash Fink had cut into the man's cheek had healed badly, Jed could see. Bill Carpenter's face, what with the livid burn down one side of it, and the knife scar, twisting like a trail drawn on a map down the other, looked like something out of a skull varnish-induced nightmare.

"Wanna talk to Jed," Carpenter said thickly. During the healing the skin had puckered around his mouth, distorting his speech. "Alone, says I," he spat, glaring hatefully at Fink.

"Beat it," Fink muttered.

But Carpenter was not to be dismissed. From out of nowhere it seemed, Tom Talbot appeared. As Jed looked around, the majority of both crews gathered around in a rough circle.

"Right then," Carpenter leered. "I ain't afraid of sayin' it in front of ya, Mike. The boys and me have been thinkin' that it's time for a new patron of these here two boats. Jed, we wants ya to take the General a message from us. Tell em that me and Talbot here is to be the two new patrons. Right? You tell em that. Fink is out. Tell em that we're willin' to follow his orders once we're put in charge and promised Fink's wages split in two."

"Talbot?" Fink asked in an even, calm voice. "Tommy? You in on this with him?"

Talbot nodded, his wispy blond hair standing up in the river's breeze like a brave's head feathers. "I am, Mikey. I told ya long before. It's hell to cut yer friend over a whore. . . ."

"And what's to happen to me, boys?" Fink shouted.

There was a general rumbling among the mob of crewmen, but it was Talbot who spoke up. "Mikey, you can go ashore, with the trappers." Carpenter began to object, but Talbot silenced him with a look of warning. "You can go ashore, Mikey, unharmed. Fair enough?"

"Well, now," Fink drawled, still sitting next to Jed. "That might be fair enough for some, but it ain't the keelboat man's way."

"Mikey, it's yer only chance," Talbot warned. "Take it!"

"Now Tommy, you hush up," Fink said absently. "I ain't addressin' myself to you, cause you ain't the ringleader here—" Fink's thick, gnarled finger shot out to point toward Carpenter, who involuntarily took several steps back until he came up against a big, bearded crew member. "It's him!" Fink roared in his deep, powerful, patron's voice.

It was the voice Fink used when exhorting his men to pole, and at once it became clear that Carpenter had overplayed his hand. His attempt to take over the boats had come too soon, probably hastened by Jed's appearance. It was a desperate gamble, and it looked like he was fated to lose. Jed examined the faces of the crew. He came to the conclusion that they were not behind Carpenter so much as they were merely looking forward to being entertained by the challenge, and its inherent promise of violence.

The crew member Carpenter had butted up against shoved him forward, back into the center of the circle. Fink regarded his one-time friend as he slowly climbed to his feet. "You cried your tale to Jed, but Jed don't decide who gets to be patron." He was so drunk that he staggered more than walked toward Carpenter, who had begun stroking the knife scar along his cheek as if to gain some new courage from it. "You know the way keelboat men pick their leaders, Billy," Fink laughed as he towered over his opponent.

"I can't take you in a fight, Mike," Carpenter wavered. He looked around him for support. "A fist fight don't prove nothin'," he crowed, and then a sly look came across his ravaged features. "Shootin' is good. A man's size don't come into account when it's shootin' time. . . ."

"Aye, Billy. Shootin' it'll be," Mike grinned, nodding as the crowd around them cheered their approval.

"Don't do it, you fools!" Jed shouted, jumping to

his feet. Several pairs of hands locked his arms behind his back. He was helpless as Fink pulled Jed's brace of pistols from his belt and held them up to the crowd.

"We'll shoot cups, Billy. How does that suit ya? Me at one end, and you at the other," Fink said, pointing with the guns to the roof of the cargo box.

Carpenter's face fell. "I wanted a duel," he began, but his complaints were drowned out by the crews.

"You's overruled, Billy," Fink said in a parody of an apology. "Shootin' cups, it is. Now don't look so down, Bill. You may git the first shot. I'll tell ya what. Let's sky a copper to see who does."

A coin was duly produced, and Fink spun it into the air.

"Heads!" Carpenter screeched as it clattered to the wood deck, bounced once, and then settled.

"Tails, Bill," Fink gently said as necks craned to gape at the coin. "You lose, boy."

The color drained from Carpenter's face, so that all that seemed left was his scars. "Tommy?" he called in a trembling voice. "All my goods and wages is to go to you. I say it afore all these here witnesses."

"Go on now," someone from the crowd called out gruffly. "You ain't about to die. Shootin' cups, is all. Mike's a deadeye shot. Then it's yer turn, 'til one of ya misses, and he's the loser."

"A dollar of me comin' wages on Carpenter!" someone else shouted. "I say he's a better shooter than Fink!"

"I'll take that!" came an answering yell. Soon the two boats were ringing with the wagering of the excited men.

Jed stood, his arms still pinioned. Sweat was pouring from him. "Don't kill him, Mike!" he begged as the patron swaggered past him to climb up to the roof of the cargo box.

Fink fixed one bloodshot eye on the young trap-per. "Shut up, Jed," he snarled. "This here's my terri-tory, I tell ya. Hold em good!" he instructed Jed's captors.

Carpenter stood at one end of the cargo box's flat roof. One of Jed's pistols hung impotently from his right hand. On top of his head was balanced a tin cup filled with skull varnish. Fifty paces away, Fink stood, ready to take aim and blast the cup from Carpenter's head with Jed's other gun.

"Ya all know the rules!" Fink bellowed. "Iffen I hit the cup, Billy's got to match my shot!" Now Fink's drink-sodden voice grew serious. "I now swear on the river that iffen I lose I'll sign off in favor of Carpen-ter!"

The crews expressed their satisfaction with the deal with shouts of "Let's get on with it!"

But Fink took his time. Once he began to sight down the barrel of his pistol, only to turn the move-ment into a yawning stretch. His mugging provoked laughter from the crews.

Jed watched it all with queasy fascination. He caught Talbot's eye, but the other only shook his head in resignation. Gesturing toward Carpenter's shivering form, he drew his finger across his throat.

Now Fink had his gunhand extended. He squinted down the barrel of the weapon. All signs of drunken-ness seemed to have left him. He was rock steady, un-wavering as he pointed his gun at his target fifty paces away. "Hold steady, now, Billy," he murmured. "Don't go spillin' that skull varnish. I'll want some presently."

He fired the pistol. The bullet took Carpenter square in the forehead, shattering his skull like a ripe melon. The body somersaulted backward, blood spew-ing from yet another jagged crack in his face.

"Why Billy," Fink said, his voice loathsome with

feigned hurt. "You've gone and spilled the whisky!" He strode to the body, and picked up Jed's other pistol, wiping a spot of Carpenter's blood off of it against his shirt. "Well fellows," he called. "Looks like I lost!"

Shocked silence. Then one of the men began to titter at Fink's joke. Soon, more joined in, and jugs of skull varnish began to be passed.

"I don't know how it happened, boys!" Fink told the crews. "He musta moved, he did!"

Jed stared at the crew. This was a lawless land. He knew that nobody would dare accuse Fink of murder. That crime would go unpunished.

"The only thing is, while I lost, Carpenter, poor boy, is no more," Fink continued on. "I can't sign off as patron to him now! Anybody else care to play shootin' the cups with me?"

None of the men in either crew would meet his level gaze as he hefted Jed's still-loaded pistol. "How about you, Tommy?" Fink called to Talbot as Jed was released.

"No, Mike," Talbot said, his eyes staring at the deck.

"Then I reckon you no longer want to be patron?"

"That's right, Mike."

"You sure, now, Tommy?"

But Talbot was already on his way down into the hold.

Fink climbed down off the roof to hand the pistols back to Jed.

"You didn't have to kill him, Mike," Jed said, his voice loaded with accusation.

"To hell with you and what you think, boy!" Fink sneered. "Go back and tell your General what's happened. Let him know that Mike Fink is waitin' on 'em to shove off outta here!"

"Atta boy, Mike! You tell em!" came from a couple of crew members drifting by.

Jed turned to go, but Fink grabbed his shoulder and spun him around. "Listen to me, Jed," he said in quieter tones. "I still take my orders from the General. Don't go bein' fooled by what I says in front of the boys. I got command of 'em only for as long as I control 'em. They's tough, but they's cowards. Iffen you gets Ree trouble, these crews may not be here when you need em. Understand, boy? I'll be here for ya iffen I can, but I got only so much control over my crews."

"And shooting Carpenter, Mike?" Jed asked in anger. "Was that just a ruse as well?"

"Dammit, he was my friend, not yours," Fink mumbled. He began to turn away, but then eyed Jed with curiosity. "You ever kill a man? Or ever even see one killed before?"

"N-No," Jed admitted.

"Hell, boy," Fink snorted. "That explains it then. Don't go shamin' a man for somethin' you don't know nothun about, you hear? Not until you learns that there's things to be done that often times a man don't want to do."

He watched as Jed made his way back to his skiff. "Just remember to let the General know," Fink warned. "You think you got troubles jest dealen with the Rees, but hell, I got worse savages in these here two crews your old General gave me."

What Fink had told him was true, Jed mused as he rowed back to the beach. The crews were more uncivilized than the Rees. Jed felt sickened and tainted.

Chapter 13

Cabanne coughed and gagged, thinking that this calumet smoking was the nastiest part of friendly relations with the Rees. Other tribes at least smoked *kinni-kinnick,* the inner bark of the red willow, which, when mixed with tobacco and smoked, produced an effect comparable to a long, healthy draught of Young Cayewa's fine cognac. But the damn Rees didn't go in for that sort of thing. At least not the older, religious ones. It was a different story for the younger braves, as the French man well knew.

To Grey Eyes, he ceremoniously said, "We smoke the pipe of peace so that the Arikara nation and Young Cayewa will be joined together in harmony."

Grey Eyes took the calumet from him and puffed on it, making great billowing clouds of smoke. "May your wishes float to Grandfather, and so, be acknowledged," he said out of politeness, with no real warmth in his voice, as the acrid fumes rose toward the hole cut into his lodge's ceiling. He nodded, and put the calumet back in its place between them. His posture relaxed as he eyed Cabanne. The visitor was foul-smelling, his manner unpleasant. "What do you wish to tell me?" the Guardian asked, indicating that the ceremony was over, and that they could get down to business.

"My Guvner, Cayewa, wonders why you make peace with the Americans. They have given your people trinkets, but Cayewa has brought the young braves of Bear's village rifles and ammunition."

"All whites are the same," Grey Eyes replied. "We wish harmony with all whites."

"All whites are not the same, Guardian," Cabanne responded, careful to keep his voice filled with respect. "Some whites bring the Arikara nation gifts fit only for squaws, other whites lead the Arikara nation to the spoils of victory worthy of them. I myself led the braves of Bear's village to a village populated by bad whites. When Bear's young braves were finished, they had scalps for their coup poles, and guns and ammunition. These are gifts fit for men. These are my gifts. Trinkets are gifts for women. Those are their gifts. All whites are not the same, Guardian."

The raid on Pilcher's fort had indeed garnered Bear's braves rifles and shot and scalps, but it had also rewarded Cabanne with the spoils of Pilcher's boys' traps. There'd been four packs of beavers in the fort: three hundred and twenty pelts. That much fur would fetch seven hundred dollars. Cabanne had instructed his four men to cache the fur packs in a safe place until they were ready to transport them back to Fort Kiowa. Supplying the heathens with skull varnish had started out as merely an instigative ploy, but it looked as if it might well turn out to be a highly profitable one. Why, the Rees themselves could be turned into trapper slaves, turning over their fur packs for kegs of the addictive skull varnish. It would do his heart good to stand over these savages, whipping the pride out of their stinking hides. . . .

"You brought Bear's young braves another gift, or

perhaps curse. You brought them strong drink." Grey Eyes scowled. "It is another of the whites' curses, like the poison disease once brought to the Arikara nation. This strong drink dulls the sound of the world inside men. This strong drink makes right-thinking people think wrong. It weakens the Law so that the Arikara nation can no longer hear it or see it in the voices and manners of their Guardians."

"Bear does not believe that," Cabanne said. "Bear—who is old and wise and the Guardian of the prosperous upper village—wished his braves to enjoy the benefits of skull varnish before they went to help themselves to honor and weapons at the cost of the bad whites."

Grey Eyes pondered the situation. He had his doubts about what Bear believed or didn't believe, about what the old Guardian even knew. True, he had bragged to Grey Eyes about the accomplishments of his young men, had even admitted that he knew about it, and approved of their use of the whites' strong drink. But times were crucial between the two villages right now. The father had a lot to gain or lose once the daughter became the wife of the Guardian of the lower village. It would not do for the old man to admit to weakness or ignorance concerning his people at such a time.

"I have brought Grey Eyes a gift of skull varnish," Cabanne said. He made a great show of removing a shiny red, ceramic jug of the stuff from his pack. The color alone should intrigue the savage, Cayewa had explained to him. "I have brought this so that Grey Eyes can learn of its fine magic."

Sighing to himself, Grey Eyes looked about his lodge, at his coup pole, his weapons, at all his implements and badges of his rank, of his position. Never had the weight of his responsibility felt so heavy upon his shoulders. Never had the world seemed so at odds with what was handed down in the Law. His vision of the flames turning against him flitted through his mind, but he pushed the haunting doubts away. *The now, concentrate on the sound of now—*

"The Arikara nation wishes to be in harmony with all whites." He carefully chose each word as he spoke to this emissary from Young Cayewa. "If, indeed, there are different kinds of whites, I will make a separate peace with each tribe. . . ."

"But not with the bad whites," Cabanne interrupted. He saw Grey Eyes' angry scowl, and shut up fast.

"By visiting Bear's village, and by leading his young braves from my pronouncement of peace by means of strong drink and promises of glory, you have angered me. The pronouncements of the Guardian of the Arikara nation are not to be flouted by ignorant whites. You have ridden into this village on a fine horse. You will walk out of this village without it."

"Now just you hold on, there. . . ." Cabanne growled.

"Your horse is the penalty you shall pay for disregarding my will," Grey Eyes continued matter-of-factly. "Should you say one more word in objection to this I shall slit your throat, for all whites are but lowly vermin to the Arikara people. And I shall still keep the horse," he added as an afterthought.

Cabanne felt his temples throb with anger. *Oh, I could wrap my hands around your throat and choke the life out of you, savage. Oh, killing you will one day be my finest kill of all. . . . Vermin, am I? You sit there in your loincloth and feathers, and call me ignorant, and vermin? You stinking heathen, can you even dream of how your future and your children's futures are in the hands of men like myself?*

At that moment, Cabanne's hatred was a living,

palpable thing, a wormy, scuttling insect with bile for blood, threatening to gnaw his own gut to pieces if he didn't reach out and snap the filthy, son-of-a-whore Ree 'Guvner's neck—

Grey Eyes sat through the silence, his face as filled with guileless curiosity as a child's as he watched the white work his way through the emotions that so easily took possession of his weak, animal will. There was no fear on his part of an attack by Cabanne. Grey Eyes did not believe that he was so stupid as to commit suicide.

Presently, Cabanne got control of himself by promising his bitter anger that there would be a later time, when all debts would be paid. "I accept the Guardian's judgment concerning my trespass," he said in his meekest voice. "I thank the Guardian for his mercy."

Grey Eyes nodded. "You are dismissed," he announced, turning his face away from the white to signal the end of their conference.

"But if it pleases the Guardian, if one white is punished for a trespass, shouldn't another white be punished as well?" Cabanne asked craftily.

Without looking his way, Grey Eyes ordered, "Speak of this."

Here's where if I'm not careful, it'll be my scalp that's taken, and not Jed Smith's. "If I speak of this," Cabanne began carefully, "I fear I will bring down upon myself the Guardian's great anger, for the tale I have to tell is a sad, sad one." Cabanne waited, his trap set.

"Who does this tale concern?" Grey Eyes asked.

Ah, so you only nibble at my bait. "It concerns one of the bad whites camped along the beach," he said. "And the princess."

Grey Eyes felt the pain and sorrow begin in his

heart even as he said, "Tell me what you know, white. I command it."

I've hooked you now! Cabanne gloated to himself. To have simply come out and told the Guardian what he knew would have been to invite the savage's wrath down upon him. But now he was safe. According to the insane Arikara logic, no man could be punished for bad news he'd been commanded to deliver. . . . Soon he'd be out of this foul lodge, and on his way back to camp, where he'd be safe with Tooth. *Now I will skin your heart, your soul, savage. I'm a hairbreadth from enjoying the princess's favors, and causing my enemy's death.*

Careful to keep all signs of amusement buried, Cabanne skillfully spun out the tale of what he had witnessed between the young trapper and the beautiful princess the previous night.

The summons had come to her in the form of a young brave who had stopped no less than thirty feet from where she sat, surrounded by her servant maidens. The young brave bowed his head most respectfully as he waited for one of her maidens to come hear him.

She set down her sewing and waited for her servant to come relay the message. The girl beamed as she told her that the Guardian of the Arikara nation bid Guardian Bear's daughter to come see him at once.

All the other maidens put their fingers across their lips as they giggled and blushed over the delicious joke inherent in such an urgent summons from a man to a woman.

The princess, however, did not smile. She had been Grey Eyes' betrothed for many years, ever since they'd first seen each other, long before the pronouncement had made it official. She understood him quite well. She knew of the visions that guided him, the sacred flames which he carried in his heart and which kindled his soul. But there was more at stake than passion. Their union would reunite the nation. There was no question of the marriage.

It was because she knew him so well that her spirit was dark and heavy. Forces she could not control had begun to wreak havoc on the Arikara nation. Today she felt these forces in Grey Eyes' summons, which was cold, the summons of a Guardian to a princess, not of a man to his woman. Last night she had felt these forces in the white man's warm kiss. . . .

She rose and made her way into her lodge to dress. She would wear her finest frock to go see him. The dress was cut from scarlet cloth, bolts of which had been left in tribute by keelboats passing through the nation over the years. It was covered across the breast and back with rows of elk teeth and wondrously delicate sea shells. She herself had never seen this marvelous thing called the "sea," but her father had, long ago, when he was a young man and had gone wandering. When he'd returned he had a pouch full of the precious ornaments. For many nights he'd entertained the entire village with his tales of what he'd seen and heard, but nothing fascinated the nation as much as his description of this body of water which made even the rushing, roaring Stream of Life upon which their village was situated seem like a little trickle. One village elder had offered her father three horses for the pouch of shells! But he had refused the offer. He had said that these precious things were for the enjoyment of his wife. . . .

When her mother had passed on, the shells had been given to her. She had painstakingly embroidered them onto the dress, along with the elks teeth, which themselves were worth the price of a horse.

She would wear this dress to confront Grey Eyes, and follow the letter of the Law. She would give Grey Eyes respect, proper protocol—

Your heart? Can you still give him your heart?

At one time the princess would have consulted her father concerning her visit. But that was when they were both younger, and Bear was more vigorous. Her father, brave strong Bear—how old and frail he had become! Long ago it seemed, when Grey Eyes had made his first overtures of friendship between the two villages, and begun his initial courtship of her, Bear had sighed with relief and practically handed over the protection of the upper town into his young and capable hands. Bear had no Second-In-Command; he had said there was no need for one, that it would only cause anger between the brave he might choose and the lower town's Little Soldier. All the elders had agreed that this was a wise decision. Grey Eyes would care for them all.

But the elders had been wrong. Her father had been wrong. The lack of authority in the village had led the younger braves to defy the ban on combat. They had even disobeyed the Law against the taking of the whites' strong drink. Elements in the village were no longer right thinking, but still her father slept the sleep of an old man. . . .

The princess's heart lifted. Perhaps Grey Eyes only wanted to discuss arrangements for the upper village. She murmured a fervent prayer that this be so. This she could discuss. Her opinions would draw her closer to him.

She chose to walk the distance between the two villages. Surrounded by her retinue of young girls, protected by three of her father's warrior braves, who hung back but kept their weapons at the ready, she strolled through the barren space now littered with the aftermath of the glorious feast.

Women from both towns were already at work hoeing the remains of the foods left over into the earth. The ground, thus fertilized, would be ready for planting come the next growing season. From the ghost of the feast would spring lush greenery, food plants for the new children to come to the reunited villages. This was right thinking at its best. This was what made Grey Eyes the finest Guardian in the history of the Arikara Nation.

He was in his lodge. As she entered she smelled three things: the sharp smell of the calumet, the pungency of incense burned to purify the air, and, to her guilty horror, the scent of white man mixed with that of dog.

Grey Eyes was sitting cross-legged, his fine body dressed only in loincloth; in his hair he wore the white feathers of his rank. The fire was banked high despite the warmth and earliness of the day. He didn't look at her when she came in, but only continued his staring into the fire. She wondered what he was seeing in the flames. . . .

"Sit, daughter of Bear, Guardian of the Arikara Nation," Grey Eyes said, still without looking at her.

So, it was to be official titles and no endearments, she thought. She took her place beside him, but so clearly apart from him. Now the fine dress she had worn so proudly seemed ragged, dirty. The joy had gone out of it, the way the soul leaves the body upon death.

She sat tall, and steeled herself, for she was a princess. A princess's pride would ride her rampaging emotions, guiding, if not controlling them, so that they would take her heart where she wanted it to go, the very way she herself could expertly guide, if not control by force, a galloping horse. But at the same time, her woman's soul cried out in mourning over the tragic loss—the very characteristics that made Grey Eyes the man he was, would force him to behave in such a manner that could only drive her further and further from him.

"Did the princess know of the attack upon the whites?" he asked in his soft voice, still staring into the flames.

"Guardian, there was talk. Young men like to talk about things before those things are accomplished."

"The princess did not tell her father?"

"Guardian, it is not for a woman to interfere in the natural order of things."

"The princess did not lend her influence to prevent this attack?"

"Guardian, it is not for a woman to interfere in the natural order of things."

"The princess knew my feelings concerning this matter?"

Now she was silent. She knew he needed no answer. That her answers did not matter. He was still staring into the fire, and could see her responses in the flames, before she herself could mouth them. Was he not Grey Eyes, whose ally was the flames that purify?

"Did the princess enjoy the feast?"

"Yes," she said, too quickly.

"The princess wandered off. . . ." He let the sentence hang unfinished in the air, let the silence, intensified by the crackle of the fire, do its work. He was a man who could listen to the sound of *now,* but all women, no matter how right thinking, tended to let the jangle of their feminine thoughts drown out the sound.

"I wished to be alone with my thoughts, and so wandered off—Guardian!" she added as an after-thought, quickly, but of course, much too late for correct protocol. She cursed at herself for allowing him to unnerve her, and then cursed at herself for thinking that it mattered. She saw the direction in which he was going, and wanted to cry out a warning. Didn't he understand that if he won this game, he would lose?

"But the princess was not alone with her thoughts," there was anger in his voice, his fists were squeezed so tight his knuckles had gone white.

She looked at his profile. The very blood in his temple was pulsing in anger and frustration. The intensity of the moment was unbearable—full of pain, but also giddy pleasure. She had never felt so alive as she did now, caught in the crossing currents of the loves that two so totally different men held for her. She felt that jewel of pleasure a woman can find in even the most tragic of circumstances if she at least knows that, out of it all, she has managed to place her mark upon a man. She now focused her entire being on this flickering of pleasure. It embodied the beauty of being alive; its succor would warm her against the frost of the coming sorrow. "Guardian," she said almost as if in triumph, "I was not alone."

Finally Grey Eyes turned his face toward her. Fiercely angry as he was, it was not her words themselves that had broken his resolve. It was the sound of her voice. His realization, when it came, was so bitter he thought he would surely have to weep. How could it be that in her betrayal of his love, she had found the music of now?

She saw the blow coming as his hand rose toward her face, but merely locked herself in place, refusing to give him the satisfaction of dodging or flinching. Still, when he hit her, the slap was like a thunderclap. Her head rocked sideways on her neck, and dazed, she felt herself slump away from him. Her head came to rest upon the thick, furred surface of the pte rug, and for an instant her vision was as dark as night, although filled with as many sparkling pinpoints of stars.

She came to almost immediately, and was rising up on one elbow when he reached out to pull her into position for yet another slap. His fingers found the front of her dress, and as he jerked her up, his other hand raised and ready to come down on her, her bodice ripped.

The precious sea shells shattered and fell to the rug, their beauty vanished. She stared unfeelingly at the dull shards; so much had been lost, they suddenly melted into the nothingness of yesterday.

Grey Eyes stared at her, but she made no attempt to cover her bared breasts. He reached out, gently now, to finger the small gold cross that rested in her cleavage. As he turned it against the light it glittered like a tiny spark of fire.

"You wear that for him?" he asked, his voice thick.

Her cheek was on fire where he had struck her. She felt the pain seeping through her head. "Where is your protocol?" she spat, and at once was sorry for her sharp tongue. Through no fault of his own, he had been robbed of so much. Through her weakness, she had led the savior of her nation into a maze from which he might never find his way back to right thinking.

Grey Eyes slowly lifted his hand to turn her head. He inspected the bruise which already discolored her cheek. His touch—which she had longed for and dreamed of for so many years—now only repulsed her. He must have seen it in her eyes, for he let his hand fall to his side.

"I have struck you, princess, daughter of Guardian Bear," his tone was dreamy, the tone of a warrior brave just after a battle, when what was so vivid and real has already passed into memory. "There is no excuse for me, princess—"

"Guardian—"

"No!" he shouted in pain.

She understood. His announcement would be made to the nation when the time was right, but for now, she, who had witnessed his fall, would keep his secret. He was no longer Guardian of the Arikara Nation. He had fallen from the string of his balanced life. An Arikara warrior brave who had struck a woman could be forgiven, but he could no longer represent the Law to his people.

"Princess, daughter of Guardian Bear," he said. "There can be no wedding."

"There can be no wedding," she sadly agreed, wondering why it was that since their union had become impossible, she wanted it so much more. . . . "Our nation will suffer for our foolishness. . . ."

"It will suffer."

She pulled a robe from the floor and wrapped it about herself to conceal her nakedness. When she rose he made no move to detain her. At the door of the lodge she turned back. He once again seemed lost in his flickering flames. "Will you kill him?"

Grey Eyes smiled. "Perhaps he will kill me."

"To take his life is to take mine."

Grey Eyes looked up at her. Her golden hair was a loose wave against the shiny blackness of the furred robe. She was shivering, hunched over, vulnerable, so beautiful. "Leave me," he said. When she did, his devastation was complete.

It is the accursed whites. He watched the flames stand attentive to his misery. *All they touch is spoiled. I had welcomed them in peace, ready to forget the hor-ror and misery they had brought down upon the na-*

tion, ready to let go of the past while a new beginning was shaped for my people.

"There will be no new beginning," the flames crackled gleefully. "Grey Eyes! Your heart is no longer pure! It burns with a different flame."

It was the white trapper who had no woman of his own kind who had come to rob the princess from him, the way the smirking ravens come to rob the fields of corn meant for Arikara babies, Grey Eyes thought. *And I will see no babies. . . .*

"What can a man own?" the flames blazed. "The more he desires, the less he has. . . ."

"I desire vengeance," he told the flames. Once the whites destroyed my people. Carefully, patiently, I cultivated a new beginning. That seedling has been crushed beneath the boot of a white's lust. *Now I will destroy his tribe, as he has doomed mine.*

"Grey Eyes! We, the flames that sustained you, will now eat you up! As your inner flame reduces you to ash, the smoke will rise up to sting Grandfather's eye."

". . . To take his life is to take mine," the princess had said. So be it. Once I was Guardian, now I am a walking dead man, a ghost in the world, remaining only until I take vengeance. Let the princess die, as I will die, as her white will die. *As our passions have mingled and entwined, so will our deaths.*

"Zealous flames," Grey Eyes murmured. "How you blacken all I have lived for. How true you lately told me of my fate. . . ."

Now the flames were eloquent in their silence as they crackled in appreciation.

"No longer am I Guardian," Grey Eyes told them. "Now I am but Arikara warrior brave." He held up his skinning knife in salutation. "A warrior brave is cunning. I will fool my people into thinking I am still

Guardian. I will lead them down upon the white tribe fouling my village."

"Grey Eyes," the crimson embers smoldered, hissing softly, like crafty, red foxes. "Grandfather's eye will cry for your people, for the flames of the real world will have your nation. . . ."

But the warrior brave was no longer listening. He brought the hilt of his knife down hard on the red ceramic jug of skull varnish left by Cabanne.

It cracked open, a rounded red heart spilling its contents. It shattered, the wet pieces of crimson clay resembling pools of blood.

Chapter 14

The three skiffs were ferried to the keelboats and back, bringing ashore the boxes of goods General Ashley offered the Rees in exchange for horses. Trading had been going on for the better part of this bright, sunny day. It was the first contact between the Ashley-Henry expedition and the Indians since the feast, two nights ago.

Jed watched as the boxes were hoisted onto the shoulders of braves. The goods snaked up the ridge, to vanish behind the barricade.

Ashley sat across from Bear on a pte robe spread upon the beach. The old Ree Guvner seemed to become increasingly feeble as the day wore on. Three times he raised his trembling, gnarled hand to halt the proceedings. His attendants would then half-carry his frail form back up the ridge so that he could rest in his lodge.

These delays were driving Ashley to distraction. After seven hours of dickering with the Rees, he had garnered only nineteen horses and a few pte robes.

"He's hurtin' bad inside, General," Eddie Rose shrugged. "He's too proud to let on how poorly his health is. He's just as much in a hurry as we is. Why he's doin' this alone, beats me."

Jed wandered toward them. "Where's Grey Eyes do you think?"

"Where is he?" Eddie softly echoed the question. "It right bothers me, it does. Both Guvners oughta be down here. General, I'd be prepared for anything iffen this was my shindig."

"Why would they give us any horses at all if they were up to no good, boys?" Ashley snorted. "I don't see trouble. Maybe old Bear is negotiating for both villages because of his age."

"I don't see it," Jed began.

Ashley shot him a dirty look. "In some cultures age is considered a sign of wisdom," he growled.

Eddie Rose laughed. "No offense, General, but the Rees figure it's better for old folks to advise than do. And my advice is get yerself a fix on Grey Eyes. He's the key to whatever it is that's gonna happen to us hereabouts."

The distant sound of hammering, and the screech of wood being pulled apart traveled across the water from the keelboats. Mike Fink and his men were knocking down the now empty cargo boxes to make room for the horses. The goods and supplies set aside for the expedition's use had all been stowed below deck. Without the immense cargo boxes, one of which still bore drops of Bill Carpenter's blood, each keelboat would become, in effect, a huge barge with an open flat deck. As many horses as could be fitted on these flat rafts would then be transported the final distance up river between here and the expedition's destination, the outpost to be built by Ashley's partner, Major Henry. The fort was to be located at the mouth of the Yellowstone River, where it connected with the Missouri. At that junction of these two rivers began the Rocky

Mountains. The horses that couldn't be squeezed onto the boats would have to be taken via the overland route, a dangerous and arduous journey, one that would severely deplete the animals' stamina.

Jed wandered the length of the beach. A veritable village of canvas had sprung up along the water line. All of the trappers had insisted on staying on shore during the negotiations. Part of it had been their natural reluctance to want to mix with their inferiors, the keelboat crews. But the trappers—most of whom had lost friends or associates to Ree war parties over the years—were all suspicious of the nation's sudden hospitality. They wanted to keep a close watch on the heathens.

He recalled his talk with John Clyman around the campfire the night before. "Friendly Rees ain't unheard of," John had remarked. "Hell, they changes their mood like the weather, and right now this wedding they's got planned has pulled their teeth." Clyman had nervously tugged at his full, dark beard. "What you gonna do about that cute li'l punkin, Sunblossom, boy? You plannin' on takin' her on as a wife, or jest a squaw?"

Jed had given him a surprised look, but Clyman had just laughed. "Jed, we all seen how you took a fancy to her."

"I don't know what to do," Jed had told him truthfully. "I can't make my move until we've got our horses. Then, I've been thinking about waiting around here until after all you boys shove off, then going in to get her. That is, iffen she's willing," he added.

"Squaws is always willin'," Clyman laughed.

"This one's royalty, John. I'd be pleased iffen you'd watch out how you speak about her."

"Sure thing, boy," Clyman chuckled, holding up his hands in surrender. "I can tell you from experience that squaws make fine trappin' partners. You and her, could bring in jest as many pelts as two men. Only thing of it is, you couldn't rightly settle in at Fort Henry, not with a punkin like that, and all the boys around with their tongues lollin' like wolves."

Jed shrugged. "I tell you true, I was planning on cutting out on my own once we reach the Yellowstone, anyway. No offense, John. But I came all this way to be a wilderness man. Company's nice, once and a while, but I'd rather it'd just be me and the mountains and my traps around me."

Clyman nodded sagely. "Unlessen you wins your Sunblossom. . . ."

"Unlessen," Jed agreed. "But I haven't seen her since—" he stopped, uncertain whether to confide in Clyman.

"Since you rescued her from the pte?"

"John, I met her during the night of the feast. I wooed her then. And I think I won her. She even gave me a clue about what had gone on back down the river, at Pilcher's fort, not that she sounded too broken up about it. . . ."

Clyman had dismissed Jed's worry. "She's a Ree, and has got to act all highfalutin. But take it from me, no woman anywhere in the world is happy when menfolk resort to war. Anyways, even if she is royalty, and did know about the attack in advance, there wouldn't have been a thing she coulda done about it." Clyman's face darkened. "What worries me is that there's maybe some connection between your wooin' her, and Grey Eyes not comin' down to parley. Have you mentioned this to the General?"

"No, of course not," Jed had frowned.

"I reckon you wouldn't . . . not at all," Clyman had muttered. "Well, there's nothin' for it but to hope for the best."

As Jed got up Clyman had grabbed his shoulder. "Listen to me, boy," he began, his beard-shrouded face half in shadow and half-lit by the campfire, "stay away from that punkin until we're all of us free and clear of this damned place. Iffen Grey Eyes gets wind of yer romance, it'll be war for sure."

Now, as Jed paced the beach, he pondered what his heart had gotten himself, and the trappers, involved in. . . . He gazed at the nineteen horses standing hobbled against the wind. Nineteen horses, and they needed at least fifty. . . . Where was that old man Bear? Let this trading be done with before his nerves were worn clear through.

He looked up the ridge, staring at the barricade silhouetted against the bright, blue sky. Sunblossom was up there somewhere. . . . Was she wearing his cross? Was it around her neck, nestled against her sweet breasts, pressed against her heart, like a hidden, secret promise of future love?

"Jed!"

It was Hiram Angus, the fringe of white hair around his ears flapping as he scrambled along the beach. Jed set off at a run to meet him. A sense of trepidation had begun to flow through the young trapper, as if he were being stalked by an animal, like the one on that dark path near the stream, with the smell of death padding around him on four paws.

"Best git over to Ashley," Hiram managed between huge gulps of air. "We all gots to make a plan. Bear ain't negotiatin' for the villages no more. Word is, Grey Eyes is comin' down."

Chapter 15

Just the sight of him sitting there made the trappers lose heart.

Bear had been yielding against Ashley's spirited bargaining. Each time the General had relayed his terms through Eddie Rose, the old Guvner had relented a little bit more. The way things had been going, it had seemed as if the expedition would have had their fifty horses for a minimal amount of goods.

The old man had clearly wanted the expedition satisfied and out of the territory as soon as possible. Eddie Rose had seen through Bear's haste to several likely truths: He was more concerned with his daughter's coming wedding than dickering over a handful of horses; that he was in an embarrassing bind over the fact that the wedding was to be celebrated and honored by a ban on warfare, while his own braves had attacked Pilcher's; and finally, that as far as he was concerned, the Ashley-Henry expedition was ignorant of the massacre, and the old Guvner wanted the whites gone before they found out, and any further unpleasantness could mar the wedding festivities.

The experienced interpreter had advised Ashley to play an old game: It amounted to turning the tables on

Bear. Most usually, it was the Indian who took his time pondering a deal. Eddie told Ashley to hem and haw. Such delays, combined with the betrayal of the Guvner's own, infirm body, would prove to be to the expedition's advantage.

But now it was Grey Eyes sitting tall and strong on the Ree side of the pte robe. The trading had been going on for more than an hour, and each offer Ashley had made for more horses had proved useless. Grey Eyes had steadfastly refused each price with disdainful silence. Not once had he looked at Jed, who was sitting just behind and to the left side of Ashley.

"What now, Eddie?" Ashley muttered to the interpreter on his right. "If I offer anymore per horse, I won't have enough for the full fifty."

"Now we ask him what he wants, I reckon," Eddie spat, making no pretense of hiding his displeasure at the idea. Ashley nodded reluctantly. Allowing the Ree to express his wants was tantamount to letting him take the offensive. "He's wearing more clothes than I thought these savages knew what to do with," Ashley wondered out loud. "What's he all duded up for?"

Grey Eyes wore thick, rawhide leggings, and a long-sleeved deerskin shirt. Around his waist he had a wide, beaded belt from which hung a long, curved, skinning knife, bullet pouch, and powder horn. Across his lap rested a rifle. His white headfeathers fluttered in the breeze.

It was Jed who answered Ashley's question. "He's dressed for war. Ain't he, Eddie?"

"Hell, boy, you're the expert, ain'tcha?"

Grey Eyes' Second, the short, well-muscled Little Soldier, began to whisper in Grey Eyes' ear. The Guvner took no notice of it. At the sound of Jed's voice his eyes had shifted over to stare at the young trapper. After a moment he pushed away his Second and began to speak. His voice was loud and deep. It carried all the way up to the barricade, around which braves had congregated, and all the way down to the camp of tents Ashley's men had set up. Eddie Rose hissed a translation to Ashley as the Guvner spoke. But Jed needed no help in understanding the Ree's cadenced words, which were spoken without the Guvner ever shifting his gaze from the young trapper's eyes.

"When your tribe came here the Arikara nation welcomed you in peace. The nation and your tribe hunted pte together, the nation and your tribe feasted together, all in celebration of the rebirth of the Arikara people—"

"He's not mentioned Jed's rescue of his bride-to-be. Should we remind him?" Ashley whispered.

"Wait for it," Eddie Rose muttered, glancing at Jed.

"The Arikara nation has made two overtures of friendship," Grey Eyes continued. "The white tribe has made only one, when this young brave saved the daughter of Bear, Guardian of the upper village—"

Jed stared at Grey Eyes' face, but could read no emotion there. Did the Ree Guvner know? Every instinct Jed possessed told him "yes," and at once he was overwhelmed with the urge to save Sunblossom. What might this savage do to her? *What had he already done?*

"The Arikara nation demands another overture of friendship." Grey Eyes paused. "Of trust." His gaze bored into Jed. "The honor of the nation demands this: For every horse the price will be the last offered by the white Guardian, plus three rifles, and with each, fifty balls, and powder."

Loud cheers, sounding like ominous, distant thunder, came from the Rees along the barricade as Grey Eyes slowly mouthed the three English words of weaponry.

"Why the damned heathen!" Ashley shouted. "Eddie! Tell him—"

"I'll tell him we'll think about it," Eddie urged. "General, we need time to get ready, to plan . . ." he trailed off, miserable.

"What is the whites' answer?" Grey Eyes demanded.

"The Guardian of the Arikara nation has made his request. Allow our Guardian to consider . . . the offer," Eddie stuttered.

"Tomorrow, noon," Grey Eyes decreed. He rose and made his way back toward the ridge. Behind the barricade the Rees began a soft chant that slowly, agonizingly, grew ever louder.

"Ninety-odd rifles, plus ammunition!" Ashley laughed bitterly. "Does he really expect us to give him that?"

"No, sir," Jed said, his voice hard and determined. "He doesn't expect that at all. He expects us to refuse. That way, it's us that broke the peace, not him."

"Then they can come down on us," Eddie murmured.

They sat in silence for a moment, listening to the Rees' chants of war.

"Hell," Jed sighed. "Reckon Grey Eyes and me have some private parleying to do."

Chapter 16

Jed began to climb the ridge in the darkness. The night had turned cloudy, blanketing the moon. He thanked God for that. The Ree sentries walking the barricade were just as anxious as the trappers on the beach. Jed had ordered a double watch throughout the evening.

Not that the trappers felt much like sleeping. To a man, they'd understood the real intent of Grey Eyes' ultimatum, the real intent of the horrific Ree war chants that had thundered in their ears until midnight.

The scrub brush, a hellish tangle of burrs and nettles, sliced through Jed's hide gloves, and scraped his face. Above him, there came the sound of a footstep—he pressed himself into a hollow, trusting to the inky darkness for protection.

The footstep did not repeat. Had he really heard it? Was it his imagination? *Get hold of yourself!*

Jed willed himself to move out of the marginal safety of the hollow. Nothing happened. It was as if his terrified body had gained a will of its own. Despite the chill of the night his clothing was soaked through with perspiration. His face was dripping wet. Twigs and leaves stuck to his nose and chin as he hugged the earth.

Only half-way up. Far to go.

And when he reached the barricade the nightmare would truly begin. Undetected, he had to steal through the village, and like a ghost, had to find his way to Grey Eyes' lodge. His goal was not to kill, but to save lives. The lives of the trappers below, the lives of Ree warrior braves. Jed was on his way to Grey Eyes in order to talk of peace, but the Arikara concept of truce was not based on white flags. A truce parley had to be earned by stealth.

"You can't ask for a truce," Eddie Rose had said. "Jed, with the Rees, you got to steal it." He'd stomped over to the table on which the coffeepot sat and poured himself a tin cup full of the strong brew.

Ashley had said nothing during the exchange between Jed and the old interpreter. He'd leaned back in his chair and stared, as if he could see through the walls of his tent to the source of the seemingly endless chanting coming down from the ridge. He shifted his gaze to Hiram, to Eddie, and then to Charbonneau, the strange, quiet Frenchman. As always, he had that slight smile playing at the corners of his mouth, as if the Ree death waiting for them all was only a child's joke.

And then there was Jed Smith. Ashley made yet another attempt to control his temper. He knew it would do no good to rage at the man. His experience back in St. Louis, with his partner Major Henry had taught him that. Henry had been a trapper, a wilderness man, for years before the duo had embarked upon their munitions business, the actual start of their partnership. From that relationship Ashley had learned that there existed no more stubborn, more independent breed of man than those who chose to find his living in the wilds. If you told a wilderness man "yes," he'd say "no"; "right" he'd go "left"; "retreat," he'd "charge"; "do not," he'd "do."

There hadn't been the trace of an apology, not the least bit of embarrassment or even goddamned humility in Jed's demeanor as he'd said, "General, I've fallen in love with the princess, and I reckon she feels the same about me. Or maybe she doesn't yet, but that's my business. I reckon I'm causing you and the boys some trouble about all this, but it can't be helped. Maybe old Grey Eyes and me could have it out without getting his boys and our boys into the tussle. If that's a possibility, I'm willing to give it a go."

"That's my boy!" Hiram had crowed, his blue eyes twinkling. "Fightin' proud, fightin' proud he is!" His walnut colored, bald head, had wrinkled with pleasure as he nudged Eddie Rose in the ribs.

Eddie's ferret features had split into a wide grin. "Ain't love grand?" he'd smirked.

Yes, Jedediah was a wilderness man, all right, Ashley thought to himself. The fact that Jed probably wasn't going to live long enough to see the Rockies was merely a technicality. The art of being such a man was, after all, just a state of mind. . . .

"All right, Jed," Ashley sighed. "You signed on with me to pull furs, but I never said you couldn't pull a wife at the same time. Remind me to put something about that into the contract for next time. Assuming there is a next time," he growled. "Boys," he addressed the gathering at large. "What are the options?"

"We could pull out tonight," Eddie offered hopefully. "Pack right up and shove off." He was the only one experienced in battling Rees, and so was the most enthusiastic advocate of turning tail under cover of darkness. "One on one, them heathens would give us a tough enough fight. But the odds is more like ten to one."

"Iffen it comes to a fight, we're their meat," Hiram agreed.

"And without the horses, the expedition is crippled," Ashley pointed out. "Henry is most likely pulling beaver up by the Yellowstone, but to really branch out, he needs these horses."

Jed broke in. "There's no way we could load the nineteen we got onto the boats in the dark. If we pulled out now it'd have to be without them. And that's not a possibility."

"You are all forgetting something else," Charbonneau quietly said. "The Rees have created a natural barrier in the river comparable to their land barricade protecting their villages. Did not your patron inform you that the only way to navigate the danger is by poling?"

"He did," Jed said. "And that will be tough enough in daylight, impossible in the dark."

"Well, then we ain't goin' nowhere," Eddie listlessly said.

"I'll issue an order to load the horses we do have at daybreak," Ashley decided. "That way, we can make our escape if we have to."

"We'll have to," Eddie nodded. "Loadin' the horses will be all the answer Grey Eyes needs to come down on us."

Ashley, the skin of his chin red and raw from his nervous tugging at his goatee, literally bounced with frustration in his chair. "I'm a businessman! There's got to be a way to talk to Grey Eyes, to make him understand the futility of fighting." He turned to Eddie Rose. "Explain to me why we can't ask for a truce to discuss this business with Jed and the princess. . . ."

Eddie cleared his throat, and looked around the tent. "Well now, first of all, we ain't sure that's the burr under his saddle, but this hoss figures it is. All right, now, there's no way a Ree Guvner is gonna discuss that sorta personal thing with you, General. Iffen he'd talk to anybody about it it'd be Jed here. But Jed can't go wavin' no white flag to the Rees, as if theys civilized people, cause the Rees believe that a truce has to be stolen from them."

"Christ, these heathens have a lot of rules. . . ." Ashley muttered to no one in particular.

"For an uncivilized people," Charbonneau added wryly.

But Eddie Rose was warmed up now, and not about to give up the floor. "Iffen Jed here could get the drop on Grey Eyes, then the heathen would be honorbound to hear what Jed had to say. Just like in our kind of white flag truce. Now, Jed couldn't ask for, let's say, the rest of the horses at a fair price, and the princess, cause Grey Eyes would most likely rather die than give all that up. There'd be no honor in giving in totally. But Grey Eyes would be honor-bound to at least consider any reasonable request that Jed might make. Like a one-on-one battle. Jed would've earned that much, simply by being able to get the drop on the Ree." Eddie surveyed the dour faces in the tent. "Well, that's what passes for gettin' a Ree's attention in a truce-like situation, anyhow."

"So if I were to sneak into the village and catch Grey Eyes unaware, he'd at least listen to what I had to say, and most likely give me safe passage out, and back down the ridge?" Jed asked.

"For sure," Eddie said. "He might not agree, but by catchin' him unaware, you'd have earned your say. Then he'd have to escort you home."

"I'll do it then," Jed shrugged.

"And git yer fool head blowed off before you git within a hundred yards of the Guvner's lodge," Hiram muttered. "Don't go forgettin', ya don't git no points for tryin'."

Jed got to his feet, and began to pace around the small tent as he spoke. "I got us into this. She's my woman, or at least I hope she'll be, and if I win her, I'm certainly not going to share her with any of you, so I reckon it isn't fair for me to expect you to share in the fighting for her."

"Maybe it ain't about what you expect, boy," Hiram said quietly. "Maybe we're volunteerin'."

"Oh Christ!" Eddie Rose moped, but he didn't contradict Hiram. There wasn't a hell of a lot that could band a bunch of lone wolves like trappers together, but no matter what the beef was about, whites stood with whites against Indians. It was the wilderness man's way.

It was Jed who settled the question. "If I can get to Grey Eyes, and talk him into a one-on-one, he'll most likely agree to letting the General have his horses, no matter what the outcome. If he wins, it's over and done with, he's got his honor back, or whatever, and things are back to normal. If I win, he's got to leave orders that we're all to be unharmed. Right, Eddie?"

"In all my time, I've never heard of a Ree lyin', or going back on his word. It just don't happen."

"Then it's settled. I've got to try," Jed smiled. "Even if I don't get to him, it's worth a try." He turned to Ashley. "And it's the least I can do for causing this mess."

"Can you do it?" Ashley asked flatly.

"I'm a fetchin' Jimmy Beck," Hiram announced. "He's the best at this, of all of us. This isn't about bein' a hunter, Jed, this is about bein' the hunted."

"He's so little, sneakin' comes natural to 'im," Eddie Rose grinned.

Stealth came easily to Jed Smith, too. He still remained motionless in the hollow, listening for sounds, but hearing nothing but the occasional hoot of an owl, and the liquid flapping of leathery bat wings. His sweat had dried and his cramped muscles had begun to feel the night's damp chill.

"*Move but don't think. Let yer senses be all,*" tiny Jimmy Beck had said, his middle-aged, blue eyes dead serious in his little boy's freckled face. "*Yer 'imagination's yer own worst enemy, boy.*"

Ever so slowly and quietly, Jed pulled himself from the safety of the hollow, realizing its sanctuary was merely an illusion. "*When you think yer safe, that's when yer not—*" Scuttling along with his belly scraping in the dirt, like the countless, many-legged night things sharing the vegetation with him, Jed reached the thorny wall of the barricade. Again, like some night insect, he pressed himself against its base, a centipede under a log.

"*Lookit me, Jed. On me toes I barely make five and a half feet. Me two arms together don't make one a yers. I don't think like the wolf, I think like the rabbit. Me weapon's not in me muscles, it's in me senses: eyes, ears, nose. . . .*"

Jed sniffed the night air. The scent of Ree was all around; he was drowning in it.

"*Don't worry boy,*" Eddie's freckles had danced as he grinned. "*Yer heart will be beatin' like all get-out. It'll sound like God's drums at least. But theys can't hear it.*"

Jed slid along the barricade's wall, looking for a weak portion in which to push through. "*The odds'll shift a tiny bit yer way oncen you get to the barricade,*" Eddie had told him. "*The Ree sentries'll watch the ridge, but they'll count on the thorns of the barricade to give 'em close-up protection. They'll be thinking like wolves, not like rabbits.*"

Jed found his spot. The weave of wood and thornbush was there, but more sparse than anywhere else he'd passed. It would have to do.

"You got to listen like yer life depends on it, not like there's only a meal in it for yer," Jimmy had warned. *"You IS the meal."*

"Breathe through yer nose," the tiny trapper had instructed. *"Short breaths that don't fill your head with lots of noise. Then listen. Close yer eyes and send yer hearing out of your two ears like scouts to git the lay of the land.*

Jed closed his eyes. Off to his right he heard the slumbering snort and huff of the horses in the Rees' stockade. With a shock he realized that the Ree corrals were more than a hundred yards away.

"Iffen you try, magic things will happen, Jed. . . ." Jimmy's smile was filled with admiration. *"I can tell. You got it all. Nothin' I can teach you. You was born with it. Ain't nothin' like a true, blue wilderness man. He's the wolf that can think like a rabbit."*

Jed listened. Off to the left, footsteps. He gauged them for a split second as he huddled in the dark. The footsteps faded away. Silence, but still he listened hard. He strained and squeezed his ears for the tiniest sound, until even the natural night-time noises faded, and a cottony roar born of his own effort began to sound in his head.

He pried apart the vines and wood blocking his way through the barricade, unmindful of the pain as the needle-sharp thorns punctured his already shredded gloves. Holding his knife at the ready, he slipped through, eyes swiveling in his head, and ears searching for sight or sound of an alerted sentry.

"Don't worry about dogs. They keep em away from the barricade. Rees got noses as good as dogs.

*They don't want the animals paddin' around coverin'
up any noises you might be makin'."*

Jed froze where he was, hunched over, actually
inside the barricade, a roof of thorns over his head.
The footsteps he had heard fading were now growing
louder.

A Ree sentry was approaching.

He can't see me, Jed thought. But he knows I'm
here.

The Ree was tall and broad-shouldered. He carried a fusil in his right hand, and a knife in his left. He
was using the short, squat barrel of his shotgun the
way a blind man uses his cane, waving it in an arc
from left to right and back again.

Jed stayed right where he was inside the barricade. The least bit of movement would pinpoint his
position. All the Ree would have to do would be aim
his fusil in Jed's general direction. The gun's shot pat-
tern would do the rest.

The Ree was five feet away. Jed thanked God
again, this time for already having his knife in his
hand, ready to be used.

The Ree took another step closer. *This isn't murder*, Jed told himself. *It's this sentry or me. It isn't
murder.* The sentry couldn't be allowed to shout, or
fire his cocked weapon. The gun was the trickiest part.
Even a dead man can pull a trigger in reflex. . . .

The Ree was now standing parallel to Jed. The
barrel of the fusil was actually past him, but the sentry's body was blocking his exit from the shelter of the
barricade. *Let him take just another step. Then get the
gun with your left hand, use the knife in your
right. . . .*

The Ree was two paces in front of him. Jed
launched himself, but even as he did the sentry began
to whirl. Jed managed to jam his left thumb into the

space between the cocked hammer and the load. The Ree pulled the trigger, and Jed felt the hammer smash into his nail.

The Ree's mouth was gaping, ready to shout, and his left hand had begun to push his own knife toward Jed's ribs. Jed's blade was inches from the sentry's throat: *"Push it in edge toward you, then pull. The heathen's throat will come out with it, clean as a whistle."*

But at the last instant Jed swiveled his wrist, to bring the hilt of his Bowie slamming against the Ree's jaw. The shout never came, turned into a gasp as the sentry crumpled to his knees. Jed hit him again, this time whipping the hilt against the Ree's temple. The sentry collapsed, unconscious.

Jed felt his own muscles turn to water. The fusil was still hanging from his left thumb. He clicked its hammer back to release himself, then carefully set it down, beside the fallen Ree. *"That's one you owe me, partner,"* he thought, and then set off, heading toward the corrals where the horses were kept.

Grey Eyes' lodge was somewhere in the block of cabins two rows behind the corrals. Jed had remembered seeing it the first time he had visited the village with Ashley, Eddie Rose, and the others. Jed had remarked that the lodge was larger than all the others. and that's when the interpreter had identified it.

The horses eyed him nervously, jerking their heads as he crouched beside the rough-hewn logs of the corral. Jimmy Beck had said that it wasn't likely that Jed would run into any guards once he got past the barricade. The Rees were hardly worrying about the trappers attacking them, after all. The corrals marked the end of the lower village. Jed wouldn't have to worry about anybody coming at him from the direction of the barren no-man's land between the two towns, and so, could concentrate on covering his left-hand side as he made his way along the deserted path to Grey Eyes' lodge.

"*Them lodges will be buttoned up tight. Rees sleep real sound when theys at home.*" Jimmy had chuckled. "*You won't run into nobody. You'll be clear until you get to Grey Eyes' lodge. That's when things will get sticky again.*"

Jed thought about how it would be. The door would be shut, and he knew there would be no way in hell he could open it without awakening the man. It would take Grey Eyes a moment to go from being asleep to being awake. That was all the time Jed had to hurl himself on top of the Guvner, press his knife to his throat, and hiss the two words that were synonymous in the Ree tongue: "*Live, listen.*"

After that, if Jed got to that, he could relax. Grey Eyes would hear him out, maybe even give him some sort of gift to commemorate the event. He'd tell Jed when he'd give his decision, and then summon an escort to see that he got safely past the barricade. Jed might have slaughtered ten braves along the way to the Guvner's lodge, but that wouldn't matter. Grey Eyes might immediately refuse Jed's request, telling him that he still intended to massacre the entire expedition unless the guns were handed over, and that wouldn't matter. Jed would still be treated with honor and respect for having forced the truce in the first place.

As he rose from his crouch to start the final dash, it occurred to him that perhaps Grey Eyes would be awake when he pulled open that door. In that case, the Guvner's hurled knife would find his heart as he passed through the opening, his silhouette a perfectly framed target backlit by starlight through the doorway.

Jed grinned to himself. Sweet dreams, *Guardian of the Arikara Nation*—

The figure came at him from the shadows, *from the right*!, locking its strength around his lower legs, so that Jed fell forward. His knife went flying as his arms stretched out and his fingers spread wide in a reflex attempt to break his fall. The air went out of him as his belly thudded into the dirt.

His attacker seemed small and light, but he was very fast as he scrambled up along Jed's spine like a chill. Fingers entwined themselves in Jed's hair. His head was jerked back. Even as Jed twisted around he knew it was too late. The knife blade felt freezingly cold against the hot, trembling skin of his throat.

"When you think yer safe, that's when yer not."

Chapter 17

"He'll never let us, I say," Wilkie Booth, first mate on the *Yellowstone Packet*, tipped the jug of skull varnish to his lips and kept it there until every drop of the potent brew had been drained. He tossed the empty jug overboard. It was lost sight of on this dark, moonless night before it even hit the water.

"Mike 'ud skin us alive if we tried to git us some tonight." Wilkie's sallow, pock-marked face took on the expression of a bull snake. It was Wilkie's way of smiling. "But damn, boys, it 'ud surely be worth it. I powerful miss them squaws we had back at ole Atkinson."

"That was a fine enough place," Rick Boe agreed. He was a young, good-looking fellow, well-built and strong, and always ready for a fight—just the right requirements for the job of keelboat man. He knew how and when to turn on the charm. He was invariably one of those lucky cusses who always became the pet of the whorehouse, often even getting some for free, but he was such a good-natured chum that the other boys never held it against him. "I once overheard Eddie Rose tellin' somebody that he'd taken a Ree for a wife a long time ago. . . ." Rick looked about him to make sure he had his audience's attention. "Rose said it was the best he'd ever had. And he's had a lot. . . ." That last was delivered with a sagacious nod. In actuality, Rick Boe had heard Eddie Rose say no such thing, and if he had ever asked the old interpreter, he would have found out that the Rees were the one tribe where a white man had to be celibate if he wanted to live in a village. Whites could barter or buy a Ree female, but they then had to take her far away from the home territory. As with all things concerning the Rees, the transaction had to be conducted honorably, and with utmost courtesy. More than one trapper, made hasty by passion, had been killed by the father of the very girl he was courting.

"Well then. If theys out there waitin' for us, I'd say we river boys oughta go show 'em a good time," Wilkie Booth announced. There were six of them sitting around the rear deck of the *Packet*. They'd spent a long, hard day tearing out the cargo box. Now they had worked their way through the evening meal, several cigars, and two jugs of varnish. It was just a little after two in the morning, but the night was still young, for all thoughts of sleep had been banished by the raucous sound of the Rees' chants that had previously floated across the water.

To the riverboat men, who were ignorant of the goings on between Grey Eyes and the expedition, the chants were evidence of yet another sumptuous feast like the one they had already missed, through nobody's fault but their own of course.

"Them heathen is sure a festive bunch," one of the others in the circle offered.

"Then hell, let's go!" Wilkie slapped his knee. As far as he was concerned, the case was closed.

"I don't know," Rick wavered. "Let's ask Mike."

"Ricky, I tell ya, them Ree girls, pretty as can be, will make you a chief," Wilkie teased.

"With his war lance," one of the others clownishly offered to the amusement of the group.

Rick smiled his easy smile, the one that signified that such ribbing didn't bother him since what they were teasing would most likely come true. "I still say we ask Mikey," he insisted. "If Mikey comes, ole General Ashley won't say boo!"

That made sense to Wilkie. Also, he'd have felt uneasy, being Fink's first mate and all, not asking his patron to come along for some fun. And it was important that Rick be satisfied and come along, as well. Rick's handsome face had bought them all a good time more than once.

Mike was found down in the cargo hold below deck. He'd worked out a regular little bedroom for himself, stringing up a hammock and piling crates and boxes up into two walls jutting out from the inner hull. A lantern hung from one of the timbers which spanned the width of the hull, supporting the deck planks. In all, it was a cozy, if not well-ventilated, hideout. Fink kept a pistol and knife in the hammock with him. Since the late Carpenter's ill-fated insurrection, Fink wanted walls around him when he slept. He still didn't trust Talbot to let things lie.

Mike pondered his men's idea. Ashley had never actually forbade the keelboat men from coming ashore; it had been their own decision. He too had heard the chants, and had also attributed them to yet another "party" between the heathens—and their women—and the trappers. A bit of whorin' would do all the boys some good. It'd take the spunk out of them, make them easier to control. And maybe Talbot would come along. A bit of good whorin', to wipe out the bad thing at Atkinson, the bad thing that was the cause of the falling out between himself and Carpenter, might do to bury the hatchet between himself and his old friend Tommy.

Mike swung down from his hammock. He tucked his pistol and knife into his belt and said, "Let's go fellows, but only us and the few you blabbed to. And I'll see if ole Tommy Talbot wants to come. Iffen it works out, we'll take the rest of the fellows tomorrow."

Of the original six, only four—Rick Boe, Wilkie Booth, and two others—were actually sober enough to leave the keelboat. They searched all over both keelboats, careful not to awaken the slumbering crews, and finally found Talbot curled up in a corner of the *Rocky Mountains*. Fink shook him, but got no response. Wilkie pointed out the empty keg of skull varnish lying beside Talbot, and said, "Come on Mike. He's dead to the world tonight."

The largest and smallest skiffs were at the beach. The ten man boat was tied along side the *Packet* however, and it was this skiff that the five river men used to reach the shore.

Halfway there, Fink said softly, "Pull hard boys, I want to land upstream of the tents."

Wilkie Booth groaned. "Mike this rowin' is gonna sober us up." He and the others tried to row as quietly as possible as they strained hard to keep their skiff from being swept downstream. "We get too close to that whirlpool, we're gonna get wet, Mikey."

"Pull hard, I said," Fink growled lowly. He held up a full jug of skull varnish. "This'll keep us from gettin' sober. We'll stay well away of the whirlpool. I just wants us to land upriver of General Ashley. I ain't in the mood to start jawin' with that ole billy goat."

The other men quietly snickered at that. Mike Fink nodded to himself in satisfaction. "Here, let's all us have a drink while we're pullin'." He handed the jug to the nearest man, and leaned back in the bow of the boat. The truth was that Mike was uneasy about what Jed had witnessed concerning Carpenter's demise. Had Jed mentioned the shooting to Ashley? He didn't think so. The boy had changed since St. Louis. Back there, he'd been the sort to go tattle on a man in the hopes of having a crust thrown to him by his employer. But now, Jed had taken on the characteristics of the older, experienced wilderness men. They were a close-mouthed lot, and what they couldn't settle for themselves, they learned to live with. In any event, they didn't go complaining to their employers or the law, the very two things they'd come to the wilderness to gain freedom from. Yes, Jed had more than likely kept his mouth shut, Mike told himself. After all, the young trapper owed him his life. That ole grizz almost had him for lunch. . . .

Mike wouldn't have cared one way or another about what Ashley knew if he'd had a solid, decent crew behind him. But his boys were mostly yellow, and wouldn't stand by him in a fracas, should "billy goat" Ashley get a mite frisky, and decide that Mike Fink was for hanging. Such punishments for rash deeds were rarely handed down by expedition leaders due to the balance of power between the trappers and the keelboat contingent, but they had been known to happen when the crime was particularly onerous, or the expedition's leader particularly religious.

"We're comin' in to shore, Mikey," Wilkie whispered. The first mate hoarsely called out orders to the other rowers.

"Keep yer voices low," Mike hissed. "Seems mighty quiet right now." They were about two hundred yards upriver from the tents, and their keelboats in the middle of the channel. "You all got yer knives?"

They all had them. Guns were playthings to river

men, who did not hunt for their bread and board. In the close quarters of a keelboat, a knife was the deadliest weapon.

"Here's the way I see it," Fink whispered. "We go up that ridge, quiet like, and see what's what."

"Where do we find the door in that there wall?" Rick asked.

"Door?" Wilkie sneered. "We don't need no doors, we needs whores!"

Mike hushed the chorus of "yeas!" a less enthusiastic chorus than when the subject was first brought up back at the *Yellowstone Packet.*

"You ain't afraid, is ya, Mikey?" Wilkie asked softly.

Damn right I am, Mike thought. "Hell no, I ain't afraid. Any man says I is, will swim back to them keelboats.

"All right!" Wilkie softly laughed. "Let's go boys!" He stepped out of the skiff.

"Wait for me, first mate," Mike muttered, and stepped ashore.

The three Arikara sentries first heard the noisy keelboat men when they were just halfway up the ridge. One of the sentries went to fetch Little Soldier for instructions. Their orders had been to kill any whites attempting entry into the village. But that had applied to trappers, not to the whites who lived on the water. These five whites carried no rifles, but rather knives.

When Little Soldier came he surprised them. These whites were not honorable men, he told his three sentries. These whites showed no respect for the Arikaras as worthy foes. Did these whites not huff and snort their way up the ridge like pte? There! Even now, one of the fools was whining to his companions, probably because of the nettles hooking into his skin. He would whine much louder before his life was finished. . . .

"These whites are for the women," Little Soldier decreed. "Try to take them alive."

Two of the sentries put down their rifles and went to fetch their bows.

Fink and the other four had reached the barricade. They could hear horses whinnying close by, off to their right.

"How we gettin' through, Mikey?" Rick Boe whined. His hands felt like twin pincushions, so filled with the spikes of nettles and burrs were they, and his initial drunken glow had worn off to be replaced by the sour, aching feeling of an early hangover brought on by physical exertion. He was ready to turn tail and head back to the keelboats and sleep, and he would've, if it wasn't for his fear of the razzing he'd have to endure when word got around the next day that the great Rick Boe had backed out of some whorin'.

"I don't see no doorway," Fink muttered, peering through the darkness. "Hell, let's just climb over."

They were all bleeding by the time they'd managed to blunder their way over the barricade.

"Where is everybody?" Wilkie asked. The jug of skull varnish dangled from his right hand. He bent to put it down, and in that instant, heard the swoosh of an arrow pass over his head. It embedded itself in the throat of one of the men behind him.

Rick Boe screamed at the sight of the boatman clawing at the shaft jutting out from his neck, and then screamed even louder as an arrow entered the back of his knee, spilling him to the ground. He moaned and squirmed, his right hand blindly waving his knife in the air around him.

Wilkie Booth ran toward his fallen comrade, but was intercepted by a Ree armed with a knife of his own. The sentry jabbed at him, but Wilkie dodged and then feinted with his blade. The Ree dropped his guard to protect his belly, and in that moment Wilkie drove his Bowie deep into the sentry's heart.

"Let's go!" Mike shouted. A Ree hurled himself at the keelboat patron's legs, bringing him down. Mike and the Ree rolled on the ground, but very quickly Mike was able to get himself into position. Straddling the Ree, he put his big hands around his adversary's neck and jerked him forward to smash the top of his head against the Ree's face. Blood leaked from the sentry's nose as he sagged back in Mike's grip. The patron let him go, pulled his knife from his belt, and slit the unconscious Ree's throat.

"Help me!" Rick Boe howled. "Wilkie! Mike!" He began to crawl toward the barricade.

Mike regained his feet and dashed for the barricade, with Wilkie Booth and the remaining keelboat man fast behind. It had all happened so fast, Mike thought in panic. There'd been little noise, just the keelboat men's nightmare-like shouts, the insectile hum of the arrows, and the abrupt gasps of dying men.

Wilkie Booth looked over his shoulder as he ran. He felt real pity for Rick, and wished he could rescue him, but the odds just didn't allow for it. Dying beside Rick wouldn't change a thing for the boy. . . .

Mike had looked back at the same time. He saw a Ree rush out of the darkness and then pause, in preparation for throwing his knife at Booth.

"Wilkie, look out!" Mike shouted. At the same time, an arrow hummed out of the shadows to drop the third keelboat man. Mike pulled his pistol from his belt and stopped to fire at the Ree, just as the heathen's throwing arm was whipping his blade forward. The pistol's report shattered the darkness like a cannon blast. The bullet punched a wide, bloody hole into the Ree's chest, forcing his throw to go off. Wilkie screamed in pain as the Ree blade, meant for his back, buried itself high up in the muscle of his meaty, left shoulder. He somersaulted over the barricade, fear and pain adding an extra spring to his legs. Mike Fink was right behind him, and the two rolled down the ridge, moaning and crying, thanking the Good Lord above for the protection of darkness.

Rick Boe crawled about like a bird with a broken wing. He swiveled his head wildly as a rapidly growing number of Rees encircled him. At first he menaced them with his knife, but he knew he had no chance with that kind of stand-off. He quickly threw his blade down and began to babble for mercy.

"Somebody say somethin'!" He began to weep. He was dead for sure, as dead as the other two keelboat men, whose still bodies each had an arrow jutting out in an obscene reminder of why they had come to the cursed village in the first place.

"Why don't somebody help me?" he begged. "Friends . . . I . . . Get General Ashley! I'm hurt. What's goin' on here?"

The circle of braves parted. Figures were approaching. Rick squinted to make them out. "Oh, thank God," he sobbed. They'd understood. The arrow in his leg burned and throbbed like fire, but they'd know what to do. He'd be back at the boat in no time. . . . And he'd never leave it until they'd made civilization again.

Rick Boe held out his arms to the five squaws looking down at him. As they bent to him, he gave them his best smile.

Chapter 18

Jed waited for his attacker to slice that hideous, red, wet smile into his throat. He had no chance. There was no way to beat the Ree. Jed's least movement would drive the sharply angled, upthrust blade into himself.

"Get it done with," he whispered wearily. Eddie Rose's tales of Ree torture came back to him. *Please*, Jed prayed. *Let it be a clean death*. In Ree he said, "Why do you wait, Arikara brave?"

"*Je-ed?*" A woman's voice.

The blade dropped away from his neck. Jed twisted around to stare into Sunblossom's face.

Her brown eyes widened in shock and surprise, but even as Jed stared, the princess regained her composure. Her expression changed to one of wicked pleasure. "I have captured you, *Jed*." She held up her knife. "Once you rescued me, but twice now, I have given you back your life." She pressed herself tightly against him, blushing at her own boldness. "You must rescue me, again," she said demurely.

"What are you doing here?" Jed demanded.

Her look was skeptical: *Whose territory is this?*

"I was on my way to Grey Eyes' lodge. To capture a truce."

"Then I truly have given you back your life again," she mocked. "Only kindly Grandfather could be watching over you. It was He that kept you from the sentries and delivered you to me."

Her amusement, and taunts stung Jed's pride. "Do not be too sure, princess. I overpowered one of your sentries. Back by the barricade. He never even heard me coming. . . ."

Now her look of surprise had returned. "Did you kill him, *Jed*?" she asked. There was sadness in her voice. To care for a white, *the slaughterer of her people*—

"No," Jed said harshly. He was afraid of her reaction, wary that she would see his compassion, his reluctance to take a human life as a sign of unmanliness. How far apart were their worlds of morality? "I did not kill the sentry. It was not . . . necessary. I overpowered him, I hit him. He sleeps now, but he will live."

The princess gazed at this man who had come to change her life, the way a dam can change the course of a river. This man had stolen her thoughts, captured her dreams, had taken Grey Eyes' place. *This man*— The realization swept through her. She had stopped thinking of him as a white. Now she saw him, in both her mind and heart, as a man.

"Warrior brave of your people," she said solemnly. "Daughter of Bear, Guardian of the upper village, thanks you for the life of the Arikara warrior brave."

"And my reward?" Jed smiled.

"Reward . . ." She pondered it a moment, and then brought her face toward his. Jed put his arms around her and pulled her close. Her lips were cool and moist. Her mouth was sweet. The kiss hinted at an eternity of pleasure. Jed's heart began to race.

At last, Sunblossom broke away. "You must go," she breathed. "You are brave, but you would never steal Grey Eyes' truce. He would kill you."

"I have got to try." Jed hugged her tight. "It is our only chance."

Our chance. Of course, Sunblossom thought. He was referring to his tribe of whites. "Were you going to ask for mercy from the Guardian? Oh, but you do not understand. . . ." her tone was wistful. "He would never grant you mercy—"

"I was going to challenge him to combat. Just the two of us."

"Why would you do such a thing?" she asked, horrified. "It would mean your death."

"To win you," Jed told her softly. "For *love*," he murmured, using the English word for that term of endearment that had no counterpart in the Arikara tongue.

"*Lo-ve* . . ." The princess's voice was child-like.

"I wish to take you for my wife," Jed told her. "I mean to have you."

Sunblossom began to weep. "This is not possible. Grey Eyes would never permit such a thing. For reasons you could not understand. You would be killed—"

"Do you wish to be my wife?"

"Our people are now at war because of this passion between us."

"Our love," Jed gently corrected.

"Our love," Sunblossom smiled through her tears. "But it is dreaming. There are so many pleasant dreams. The sweetest are the most fleeting."

"Do you want to marry me?"

Sunblossom gazed at him. "You do not understand. You do not acknowledge my world. But you are living in it."

"Answer me straight, woman," Jed demanded. "*Do* you?"

She gave the slightest of nods, and then quickly said, as if in contradiction, "It would be a delicious dream."

"That is why I have got to get to the Guardian," Jed said elatedly. Do you not understand? To make that dream happen. What is life for except to get after those dreams?"

To live the dream one is given, she thought. She brushed his cheek with her fingers, and said nothing.

A shrill scream pierced the night, paralyzing the two. The princess was the first to react.

"You must escape," she begged, her eyes filled with fear.

In English came the shout, "Let's go!" followed by panicked pleas from yet another white: "Help me! Wilkie! Mike!"

"Oh Christ!"Jed swore. "It's some of Mike Fink's boys!"

"The chance for a truce has been lost!" the princess told him. "The entire village will soon be awake!"

"My comrades—" Jed started in the direction of the noise.

Her fingers were like claws locked around his arm. "They are dead, or soon will be," she cried. "Listen to me. I am here because I was on my way to reach you with a warning. Beware of treachery, from your own kind, and from my people. Grey Eyes was visited by a white. He has been much in my village of late. He is very big, with much hair on his face. He has a pet, half dog and half wolf. He gave my father's braves strong drink. It caused them to—" she stopped abruptly, and looked at Jed uneasily. "It caused them to do wrong. This white told Grey Eyes of our meeting during the night of the feast.

"His name is Cabanne," Jed nodded. "I know him." He remembered the scent of dog, of man, and of death that night back along the path. "Cabanne is a butcher of men. Once I could have killed him. He will pay for his treachery."

"Now all of my people are your enemies." The princess shook her head. "It is hopeless. Flee. Tell your tribe to flee for their lives. The Arikara Nation wishes your deaths."

Jed smiled. His fingers gently cupped her lovely face. "But we are lovers, right woman?"

Whatever she whispered in return was lost in the explosion of a pistol firing its charge. "Hurry!" The princess urgently cried. "Oh, if you—love—me, go! I beg you!"

Jed ran a zig-zag course toward the distant barricade. At every moment he expected to feel the bite of an arrow, or the flattening punch of a rifle ball. His back fairly itched as it awaited the sensations. There were many shouts now, Ree shouts. In English he heard one last, heart-rending plea for mercy.

He dived over the barricade. As he tumbled down the ridge he grasped great handfuls of brush, tearing the vegetation from the earth to slow his fall. As soon as he could, he got to his feet and ran straight down the incline. Once he reached the beach, he began to lope along the waterline, back toward the tents.

Chapter 19

Mike Fink and Wilkie Booth reached the waterline. The skiff was where they'd left it, dragged ashore and beached. Before pushing the boat into the water, Mike evaluated the condition of Wilkie. The damned Ree blade was still embedded in the first mate's shoulder. Their hasty, headlong rush down the ridge had widened the wound. Wilkie's shirt was sodden with blood.

"I can't go on," Booth groaned, falling to his knees. He reached around himself with both hands, trying for a grip on the hilt of the knife, but he couldn't get the needed leverage to pull it out of his shoulder. "Mikey, get it out of me," he begged. "I can't stand it."

Mike looked up sharply. Who was that crashing down the ridge after them? Dark as it was, he was sure he could see the Ree war party of scalping heathens on their way to catch him. "Can't do it, Wilkie. No time!"

"Mike! Don't leave me here!" Wilkie moaned.

"Make for the tents, thataway!" Fink called over his shoulder. He glared at the big, ten-man skiff. No way in hell could he handle that boat alone against the river's rushing current. He'd be swept into the whirlpool for sure.

"I'm gonna swim for it, Wilkie!"

"No Mike! Listen! Help me get to the tents. We'll both be safe there," Wilkie desperately argued.

"You hole up at the tents, man," Mike growled. "Them Rees is gonna come down on those trappers for sure. I ain't gonna feel safe 'til I gots water and a keelboat's thick hull between me and them." With that he snatched off his boots and dumped them into the skiff, hoping to retrieve them later. He then waded into the icy-cold water and began to swim.

"Mikey . . ." Booth's call was weak. He slumped against the hull of the skiff, and tried again to get hold of the knife tormenting him. It was no good. The hilt was too slippery with his own blood. *I don't want to die*, he thought. *Help me, God!*

A hand touched his aching shoulder. Wilkie began to scream, but a hand clapped over his mouth, cutting it off. He closed his eyes, ready to die.

"Take it easy," Jed whispered. "Get up now, and we'll get back to the tents."

"Thank God! Oh, thank you, Lord!" Wilkie sang ecstatically once Jed removed his hand from the keelboat man's mouth. "I'm saved!"

"You're almost saved," Jed warned him sharply. "Now shut up! There could be Rees between us and the tents." He half carried Booth along the waterline, keeping his eyes and ears open for any sign of the enemy.

Mike Fink kicked against the current, his powerful arms and legs driving him on toward the safety of the keelboats. His pistol fell from his belt as he swam. He unbuckled his belt to let his knife drop away, too. Nothing mattered to him but to reach the sanctuary of the little citadel he had built for himself in the hold of the *Yellowstone Packet*.

The river tried its best to take him. The current tried to sweep him sideways, while the water itself turned his clothes into heavy dead weight. Mike swam on. Although many keelboat men never bothered to learn, Mike was born a swimmer. There was no facet of river life he didn't know and love.

Exhausted, he reached the side of the *Packet*, and then treaded water and dog-paddled along the length of the keel until he found a rope hanging down from the deck, its end floating in the waves like a water serpent. He hauled himself up, arm over arm, until his numbed legs could get a foothold against the hull. Then he swung himself over, and dropped, half-dead from the effort, onto the deck. Once he caught his breath, he stumbled toward the hold. The water dripping from his clothes squished with each step. His trembling, exhausted arms refused to bend, and his frozen fingers seemed unable to wrap themselves around the brass ring of the trap door.

His mind was a stupified, half-drunk haze out of which swam the images of his friends' deaths. But what could he have done?

He managed to open the door, and half walked, half fell down the five steps of the squat ladder which led into the hold. He peeled off his clothes as he made his way to the hammock. There was a blanket there. He would be warm, at last.

Naked, he found the jug of skull varnish cached by the hammock. He pulled the cork with his teeth and took a long drink. The stuff burned its way down his gullet, warming his innards. With a sigh he settled himself into his hammock and reached down to search for the matches he knew were somewhere around.

Mike found them. He struck one against the rough planking of the floor, and reached up with the flaring match to light the lantern.

He screamed.

Staring down at him, his eyes demonic, a knife clenched between his teeth, was Tom Talbot. He had wedged himself between the timbers, bracing himself with his arms and legs like some man-sized, evil spider.

Talbot let go his hold and dropped down onto Mike's belly.

"*TOM-M-M!*" Mike's cry became one long, gurgling, hoarse exhalation as Talbot stabbed him three times fast in the chest. Then, as Mike Fink's eyes began to dim, Talbot lovingly, languidly, slit his throat.

As Mike Fink drowned in his own blood, Talbot whispered in his ear, admonishing him, "I told you, Mikey. You don't cut yer friend Billy Carpenter fer a whore!"

Chapter 20

Dawn came, but the sky only lightened to grey. The blanket of clouds that had shielded the moon remained, a ceiling of dingy cotton from which hung tendrils of fog.

The overcast sky seemed to suffocate. The air itself was a palpable, clammy thing that gummed the men's leather garments, and collected into glistening droplets on their metal tools and weapons.

There was no wind, so the roar of the river seemed amplified. The sound of it in the trappers' ears made them want to leap out of their skins.

Even the horses hobbled on the beach felt trepidation as the air pressure surged and dropped. They shied and nipped at each other, showing the whites of their eyes.

Then it began to rain.

The river took on the sound of glass being pulverized by a thousand hammers as the rain pelted down. The horses hung their heads to the ground and planted their hoofs as the now wailing wind swayed their big bodies from side to side like living sails.

In this weather man emulated beast. The trappers walked with heads down and their rifles slung butt up, to protect the barrels from the rain. Those that had them walked wrapped in pte robes. For a time the protection of the canvas tents held, but as the early morning hours wore on, the saturated cloth roofs began to let the moisture soak through.

Ashley again gathered his four advisers to discuss their plight. The General was pleased to be able to include Jed in the council. Last evening they had all feared the worst when that single pistol blast echoed down from the ridge. Ashley, Hiram, Eddie Rose, and Charbonneau had all peered up at the barricade that stood like an impenetrable, black curtain. They could only wonder what that lone report signified. Jed, they knew, had not carried a firearm. Would they ever see the young trapper again?

Only Hiram Angus did not appear worried. "Iffen he'd died this hoss woulda felt it," he adamantly argued.

When Jed had returned, with the wounded Wilkie Booth in tow, the reunion was joyous. The keelboat man was taken away by several trappers who cleansed and bound his injury. Jed told whomever wanted to listen of his adventures in the Ree village, but drew General Ashley aside to tell privately of Cabanne's hand in both the Pilcher massacre and their present plight.

"I thought as much, boy," Ashley had nodded. "Hell, a man like Charbonneau shows up and offers to work for me, I had to figure some awful dirty doings was going on back at the French Company."

"I'm going to kill Cabanne," Jed had told him.

"Mighty strong words from a fellow who goes around knocking Rees on the head 'cause he can't bear to spill a little heathen blood," Ashley had grinned. "From what I've heard, Cabanne doesn't die too easily. Anyway, he's just a no-account who works for Brazeau. Killing Cabanne is like pulling a serpent's fangs. They'll just grow back as long as the snake's left alive."

Jed turned away in frustration. Brazeau was protected by his friends back in Washington. Still, there had to be a way to get to the evil bastard. Let the Frenchman use President Monroe himself as a shield, Jed would find a way to get to him. . . .

One by one, Hiram, Eddie Rose and Charbonneau had tramped into Ashley's tent. They rubbed their hands before the small fire, shivering in their sodden clothes.

Jed was the first to speak as the others took their seats. "As you know, I never made it to the Guvner's lodge. And now our time is up. It's almost noon."

"No way we can load the horses in this storm," Eddie Rose said disgustedly. "Them keelboats out there is bobbing like driftwood."

"The river is rough enough with jest the current to contend with," Hiram agreed. "Wonder if Fink managed to make it back to them boats."

"We'll find out soon enough," Ashley quietly said.

Jed stiffened. He'd never heard the expedition leader sound so dejected.

"I'm going to order that the men begin striking the tents," Ashley continued. "I want the skiffs loaded up and on their way back to the keelboats as soon as possible." Here he smiled. "At least we can be thankful to Fink for bringing us the third skiff."

"What about the horses?" Jed demanded.

"We leave them. I'm counting on the Rees holding their fire because of the horses. If they see us leaving without them maybe they'll let us go. . . ." Ashley trailed off. He shrugged, the gesture as eloquent as any words.

The four men stared at him, silent. Not having the

horses was tantamount to condemning the entire expedition.

"What about Major Henry?" Jed asked. "Your partner has done his part. He's got us a fine fort most likely. You going to fail him this way?"

"What would you have me do, boy?" Ashley exploded. He jumped to his feet and rushed toward Jed, to stand over him. "This expedition has been queered from without and within," he spat, his face dark with anger.

Jed rubbed his bloodshot eyes. When was the last time he'd slept, he wondered? He stood up, and gently put both hands on Ashley's shoulders, holding him at arms length. They stood like that a moment, with the only sound coming from the rain drumming down on the sagging tent roof.

"I'm sorry, Jed," Ashley finally said. "It's been a long—I—"

"Here's what we can do, General." Jed looked about the tent, addressing them all. "I can ask for some volunteers to help me lead the horses overland to the Yellowstone. Maybe you boys that stay here could work a holding action, giving me a bit of a head start."

"Rees would catch up to you in no time," Hiram glowered.

"Maybe," Jed agreed. "But it's a chance to get some of those horses where Major Henry is waiting for them. Maybe I could send a man ahead of me. He could bring back half of Henry's trappers to escort me the rest of the way. . . ."

"It's possible. . . ." Ashley mused. "How many trappers would you need?"

"Half a dozen, maybe," Jed replied. "That ought to be enough. At any one time, six horses would be ridden, and the rest led. We'd have fresh mounts all the time by rotating the horses. That way—given a bit of a head start—we just might be able to stay out in front of the Ree war party that'd be on our tail."

"But you cannot ride the entire journey," Charbonneau interjected. "Much of the terrain is too rough. You would have to walk the steeds."

"If we have to walk, so do the Rees," Jed replied. A slight smile played across his lips. "You sound like you know the route pretty well. Reckon I could use a fellow like you on this jaunt."

Charbonneau smiled back, his blue eyes twinkling. "At your service, monsieur."

"Hot damn!" Hiram Angus crowed, smacking his knee. "I'm a goin' too! My arse is gettin' mighty sore settin' around here."

Charbonneau caught Jed's eye, and quickly shook his head.

"I'm sorry, Hiram," Jed murmured. "Not you."

"Cause I'm too old? Is that it?" Hiram raged. "I can still whup yer butt, son!"

"Old friend," Charbonneau softly intervened. "We are both too old, but I know the route better than you. Better than anyone else here. It is I who must go. But any more men of my age would seriously jeopardize the chances of survival."

"Rain's letting up," Jed said. "Let's get ready."

It was while the tents were being struck, and Jed and his five volunteers were loading their gear onto the horses, that the screams began. The rain had stopped. Now there was only a light mist carried along by the river's constant, stiff breeze. Even as the mist continued, the sun poked its way through the clouds.

The screams fell like a curse upon the trappers. It was one man. He wailed and begged for mercy in English. It was Rick Boe.

Ashley strode about the beach, snarling in exasperation. All about him the trappers had become rooted where they stood, staring up at the barricade, leaving tents half down, and goods and supplies unattended.

"What are they doin' to 'em?" Wilkie Booth cried fearfully. "Somebody tell me!" His question traveled the length of the camp, and hung in the air.

Eddie Rose came up behind Ashley. "They let the women torture prisoners they consider to be cowardly. First they use sticks to poke his eyes out. Then they peel his skin off, bit by bit."

"We gotta do somethin'," one of the trappers urged. At once there was a rumble of agreement among the men. Encouraged, the man continued with added forcefulness. "I say we go up there and put the poor lad out of his misery! And take a few Ree scalps in payment!"

"Looks like we got a mutiny on our hands, General," Hiram quietly warned as Rick Boe's wails of agony continued to fall down upon the men. "Can't say that I blames 'em," snorted the old trapper. "Damned heathens."

Ashley pushed himself into the center of the mob of men. "Listen to me! All of you!" he shouted. "Pack up your gear. The storm has broke. We can be off!"

"Not without makin' 'em pay!" John Clyman yelled back, to the cheers of the other men. "Let's get us all the horses we need, boys! I say we show 'em what a trappers' war is all about!"

The mob of men broke apart, leaving Ashley where he stood. Jed came up to him. "We've lost them, General. My volunteers as well. They want to stay and fight."

"The fools," Ashley muttered.

"They're playin' right into the Rees' hands, all right," Eddie Rose agreed as he joined them. "Old

Grey Eyes figured the trappers wouldn't turn tail with a white yappin' away like that. He's a smart one, that Guvner is."

Rick Boe's screams had long since lost any semblance of humanness. Again and again his howl came, to penetrate the souls of the trappers. It rose and fell in nightmare rhythm, setting teeth on edge, scraping raw the men's already jangled nerves.

Bill Sublette joined John Clyman on the beach. The latter was behind several boxes of supplies he'd stacked up to form a makeshift blind.

"Lot of activity up there," Clyman drawled to his friend. He rested the long barrel of his Hawkens gun on the boxes and squinted down the sights. "Reckon I could pick me off one of them braves."

Sublette turned his gaunt face up toward the sun, now shining brightly in a sky only streaked with the last grey remnants of the storm. "It's about noon," he said. "Reckon it's time for the General to give his answer. . . ."

To the shock of all the trappers, Rick Boe's animal-like keening was abruptly cut off. To a man they all again stared up at that barricade along which Rees swarmed like ants.

"Look!" one of the trappers called.

A round object arched up over the barricade to fall upon the ridge. It bounced down the incline and rolled to a stop on the beach.

"Oh Lord!" cried little Jimmy Beck. "It's his head!"

Rick Boe's head sat in the sand as if he'd been buried up to his neck. Its empty, bloodied eye sockets stared at the men, as if in rebuke. The mouth was locked open. Rick Boe's severed head would howl forever in a silent grimace of anguish.

There was a moment of total stillness. The men

on both sides of the barricade looked at each other. It was time to come to grips with the finality of the situation.

"Reckon it's about time we give 'em that answer, Billy," John Clyman muttered. He pulled the trigger of his rifle. The Hawkens boomed and a moment later, a Ree brave crashed through the wall of wood and thorns, to roll several feet down the ridge before his descent was broken by a clump of nettles.

"No more shooting!" Ashley bellowed. He began to run toward Clyman's position. "Find cover!" he screamed at his men, who stood out in the open on the beach like so many clay targets.

"Toussaint!" Jed was running toward the Frenchman who was standing by the unhobbled horses. "Run them this way, along the beach!" Jed shouted. "Get them into the water! Swim them to the boats!"

Shouting and screaming, Charbonneau fired his pistol into the air, spooking the herd of nineteen horses into a fast gallop down the beach.

A sheet of flame licked out from the barricade, accompanied by rolling thunder, as the Rees fired their rifles. Spouts of sand kicked up all along the beach, and now there were howls of pain as trappers went down, wounded or dead. Jed saw Jimmy Beck fire his guns as he dashed for cover, only to be slapped down to the sand by a Ree ball.

Jed zig-zagged down the beach. The Rees were firing at will. The reports of their guns came in a rapid, stuttering series, like stringed firecrackers, to slow sporadically, as some paused to reload.

The frenzied horses splashed into the river, kicking and straining against the current. General Ashley shouted orders to several men to man one of the skiffs and guide the horses toward the keelboats.

John Clyman went down clutching his shoulder.

Bill Sublette half carried him toward the waterline, Ree balls kicking up dirt at his heels.

The horses swam on, their necks arched up out of the water. A series of rifle balls began splashing into the river around the screaming animals. The water began to turn red with their blood.

"They are rushing us!" Charbonneau shouted. He fired his Hawkens gun, punching a Ree back down behind the barricade.

Jed aimed and fired, dropping a Ree charging down the ridge. Groups were hurling themselves over the thorn wall, under the protective firing cover of those still behind the barricade.

Clouds of grey gunsmoke hung like fog around the top of the ridge as warrior braves scuttled down toward the beach. The trappers sent a withering fire up to meet them, Hawkens guns and pistols erupting in flame as soon as they could be reloaded—

But it was no good. For every Ree knocked down two more seemed to spring up to take his place. Hurtling down that ridge was an army that could not be stopped by the volleys of the few trappers left to defend their position.

"Swim for your lives!" Ashley shouted. The first, large, over-crowded skiff was making its way toward the keelboats. Jed could see the crews standing about the decks of the barges, staring at the grisly scene of carnage taking place on the beach. There was no way any of the skiffs could make a return trip for the rest of the men stranded on the beach. It would be swim or die.

Jed caught Ashley's eye, and by hand signals told the General to grab a place on the last big skiff, just now bouncing out into the current. Charbonneau was in that boat as well, Jed was glad to see. The overloaded skiff rode low in the water as it nosed its way into the channel, cutting through the crimson slick clogged with the floating bodies of slain horses.

Jed fired from a standing position, killing another Ree. It registered in his mind that in the space of a few moments he had killed two men. He drew his pistols, went down on one knee, and fired first one and then the other, crumpling another pair of braves.

The beach was littered with the bloodied corpses of trappers. The nine or so men left on the beach were using the still forms of their fallen comrades for cover. Jed made his way toward Hiram and another trapper. The two were hiding behind a cache of crates. As he reached their position, the man beside Hiram was flung backward, his chest collapsing beneath the hail of Ree balls.

Hiram grinned by way of welcome as Jed fired his rifle, knocking down one of the first of the Ree braves to reach the beach. Hiram pulled his pistols and fired both at once. There were now so many heathens rushing toward their position that he couldn't miss.

Jed reloaded his guns, the flesh of his fingers and palms blistering as he juggled the red-hot barrels of his weapons.

Hiram fired his rifle, gut-shooting a charging Ree. He looked back toward the river. "Reckon we lost all the mounts, boy—"

Another wave of fire erupted from the ridge. Out of the corner of his eye Jed saw the line of trappers off to his left peppered by the swarm of lead. They slumped down behind their flimsy cover of canvas and crates.

"Time to get the hell out of here!" Jed muttered. "Let's get wet, Hiram!" He pointed his rifle and jerked the trigger, to bring down a Ree almost at his feet.

There'd been no answer from the man beside him. "Hiram!" Jed demanded.

The old trapper was leaning against the crates. He was fumbling with his rifle, trying to reload it, but his hands were sticky with the blood pouring out of the hole in his chest. "Git, boy," he smiled weakly. The rifle slipped from his grasp as his head came to rest against Jed's shoulder. "Son," he gasped, his voice thick, a pink bubble of blood expanding from his lips, "Son, I give you the mountains!"

A Ree hurtled over the stack of crates, his momentum slamming Jed to the sand. The two men grappled for position. The brave was strong, but he was no match for Jed's raw fury. The young trapper grasped the Ree's chin and the back of his head. He twisted. There was an audible click as Jed snapped the brave's neck.

Still straddling the Ree's body, Jed stared at Hiram. His closest friend, his mentor, was dead.

Two more braves came over the crates. Jed shot these two with his pistols, not even looking as they fell past him. Springing to his feet, he splintered the hardwood butts of both handguns against the face of yet another warrior brave, and began to run in a crouch toward the water.

A Ree tackled him. Clawing for purchase in the sand, Jed slammed the side of his moccasin into the bridge of the other's nose. The brave's hands fell away, and Jed raced on.

Ree sharp-shooters were firing at him, but the clouds of smoke from their own endless volleys obscured their vision. The braves chasing him were armed only with clubs and knives. He splashed into the river, hearing the hard breathing of a brave just behind him. Jed turned to face the warrior, drawing his knife as he did so, but the brave was suddenly propelled forward to fall dead, literally in Jed's arms, slain by a stray shot fired by one of his own tribesmen.

Jed kicked out, afloat at last. With strong, steady strokes he swam toward the keelboats.

"Give him covering fire!" Ashley ordered his men in a hoarse, breaking voice. The General's knuckles whitened in frustration as he gripped the makeshift railing that had been erected along the sides of the *Yellowstone Packet*, the railing that would have been used as the hitching posts for the horses. . . .

Behind him the two keelboat crews were hurling the planks that had formed the platform between the two barges into the water. "Prepare to get under way!" Ashley called.

Several Hawkens guns boomed, and the two Rees that were swimming in pursuit of Jed disappeared beneath the surface, only to reappear as corpses bobbing and dipping in a dead-men's float.

Now the only adversary Jed had was the river itself. Ashley watched as the young trapper began to founder.

"Come on, boy! Swim! Get to me!" Ashley urged as Jed's progress slowed. "Fight it, Jed!"

He couldn't afford to lose another man, and especially not Jed. He'd lost so many. . . . He'd lost his best. . . .

Ashley began to weep, the tears rolling down his cheeks. The others stepped away from him as he stood ramrod straight, crying.

Eddie Rose was dead. Jimmy Beck was dead. And Hiram Angus, and twenty-two others. All dead, or soon to be, once the Rees were done with them. Off in a corner, Bill Sublette—a tourniquet wrapped around his leg—sat with his arm supporting John Cly-

man, whose right shoulder had been shattered by a rifle ball.

Jed was ten yards away. Ashley could see the young man's face distorted with exhaustion.

"Now!" Ashley shouted, and the two trappers who had been poised and ready flung themselves into the water to meet the lone swimmer.

Bullets began to plow into the wood of the barge. The Ree sharpshooters had come down to the water-line.

The men flung themselves to the deck, but they had little cover on the floating platform. Those that could, returned the fire as Jed was towed to the side of the keelboat by his two comrades.

The moment the trio was hauled aboard, Ashley screamed, "Cut the ropes!"

The keelboat men slammed their hatchets down upon the anchor lines. Freed, the *Yellowstone Packet* and *Rocky Mountains* began to float downstream.

Jed coughed up water as he lay on the deck. His clothes and body dripped river water dyed pinkish red. He wondered if any of the blood was his own. His body was too numb from the cold to register pain from any wound he might have suffered during his flight. The sky above seemed to be twirling. Then his vision began to darken as a great roar grew ever louder in his ears.

Strong, but gentle hands were cradling his head. Jed peered up into the calm face of Charbonneau. The elderly Frenchman's visage seemed to metamorphose into Hiram's—

But not Hiram's. Never again! Dead—

Then Ashley was bending over him. The General's anxious eyes scanned Jed's body for sign of injury.

"I'm— Am I all right?" Jed asked, his voice barely a whisper.

Ashley nodded somberly.

"How bad— How bad are we? How many we lose?"

Ashley didn't answer. He didn't need to. Jed saw the enormity of it all in the man's stricken eyes and sagging face.

Then the blackness in front of Jed deepened, and the deck felt as soft as the bed in the guestroom in the Simons' house. The bed he'd slept in with Louisa, a thousand years ago.

"My love forever. . . . That's all one person can give another. . . ."

"I give you the mountains," Hiram said.

"Don't hurt the princess," Jed murmured, and then the blackness was complete. He slept a flat, dreamless sleep, dark as death.

Grey Eyes solemnly made his way down the ridge. Before him was an awesome tableau of carnage. His braves were taking the scalps of the dead, and collecting their weapons. Off to one side, his finest men were quickly and efficiently executing the wounded trappers as befitted their status as honored foes.

The whites had fought well. During the charge down the ridge thirty warrior braves had been wounded, sixteen fatally. Five more had died in pursuit of the whites as they made for their big boats.

Grey Eyes beckoned Little Soldier to his side. "Tell the braves that the man who brings me the scalp I seek will be awarded much honor."

"Yes, Guardian." Little Soldier bowed, and went to relay the message.

Grey Eyes watched the departure of his Second.

Little Soldier was a fine warrior, a right-thinking man of the Arikara nation, thought Grey Eyes. He will make a good Guardian. The nation would know of the change very soon. Grey Eyes would call in his Second, inform him, and then walk through both villages.

He would walk the length of his nation without the white feathers in his hair. He would walk reciting the story of his own fall from grace, and Little Soldier's rise. The elders would stare at him with baleful expressions on their wizened faces. They would mutter among themselves, but in the end they would accede to his wishes, formally making Little Soldier Guardian.

All that would be done very soon. Ashes would be sprinkled about the lodges, to symbolize how all of Grey Eyes's dreams had come to nothing. He would leave in disgrace, in the middle of the night, so that none would see him go. His name would pass into dark legend. It would die, for dark legends are never told around the fire.

But first he wanted a talisman to take with him on his lone journey into the mountains. He did not expect to live very long once he left, for the Law stated that the Arikara brave's strength comes from the Nation, and not from himself. Without the Nation, the Arikara brave was nothing, and all of his foes could feast on him.

Grey Eyes no longer cared if his enemies feasted upon him. Never again could he look upon the princess without having his pleasure tainted by shame. Never again could he feel the wondrous linkage to his Nation without having it shattered by the memory of his own disgraceful failure.

He would die while meditating, alone and cold, in the mountains. But before death came, the object of his meditation would bring him bitter comfort. The princess would lose him as a husband, but she would also have lost her white. Grey Eyes would die with the satisfaction of knowing he had made her twice a widow, for the white's scalp would be hanging from his belt when he himself perished.

Little Soldier approached. "Guardian, his body is not among those on the beach. He must have escaped."

Grey Eyes turned away. Other braves had gathered behind Little Soldier, and it was imperative that they not see their Guardian's composure melt into the hysterical rage of a shrewish squaw. *How far I have fallen*, Grey Eyes thought as he stared down at his trembling hands. It will be better this way, he told himself. The hunt will be prolonged. The whites are still within your grasp. *He* is still within your reach.

He turned to face his minions. "Send scouts on horseback to follow the whites downstream. They are to spy on the whites, and to bring back word of their actions."

"Guardian," Little Soldier began in perplexed tones. "The whites have left the Arikara nation—"

"Guardian," another of the braves interjected. "We have lost many braves. The nation must mourn—"

"No! The whites must be pursued!" Grey Eyes heard his own voice sounding much too loud, too high-pitched. The appalled looks on the faces of the others stung him like hornets. "The whites mean to do us more harm," he said by way of an explanation, but the words were barely out of his mouth when he realized, in horror, that he had trapped himself. He could see the question in Little Soldier's eyes—*What harm have they done us?*

Little Soldier stared at the Guardian, but said nothing. He nodded once, and went off to see to it that the orders were carried out. The group of braves followed, openly talking about what they had just witnessed.

They see how lost I am, Grey Eyes thought as he watched them go.

By Law, Little Soldier now would soon be forced to challenge his authority in the interest of the nation. If that happened, he would be prematurely stripped of his position, and the white's scalp would be lost to him. The white might even live to marry the princess, turning his own fate into a joke to be laughed at throughout the nation.

"Wherever you are, white, that will not happen," Grey Eyes whispered, lost in the private hell of his anguish. "On her life, itself, I swear to have your scalp. . . ."

Chapter 21

She sat in the darkness wrapped in robes, and did not look up when the maiden entered the lodge. Instead, she stared into thin air, trying with all of her will to still her pounding heart, and to keep her mind empty, so as not to build up false hope. She had sent her servant to the lower village for word of the attack upon the whites, and the fate of one white in particular. That had been hours ago, when it was still light outside. Now it was dark. She had tried during her eternity of waiting not to think of the deepening shadows as an omen.

"He lives, princess."

She fought back tears of relief and joy welling in her eyes. This young girl knew too much about her mistress's emotions as it was. "You are sure of this?" she asked, fighting to keep her feelings out of her voice.

"The braves found no sign of him among the dead."

"Then he was able to escape," the princess breathed. He was alive! Was he thinking of her right now? The time had crept by so slowly, but now it seemed to stand still.

"But there is troubling news, as well, princess," the maiden frowned.

Coldness crept upon the princess, wilting the joy in her heart the way the fall's first frost steals the green-life from the trees.

"The Guardian has sent spies to learn of the whites' actions," the maiden continued. "It is said that the Guardian wishes to pursue the whites, pursue them beyond the boundaries of the nation. . . ."

Of course, the princess thought. How could she ever have imagined that he would let the matter rest without gaining vengeance? Grey Eyes' life was over. Now he struggled to save the memory his people would have of him. He was a wronged Arikara brave fallen from grace. The only power he had left was the power to destroy. Even a woman could understand, if not accept, the tenent that "it was better to pass into the oblivion of dark legend than be remembered and laughed at."

"The Guardian has called for a gathering tonight. The plunder taken from the whites will be distributed among the braves or their families." The maiden's brown eyes opened wide, like the doe in the forest that hears the snap of a twig, and in that sound, the birth of its death. "It is said that the Guardian means to announce that Shadows will be sent after the whites."

"Leave me."

"Princess—"

"Leave me!" She dismissed her servant with a wave of her hand. She sat back so that her face was cloaked in darkness. "I will summon you if I wish anything. Do not come to me tonight unless you are so summoned."

The maiden bowed and backed out of the lodge. She quietly shut the door, leaving the princess in darkness except for the beam of moonlight which streamed down through the lodge's smoke-hole.

Never before, she mused as the inky shadows danced and whirled in the miniature prisms of her tears, never before had Shadows been sent after whites. To do so was to confirm the whites as humans, for Shadows could not be used against mere animals.

Warrior braves would be chosen by their rank, and their pleas, and in a group of three, they would be sent to trail their victims. They would set aside their rifles or fusils and use the sacred, silent weapons: knife, bow, fists. They would shadow their victims until they gave the sleep of death to them. The Shadows had no care for their own safety, for they were dead men from the moment that they were given the honor of being chosen, just as their victims were dead men from that moment. The Shadows embodied death itself. They had agreed to give up their positive force of life, to become death's tools. As such, they could never again return to the life of the nation. When their gifts of death had been delivered, they faded away into the mountains, the way shadows faded with the coming of the sun.

But these men would not be forgotten. Songs were created to honor the memory of men who became Shadows.

No victim had ever escaped the Shadows. If one Shadow was somehow killed before he could deliver death, there was the second and third to carry on. If all three Shadows should be slain, three more would be sent.

Never in the history of the Arikara nation had it been necessary to send more than the initial three Shadows.

Once three Shadows killed a war party of thirty Sioux. The three had run around and around the camp

of the war party, making no noise except for the twang
of their bow strings; and the hum of their arrows. The
song told of how the Shadows had closed their eyes
during their attack, so as to allow death to more fully
take control of their bodies. In this manner, they neither stumbled nor lost their way, and neither did their
arrows. Each Shadow fired ten; each arrow found its
Sioux target. The strength drained from the Sioux
braves, and they cried and held up their medicine bags
in an attempt to ward off the Shadows. Their medicine
bags proved impotent against the Shadows.

From that day on, the Sioux had much respect
when they trod upon the ground of the Arikara nation.
From that day on, the Sioux brave stepped from the
path when an Arikara approached.

The princess began to weep for her beloved's life,
for there was no doubt in her mind that Jed was as
good as dead. The Shadows would be chosen tonight,
at the gathering, but they could not set off until the following evening. All day tomorrow would be spent in
ritual and sacrament in order to turn the braves into
Shadows.

That meant she had time to reach Jed. To be with
him, and love him, and finally, die with him, when the
Shadows came. She would leave tonight, while all the
braves were at the gathering, and the women and children were sleeping. She had already given commands
to her servants that she not be disturbed. It would be a
simple matter to slip from the deserted upper village,
and then double back to the river's bank, to follow its
winding course to the whites' new camp.

She would not tell Jed of the Shadows, for that
would blight the precious little happiness they would
have before the end came.

He was a white, and so did not hear the sound of
now, but now was all they could have. He would talk

in his white man's way of the glorious future, never realizing that the future was always only a dream from
which death could awaken the sleeper at any moment.

    She would see to it that he slept soundly until the
Shadows came to send them both wide-eyed, and
awake, into death.

Chapter 22

There was the sound of creaking wood, matched in rhythm to the boat's inexorable rising and falling. The river's noises and surges had entered into his being.

He opened his eyes. It was dark. Above him the moon filled his vision with silvery light.

Other noises beyond those of the river and the barge itself had snatched Jed from sleep. There were the crickets fiddling their night music, the soft murmurs of men talking among themselves.

He sat up. Horribly, there were also the stifled moans of strong men fighting their pain. Their eerie, muffled cries turned the boats into a quiet, floating asylum.

Rubbing his eyes, which felt as if they'd been filled with the coarse sand from that accursed beach, Jed got to his feet and went in search of General Ashley. By the light of the torches and candles placed about both boats, Jed found Ashley stumbling about, tending to the wounded. The man was half-asleep on his feet.

"So you're awake, eh? Fine, Jed. I need you."

"How many wounded are there?"

Ashley took hold of Jed's arm, "Come with me,

boy. Coffee over here." He led Jed to a small cook-fire set up on a square of tin. Its warmth and light lent an agreeable ambiance to that corner of the *Yellowstone Packet.*

Ashley eyed his young charge. "You cold, boy? Didn't have blankets to spare for you—" he brought his hand up to his mouth too late to block a jaw-stretching yawn. "—Needed all we had to comfort the wounded. Got to do all I can for the poor souls—"

"How many of them are there?" Jed repeated patiently.

"Six. Sublette and Clyman were hit on the beach. Four others were hit after they'd reached the barges. None looks like they'll die, although I'm worried lest gangrene seize the wounds." His bemused expression faded, and his eyes looked away from Jed. "But then there's Clyman. He's worse off of all. 'The Green' will have him for sure. The others have holes in them I can wash out with river water, but Clyman's arm . . ." he shrugged. "Hiram was our medico. Boy, I don't know what to do. . . ."

Jed knew what he had to say, but he put off taking on the dreaded responsibility by asking another question. "Where's Mike? Maybe he has the training."

Ashley looked at him queerly. "Fink is dead," he said.

Jed sat silent, shocked, as two other figures left the shadows to close in around the fire, approaching at the sound of the talk about Fink the way jackals approach at the sound of gunfire, in order to partake of the slain prey.

"Mikey's dead all right," Tom Talbot said, his fair face flickering like a demon's in the small light of the fire. "Killed by the heathens, he was."

"Not at all," Wilkie Booth spat sullenly, taking his place by the fire. "We got out of that together."

Talbot shrugged, addressing himself to Jed. "Then I guess he drowned himself while swimmin' to the boats. Sorry Jed, I knew he was yer friend as much as he was mine, but he ain't here no more." He smiled. "I am."

"I've made Talbot the new patron," Ashley quietly said. "He's got experience, and it's important that order among the crews be maintained until we're out of this predicament."

Wilkie opened his mouth to say something, but then thought better of it. The fact that the General had made Talbot the new patron was news to him. No sense making a fuss about what was over and done with, he decided, and no sense in contradicting the new patron. Talbot was going to need an experienced hand to take charge of the *Rocky Mountains*, and that was a job that pulled a larger cut of pay. "I told Mike he'd never make that swim," Wilkie sighed.

Jed ignored Booth, and stared at Talbot. The latter was unable to meet his steady gaze. "As far as I'm concerned Mike brought his demise upon himself," Jed said. "He was a cruel, violent man. Once he saved my life because I had done him a favor. He understood payment in kind, and for that, I respected him. Because he understood 'an eye for an eye,' I think he probably understood, and accepted, his fate."

Talbot gratefully nodded at Jed. Without another word, he got up and left the gathering. Wilkie tagged along behind like a puppy.

"You know something I don't, boy?" Ashley grumbled between sips of his coffee.

"Maybe," Jed said laconically. "This hoss reckoned there be things you didn't *want* to know about."

Ashley nodded, grinning. For a moment, the strain and fatigue left his sagging features. "Whenever you start in with that wilderness man argot, I figure there's skeletons better left buried, all right."

The two men were silent for a moment, sipping their coffee. But the silence only made the soft groans of the wounded men more unbearable.

Jed gestured with his tin cup toward the wounded. "Reckon I can do something for them."

Ashley nodded shrewdly. "Reckon so."

"I had a little of the medico's training from my tutor," Jed continued. "He was a physician, you know. . . ."

"I knew."

"Damn!" Jed exploded. "So why didn't you just come out and ask me?"

Ashley shook his head. "You don't ask a man to take on what you just volunteered for, boy."

Jed nodded. "Reckon I better tend to Clyman first."

"Reckon so."

John Clyman was lying shirtless on a pile of bedding. A large bundle of cloth had been tightly strapped on both sides of his right shoulder. The cloth was wound around his arm down to the elbow. Clyman was awake. His face was pale, white as ivory above the black mass of his beard.

Jed carefully cut away the dressing. Already he could feel himself starting to panic. He knew so little of the healer's art, and so many men's lives were in the balance.

"Christ," Jed muttered. He began to gag. The arm bone itself was untouched, but only a few raw strands of flesh remained of the muscle and tendons. He wiped the back of his sleeve—already sticky with Clyman's blood—across his sweating forehead. "Where's Charbonneau?" he asked Ashley, who was peering over his shoulder at Clyman.

"Sleeping," the General replied. "He ain't as young as the rest of us," he snorted disdainfully.

"Sleeping is what you ought to be doing," Jed said, as he began to slice away the packing around Clyman's shoulder.

"Sure," Ashley chuckled. "I'll sleep when these here boys of mine are tended to."

Jed jerked back as John Clyman's blood squirted out of a severed artery to splatter across the front of his shirt. He reached out for a rag to wipe himself. It was already crusted with the clotted blood of the other wounded trappers. Jed sat back on his heels, fighting the dizziness and nausea which threatened to envelope him. Clyman's shoulder was a hellish mess, pulverized by the heavy impact of the Ree rifle bullet.

"Jed? How bad is it?" Clyman gasped. His voice was distant, hazy, floating upon the long draughts of skull varnish poured into his gullet to ease the pain. "Come on, Jed. No fibbin', now. Is I gonna die?"

Jed shook his head, and once again peered into the wound. "John, it's all smashed up around your shoulder. And your arm." He anxiously scanned the wounded man's face, to see if any of what he was saying was penetrating the fog created by the skull varnish. "John, I'm sorry, man. I don't know how to fix it. If I don't take your arm off, you'll die."

"Can you do it, Jed?" Ashley harshly asked. "You know what to do?"

"He's got no chance at all, otherwise," Jed answered. "I'll need a darning needle, like the ones we use to stitch leather, and the thread that goes with it. I can pull this flap of skin over, and sew it down to cover the hole." He was feeling faint again, and took deep breaths to calm himself. "And I need a saw, and gunpowder. And plenty of skull varnish. Soak everything in skull varnish—" Tears choked Jed now. "Put

a flat-bottomed pan over that there fire," he managed
between sobs that he couldn't stifle. "Get its bottom
red hot—"

Ashley said nothing, but went off to do what was
required. Clyman reached up with his left hand, and
pulled Jed down so that he could whisper in the younger man's ear. "Don't take on so, boy. You'll do yer
finest for me, I knows it. But see to the others first,"
Clyman demanded. "Ole Bill over thar's got a ball in
his leg. Hell, iffen I gotta lose my arm, I can wait a
while. Ain't gonna get no worse. . . ."

Jed nodded, and went off to examine the five
other wounded men.

Sublette was smoking a pipe, his leg bandaged
tightly around the thigh stretched out in front of him.
"Ain't so bad, Jed. Ball's lodged in thar against the
bone. Jest needs to be dug out." A sheepish expression
crossed the gaunt mountain man's face. "When I was
younger I coulda done it myself."

Jed called, "I need the General, and anybody else
willing to help."

Several of the trappers approached, clearly
pleased that someone had taken charge. One of the
keelboat men bashfully explained that he was expert at
sewing up sails, and so maybe, if canvas was like flesh,
he could help. They all knew how to dig a lead ball out
with a knife blade, but Jed showed them how to pour
gunpowder into the hole and ignite it, thus cauterizing
the wound instead of infecting it with river water. This
was done on the other four wounded, all of whom had
been lucky enough to have taken their injuries without
suffering broken bones, or damaged vital organs. As
each bullet was removed, and each bloody hole burned
clean, the keelboat man sewed up the opening with
needle and thread soaked in skull varnish. The wound
was then bandaged with cloth torn into strips.

All five of the wounded refused their ration of skull varnish to be drunk against the pain. To a man they begged that it be given to John Clyman, who, as Sublette put it, "was the only one of us going to have more than a man's share of hurtin'."

Still, only Sublette had no need of strong hands to hold him down while the operation was performed. He held himself rock-steady while Jed dug the bullet out of his leg, and uttered not a sound as the caustic gunpowder was patted into his wound, and then lit afire.

Jed worked on John Clyman for three hours. Charbonneau, who had since awakened, assisted Jed. Mercifully, Clyman had passed out during the interim between Jed's first examination and the actual operation.

The saw Jed used to cut through the arm bone had to have finer teeth filed into it to make a clean cut. As soon as the arm was off, the glowing red buttom of the pot that had been sitting in the fire was pressed against the stump, to sear the end of the bone closed. Loose skin was sewn over and around the stump, as it was across the shattered area of the shoulder, but not before gunpowder was applied and lit to cauterize the shoulder socket.

It was just midnight when a hollow-eyed, silent Jed sat by the cook-fire, another cup of coffee cradled in his slightly shaking hands. Charbonneau and Ashley sat with him.

"I've been talking to Talbot," Ashley began. "He says his crews demand that they be allowed to return to Fort Atkinson. They're still powerful afraid of the Rees." He leaned over the side of the railing to spit into the river. "Damn greenhorns think the Rees is gonna sneak up on 'em in their sleep and take their hair."

"There is no possibility of that," Charbonneau

said. "The Rees have finished with us. Out of sight, out of mind."

"But I'm not finished with them," Jed muttered. "My woman is back there." He looked at Ashley. "What are you going to do, General?"

"I started out with sixty good men. Now I've got twenty-nine, who are sound of body," Ashley stared down into his tin cup. "I've lost my best, to add to it. . . ." He shook himself, and carried on brusquely. "Here's how it lays. I've made a deal with Talbot. Me and the boys who want to stay—"

"That will be all of the trappers," Charbonneau said.

"—Will stay. Talbot will take the *Yellowstone Packet* downriver, back to Fort Atkinson, with a message from me to Colonel Leavenworth. Jed, when we met with him, he said that the only thing stopping him from marching on the Rees was a lack of evidence as to their foul play. Well," he muttered softly, "when Talbot reaches him with my letter, he'll have his evidence."

"So we just wait around until the army gets here?" Jed grumbled.

"Some of us do," Ashley replied. He reached into his pocket and produced a rolled-up scroll. He spread the scrap of parchment before them. It was a map, crudely drawn, but it showed the Missouri, the Ree villages, the expedition's present position, and a dotted line which traveled overland. The line crossed the Little Missouri River, and then traveled on to the Yellowstone. It traveled up that river, to an 'X' that represented the fort that Major Henry was to have built at the mouth of Yellowstone, where that river split from the Missouri.

"This is the route you and Charbonneau were going to take to Henry," Ashley said. "I'm going to call for a volunteer to travel it on foot, to reach my partner, and inform him of what's happened. He's got enough good men up there to sent down a rescue expedition of his own." Ashley looked up from the map to Jed and Charbonneau. "With a party of boys coming down the Yellowstone, and an Army expedition coming up the Missouri, we'll have the Rees in a trap. That barricade won't do much for them with Colonel Leavenworth's cannons knocking into it from the front, and Major Henry's boys blasting into them from the rear."

"I'm still going, I reckon," Jed said. "I don't much cotton to sitting around here. I want to be out in the woods."

"And I know the way," Charbonneau said. "That map will be useless once we're in the wilderness."

Jed looked at the old trapper suspiciously. "No offense," he said, "but we're talking about walking, not riding. Are you up to it?"

Charbonneau smiled. "There are two routes. One for horses, down along the plains area," he gestured at the map. "It is longer, but flat. Then there is a shorter route, along the high country, across ridges, and through forests. That is the one we will take, Jed."

"I guess that tells me," Jed grinned. "Rather have you than anyone else, I reckon. We'll set off in two hours or so. That will give us some traveling time before dawn." He got up and stretched. "Seeing as you've slept, Toussaint, would you see to our gear?"

"Yes, Jed."

"I'm going to get some rest." He moved off to find himself a spot to nap.

"Watch out for him," Ashley urged Charbonneau. "Keep him from doing anything foolish concerning that lady love of his back at the villages."

"Do not worry," Charbonneau said. He ran his hands through his grey-blond hair, the better part of his mind already preoccupied with mental lists of equipment and weapons. He sorted and resorted the lists in his thoughts, paring down the loads so that they could easily be carried on the tough, overland trek. "He will do nothing about his personal matter until he has fulfilled his obligation to the expedition."

"Aye, I reckon so," Ashley admitted. "He's a good one, all right. Make him listen to you, Toussaint," he glowered.

"*Oui, Général,*" Charbonneau chuckled. "He will listen to an old hand like me." He smiled in Jed's direction. "Like all youths," the Frenchman reflected, "he finds only those his own age threatening."

"His own age, eh?" Ashley laughed. He held his hands up, looking at his gnarled fingers and swollen knuckles in the firelight. "Damn, it all belongs to the young ones, don't it? We're too old. I can't stop myself from longing for my soft bed and snug house back in St Louis. I've had my fill of the wilderness. If I ever make it through this adventure, I'll never leave home again. But Jed there. He can't hardly stand to be out of the rugged country. It nourishes him."

"It all belongs to the young," Charbonneau agreed. He got up, the joints of his knees creaking in complaint as he did so. "It may belong to them, but do not retire from the fray just yet, old man." He smiled wearily down at Ashley. "It remains for us relics to help the young take possession of it."

"I ain't retiring until you do, Frenchie," Ashley pretended to scowl. He reached out his hand, and Charbonneau helped him to his feet.

Chapter 23

It was nearing midnight as Cabanne approached the upper village of the Rees. He had left three of his men back at his camp deep in the forest, in order to guard their precious horses. There were five steeds left, now that the Frenchman had lost his best mount to Grey Eyes. The supplies they had been carrying were almost gone, and the heavy fur packs they'd taken from the dead men at Pilcher's fort had been cached until they could be retrieved at a more advantageous moment.

Tonight, Cabanne's mind was on softer, more entertaining plunder. Tonight he would take Grey Eyes' fine female for his own enjoyment. When he was done with her, he'd take even more pleasure in witnessing the Ree Guardian and Jed Smith kill each other over her fair corpse.

Cabanne and the one man he had chosen to accompany him, an Englishman, named Teddy, hurried through the now-barren growing fields of the Rees, toward the first row of lodges. Tooth was running ahead of them. The big dog was ranging far and wide, its brain filled with hot, animal excitement that was born of wafting scents which promised violent confrontation, and the joy of killing.

Cabanne and Teddy moved on, alert for any sign
of a sentry, although none was expected. Grey Eyes
had summoned every brave to the gathering in the
lower village. Even now, the two intruders, who had
grown quite familiar with the lay-outs of both villages,
could hear the heathens chanting and roaring over the
division of the goods and gear stripped from the Ashley-Henry expedition's dead trappers.

The mud sucked at their moccasins, the liquid
sound the only thing breaking the silence of the night.
Both men had their knives in hand. Guns would be
used only as a last resort, to aid in their escape.

Ahead they heard a sudden, rapid yapping. One
of the Rees' mutts had picked up Tooth's scent.

"We've been found out," Teddy scowled, stopping
short. The two sides of his face were out of balance
with each other, the result of being sewn back together
by Teddy himself after he was mauled by a grizzly.
Now his lopsided leer was even more grotesque due to
his twisted expression of fear. He was a big man,
though not as big as Cabanne. He trembled slightly, for
Teddy was no greenhorn. He knew what the Rees
would do to them if they were caught. He'd already
vowed to himself to pull his pistol and fire it into his
own head if he were surrounded. Death made for a ros-
ier future than torture at the hands of squaws. "Lets
us quit this, Cabanne. They'll bag us for sure, now.
We've lost the chance, 'tis certain, man—"

At that moment the high-pitched yapping was
abruptly cut off. Tooth appeared. And hanging from
his jaw was the Ree mutt, limp, broken, dead. Tooth
proudly displayed his kill to his master the way a tabby
exhibits a mouse.

Cabanne and Teddy waited, but no other dog
picked up the alarm. The Frenchman nodded to himself and nudged his follower.

"What's happened?" Teddy marveled. "Usually the other dogs join in. . . ."

"They are afraid of Tooth," Cabanne proudly said. "It has happened before like this. The other dogs of the village will silently huddle against the lodges until he is gone, for his fierce scent is in the air, mixed with the smell of the dead one. For now, Tooth rules the dogs of the Rees."

The big Frenchman moved on confidently. Now that the village's alarm system was silenced, the advantage lay with the intruders.

For all his size, Cabanne moved as silently as a ghost once the village had been penetrated. He flitted from the protective shadows of one lodge to the next with Teddy behind him and Tooth ahead prowling and sniffing for signs of any man or beast foolish enough to challenge their progress.

"That is Bear's lodge," Cabanne whispered. "The princess's is next door."

"Will she have servants with her?" Teddy asked suspiciously. "If so, we'll have to slit their throats afore they yell a warning."

"No maidens sleep with the princess in her lodge," Cabanne told him. "The girls that serve her live nearby, with their own families. All of them should be sleeping soundly, by now. If not," Cabanne shrugged, "it is your task to make sure no shout of warning or alarm is given."

Teddy nodded. "And I'll do it well," he muttered. "Anything to get this over and done with—"

His remark was cut short, slammed back into his mouth by the back of Cabanne's hand. Teddy staggered away. He brought two fingers up to comfort his bleeding lip. He uttered no exclamation of pain, nor did he even ponder the possibility of retaliating. To attempt to defend oneself against Cabanne would be as futile a gesture as the challenge issued by the hapless Ree mongrel to Tooth. Instead, Teddy only lisped through his broken mouth, "Why?"

"Your fear is making you talk too much," Cabanne hissed.

Far away, in the lower village, the Rees' ceremonial drums were pounding in unison with Teddy's panicked heart. He stared at Cabanne's broad back.

"In the Rockies, the big cats hunt," Cabanne whispered as he watched Bear's lodge for any sign of activity. "After they kill, they carry their prey to a safe sanctuary before they begin to feast." The Frenchman straightened up. "Now we shall do the same with our sweet meat."

He began to run toward the lodge, moving faster and faster, the way the big cats of the mountains move, muscles pumping with innate certainty as the creature runs down its prey. Teddy scurried after him, as much the Frenchman's servant and pet as Tooth, who now stood on stiff legs, the grey curls of fur along his thick, humped spine rising. The dog's nose was pointed toward the fields from which they'd come, and a growl, faint but ominous, was emanating from his throat.

Cabanne flattened himself against the side of Bear's lodge. After pausing to catch their wind, they slipped around the back to the princess's cabin. With more speed and agility than Teddy had thought possible for such a large man, Cabanne pushed open the door of the princess's lodge and swung himself through.

Teddy anxiously watched and waited, making sure to keep a sharp eye for any sign of discovery. There was nothing but eerie silence—silence all around, from the village, from Bear's lodge, from the black doorway of the princess's lodge. It must have gone well, Teddy thought. By now Cabanne has struck her unconscious. He'll carry her out and we'll flee the village.

For the first time since Cabanne had ordered him to come along, Teddy began to relax. He'd earned himself the right to have her second, after Cabanne had tired of her. She was a pretty one, Cabanne had said. With fair hair! And a fine figure! Teddy had not had a woman since a brief sojourn at Fort Atkinson. That had been more than a year ago, and even then, he'd had to settle for the basest of the squaw whores, that being all he could afford. No good-looking woman had ever lain with him on account of his claw-savaged face. But now he would have a princess—

Cabanne tore out of the lodge. The look of pure, frustrated rage on his face made Teddy take several, quick steps back.

"The lodge is empty!" Cabanne snarled. "She is not here—"

"Damn, all this for nothing," Teddy began to whine, but he stopped as Cabanne held up one, silencing hand. He followed the Frenchman's gaze to Tooth, who was now frozen like a statue. From tail to nose, the huge dog was one straight, unbroken line which pointed into the fields.

Cabanne smiled. Teddy knew what that smile signified. He shuddered.

"Fetch," Cabanne said.

Tooth moved off, loping slowly at first, but then gathering speed as he vanished into the dark fields.

She had waited until close to midnight, so as to be certain that all the women and children who inhabited the lodges close by hers would be sound asleep. All of the men, including her father, would be attending the gathering. Word of what the Guardian had decreed swept through both villages. If Grey Eyes did indeed

summon Shadows to chase whites, it would mark a first
in the annals of Arikara history. No man would
willingly miss such an event.

She had dressed in sturdy but soft deerskin, with a
cloak of the same to protect her from the night's chill.
In her belt she carried two knives. Her own skinning
blade, and the whites' knife that Jed had dropped when
she'd by chance cut short his attempt to steal a truce
from Grey Eyes. Grandfather had smiled at that time,
she now realized. Even if Jed had succeeded in taking
the Guardian by surprise—in itself, an unlikely
event—the requested truce would have been inval-
idated by the intrusion of the other whites into the village. Jed would have suffered the same torture as the
young white taken captive. Jed's head would have accompanied that of the young white on its final journey
down the ridge.

She had slipped from the lodge and began to run
toward the fields. Once there she could relax a bit. It
was unlikely any one would spot her, and the protection of the forest was only a few steps away.

She had been trudging her way through the first
section of the growing area when she had heard the village dog bark. She froze, uncertain of what to do. To
run would invite the foolish dog to chase her. She was
not afraid of the dog; once it reached her it would only
wag its tail and frolic about her legs, but its noisy pursuit would invite the attendance of the village's other
dogs, and her escape to Jed would be foiled. But she
couldn't stand here all night, like a silly old
woman. . . .

As she pondered her predicament, the dog was
suddenly silenced. Strangely, none of the other dogs
had picked up her scent. Now there was nothing but
quiet coming from the direction of the lodges.

Slowly, carefully, so as to make no further noise,

the princess began to pick her way through the fields. The way was muddy and damp, but she ignored her discomfort and banished her night fears of wolves by concentrating on Jed, his touch, his warmth, his joy when he first saw her during the pte hunt, his joy to come when she presented herself to him.

She could imagine her maidens' confusion come the morning. They would rush to the lower village, the poor girls by then in a quandary. To interrupt the sacred ceremonies of turning warrior braves into Shadows would be unthinkable. Grey Eyes, Bear, and Little Soldier would be sequestered with the three volunteers who had uttered the words which had at once garnered them great honor, and also sealed their doom: *People of the Arikara Nation, I am Shadow*—

The princess smiled to herself. She would have at least a day before her absence could be made known to anyone who could do anything about it. Yet if her journey was to be long, a day would not be enough of a lead. A search party mounted on horses would easily overtake her. But she counted on the whites' boats being just a day down the river.

A new sound quickly grew behind her. She stopped, and held her own breath, in order to better hear. The steady thud of four legs, and harsh, rasping breathing grew increasingly louder. It was like the worst nightmare she had ever had, to be caught standing there alone, in the darkness, while some animal thing was fast charging toward her out of the black.

She knew instinctively, as she stared with wide eyes, that what was stalking her was no village dog. She turned and began to run toward the distant trees of the forest. She knew that the woods would offer a lone woman precious little protection against whatever it was that was after her. But the mere comfort of having a tree trunk to lean against, and thus protect her back, was infinitely better than being exposed and vulnerable on all sides as she was here, in the open fields.

The animal slammed into the back of her legs, knocking her flat into the mud. She screamed at the animal's first touch; fully expecting to feel its fangs, but it only careered around and around her in an ever-widening circle. She'd not gotten a clear look at it, but what she'd seen was enough. It was as big as a wolf, although she'd never heard of the beasts wandering alone so close to a village unless they were sick. Arikara legend told of wolves playing with their victims like tame dogs before they made their kill. This must be what was happening to her now, she thought as she got to her feet and began once again to run toward the line of trees.

The animal cut close in front of her, heading her off, *steering her,* she realized. She pulled her skinning knife from her belt as she stumbled on, her damp, muddy skirt slowing her progress, as did the slick soles of her moccasins against the slippery mud.

The animal slammed into her once again, and again she fell, this time to her knees. As the beast passed she slashed out with her blade, but the wolf twisted away, nimbly dodging her thrust.

The princess once again found her footing in the mire of the field. She felt the bitter desperation of the deer, which will, up to the very last moment of its life, turn in a brave attempt to bite the very predator sinking its fangs and claws into its haunches. She stumbled on, too exhausted now from the buffeting she'd suffered from the beast to run. She kept her eyes on the animal as it flew around her. This time she would be ready and waiting for its attack.

It had twisted around at full gallop to angle in at her again. This time she turned to meet it, her knife at the ready. But at the last moment, it veered away from her. The princess began to sob. A moment ago she wouldn't have believed it possible to be more frightened, but now she was. The beast had been forced to slow in order to make its change in direction, and when it had, her staring eyes had seen it clearly.

It was no wolf, but even worse. It was the killer dog that belonged to the foul white who had told Grey Eyes of her meeting with Jed.

Suddenly a hand came from behind her to seize her wrist. The hand twisted, and she screamed in pain, her fingers on fire, as the blade dropped from her grip. She was spun around to stare up into the laughing, bearded face of the white Jed had called Cabanne.

"My dog has brought you to heel, pretty one," he said in Ree. "Come quietly now, else I will have to hurt—"

Sunblossom opened her mouth to scream, but Cabanne brought his right arm up across his chest, and swung, the back of his hand catching the side of her head. She lost her footing and fell hard into the mud. A wave of blackness engulfed her.

Cabanne stood laughing and petting Tooth, who was romping in front of his master, unwilling to believe that the fun was over so soon.

Teddy went to her and bent down to peer at her still form. "Put her to sleep right proper, you did."

"She'll be all right. Right enough for our purposes," Cabanne said.

"Wonder where she was off to?" Teddy mused as he hoisted the princess up and slung her over his shoulder. He felt his own excitement as one hand gripped her across the muddied, slippery backs of her thighs, and the other pressed into her buttocks, round and firm through the tightly stretched deerskin.

"Where she was intending to go is no longer of

any meaning," Cabanne said. "I have her now." He began to walk toward the forest, with Tooth ranging ahead of him, and Teddy, with his burden, following behind.

Chapter 24

Grey Eyes stared at his Second who sat across from him. Neither had spoken for the last hour. The seed of disagreement between them had since blossomed into the rage-red flower of anger. Accordingly, neither trusted himself to speak.

The dark corners of the Guardian's lodge began to brighten as the sun found its path in the sky. The momentary glare stabbed into the eyes of the tired men. Now the beams served to offset the blue swirls of calumet smoke which hung like ghosts in the air, and the acrid fumes of the herbs which slowly smoldered in the pots. The incense bit into their nostrils, but the two still breathed deeply so as to partake of the herbs' powers of purification.

Another hour passed. The fire between them, which had once been banked high, had now shrunk to a few glowing embers.

The three warrior braves chosen to become Shadows were also in meditation. Each brave was sequestered in a different lodge, and each was at this moment—as he had been for most of the early morning hours—staring down at his weapons laid across his lap.

In a few hours the Guardian and Ranking Second would join them for the beginning of an intricate ceremony which would go on for all of the day. If even one part of the sacred ritual was incorrectly performed, the magic would not happen, and the men would not receive the shadowy powers that came with the embodiment of death.

But the rituals and ceremonies had always been correctly performed, for always there had been harmony in the hearts of the Guardian, Ranking Second and nominated Shadows.

Until today.

The spies had returned during last night's gathering. They had reported the two whites' departure from the boats, and then the larger boat's departure from the nation. The smaller had remained, and with it, the surviving whites from the camp on the beach. The whites' Guardian, with the face of a goat, remained with his tribe. The two who had departed inland were the old one with the fair hair, and the young white whose scalp the Guardian of the nation had earlier coveted.

"This is wrong!" Little Soldier suddenly said, leaping to his feet.

Grey Eyes allowed no emotion to show, but he felt exhilaration. Little Soldier's anxiety had forced him to break the silence first. He would lose this confrontation. "Sit down," Grey Eyes said.

Little Soldier began to make for the door, but then stopped, caught between his desire to be clear of this bad magic, and his loyalty to the man seated before him. *This was wrong*, he repeated to himself. *There was death waiting in this room. . . .*

"Sit down, Second," Grey Eyes formally requested.

Little Soldier stared into the other's eyes, and took a long time answering. "Yes . . . Guardian."

It was good, Grey Eyes thought as his Second again took his seat. Even though it meant the contradiction of his desires, he had to marvel lovingly at the way the Law was all-powerful, the way Grandfather Himself was all-knowing. As Guardian he had fallen from grace, and although no one but the princess knew of this, Little Soldier, as a right-thinking man, had already begun to sense it for himself. Soon, the Ranking Brave would no longer use his title when addressing him, and justly so. But before that happened, Grey Eyes himself would hand down the white feathers of office. He had only one last use for them—

"Guardian, it is wrong to call the Shadows to deal with whites. The magic can only be insulted at this petty use," Little Soldier exhorted. "The whites are not worthy enemies of the Arikara nation."

"But if they could destroy our nation?" Grey Eyes waited, but his Second only watched and waited himself. "If they could scatter us to the winds, so that even the Sioux, whose women rut with the whites like dogs in heat could laugh at us? So that the Assiniboine people to the west and the Mandan and Hidatsa to the north, who now only whisper our name so as not to insult us, could spit on our weapons and trample the white feathers which represent our right-thinking and Law? If the whites could cause all that to happen to the Arikara nation, would they then be worthy enough enemies for the Shadows?"

"You believe the whites are capable of this?"

"I believe the whites were sent to us as a test," Grey Eyes replied, and thinking, *I have failed.*

"Do you believe they are humans?" Little Soldier asked warily.

"No," Grey Eyes lied.

"Then, Guardian, it is madness to send Shadows after the two whites traveling overland. As soon as our spies informed us of their departure, you began to lust after their blood. Of what importance are these two whites?"

"The young white is important to me," Grey Eyes muttered. "I wish his death—"

"Why?"

"Do you question my wishes?" Grey Eyes asked quietly. "Answer me, Second." Once again he let that cleverest of tricksters, silence, do its dirty work. But even as he did, Grey Eyes felt anguish—both in his heart, and in the heart of his Second. As Guardian, he had twisted the Law into a devilish shape: Noble Little Soldier now had to choose between his own right thinking, and his vow of obeisance to the office which the white feathers represented.

"I do not question the wishes of my Guardian," Little Soldier whispered. "I will uphold the Law."

"The Shadows will give death to the young white. They must also kill the old, of course," Grey Eyes sighed. "Is all between us resolved?"

"Guardian, a request."

"Speak."

"Guardian, as Second and Ranking Brave of the nation, I request that I be allowed to lead a war party downriver. I will slay the whites camped, and then I will overtake and slay the whites on the big boat. It is madness to allow some who were present during our battle to survive. They will relay their song of defeat to other whites, who may come to avenge their brothers."

"You believe that the whites have brothers?"

"I believe that they band together the way pte and wolves band together. They are not human, but they travel in herds and packs. . . . Larger and larger herds and packs every day, I fear. We must not allow any of them to remain alive. I feel the fate of the nation depends on this."

Grey Eyes smiled to himself as his Second sat waiting for his answer. *You will be a wise Guardian, Little Soldier,* he thought. *You will have to be wise to preserve the nation from the treachery I find myself doing it.*

"Before I give you my answer, Second, I issue you two commands," the Guardian began. "The first is that you say nothing of what I am about to tell you to anyone. The last is that you ask no further questions, and make no further requests until after the ritual of the Shadows is finished. Do you agree?"

"I agree."

"Second, I cannot allow you to risk your life on such a dangerous excursion. You will be needed here, in the Nation, by the sun's next coming. Then you may choose a war party—"

"By then it will be too late!" Little Soldier cried. "Their lead will be great. Oh, Guardian, I fear for the nation—"

And so do I, Grey Eyes thought, fighting back tears of his own.

"Guardian," Little Soldier whispered. "Remember your vision. The flames, Guardian, the flames. . . ."

"Remember my commands, Second. No more questions, no more requests."

Little Soldier nodded miserably. He watched the Guardian rise, and then stood up himself. It was time to begin the ritual of the Shadows.

Chapter 25

The princess lay wide-awake, listening to the snores of her captors.

It was the brightest part of the day, but in the forest the sun lost most of its strength. Each leaf and branch of the tall cottonwoods and aspens blocked the warming rays, shuttering the sun's intensity, so that the dappled, mottled beams filtering through the greenery gave the landscape a cool, soft, verdant glow.

They'd ridden for hours, she guessed. They'd kept just to the edge of the forest, but traveled the relatively level ground of the neighboring grasslands so as to allow their mounts stable footing. They had not been able to move at a gallop, for there were only five horses for the five men, their supplies, and herself.

She winced in pain as she attempted to turn on her side. The shift in position was not easy, for they had hobbled her feet together so as to prevent her escape while they slept. She could crawl, but not walk. Cabanne had told her she was allowed to crawl all she wanted. . . .

She sat up, and this time the pain was so great that she had to bite down on the back of her hand to keep from moaning. They had strapped her stomach-down across the bags of supplies packed upon the fifth horse. Her stomach absorbed an extraordinary amount of physical punishment. She was also humiliated by the white in the saddle who twisted around to taunt her in his incomprehensible tongue. Surely he reined his mount toward the roughest part of the route.

Now her belly was a mass of bruises. Each breath she took, each movement she made, felt as if a knife were twisting itself around in her stomach and sides.

She'd fought hard against it, but after a while the pain had grown stronger than her pride. Each step the horse took pounded the hard-packed bags into her, and each step forced a high-pitched whine of agony out of her throat. The torture seemed to go on forever, but finally, as the noon hour approached, Cabanne ordered his men to halt, dismount, and lead their horses deeper into the forest. They dragged her down to the ground. She'd been slightly relieved then, for they were apparantly too exhausted to rape her. They ate some of their dried meat, giving her none, not that she could have kept food down, and then spread out their robes and fell almost instantly asleep.

The huge dog had sat close by her for a time, his yellow eyes watching her, but she understood the ways of animals, especially predators. She'd kept rock-still, and soon the dog had tired of her lack of movement, and had gone off somewhere, probably to hunt down a rabbit for his empty gut. But there was no telling how long the white's dog would stay away. She had to do something now.

The forest was by no means silent. Birds chirped loudly. Squirrels and chipmunks had come out of their holes now that the hound was gone. They chattered noisily at each other, like old women in the growing fields, their feud over scraps of food never-ending.

The whites slept soundly through all this, most

likely secure in the knowledge of their strength, their lead-time, the fact that they were well-hidden, and the fact that she herself could not escape.

The white nearest her, one of the smaller, older ones, was lying on his back, his robe thrown open. He was sound asleep. If she moved very quietly, and if her hands did not tremble too much, she could nudge free the knife in his belt. Her own knives—the skinning blade, and the knife that Jed had left behind—had been taken from her.

She stared at the sleeping white, at the knife in his belt. *Go on*, she ordered herself. *Are you a Sioux whore, or are you an Arikara princess? Will you die dishonored, to pass into dark legend? Or will your people sing the story of your courage to children you yourself shall never see?*

One of the other whites stirred in his sleep, his breath coming in raspy snorts as he squirmed about in his soft pte robes. She held her breath, but the white did not awaken. Nor did any of the others, Cabanne included, lying farthest from her in the clearing of their camp roofed-in by the trees.

Go now, she urged her unwilling muscles. *Before the dog returns!*

She began to crawl toward the nearest white. Her hobbled legs trailed uselessly behind her, like the straw sleds her people hitched to horses during the long rides toward the pte herds. Each foot of ground gained cost her incredible pain. She assumed she was seriously injured inside from the punishment her belly had taken. She began to cry, but silently, the only noise the soft plop of her tears falling to the dirt.

A woman hurt in her belly could not have children. No man would want such a woman. Jed would not want her.

But she would never see Jed. She would die here.

Among these animal whites. That was certain. The only uncertainty was whether she was *truly* Arikara, and therefore worthy of her title among her people. If she was, she would manage to wreak her vengeance upon these animals for taking her. It she could, perhaps that would even goad them into killing her now, out of anger, before they thought to sexually violate her.

Her hand reached out. Her fingers hovered just above the hilt of the knife in the white's belt. The handle of the blade was of carved elk horn. The white and tan handle rose and fell with its owner's steady, rhythmic snoring.

But the princess breathed not at all as she deftly plucked the knife from the belt. As she did, she watched the face of the white. His greasy, sparsely whiskered, slack countenance never changed.

Her first impulse was to plunge the blade into his chest, but what good would that do? His death rattle would awaken the others, who would disarm her and then either kill her or take her along with them. And with one less man they could ride even faster, so that there would be no hope of rescue by an Arikara war party. She knew that such a rescue was the one thing Cabanne feared. Her people would keep him alive for many days as they whittled his big body away in punishment for stealing her.

No. She could not kill all five of these animals. That meant that she could kill none of them.

Nor could she cut through the hobble around her ankles. The thongs were many. They had been soaked in water, and then interwound, to dry as hard as metal. Her own people soaked sheets of leather in such a manner, and then stretched those sheets on a small, circular wooden frame. When the sheets dried, the leather formed a strong war shield, hard enough to turn even the sharpest arrow or blade. No, there was no way she could quickly and quietly saw through the hobble with just one knife. It would take the strength of a man such as Cabanne himself to pull them apart and off her.

But she had to do something to these animals—at least slow them down, so that there would at least be a chance that her people could catch up with them, and avenge her death.

The horses. The key lay in the horses. Without them, Cabanne's lead would soon dwindle away to nothing. But the horses were hobbled as she was, and by the same, tempered leather. There seemed to be no way, and once again she felt tears come to her eyes.

Suddenly she realized what she had to do. She would show these two-legged animals what an Arikara woman was. . . .

In the distance one of the horses softly whinnied. She could see them dipping their huge heads as they gnawed and nibbled the soft grass and tender tree shoots.

She began to crawl in their direction.

Cabanne came awake first. Had he heard it, or had it been a dream? Now all was quiet, but Tooth was nudging at him with his wet nose. His eyes still closed, the Frenchman pushed the dog from him. "Away, damn you," he mumbled sleepily.

But something was wrong, he realized. His hand had come away from Tooth wet, warm, sticky.

Cabanne opened his sleep-bleared eyes. Tooth's massive head was a foot away. The dog's fur and face were stained with warm, red blood.

Cabanne brought his hand to his own face and sniffed. He knew the smell of this blood. It was horse.

The sound from his dream came again. One of

the horses gave a guttural, squalling bray of pain and terror.

"Non!" Cabanne wailed, hurling away his pte robe as he clambered to his unsteady feet. Tooth shrank back, tail between his legs as his master lumbered forward.

Teddy and the three others all shot bolt upright. They pulled their pistols from their robes, and for a split second there was no sound but the metallic *clicks* of hammers being snicked back as the men looked wildly about them for sign of danger or threat.

Cabanne was already running. "The horses!" he cried.

Teddy and the rest kicked free of their robes and ran to follow. When they reached the horses they stopped short.

"I don't believe it," Teddy gasped.

The heathen woman was on the ground in the very midst of the five horses. The beasts were still hobbled, but bucking and twisting, their bodies rising in the air. Drops of blood flew from their spindly legs as they rose up off the ground. The heathen was crawling about, squirming through those stamping hooves like a serpent. She'd gotten hold of a knife, the vixen had. She was slashing away at the legs of the steeds.

Cabanne rushed toward her, but she slithered away. As luck would have it, one of the horses, a big, dappled grey, its sweat-foamed flanks heaving in pain and terror over the little thing that stung just below the range of its vision, flung itself in the Frenchman's path. Cabanne tried to maneuver past the steed, but it was a panicked, hysterical beast. Its tiny brain could stand no touch, not even the light pressure of Cabanne's palms along its ribs. Though its front feet were hobbled, the horse kicked out like a mule with its unfettered rear legs. Cabanne threw himself back, howling in impotent rage as the heathen crawled on beneath the other mounts' legs, her knife doing its dirty work.

One of the men thrust a pistol forward toward the woman, but lowered it as Cabanne screamed a warning not to fire for fear of striking one of the horses. The Frenchman managed to reach her. She had a bone-chilling grin on her sweat and blood-stained face as she confronted Cabanne. She lunged at him with the knife, but her swipe fell short. Cabanne kicked the blade out of her hand, and dragged her by her hair away from the mounts.

"I will kill you! What have you done, cursed woman!" Cabanne demanded in Ree. His thick fingers closed about her throat. In English he shouted, "Teddy! See to the mounts!"

"Kill me!" the princess urged. She spat up at his ugly face, the spittle landing on his long, matted beard. "Kill me, vermin!"

But Cabanne, gaining control over his fury, only shook his head. He tossed her aside. "You would like that, of course," he said, the anger and hatred he felt making his voice tremble. "But then I would not get my pleasure from you. And, princess, I mean to have that. And I may need your wretched life. It may buy me back my own, should your tribe catch up with me."

Teddy approached, being careful to stay out of arms' reach of his enraged comrade. In his hand he held the blood-smeared knife.

"What's she done?" Cabanne snarled. "She can't of butchered them all that bad. She's but a woman. And we were up at the first scream."

"She's finished em, 'tis certain," Teddy shrugged, the mismatched sides of his face showing a demon's frown. "She's hamstrung em. Cut a tendon on each leg. Sliced clean through each, she did. The steeds were hobbled, so they couldn't kick. And it only took one swipe of the blade for each to complete the dirty work. I'd wager such butchering doesn't take long enough to make 'em scream."

"Then they're done for," Cabanne glowered.

"Aye. They're good for nothin' but meat for that there cur of yers, I'd say." Teddy held up the knife. "Whose is this?"

The small, older, sparse-whiskered trapper stepped forward. "It's mine," he whimpered as Cabanne fixed his glare on him. "The heathen stole it from me while I slept. It coulda been any of youse!" he cried fearfully. "Youse knows they's nothin' but thieves!"

"Give me the blade," Cabanne said evenly.

"What'll you do to me?" the smaller trapper asked as he began to back away from Cabanne. He cursed himself for being a fool and leaving his pistol on his robe. "Cabanne. . . . I'm a good 'un. Hell! Youse all knows that!" he shouted.

"Easy, Pete," Cabanne grinned. "I will just give you your blade back." His hand whipped forward, and the knife took the small man square in the chest.

Pete sat down hard. His fingers locked around the white and tan elk-horn handle of the knife that was buried to its hilt in his breast.

"Now you will not lose it again, Pete," Cabanne said as he turned away. "The rest of you, take only what you can carry easily. We must make the high country before dark. If we stay down here, the Rees will catch us. Up there, the heathens must walk, as we now must. We will climb, and then begin to double back. That is our only chance to reach Fort Kiowa."

"What's to be done with her?" Teddy asked.

"Cut away the hobble, but tie her hands tightly, and put a thong around her neck so that she can be led like the animal she is," Cabanne spat. "Hurry! The Rees on horseback could be gaining on us at this very moment!"

"What about Pete?" Teddy asked. "And the horses? Let me finish them off—" He gestured toward the small, wretched figure, now lying on his side, legs twitching and kicking as his life slowly trickled out of the knife-plugged hole in his lungs.

"Leave him be," Cabanne snarled. "Forget about the horses. Pete's death, the horses' deaths, will be a thousand times more pleasant than yours will be should the Rees get hold of us!"

Chapter 26

Jed pulled himself up the hill. He couldn't remember ever feeling so God-awful tired, but so damned good.

In the high country the air was cooler. The wind tasted of ice-blue winter in his mouth. The hills and valleys were drenched in flames of gold and scarlet. They were breathtakingly beautiful after the monotonous blue-green of the pine-wooded slopes below.

"Wait for me at the crest," Charbonneau called. "There are gifts waiting! First a surprise. And then God shall paint us a glorious sunset for our evening's entertainment."

Jed waited at this small flat clearing, one side protected by a sharp rising slope. He set down his pack and leaned against it. Tied across the top of it were the roasts and fat hams of an elk he'd dropped with one quick shot earlier in the day. What a fine supper they'd have tonight! They had flour for gravy, and plenty of coffee to drink! And tomorrow he or Charbonneau might bag partridges, or a deer for Henry's men. And there were wild fruits—berries and plums—fall-ripe and sweet for dessert. Why, a man couldn't fail to eat like a king! It was all here, in the wilderness. The whole continent lay wide open and waiting for him, like the most bountiful, beautiful woman in all of eternity.

He thought of Sunblossom, his love, waiting for him back at the villages. Her hair the color of the sun shining through the yellow leaves, her kiss as soft and cool as the murmuring breeze caressing his face. Her superstitious ways would drop away from her once he took her in hand and showed her the right way to live in this wonderful world. They would be Adam and Eve, readmitted into the Garden of Eden. Their strength would lie not in innocence—for Jed had felt the loss of that precious quality after Louisa's betrayal—but in hard work and freedom. They would make love when and where the passion seized them. They would pluck their sustenance from the land, and place upon the land their beautiful children who, Lord willing, would reap further bounty from a paradise untainted by the stink and dirt of civilization.

Again he thought of Louisa. How naive he had been to think that she could have stood beside him here! How foolish to imagine being a farmer in this violent paradise! Never would he have submitted to the shackles of a plow when the wilderness begged a man to take the best and leave the rest for the scavengers sure to be trailing behind.

What was it Hiram had shouted during the pte hunt? That there were enough buffalo to last forever? So be it, Jed decided. Enough of everything to last forever. The thought grew and grew in his mind and heart, until he felt like crowing with exhilaration.

He leaned back his head and cupped his mouth with his hands. The shout began deep in his gut and rose up, echoing against the trees and distant bluffs. It was the bellow of the great, shaggy pte, the roar of the fierce grizzly, the howl of the wolf, the cry of the cougar. It was the life-sound of all the creatures who lived in the wilderness, for their life-forces all lived in him. He was a man, and the master of all he surveyed. He was a man, and so the wilderness threw itself at his feet, making only one demand in return. That he be strong and wily enough to stay alive. The moment his strength and wiles lapsed, death would find him. But even that was a small price to pay for a few days of freedom. And what better funeral could a man have than for his bones to lie in the green, fresh grass, polished clean by nature, warmed by the savage sun?

Charbonneau slumped down beside him. He was breathing heavily, but his lined face broke into a jaw-splitting grin as he leaned back into the rays of the slowly sinking sun. He had rested but a few moments when he leapt to his feet, tugging at Jed's sleeve. "Hurry! We do not have much light left!"

How far are we going to travel today?" Jed groaned. "Let's camp here!"

"Yes, of course!" Charbonneau laughed. "Not to travel! But to see the surprise! To feast your eyes, boy! Hurry! Leave your pack!"

Jed did as he was told. Rifle in hand, he trotted along after Charbonneau, who scampered ahead, urging Jed on, his elderly body cavorting like a child's. They mounted another, smaller rise, and then splashed through an icy cold stream. Charbonneau led them up and up, over boulders and outcroppings toward the sun, as if they were going to meet it. The journey ended at a cliff. Jed looked down.

Stretching out before him were gently rolling meadows, an endless carpet made of millions of wildflowers. The colors—reddish pink, purple and yellow—overwhelmed him, as if he were staring into the eyes of the Lord Himself. The living blanket of color was bordered on one side by a forest of tall pines, and on the other by rust red cliffs, like the one on which they were standing. Far to the west, beneath an ochre and purple sky flung out like a cape of silk by the setting sun, were the jagged teeth of the Rockies themselves. They sat rigid and defiant, the continent's pride and joy. They rose toward the heavens like the church spires of the whole world.

Jed felt the image of those mountains shivering and burning inside of him, at the same time. He stretched out his arm, and pointed toward them. "There—" he said in a hoarse whisper. "I'm going to live there!"

Charbonneau put his hand on Jed's shoulder. "That is where you will soon be. I wanted you to see them for the first time, like this. I wanted you to see the flowers. For so long you've dreamed of what was waiting for you here. I wanted you to see it finally, like this. When death finds you too soon, sooner than it will find those who hide in the cities, you'll have this to think on as you die."

"And Hiram?" Jed suddenly asked. "Did he?"

"Yes," Charbonneau whispered. He tightened his grip on Jed's shoulder. "He had this to shrink his death down to man-size."

"I give you the mountains," Jed said to himself quietly. "Thank you, Hiram." In his heart, he buried his old friend.

After a few more minutes, Jed and Charbonneau slowly made their way back down the rocky cliff. They hadn't gone a few yards when the shot came rolling and rumbling from the direction of the pine forest. Both Jed and Charbonneau silently stared as the explosion's echo died away against the far cliffs.

"There are no Indians here," Charbonneau began.

Jed shook his head. "That was no *fusil,* but a Hawkens gun. That means trappers." His eyes narrowed as he stared off in the direction of the shot.

"Reckon I have reason to believe Cabanne may be hereabouts."

"Not Cabanne, Jed." Charbonneau was standing very still, his weight perfectly balanced on his feet. His rifle was in his left hand. His right knew the exact position of the knife in his belt. This big, strong, young man he liked so much was hunting something. Charbonneau stood and waited to find out what Jed considered to be his prey.

"He's left his scratchings around the Ree villages," Jed replied. He turned away from the vista to gaze at the old Frenchman. Jed could feel a tension between them. He didn't want the old Frenchman to think that he held a grudge against him by dint of his nationality. There were only two men on earth who had made themselves his enemies: Cabanne and Brazeau. "Toussaint, I mean to kill Cabanne. I reckon he was more the cause of the massacre than I was." Jed quickly filled his companion in on what he had learned from the princess concerning Cabanne and the Ree Guardian. "You're my friend. I can't get you mixed up in this."

"And you are my friend, but he is my countryman," Charbonneau frowned. "Confront him if you must, but I cannot help you in your vendetta."

"Fair enough," Jed said. "What say we go cook ourselves up some elk, and a big pot of coffee?" He held a finger up to the wind. "Breeze is blowing our way. We can make a fire and not have to worry about Cabanne smelling it."

"He will not be alone," Charbonneau warned as they made their way back to the clearing.

"But he won't be with friends, either," Jed smiled. "Reckon he and his kind—" Jed avoided referring to Brazeau by name so as not to offend Charbonneau, "don't believe in free trappers. He'll most likely have himself a few engagés along, but I don't think they'll back him much in a fight."

"And if they do?"

"I mean to kill Cabanne. I owe him a death," Jed said. "If it weren't for him, Hiram and Eddie Rose and fine Jimmy Beck would still be walking the woods. If it weren't for him John Clyman would still have his arm, and General Ashley would have his fifty horses, and maybe even, I'd have my darling Sunblossom by my side."

Charbonneau thought about what Jed had said. "Let us fix our supper, boy. I will make us up some biscuits."

They were silent through much of their meal, content to listen to the natural symphony of the night wind through the trees, the counterpoint of the crickets, and the owls, content to stare up at the clear, velvet sky and let the stars entertain them with their twinkling passion play about what really lasts, and what a man ought to be thinking about during his brief life. The lesson the stars taught was not lost on Jed. As he gazed at them he felt his angry passions gentling.

But he still couldn't banish completely thoughts of the rogue animal who had to be stopped. Cabanne had already twice crossed Jed's path, bringing misery both times. He owed it to his Sunblossom, to the Rees, to mankind, to wipe this madman from the earth. The thought of killing, however, hung very heavy on Jed's mind. Though he'd slain many Rees, he did not want to become known as a man killer, a rogue like Cabanne. The only way to avoid re-enacting the tragedy of Cain and Abel, Jed felt, was to avoid other men entirely, the way the lone wolf stayed clear of the territory of his rivals. This Jed vowed he would do. He would take his Sunblossom and live a solitary, trap-

per's life in the wilderness. After he took care of
Cabanne. . . .

He looked across the fire to where Charbonneau
was sitting quietly, smoking his pipe. They'd each
eaten an elk ham, and split between them one of the
roasts. The other, sizzled crisp, had been packed away
for the next day, along with the extra biscuits. Charbonneau had gathered some berries, and these they'd
eaten for dessert, washed down with black coffee.

"Cabanne's got his hound, you know," Charbonneau suddenly said. "A man like you can sneak up on
another fellow, providing the wind is right, but it is
something else to get the drop on a hound."

Jed pointed to a pile of boughs he had gathered
while Charbonneau was away fetching their berries.
"Fellow I used to know taught me a lot about animals.
When he used to want to gentle a horse, or calm a nervous, birthing cow, he'd rub himself all over with the
straw that beast lived in. I reckon if I smoke my
clothes with that cedar and pine, that old hellhound of
Cabanne's won't smell me coming until it's too late."

Charbonneau grinned in admiration. "Damned if
that will not work. Who taught you that? Not Hiram
Angus?"

"No." Jed stripped off his buckskin shirt and
breeches. He put the cedar and pine boughs on the fire
and waited while they smoldered to produce their pun-
gent smoke.

"Who then?" Charbonneau persisted.

"My brother." Jed draped his clothing over a
green stick and held the garments over the fire, letting
the fumes permeate the leather.

"Well now, he sounds like a fine fellow."

"He is," Jed nodded.

"Two brothers can do very fine in the wild country," Charbonneau mused. "Will he be emigrating West?"

"Don't reckon I'll ever lay eyes on him again," Jed said. "Don't know if I want to. There's more to it." Jed realized with a start that the only man he had told his story to was Hiram Angus and now Hiram was gone. "Don't want to go into it now, Toussaint."

"Bad blood between brothers is a sad thing," Charbonneau offered.

"There wasn't any clear-cut wrong," Jed said. "He didn't do anything bad to me, nor I to him, it just seemed that way from either side. We were both just set on what we wanted. And you always have to pay a price for what you want."

Charbonneau was silent for a moment. Then he began to shuck his own clothing. "Yonder direction is the way we will be going anyway," Charbonneau said. "After you finish with Cabanne, *if* you finish, it makes no sense to double all the way back here for me." He found a green stick of his own, and emulated Jed's actions. "Your fight with Cabanne is your affair, but you are going to need somebody backing you up in case those engagés decide there might be a bonus waiting for the man who back-stabbed you."

"Glad to have your back-up," Jed nodded.

"Welcome to it, Jed."

After they'd dressed, they rubbed the ashes of the cedar boughs on their skin and weapons, put out the fire, and then set off in the direction of the pine forest from which the shot had come. They walked several miles along the darkened cliffs until they found a route which allowed them to descend to the wildflower-filled meadow. At the edge of the forest they paused while Jed sniffed the air.

"I've got their fire," Jed said softly. "And I smell his hound."

"You are sure it is not the scent of wolf?" Charbonneau asked dubiously.

"I'll never forget that dog's scent," Jed muttered.

Charbonneau said nothing, but wished he were a bit younger, so that giving up his pipe could do his sense of smell some good.

Once in the forest the two became more like tracking animals than humans. They hid their packs and rifles, and continued on with only their loaded pistols and knives. The long rifle was too cumbersome to carry through the thick brush, and too slow to point and fire at close quarters.

They slithered through the forest silently. Now Charbonneau could smell the fire and the savory odor of roasted meat. He followed Jed's lead, let Jed do the tracking, while he himself concentrated on the placement of his moccasined feet, and the passage of his agile body through the dark ocean of the pine forest. How young Jed was to be on this mission of vengeance, he thought. And then there would be Brazeau, Young Cayewa himself to kill, should Cabanne be vanquished. Charbonneau was glad he was old. It would be better to die than to have to witness the final battle between these young Americans coming to claim their continent from the Europeans who had seized it. Men like Jed were giants, and they would do battle with the giants they met.

Charbonneau thought back to his younger days, when he and his beloved Sacajawea took Lewis and Clark to the Pacific. The Spaniards settled along the coast assumed the Rocky Mountains would protect them from the men in the East, but they were Europeans and had grown up round-shouldered from sharing their continent, from sharing their space. The young American giants were not interested in sharing. They wanted it all, and they would have it all. Jed would scale those mountains, and over the years others like Jedediah Smith would come to scale and live in them, until, ultimately, the mountains would become tame, and then the thousands of small, mean-spirited men would bring in their families in order to fence-in, taint and spoil the wilderness.

The giants would perish. First Brazeau, but soon, Jed Smith as well. The giants would be chopped down by men with deeds in their pockets, just as the forests would be chopped down. But until that day a man's spirit was all, and the food was for the taking, and the only laws were the laws of God and nature, and maybe these two were the same thing after all. Someday the world would lose its giants, but that day was far off, God willing. For now, Charbonneau was glad to be among them. He was glad to be a wilderness man.

Ahead, Jed paused. Charbonneau slid up behind him.

"Could Cabanne have a Ree war party escorting him?" Jed whispered. "I smell Ree."

"Not likely," Charbonneau frowned.

Jed nodded, unconvinced. "Stay here. I'll come back for you. I think they're close by."

He traveled for nearly a mile, being careful to keep the breeze blowing into his face, relying upon his senses of sight, hearing and smell, remembering all that Jimmy Beck had told him, remembering to be the wolf that thought like a rabbit.

Soon he saw the glow of their fire just ahead. Jed froze. He spent long minutes hunkered down, watching for any sign that they were aware of him. The hound was lying on its side close by the warm embers. His ears twitched in some dream, but not once did the big head lift up, or the ugly snout point in Jed's direction.

Jed moved to get a better look at the number and placement of men. He spied Cabanne's huge bulk, his

back against a pack, his legs wrapped in a robe. Three
other men formed a semi-circle closeby. A jug of skull
varnish was making the rounds between them. Jed
could see the glowing tips of twigs wavering in the air
like fireflies as the men lit and re-lit their smoking
pipes.

What Jed saw next set his heart to pounding, and
pushed hot rage up into his temples until he had to
close his eyes against the dizzying, whirling anger.
Sunblossom lay on her back, her arms cruelly pinioned
behind her, so that her body was arched on her own
wrists. Her skirt was rumpled, and up around her
thighs.

Cabanne had taken his woman and used her.
Killed her? Jed saw himself rushing into the camp. The
hound would be on his back in a second, but before its
teeth could bite through his neck he would wrench the
Frenchman's head clear off his shoulders with his bare
hands.

It was a vivid picture. Every fiber of his being
longed to make it happen. He had to clench his fists
and wage a more difficult, private battle against this
dumb male rage. She had not moved. He could only
hope she was still alive. Dark patches of dried dirt, or
blood, encrusted her legs, and her mouth. He would
now have to find a way to kill his four enemies, all
of whom had had a hand in her misery.

He watched and prayed. As if in answer to his
plea to God, her contorted body moved, but so slightly
that he thought the sight was merely the product of his
heart's devout wish. No! She was alive! One leg rose
and bent. The fire's light traced the supple line of her
thigh, and the slender rounded strength of her calf.

He nodded a silent thanks to the Lord, and
slipped back into the shadows, back through the forest
to Charbonneau.

The Frenchman revealed no expression as he listened to Jed's horrific tale. Charbonneau had seen much in his years in the wilderness, and he knew much about Cabanne. He said only four words in reply. "I will help you."

Jed looked into his eyes. "He's your countryman."

"Nationalities cease to be important," Charbonneau growled. "He has made himself into an animal. Now we will make him dead."

Jed did not insult his comrade with awkward, mumbled expressions of gratitude. "He's my meat. I mean to have his scalp. I'll kill him, and another. You'll have to be responsible for the other two."

"You are forgetting the hound," Charbonneau warned. "The hound is the equal of two men. I have seen this. You must believe me."

"I'll kill the dog," Jed said impatiently. "The dog is mine, I'll skin its fur." Every moment they waited was another moment in which Cabanne could kill Sunblossom.

"Your way will kill the princess," Charbonneau told him. "She will be among the first to die, Cabanne will see to that. Do not underestimate him. If you do, your woman will die."

Jed fought the impulse to tear away from this old man and do the job alone. And yet, what Charbonneau was saying was true; Sunblossom would be the first to suffer in a quick, savage fight. He felt like a swarm of hornets finding out that their nest had been torn apart. He fought for patience and asked, "What do you suggest?"

Tooth's head rose snarling. The hound leapt to his feet and stared intently into the shadowy silhouettes of the pines outside the faint circle of light cast by the campfire.

Cabanne and his men looked in the direction the dog was facing. Each man had his hand on a weapon. They had initially taken Tooth's alarm on faith, but now they could hear that whatever it was that was approaching, it certainly made a lot of noise. They had each long ago learned that in the wilderness, death tended to come on silent feet.

"Cabanne!" Charbonneau shouted. "*J'ai soif!* Drink! I am thirsty! Drink!" As he approached he was careful to keep his rifle pointed toward the sky.

Tooth roared a challenge and lunged. "*Non,* Tooth!" Cabanne commanded, stopping the dog in his tracks. "Toussaint?" Cabanne called, clearly astounded. "*C'est impossible!* Where did you come from?" he asked, elatedly. "Quick!" he babbled to his men, throwing down his fusil to snatch at the jug of skull-varnish. He tossed it to Charbonneau, who had slumped down by the fire.

"*Je suis fatigue,*" Charbonneau sighed heavily. He murmured a few words to Tooth, and the hound began to thump his tail against the ground. He took a swig of the skull-varnish, grimacing as the harsh liquid burned its way down his throat. "*Have you cognac, s'il vous plaît?*" he grinned.

"*Non,*" Cabanne smiled. Thoughts of cognac reminded him of the pleasures and rewards waiting back at Fort Kiowa. And Charbonneau was a good man to have on one's side in a fight. "*I am happy to see you, Toussaint—*"

All of his men still held their weapons, Cabanne saw. He realized that they did not yet comprehend that Toussaint was not a foe. "This man is Toussaint Charbonneau!"

"Well, well, is that who it is?" Teddy eyed the old fellow speculatively. He'd never seen Charbonneau before, but the man's reputation was legendary.

"Give him food!" Cabanne ordered. "What do you wish, my friend? We have meat—" he began to laugh, gesturing toward the princess who was sitting up to stare sullenly at the newcomer. "We even have a woman for you, Toussaint!" Cabanne's expression grew thoughtful. "Have you been long on our trail, my friend?"

"Long enough to know that the Rees have not yet caught up to you," Charbonneau said. "Else I would not be joining your party." He refused the chunk of roast proffered by one of the men, and took another swig from the jug. "Have you gone mad, Cabanne? You have stolen Bear's daughter. She could be none other, what with that yellow hair of hers."

"She is a fine trophy, yes?" Cabanne chuckled. "And a sweet woman. . . ."

"As long as her hands are tied," Teddy remarked, to the laughter of the others. "One of the boys tried to take her with her arms loose, and she damn neared plucked out his eyes!"

"Where are your horses?" Charbonneau asked. "How did you lose them?"

Cabanne glowered. "Enough! Tell me now why you are here. The last I saw of you was when I left Kiowa. Why did you journey upriver?"

"Young Cayewa gave me my instructions," Charbonneau began. "I was to join the Americans, claiming that I no longer wanted to toil for the French cause. I was to spy on them, and confuse and confound their cause whenever possible. By reason of my experience, I was able to become a confidant of their leader, General Ashley. I escaped with the survivors of the Ree attack upon their camp."

"Poor Toussaint," Cabanne chuckled. "You could have been killed."

"I still could be," Charbonneau frowned. "And

you as well, but not as pleasantly as a man dies in battle. Why did you take the princess?"

"To punish the Ree Guvner, and to confound a certain American," Cabanne said.

"Jed Smith?"

"Yes," Cabanne nodded. "You did your spying well, I see."

Charbonneau shrugged. "The boy made no secret of his affection for the princess." He looked at her. Her eyes were wildly darting from his face to Cabanne's at the mention of Jed's name. She was dirty, but he could see that her injuries were slight. She'd been slapped a bit, but no worse. "Have you and all your men had her?" he asked.

"All." Cabanne grunted in satisfaction.

"And you are not concerned about Jed Smith, or the Rees?"

"The Rees are far behind us," Cabanne muttered. "I look forward to taking the American's scalp."

"Want to take it now?" Charbonneau smiled. "I left him a mile back. The fool thinks I am at this moment preparing to cut the woman loose of her bonds. He thinks that I could betray a fellow Frenchman. Shall we go kill Jed Smith now, Cabanne?"

"*Avec plaisir!*" Cabanne gloated. "Ah, Toussaint! Cayewa will reward you handsomely for this!" He jumped to his feet. "Teddy, take the others and——"

"No, my friend," Charbonneau said. "Too much noise. Jed Smith is no greenhorn. Just you and me. Just the two of us. Any more coming along and he would be warned."

"Very well," Cabanne nodded. "Teddy, you and the others will stay here to guard the camp, and the princess." Fusil in hand, Cabanne followed Charbonneau into the darkness beyond the campsite.

*   *   *

Jed crawled up close to the camp. Where were
Cabanne and Charbonneau? The plan had been for
Toussaint to seem to try to force himself on the
princess, and using the protective cover of his embrace
to slide the knife into her bound hands. He was to
whisper the Ree phrase Jed had taught him: *"Wait for
a sign!"* Charbonneau was to make her understand that
soon the time would be right for her to free herself.
Her life would still be in danger during the ambush,
but at least she would have freedom of movement,
and a blade with which to defend herself. It was a
slight advantage, Charbonneau had argued, but the
best that could be done for her. And it just might be
enough to make the difference between her living or
dying.

There was no Charbonneau, no Cabanne, and no
hound. There were just the princess and the three men
left in the camp, and while Jed was confident of his
ability to take three men in an ambush situation, he
was less certain about this outcome, for all three were
sitting up with their rifles in their laps. He couldn't
even assume that Sunblossom had been given the knife.

One of the trappers set down his rifle and got to
his feet. He pulled a knife instead of his pistol from his
belt. "She'll make good cover for us, should the fellow
doubleback on Cabanne and come here," he told the
others.

"Good thinking, Teddy," one of them said. "Put
her right in the middle. That'll stop anybody from
sharp-shootin us."

Jed slid his knife from its sheath and slipped it
between his teeth. He drew both pistols and eased back
the hammers as one of them spoke.

"Reckon we ought to put out this here fire, as
well." One of them slapped a robe over the embers.

Jed slid forward. He was less than ten feet away

from them now, but he knew that the tree trunks protected him, that they could not see him as long as he lay stock still. But once he raised himself and swung the pistols up to aim, they'd spy his movement. But by then, God willing, it would be too late for them to bring their own rifles up to their shoulders. He'd shoot the two near the glowing embers, and throw his blade at the other. Even if he missed the one standing over Sunblossom, it would at least bring the odds down to one on one. This fellow named Teddy was big, but his size didn't bother Jed as much as the pistol in the man's belt.

As Teddy bent to grab hold of Sunblossom's hair, she twisted around on her back to drive her heel into his groin.

"Damn whore!" Teddy gasped in pain, clutching at himself. The other two men laughed.

Jed brought up both guns and fired. He saw the two swivel their heads his way as the reports shattered the night. He didn't look at them but let his empty pistols fall to the ground as he swung about, ready to throw his blade.

Except that the man wasn't there.

Jed stood crouched in an agony of indecision. He longed to rush into the camp to free Sunblossom, but that would expose him to the knife and pistol of the other man. He darted in anyway, leaping over the embers, to land between the two he had shot. One was quite dead, the ball having caught him in the throat, but the other was twitching and coughing, blindly reaching for the stock of his rifle. The bullet had hit him high in the belly.

His eyes swiveling in their sockets for a sign of the third, Jed quickly thrust his knife through the heart of the survivor.

"Where did the other go?" he demanded of

Sunblossom as he ran to her, and slit the leather thong
binding her wrists.

"He jumped that way!" she pointed. "Into the
forest!"

"Cabanne? And the other? The old one, with hair
the color of yours?"

"Gone there!" She pointed in the opposite direction.

"Come on!" He pulled her to her feet and half
carried her from the camp, stopping only to collect the
weapons of the three men and his own pistols.

Cabanne whirled around at the sound of Jed's pistols. "He has doubled-back upon us!" Cabanne swore.
"Hurry, Toussaint!"

"Stand very, very still, my friend," Charbonneau
warned. He swung his Hawkens gun up toward the
other's head.

"It was a ruse?" he whispered in disbelief. "Toussaint?"

"You are my countryman," Charbonneau said.
"What I am doing is pulling a ruse on Jed Smith. Let
the fusil fall to the ground, my friend. And your
knives."

Cabanne shrugged, to let the leather thong of the
sawed-off shotgun slide from his shoulder. The weapon
fell heavily to the earth. "You will kill me?" One by
one, he dropped his blades.

"No. I give you your life this one time, animal,"
Charbonneau spat. "I am saving you from Jed, this
time, although he will find you eventually. But that
will not be my concern. For France, for Young
Cayewa, I spare you. Run now! Run!"

"Toussaint," Cabanne pleaded. "With no weapons,
nothing?"

"You have your hound," Charbonneau chuckled.

Some yards away, a branch snapped.

"Run, Cabanne!" Charbonneau hissed. "That could be Jed Smith! He will have *your* scalp!"

Cabanne lumbered off, Tooth at his heels. Charbonneau watched them disappear into the dark. Without a gun or blade Cabanne would not attempt to ambush them. He hoped Jed had the presence of mind to collect the weapons of the three he had killed. That Jed had indeed killed all three, Charbonneau had no doubt.

There was the sound of somebody coming his way. Another twig cracked, this time from behind him. Charbonneau frowned.

Jed would never make such noise—

Charbonneau heard the hiss and spark and twisted away as the pistol exploded its ball, but he wasn't quick enough. The impact of the bullet crashing into his back made him jerk the trigger of his rifle. He cursed as the heavy ball slammed impotently into the earth.

Teddy crashed through the brush as Charbonneau collapsed. He threw down his pistol and advanced with his drawn blade. "I'll take your scalp, you damned traitor!" he screamed in rage.

Charbonneau thrust out his arm, and found Cabanne's fusil. He brought the little shotgun up, and snapped back the hammer.

Teddy stopped dead. He brought up both his hands, letting the knife drop, and tried to back pedal away. "No . . ." he began to whine.

Charbonneau pulled the trigger. The blast lifted Teddy up, and slammed him back as if he'd been caught in a gale-force wind. He fluttered to the ground, quite dead, with a large, ragged, bloody hole where his chest had been.

*　　*　　*

Cabanne paused. "Teddy!" he bellowed. There came no answer, and without a weapon, he was not about to investigate the outcome of the short-pitched battle he'd just heard. He considered his situation. Without weapons, attempting to reach Fort Kiowa was out of the question. He would return to the camp, on the slight hope that something of use could be scavaged from whatever had been left. Then he would head back toward the Ree villages. He could quite easily tell the Ree Guvner a self-serving version of the events that had taken place. Jed Smith most likely had the princess by now, and that was perfect for his story. . . .

He silently made his way through the woods, his dog beside him. He was alive, and that was what mattered in the wilderness. He was alive, and as long as that was so, he could kill. . . .

Charbonneau let the fusil fall to the ground. He could feel the blood seeping out of the hole in his back, but could feel nothing at all beneath his waist. He wondered if he could just possibly stay alive until Jed found him, just so that he could explain to the boy why he'd allowed Cabanne to escape. If he could just be allowed the time to explain. . . . He was certain the boy would understand.

If Jed had any sense at all, he'd hole up somewhere until dawn. That was what he himself would do in such a situation. Hole up with his woman. God! What he wouldn't trade for the knowledge of whether Jed had indeed saved the woman!

"If you did, marry her boy," he whispered. His only audience was an owl perched in the low branch of a pine so tall it seemed to taper off somewhere past Heaven. "Marry her. Don't let her put any foolish notions about her being spoiled into your head. That's just dumb, heathen pride. Don't listen to it! Marry her. . . ."

He thought about his own woman, gone for ever so long now. . . . That damn squaw had made him famous! He had to smile about it. It'd be good to see her again, although life was getting ever sweeter now that it was ending, and it would be sweetest of all to make it to the sunrise.

This wasn't going to be such a bad death. There was no pain, after all. He wished he could get a glimpse of the stars. But the roofing of pine was too dense. . . .

He decided to leave a message of sorts for Jed. With his palm he smoothed away as many twigs and pine cones as he could manage. There didn't seem to be much grass here, and the ground felt fairly hard-packed. It might serve. . . .

With the tip of his knife he traced the words: HAD TO FOR FRANCE. He doubted if it was legible, but what the hell, it had made him feel better.

He was swimming in the sparkling, blue waters of the Pacific when he died.

Chapter 27

Seven songs were composed by the Arikaras to tell the stories of what had happened when Grey Eyes, Guardian of the nation, was told that the daughter of Guardian Bear had been stolen. No brave but Little Soldier had the courage to confront the Guardian with the evidence.

Grey Eyes gazed down at the two knives. One was a skinning blade of Arikara design. It was the princess' weapon and tool. The other was a white's wide, curved implement, razor sharp on both edges. The knives had been found in the field, along with signs of a struggle. The princess had evidently drawn her blade to defend herself, forcing the white to drop his, but his brute strength had prevailed. She had been stolen.

That story makes the first song.

All of the nation stood silent and trembling as they listened in shock to the anguished wail that came from the Guardian's lodge. Grey Eyes howled and moaned for hours, and those of the nation who had the courage to peek into his lodge said that he cried like a child and tore at his hair the way squaws will when their warrior husbands come home stiff and dead. The older warriors took up their heavily laden coup poles and carried them to the perimeters of the nation. There they shook their poles into the sky to ward off the threat to the Arikara people. Still, the younger braves shook their heads, and the pregnant women weeped for their unborn babies. Grey Eyes was their Guardian. He was their priest, their judge, their calendar, their clock. He was the core of their nation. As they listened to him cry, they knew that their nation was sick in its heart.

That story makes the second song.

The three Shadows had since departed to bring death to the two whites, but now that it was known that the whites had taken the princess with them, the warriors and elders were thrown into a quandary. Shadows could not rescue, but only kill. What would happen when they took the lives of the whites, and then were confronted with the stolen princess? Would they recognize her? Would they be able to stop themselves from killing her? And if they could, how would she survive the trek back to the nation, unescorted, perhaps injured, or at the very least, weakened by her ordeal? The Shadows certainly could not bring her home. They were no longer human, they had sacrificed their humanity and let death become their souls in the service of their nation. The elders looked at each other and scratched their heads. The warriors stood about staring down at the ground. This crisis of spirit, this question of theology, this challenge to Arikara doctrine, to the pure sanctity of the most sacred of spells, confounded everyone. Only one of the nation could say what would happen, but instead of meditating upon the conundrum, he hid in his lodge and sobbed.

That story makes the third song.

Little Soldier, Second to the Guardian, and Ranking Brave of the nation, was powerless in this sit-

uation. If the Guardian should die, the Ranking Brave
knew what to do. If the Guardian should give up his
white feathers the Ranking Brave knew what to do.
But there was no law covering what was to be done
when the Guardian merely hid and cried. Now Little
Soldier was a wise brave. His heart was perhaps not as
pure, and his spirit not as strong as Grey Eyes', but he
was a superb warrior, and had many times proven himself a fine military tactician in conflicts with other
tribes. He understood the threat to the nation in terms
of a "trappers' war"—the surviving whites would bring
others of their pack to combat the nation, and the
Arikara warriors would have to fight the fierce whites
without the benefit of knowing that they had a strong,
righteous Guardian, without the benefit of knowing
that the nation's heart was sound. Little Soldier went to
Bear, who was old and infirm, stricken with grief himself over the theft of his daughter, but nevertheless, still
an Arikara Guardian.

"Bear, Guardian of the nation," Little Soldier de-
claimed. "The nation is soulless; the nation has no
heart. Grey Eyes weeps like a babe, you weep like one
ready for the grave. The sacred office is held by an in-
fant and an old man. I am young and strong, and can
confront the danger that threatens. I bid you, hand over
the white feathers."

All the nation held its breath, for such an auda-
cious request had never before been made by a
Ranking Brave to a Guardian.

"You have no respect for tradition," accused
Bear. "This is not the way things are done. In the
past—"

"You are no longer hearing the sound of *now*,"
Little Soldier softly said.

The chill which ran up and down Bear's crooked
spine made him realize that Little Soldier was right.

The old Guardian thanked the new. He knelt at Little Soldier's feet, and as the warrior-brave plucked the white feathers from Bear's thin, grey hair, he announced that he was Little Soldier, Ranking Brave no longer, but Little Soldier, Guardian of the Arikara nation.

The Elders quickly nodded their blessings as Little Soldier placed the white feathers in his own hair. Times were strange, but they had no desire to be left behind.

That story makes the fourth song.

Grey Eyes had become silent in his lodge. He was now like a turtle hiding in his shell. Little Soldier was indeed Guardian at long last, but he was not one to let the honor go to his head, making him foolish. Little Soldier knew that the white feathers in his hair meant only as much as the loyalty, obedience and obeisance they could garner for him from the people. A lesser man would have stamped his feet like a dumb, wild pony. A lesser man would not have understood that the thoughts of every Arikara were with the silent one hidden away in his lodge. Since Grey Eyes had ended his loud lament, no one had found the courage to again look into the lodge. Who knew what Grey Eyes had become? What sort of demon was now lurking in the shadows of his residence? Little Soldier wondered much the same thing, but he was no coward, and the white feathers demanded that he confront Grey Eyes before he attempted to issue any decrees to the nation.

"Grey Eyes! Come out!" Little Soldier hollered. He strode up to the door of the lodge and did a war dance, his moccasins pawing at the earth, and his head dipping and rearing like a bull pte issuing a challenge.

The elders were once again shocked, but hindsight later revealed that such was Little Soldier's intent. The nation was fevered. The fever had to be broken.

"Grey Eyes!" Little Soldier hollered. "Come out and pay your respects to the Guardian of the Arikara nation!"

That story makes the fifth song.

Grey Eyes came out. A huge circle had formed around his lodge, but as he pushed open his door and stepped out into the sunlight, the circle moved back, the way ripples in the river ever-widen from the point at which the tossed stone plunges into the water. Grey Eyes' long hair hung in his face. His torso was criss-crossed with long, open wounds; he had rent his own flesh, and had rubbed dirt and stinging herbs into the wounds so as to keep the pain alive. The white feathers of his office were in his hand. They were crumpled and broken. Grey Eyes gently lay them down upon the ground.

He stood straight and tall, and the eyes in his head rolled back so that only the whites showed. Like a monster's eyes they were!

He shuddered and shook like a puppet on strings, and there slowly grew on his face a hideous grin. Like a monster's leer it was!

Then Grey Eyes began to laugh. That was the most frightening thing: to hear his loud, deep, clear voice, the voice that had always been a succor to his nation.

Grey Eyes drew his knife. He slowly gouged a deep line into his wrist, but no blood flowed! He drove the point of his knife clear through the palm of his hand, but when he withdrew it the blade came out as clean and dry as if driven into dead earth, dead straw, dead wood, dead leather.

The elders moaned and the mothers covered the eyes of their children. Even Little Soldier hastily retreated, his face as pale as the snow. Well they knew this sign.

"People of the Arikara nation!" Grey Eyes roared. "I am Shadow!"

That is the story of the sixth song.

That is the story Arikara mothers told to their naughty children when they wanted them to behave. It is indeed a horrid thing to contemplate a man so miserable and torn by his passions that he could turn himself into Shadow without the aid of complex, sacred ritual. That death could embrace a man without formal invitation being issued through the nation's meditation and ceremonies. That a man's sorrow could be so deep that death—unaided—could find him and settle in, the way a swarm of bees settles into a hollow log.

"Don't do this, and don't do that," Arikara mothers would scold. "Else Death will come grab you, little one. Else Death will see how naughty you are, and make your body its lodge, as it did with Grey Eyes." The children would shiver and shake and certainly then behave.

And so did the Arikaras deal with the awfulness of what had happened to Grey Eyes. Thus they tamed the terror, clipped its claws and pulled its fangs, and relegated it—spanked—to the nursery. The terror rolled among the children. At night, it held their eyes wide, but at least it kept them quiet.

All that, of course, was when there still were Arikara mothers; when there still were Arikara children.

The seventh song concerns itself with what took place after Grey Eyes, as Shadow, gathered bow and blade and rode off in pursuit of the man who had possession of Sunblossom. This last, greatest Shadow had no worry that the three previously sent would succeed in killing the white, named Jed Smith. This Jed Smith was his, just as he now belonged to Jed Smith.

The seventh song concerns itself with the many

sides of the circle of passions formed by the union of male and female. Desire and regret, devotion and betrayal, bitterness and sweetness. Who knows where a circle begins and ends?

The seventh song concerns itself with the beginning of the end of the Arikara nation. It tells of a wave of whites dressed in blue, a blue wave so wide it was as if the sky itself had come down to wage war against the Arikaras.

In the song the whites have big thunder-guns which ride on wheels. Many warriors die. Grey Eyes' vision comes true.

The seventh song is very long. No one knows if this is so because so many things happened, or because the Arikara song-weavers instinctively knew that when the seventh song ended, there would be no others.

All seven songs were always sung together. A refrain separated each one from the next:

" 'People of the Arikara nation," *Grey Eyes roared.* "I am Shadow!' "

PART FOUR

THE SEVENTH SONG

Chapter 28

Fort Atkinson's bustling noises faded from Colonel Henry Leavenworth's mind as he pondered General Ashley's letter, brought to him by the man now standing before him.

Tom Talbot, his wispy hair falling into his eyes, stood bashful as a barefoot boy in front of the assemblage. His eyes flicked from the impassive face of the military commander to the pair of strangers occupying the arm chairs that Jed and General Ashley had sat in so many months ago.

"And so you left them there, at the mercy of the Rees," Leavenworth finally said, the ends of his handlebar moustache dipping down with his frown, like a pair of sabers. "Ashley and—" he looked down at the sheet of paper which rested on his vast expanse of belly. "—Twenty odd men, not to mention the wounded."

"Y-yes, sir," Talbot squeaked, wishing he were back on the river, any river. Damn, he should have read the letter beforehand to make sure that there was nothing in it that might cost him his hide. . . . *Well, Tommy, boy,* he thought to himself, *time to think quick and talk faster.* "Well, you see how it is, Colonel,

we figured that the only chance our poor boys 'ud
have, consider'n that theys were not about to come
back with me, was for me to git here and tell you about
it all right fast, so's that you cud rescue them . . . , Sir."

"Sergeant!"

Tom Talbot flinched as Leavenworth shouted.

There was silence in the Colonel's rough-hewn office as the four waited for the sergeant. Leavenworth
stood abruptly, the gold buttons of his uniform straining to keep his blue tunic closed across his stomach,
and bellowed impatiently again, "Sergeant!"

"On the way, sir!" came a faint voice from somewhere beyond the half-shut, oak plank door of the office.

As long as he was up, Leavenworth figured it
would do to pin-point the Ashley-Henry expedition's
position on the river. He turned to his map. "Would
you say they're about here, Talbot?"

Tom looked at the barren beige, upon which the
sky-blue strand which must be the Missouri, meandered upward. Leavenworth was pointing at a spot
about three inches below a painted-in, large tepee of a
sort Talbot had never seen. "That ud be about right,
Colonel. You really can't miss 'em. Theys on the river,
you see."

"Ah, thank you for joining us, Sergeant," Leavenworth remarked to the tall, bearded soldier who appeared in the doorway. He entered to stand just behind
Talbot.

Tom glanced back at the fellow hovering over
him. "Is I under arrest, Colonel?" he meekly asked.

Leavenworth regarded the patron. "You deserted
your employer. Left him and his surviving men in the
wilderness, at the mercy of wild beasts and savages!"

"But we agreed—" Talbot began.

"Silence!" Leavenworth thundered.

"Yes, sir," Talbot whined. He resumed staring at the floor.

"However, you did indeed bring me word of the expedition's plight. That counts in your favor, Mr. Talbot."

"Colonel. I swear that General Ashley is alive and well, and that I begged him to come along with us. Ask any of my crew. I certainly did—" Talbot beamed at the commander. "And I'd do anything reasonable to help him out."

"Splendid, Mr. Talbot," Leavenworth nodded. "Sergeant, escort Mr. Talbot back to the guard house."

"How long you gonna hold me and my boys?" Talbot groaned. "We ain't done no wrong—"

"Sergeant?"

The big soldier saluted, and clamping a firm hand on Talbot's collar, jerked him away toward the door.

"And ask Lieutenant O'Fallon to join us, would you?" Leavenworth added. The sergeant nodded and left the office, prisoner in tow.

Leavenworth sighed and pulled open the side drawer of his desk. He removed a half-empty bottle of brandy and three none-too-clean glasses, pulled the cork on the bottle with his teeth, and poured out three generous measures of the liquor. He came around to the front of the desk, a glass in each hand, and offered one to the nearest of his guests. "Mr. Pilcher?"

"Don't mind iffen I do," the lanky, hawk-nosed, trapper said. The glass disappeared in his ham-like, calloused hand.

Colonel Leavenworth offered the second glass to his other guest. "Monsieur Brazeau? I do apologize for it not being the fine cognac of your native land," he said ingratiatingly.

Brazeau dipped his head politely. The tight skin of

his bald scalp glistened ivory-yellow in the sunlight coming through the office's window.

Josh Pilcher drained his glass and got up to set it on Leavenworth's desk. He was six-feet, two-inches tall, and weighed in at two-forty. His deerskin shirt and pants were fringed, and his wide, leather belt squeaked against the brace of pistols tucked at his waist as he paced the length of the office. The floorboards beneath his moccasins groaned at his weight. When he spoke for any length of time, his voice broke. This incongruous, high-pitched change in tone made Pilcher sound like an adolescent on the verge of becoming a man, but few dared laugh when his voice so cracked. The damage to his larynx had come about when a big bitch of a wolf had clamped her jaws on his neck. She'd had her back leg caught in one of Pilcher's traps, and so was mad but relatively immobile. He'd managed to wrestle free. The story goes that he then gave the bitch as good as he got. With one hand he muzzled shut her jaws, pointed her snout up toward the sun, and locked his own teeth into her exposed neck, tearing out her throat.

"Well now, Colonel," Pilcher began. "When my boys became the Rees' meat, you said yer hands was tied. You gonna let Ashley's boys go the same way, or are you gonna do somethin' about it?"

Leavenworth pondered the situation. Sorely tempted as he was to lead a punitive expedition against the Rees, two things stood in his way. First of all, he had no mandate from Washington for such an action. Second, he had virtually no experience as an Indian fighter, although he did covet the reputation of being such. "Monsieur Brazeau? What do you say?"

Brazeau smiled. "As an agent of France, I hesitate to become involved in a matter between the United

States and its citizens. However, the Rees *are* a nuisance. . . ."

Pilcher stomped over to Leavenworth's desk. "Except yer boys seems to get along fine with the heathens, Cayewa," he snorted. "Why is that, do you think?" He hefted the brandy bottle and glanced inquiringly at Leavenworth, who nodded, holding out his own glass for a refill. "Jest why do you think that Rees war party went by yer Fort Kiowa to wipe out my outpost?"

Brazeau remained silent. His impassive features revealed nothing. He drained the last of the brandy from his glass, but shook his head at the offer of more.

"I asked you a question, Cayewa," Josh hissed.

"And I have chosen not to answer it," Brazeau barked. The thick cords of his neck stood out in his anger. "I do not answer Americans' questions. I am an agent of the French government and have immunity from American authority. Is that not so, Colonel Leavenworth? Has not your own Commander-in-Chief, President Monroe, informed you to that effect?"

"He has," Leavenworth droned.

Pilcher drained his glass, and slammed it down on the desk. He confronted Brazeau, pointing a thick, blunt finger into the Frenchman's face. "One of these days, Cayewa, one of these days you'll be goin' back to that there Frenchie government o' yers, in a box. Iffen President Monroe don't like that, he can jest pull on a pair of buckskins and come tell me about it."

"Mr. Pilcher," Colonel Leavenworth warned. "I must ask that you refrain from threatening Mr. Brazeau. As an officer of the United States Army, it is my duty to protect diplomatic personnel." The Commander tried to catch Pilcher's eye. He hoped that the tone of his voice had made it clear that he was on the side of his fellow American.

"I do not need your protection, Colonel Leavenworth," Brazeau snarled. His hand rested on the metal-capped butt of the pistol in his belt.

"Gentlemen, I did not call you here to argue," Leavenworth said. "Monsieur Brazeau, I ask you, man to man. What is your feeling concerning a punitive expedition against the Rees, mounted from this fort?"

Brazeau thought about it. Pilcher, for all of his loud talk, was finished as competition in the fur trade. Brazeau's own men could move in and claim Pilcher's trap lines as their own. That left only two other presences on the river: the Ashley-Henry expedition and the Rees. Brazeau had no doubt that he and Cabanne—along with Fort Kiowa's engagés—could dispose of the former, and here was the United States Government, graciously asking his permission to wipe out the latter! With the Rees gone, the entire river's treasure would soon belong to France. Let the fools here hold official title to it. France would reap the furs. . . . "Colonel Leavenworth, I totally agree that the Ree situation has gotten out of hand. As an outsider, I can only hope that you will see fit to punish them for their violent ways."

Leavenworth nodded, satisfied. "So I can count on your official support of my actions, should Washington question them?"

"My good Colonel," Brazeau drawled. "I will go so far as write to my people in your capital, expressing my full support and gratitude for the way you are protecting both the interests of your own country, and France." He paused as a twisted grin came to his thick lips. "Indeed, I have one hundred men to lend to the cause. My engagés will fight side by side with your men."

"And that'll mean you'll share in the fur plunder taken from the Rees," Pilcher said.

Brazeau only shrugged as Leavenworth said,

"Well, that's all right, Josh. He's entitled to a share if he helps. And I'll need your help as a guide. . . ."

Pilcher nodded. "Too damn late to do my company any good, but a share of the Rees' furs could keep me from goin' bankrupt. But I'd do it jest for the plain joy of slaughterin' them heathens they way they slaughtered my boys. Count me in, Colonel."

There was a knock at the door, and a young, blond-haired soldier entered, lieutenant's bars on his shoulders, a saber rattling at his waist. He came to attention as he centered himself precisely in front of Leavenworth's desk. His salute was razor sharp.

The Colonel nodded in appreciation. He leaned back in his chair and spoke slowly, savoring every word. He'd dreamed of issuing such orders for a long, long time. "First off, son, I want you to tell Talbot and his scum that I'm impressing them into the service of the United States Army. They'll serve as our crews else I'll hang them for attempted murder . . . or something. . . ." Leavenworth eyed his young officer. "Got that, son?"

"Sir!" O'Fallon had some inkling of what was coming next and positively clicked his heels with joy.

"We're moving on the Ree villages, son. I want five—no—make it six regiments. Just leave a few men here to keep the peace. We'll be bringing all five six-pounders, and—what have we got? Three howitzers?"

"Three five-and-a-half inchers, sir."

"We'll take em as well. Now, we've got Talbot's *Yellowstone Packet,* but we'll need several other keelboats. There's a few sitting at the docks, their owners waiting for somebody to be able to meet their price. I want you to commandeer them. Tell the owners it's official U.S. business. If they complain, tell 'em we're at war. If they still complain, throw 'em in the guard house."

"Yes, sir!" O'Fallon beamed. This would mean captain's bars for him, for sure!

"Impress any other crewmen you find loitering about the grog-shops and whorehouses. We're going to need them." He looked over at Pilcher. "Josh, how long will it take us to get there?"

The trapper's brow furrowed. "Reckon about twenty-odd days, iffen we don't get sunk by all that heavy gunnery a yers," he chuckled.

"You heard him, son. Supplies for twenty, make it thirty days, each way of course." The Colonel reached for the brandy bottle and refilled the three glasses on his desk. When he looked up, the lieutenant was still standing at attention, his expectant face focused, staring back at him. "Well, run along, son," Leavenworth said mildly. "I want to be off in a day or so." He smiled at Pilcher and Brazeau. "Gentlemen, a toast? Oh! Lieutenant!"

O'Fallon paused in the doorway and looked back. "Sir?"

Leavenworth gestured with his glass toward his own saber, resting against the wall in the corner behind his desk. "Have a man come get that and sharpen it, will you son? Hell of a thing, a man going off to war with a blunt sword. . . ."

Chapter 29

Sunblossom was the first to find the corpses the next morning. They decided to look separately for the possible victims of last night's shots. Ted was certain they'd find Cabanne's body, but the *fusil* shot had greatly worried him. The gun belonged to Cabanne.

A swarm of buzzing flies on the other side of a bush attracted Sunblossom's attention. She cocked her rifle as she approached. There was no telling if predators or scavengers had been attracted like the flies as well. All last night, while she sat huddled by Jed's side, unable to sleep, she'd listened to the mournful howls of the wolves. Bears and jackals also lived in this forest.

She first came upon the body of the one who had helped Cabanne take her from the villages' growing field, the man with the ravaged face. Now his body was ravaged as well—torn apart by the fusil's blast and infested with flies. She was glad of that. This white had taken her most brutally. After Cabanne, that was. No one, or nothing could have been as brutal as Cabanne. He'd put his full weight upon her, his fingers wrenching a handful of her bruised and tender belly to make her surrender. He'd pried apart her legs, and roughly thrust into her. She wondered if she could ever again close her eyes and not see his coarse, bearded face. Could she ever forget the stench of his fetid body, and his foul breath? He was a monster.

She turned away from the white's body, and stumbled upon the old one, the one Jed had said was their friend.

He was lying there in a manner which suggested he had died in peace. This pleased her, for Jed thought well of him. He would be sorry when he saw that his comrade was dead.

She gave the call that Jed had taught her and waited. She knelt next to the body and kept her eyes wide and alert for any animal that might dart out of the woods. The Arikara people did not fear the dead.

While she waited for Jed, her gaze fell down upon the strange markings in the earth under her moccasins. She wondered if this was bad magic done to Jed's friend by the evil white who had killed him. She'd already obliterated half the markings and decided to wipe out the rest before Jed could see it.

Jed came and checked the bodies. He managed a smile as he took her hand.

Sunblossom did not smile back. She had locked away her heart, her thoughts of a future with this man. She had no future with this man. She had no future. She was ruined.

The strained, dark silence, the dreadful impasse between Jed and the princess lasted for many days.

At first Jed was content to let the distance between them remain, for Charbonneau's actions and his subsequent death on that violent night greatly disturbed him. Why had Toussaint led Cabanne from the site of the ambush? Was it to save him, and if so, why did he strip Cabanne of his weapons? Perhaps he had meant to kill Cabanne himself, but the third man from the camp, the one who had escaped Jed, had prevented this.

Jed would never know. When he buried the old Frenchman, he'd placed one of his own pistols upon the body, and took up Charbonneau's to carry with him. He would never forget this quiet, wise, old explorer.

Now traveling safely over the rough country was most important. The land itself seemed bitter and angry. Huge red bluffs flanked the wild ragings of an unknown river, and trees, standing solitary and stolid, like mountain men themselves, thrust their gnarled, twisted limbs into a grey sky. Hulking, heavy-boned wolves, brutes bigger than any Jed had ever before seen, prowled this no-man's land. Eagles with wings and talons powerful enough to lift the agile antelope and deer ruled the sky. Underfoot, rattlesnakes clattered their warnings to the man and woman who trod closeby. Overhead, the sun was a small, white disk whose feeble warmth warned them of winter's imminent approach.

For one week they traveled this cruel landscape. Days passed when no word was spoken between them. Jed would watch her trudging along beside him, making no complaint of the weight of the pack upon her back, or of the weapons in her hand and at her belt. She also never laughed or responded to his gestures of affection, his hesitant, gentle attempts to touch her, to make her say that she was glad to be with him. He had told her several times how glad he was to be with her.

She was growing thin. Her beautiful face seemed to have misery permanently etched upon it. Evenings were the worst times. They would make camp. Jed would roast the meat his hunting skill secured for them. Sunblossom would gather roots and berries unfamiliar to Jed, and prepare them for him. He would eat

these foods, thanking her profusely for her efforts, and
beg her to eat. She would take her share of the food to
please him, but Jed, watching her sorrowfully, saw that
she actually ate little. At such times he longed to wrap
her in his embrace. But the first and only time he had
attempted that, she had stiffened and shuddered like
some caged wild thing.

His agony at being physically and spiritually apart
from her was great, but it was less than the hell he
seemed to put her in whenever he reached out.

Then there were the nightmares.

He would watch her as she slept, watch as the
nightmares stalked and captured her. Her lovely face
would tense, her precious mouth would begin to
tremble, she would clench her small fists, and her
whole body would shiver and shake with such violence
that he couldn't help but softly call to awake her. Her
eyes would snap open, but not before that tortured,
thin whine of fear rose from her throat.

Sometime later she would manage to fall back
asleep. And sometime later the nightmares would begin
again.

Jed would sit and stare into the fire, and mourn.
Never had he felt so strong, so at the height of his
male prowess. Never had he so intensely felt the male's
natural impulses and instincts to love, cherish and protect his female, his woman, his world. And never had
he felt so helpless.

On those cold, barren nights, with no place to
spend his physical and spiritual love, Jed forged and
tempered his love into a steel-cold hate. Cabanne had
done this to her. Cabanne had broken her soul.

"One week's travel along the high, barren, ridge-
country," Charbonneau had told Jed during their first
nights together. "Then we'll angle down, due north-

west, to regain a gentler terrain. We'll reach a river.
That'll be the Little Missouri. Travel along that for a
few miles, and we'll come to a placid stretch of shallow
water. That's where we'll rest before fording the
river. . . ."

The ninth day of their travel had dawned bright
and sunny. The weather promised to be more balmy,
more like late spring than late fall.

They'd arrived at the shallows Charbonneau had
described, late the previous night. Sunblossom collapsed
into an exhausted sleep while Jed kept watch. Here
they would spent a precious day or two marshalling
their energies before pushing on to the Yellowstone,
and the last leg of their journey to Fort Henry, or, at
least, where Jed hoped he'd find Fort Henry.

Jed now napped while the princess kept watch.
He was never to know what caused him to awake, but
after much pondering, came to believe that just as living in the wilderness comes to give a man a sixth sense
about danger, so does a romance cause a man to sense
a danger to his beloved.

His eyes snapped open. Sunblossom was nowhere
around. He didn't call out, for fear of who or what
might be nearby. He grabbed his rifle and tried to pick
up her tracks.

The Little Missouri's shallows were crystal clear,
beautiful. The slow, easy water rippled across sky-blue,
glistening rocks. Above, the strong, yellow sun gave the
river the spark and glitter of diamonds. There was still
lush greenery here. The chirp of birds and buzz of bees
promised of ripe fruit nearby.

Jed scanned for danger, but saw none.

He prowled along the riverbank looking for signs.
His tread was silent. If his people back in Pennsylvania
could have seen him, they would have whispered
among themselves about this hard man who moved like

a savage, like an animal. This man would not have sparked the memory of their Jedediah.

A coughing sound came from the thicket off to his right. Jed quickly moved away from the river, toward the noise. Sunblossom was kneeling with her back to him, her buttocks resting on her heels, as if in an attitude of prayer. Jed could not help noticing the loveliness of her hour-glass form, how the soft leather of her dress folded itself to her every curve. The sight of her thus, with her pale hair down around her shoulders, thickened his emotions. *I will win you all over again, he thought to himself. I will make you forget the nightmares you've endured.*

Her hand dipped down to the ground, and rose up again. Again came the gagging cough. She was eating something. Poisoned leaves, Jed realized. She was killing herself!

His wail was beast-like, tortured, a sound from hell. The shock of it shook her with the third handful of the leaves halfway to her mouth.

Jed leaped upon her and knocked the shiny, serpent-green leaves from her hand. Sunblossom's brown eyes were wide, the pupils dilated. There were flecks of foam on her lips. She tried to speak, but couldn't for her throat was already constricted from the effects of the poison.

"No!" Jed roared in English. His fingers flew to her mouth, but she twisted away, fighting his attempts to save her. He socked her in the pit of her stomach and she belched up some of the leaves. All at once the fight went out of her, and Jed was able to pry open her jaws and thrust his fingers down her throat, making her retch more, forcing her to vomit up the loathsome green stuff, until she collapsed weak in his arms. Her head lolled on her neck and her eyes were unfocused.

How much more of the poison remained in her gullet, her mouth?

He carried her to the river and splashed into the water thigh-deep. He held her under in the icy flow for a moment, hoisted her up, and then plunged her under again, until she was soaked through.

"Let me die!" she screamed, pleading with him. This time she thrust herself under the water, as if to drown.

But she was fighting him now. Thank God for that! He sat down on a rock and hauled her across his knees. Folding back her sodden skirt to reveal her bare bottom, he began to slap her buttocks in a steady, stinging rhythm. She kicked and squalled, her face dipping in and out of the cold, clean water. Each of Jed's spanks elicited a shrill, outraged squawk from the princess, and each spank forced her mouth to take in more of the water. When she coughed it out, the plant came with it. And, though he tried to suppress it, Jed felt himself become more and more aroused.

He finally carried her from the water and back to the campsite. Her teeth chattered as he peeled off her soaked dress and wrapped her in a pte robe.

It was the first time he'd seen her flesh, seen her naked. He was thoroughly aroused by now, but he was so relieved that she was alive that he made no overtures. She was sullen, pouting and her hair was a wet, tangled mass around her face and shoulders. She hugged the robe close to herself to ward off the chill while Jed rebuilt last night's fire. Only then did he peel off his own wet clothing, and warm himself in a pte robe.

He made a strong pot of coffee and forced her to drink some. They sat there, each in a robe, cradling their tin cups in their hands. The princess was silent.

Her eyes seemed to look everywhere but into Jed's. That was all right, he thought. He could wait.

"Why did you save me?" she finally hoarsely whispered, still unable to face him. "Why did you?" She shook her head, that quick little movement conveying her sense of helplessness, of misery. And although she squeezed her eyes against them. the tears came, running down her cheeks to fall and glisten in the wooly curls of the robe.

Jed was at her side in a moment, to gently and cautiously cradle her in his arms. "I will never let you die," he said. "Put it out of your mind. It will never happen, for you are my woman."

"No," she tiredly whispered. "I am ruined. I am no longer clean."

Jed held her tightly. He could feel her shivering through the robe. It reminded him of the tiny trembling of a broken-winged bird he'd once cupped in his palms. What could he say to his woman? It didn't matter to him? He didn't care? It changed nothing? He somehow had to make her understand that he did not value her less for what had been done to her.

As gently as he could, he turned her quietly sobbing, tear streaked face to his. "Listen to me. All of those who have . . . hurt you, are dead except for Cabanne. And I swear to you, he will die for this as well. It has happened, and I grieve with you, but you are still my woman. That has not changed. It will never change." He raised her chin. "Look into my eyes," he commanded. "You will always be my woman. Do you understand?" He smiled at her. "Sunblossom," he whispered in English. "I love you."

She looked up into his face. His damp hair was thick and black. It hung as straight and sleek and shiny as the hair of her own people. He'd let his beard grow. It too was black, and joined with his shoulder-length hair to frame his face. His skin had grown golden tan, and his eyes, so bright blue, spoke to her, told her things his faltering words had only hinted at. This man grieved for her, felt her sorrow, but did not value her less. She recalled how she had come to be taken by Cabanne. She was attempting to reach this man and spend a precious few hours with him before his life was ended by the Shadows Grey Eyes had dispatched. She would die with him! Soon her own shame would be blotted out, but until then, what wrong could exist in her being the woman of this man who so passionately wanted her?

She gazed down at his strong, naked body. Timidly, as if she were afraid that this last chance for happiness was a fragile dream which she still might accidently shatter, her fingers traveled down the hard expanse of his belly, down to trail along his thighs. She thrilled to watch him grow thick and hard at her touch. His sharp intake of breath brought her eyes back to his, and in their bright blue stare, she saw desire, and passion, and, quite strangely, fear.

That this great man could possible think himself unworthy to lay with her was the crowning irony, and in her rush to comfort and reassure him, her own shame, her own terror, were quickly banished. She shrugged off the robe, and let him carefully lower her back upon it. He then pulled his robe over both of them.

Jed let his fingers trace the lines of her face. He cupped her chin in his hands and kissed that flower-sweet mouth for which he had so hungered. The touch of her hard nipples against his chest, the rub of her belly against his, her thighs against his, singed him like fire. And then there was the tortuous pleasure of her silky groin rising up to tease his hardness, capturing him so that his sinews and muscles no longer responded to his will, but were completely under her command.

She locked her legs about his back as he slid into her, and moved with slow, languid strokes. He pressed his face into the fragrant curves and hollows of her neck, as she softly mewled her passion.

Her fingers slid down to his hips to press him deeper into her, and her hot breath scalded as she pressed her mouth against his ear. She came groaning and crying, clinging to him, and he lifted her up off of the robe, howling and crying himself, as she drew from him that little piece of his soul.

When he could, he lifted himself to his elbows and gazed at her. "I love you, woman," he said in English.

Sunblossom smiled up at him. "I love you, woman," she quickly and carefully repeated.

Jed laughed out loud, while she eyed him quizzically. Merriment being contagious, it was only a moment before she too was giggling.

"I love you, Jed," he instructed her.

"I love you, Jed," she echoed. Pulling his head down, she gave him a long kiss.

"Do you, woman?" Jed asked in Arikara.

"Yes," Sunblossom said instinctively. An unmistakable look of affection came to her eyes. She clasped her arms about his neck, drawing him down for another kiss. "You are my man," she said in Arikara, and this time there was no uncertainty in her tone.

They made love twice more that afternoon. It was after that third time, while they were enjoying the sensations of just being in each other's arms, that the first Shadow came.

Sunblossom saw the Shadow peering at them from the shelter of a clump of trees, but she made no sound.

She was, after all, Arikara. There was no possibility that the Shadow could be defeated, for how can anything that lives ever defeat Death? She would not warn Jed. Let him die happy, in her embrace. As for herself, she thought as the Shadow swiftly approached on silent, cat's feet, she had her man. That was all that mattered. She saw the glint of the blade in the Shadow's hand, and squeezed shut her eyes to await Death's cold bite.

Jed heard nothing as the Shadow reached them. But Sunblossom's sudden grip on him caused him to tense and rise like a squirrel at the scent of danger. It seemed as if he had heard the faint whistle of the arrow after the fact—after it plunged to the ground and slashed his hand where his neck had been just seconds before.

He twisted around in time to lock his fingers about the Ree's right wrist and stop the thrust of the knife intended for his back. With his other hand, Jed reached up to vise-clamp his strong fingers about the Ree's throat. For one eternal moment the two combatants' awesome strength locked them in equilibrium. The two were still, a frozen, violent sculpture.

The Ree bore down on his knife hand. The tip of his blade pressed into Jed's neck. Jed squeezed hard, cracking the bones in the Ree's throat. The Ree's legs twitched violently, but Jed held on, squeezing and twisting until he broke through the neckbones. When Jed let go, the dead Ree's head flopped to the side, and then forward, like a child's rag doll.

Jed shoved the body from them. Breathless with fear and from the struggle, he glared at Sunblossom. "You must have seen him? Why did you not warn me?"

She stared at him with confusion. "He is Shadow—"

"What the hell is Shadow?" Jed demanded. He looked at the body. Two grey, charcoal-drawn lines ran horizontally across the Ree's chest. "I thought Arikara did not paint themselves."

The princess warily approached the dead body of the Shadow, coming no nearer to it than three feet, in case it suddenly rose up and grabbed her. When she turned to Jed, he knew this was some Arikara superstition. His anger toward her began to ebb as he quietly asked: "What is Shadow?"

After she explained it all, in a semi-coherent, faltering way, half born of shock, and half of the disbelief of her own eyes, Jed took her into his arms and hugged her. He kissed the top of her head, letting his eyes stray to the corpse of the Shadow.

"So much for your Angel of Death, woman," he muttered in English. He held her at arms' length, and told her the following, "Sunblossom, I told you before that I would not let you die, and I meant it. As I defeated this Shadow, I will defeat the other two. But you must warn me should you see them first. Understand?"

She nodded, and then smiled, because she knew that it was expected of her. "I will warn you. . . ." She looked at the body. "Jed, never has there been need to summon forth and dispatch more than three Shadows."

Laughing, Jed hoisted the Ree's corpse up on his shoulder and took it to a tall, near-by tree. He pushed the body up onto a fork of a low, strong branch.

Sunblossom asked "Why do you do this?"

"I wish for the other two Shadows to find this one. To see what I have done to him. No predators will get to the body for a while up there. What do you think? Will it frighten them?"

The princess's expression grew thoughtful. "It has

never occurred," she said doubtfully. "They will be angry. Rage will be wild within them." She shivered.

"That is good," Jed nodded. "Angry men make mistakes." To himself, he again muttered, "Angels of Death," and then spat in contempt upon the ground. He turned to face Sunblossom, and smiled. "Hurry now, woman, we must break camp. We have to find another place to sleep for tonight, and then tomorrow we must continue on to the Yellowstone."

"I love you, Jed." She impulsively uttered the phrase in his whites' tongue, knowing that it would please him. Then she went to do as she had been bidden, following her man.

Chapter 30

One by one, he had come upon the bodies of the Shadows Jed Smith had dispatched. The birds had led him to each corpse. From miles away he could see the spiraling distant specks in the sky, the specks that grew into the cold-eyed, humped-back buzzards that feared no animal. They would perch upon their prize with naked, orange claws, and peer at the interloper with one cocked eye, as if to say, *"Why do you come now? This is dead. Now it belongs to me. . . ."*

But perhaps the buzzards recognized the grey markings on his chest and realized that both their domains were one and the same.

He kicked the slinking jackals and snarling wolves out of his way as he approached the bodies. He felt nothing as he contemplated each familiar corpse. They were merely signposts on his road.

Storm clouds were approaching. They were coming fast, rolling and barreling in and over themselves, eating up the sky. The wind itself had stopped still out of respect for its vast, grey, muttering cousin, who was now completely staining the sky.

Jed Smith, you are the wind, Grey Eyes thought. *I am the storm.*

He began to run. He had turned his horse loose to wander home many days ago, when the trail he was following began to wind its way up into the high ridge country. He took nothing with him but his bow and quiver, and his knife. These were his only comforts, for Death does not need a soft robe in which to sleep, and Death had no use for a fire.

He could run for miles and miles. He could run all day, and make the slow, deep beats of his heart match the rhythm of his feet's cadence, and the rhyme snaking round and round his mind, *"Death's song is strong—"*

The Shadow rhyme nourished him so that he needed no food. The Shadow rhyme slaked his thirst. As he ran, sharp stones sliced through his moccasins and into the soles of his feet. He did not feel the stones, and he did not bleed. *'Death's song is strong—'* said the rhyme.

The first heavy drops of rain slashed down from the wet, smoky sky. Lightning so bright it hurt the eyes slid through the charged air to split the earth. Thunder rattled in his ears. In seconds he was soaked. But he kept running through the curtain of water.

Grey Eyes laughed in delight at the storm. Other warrior braves always feared the storms as bad omens. They were the dark half of the Great Mystery, Grandfather's bad temper. But to Grey Eyes, the storm was like the spirit which ruled him. It reinforced his power.

Death's song is strong, went the rhyme. Cold as winter's frost it was, but such cold numbed the flesh, and locked the heart's steady, red flame in a crystal shell of blue ice. Faster and faster went the rhyme in his head, and faster and faster did Grey Eyes run.

The military expedition left Fort Atkinson with much fanfare, but five days out upon the Freedom

River the winds and rain came, soaking through the blue wool tunics of the soldiers, and rotting their tempers the way damp will rot food. They snarled and fought among themselves like a pack of wild dogs.

Ten days out, during a heavy fog, one of the four keelboats—the *Bonnie Rose*—hit a shoal. As the river bit a chunk of lumber out of its hull, a full company of men and heavy crates of ammunition and weapons were tumbled into the yellow water. Unbeknownst to Lieutenant O'Fallon, the commanding officer of the *Bonnie Rose,* one of the gunpowder crates came to rest in the smoldering remains of one of the cooking fires on board. No one noticed it during the confusion of trying to right the boat and tend to the critically injured. Within minutes the crate of gunpowder exploded, shattering the *Bonnie Rose*. Most of the crew, including O'Fallon, were killed.

Colonel Leavenworth could see the bright flickerings of the fire through the mist. He had heard the shouts for help from the men on board the *Bonnie Rose,* but after the explosion, the only shouts that came were from the men on the other keelboats, wanting to know what had happened.

Leavenworth was cold. The chill which had penetrated him days ago had brought with it a constant hacking cough. It seemed his strength was steadily being drained out of him.

Pilcher came out of the mist toward him, like a ghost. "How long," Leavenworth begged, "until we reach Fort Kiowa?"

Pilcher shrugged. "Depends on where we are, Colonel. And we won't know that until the mist clears. And we won't know *that* until this wind blowin' into our faces calms."

Leavenworth looked down at his aching knuckles

and wrists. "I didn't know, I didn't imagine that it could be like this."

Talbot came up to him. "We best anchor here! We lost that boat! I can't believe it! The boats behind can't even get past that burning wreck until theys can see what they're doin'." He rushed away, leaning into the wind.

"You men call this the 'Freedom River'," Leavenworth mused aloud. "I don't understand it. How many good men have lost their lives in these hellish waters?"

Pilcher took in the Colonel's appearance. He looked into the officer's bloodshot, tired eyes. *No, you didn't understand, and you never will. Ain'tcha goin' to make a toast now, Colonel? Toast yer boys who'll be feedin' the catfish and snappin' turtles over the next few weeks? You got yerself a right fine army marchin' along the bottom of the river. The wavin' watergrass is their flags and pennants now.*

"This river is a hard thing, Colonel," Pilcher said. "It takes everything. Men come to it to be stripped down and polished clean. But one thing the river guarantees: Live or die, when it's done with you, you've got yer freedom."

Chapter 31

Over the next week, their journey upstream along the banks of the Yellowstone was hard. During that time they did not let their guard drop once, because, as they knew, the Shadows were closing in.

Jed and Sunblossom holed up behind the shelter of a boulder-strewn ridge and simply waited for the second Ree to show himself. When he came out of the woods far below, Jed took careful aim, and dropped the brave with one shot. Leaving Sunblossom safely behind with her own loaded rifle and pistol, Jed hurried down the ridge to make sure the man he had ambushed would plague them no more.

The half-ounce slug had blown a nasty hole through the Ree, but the brave was still alive. He glared up at Jed with hate-filled, black eyes, and began to crawl slowly toward the trapper.

Jed could only admire the spirit that gave the Ree the fortitude to carry on. The brave was dragging his broken, useless body along the ground, leaving bits and pieces of himself sticking to the blades of grass, and all the while, he uttered not a whisper of pain, but merely slithered toward Jed's feet.

Pity for this man surged through Jed as he

watched the Ree's fingers claw for purchase. Drawing his knife, Jed quickly stepped around behind the brave. He pulled back on the Ree's hair, and slit his throat.

Even then, the Ree took a long time to die. Jed sat with him until he did.

After that, Jed gained a great deal of respect for these Arikara Angels of Death, and resolved not to rest until he had sent the third, and last, on his way to Hell. When nights came, he told Sunblossom that he would not lay with her wrapped in their pte robes by the fire, but that she would have to lay by herself, bundled up with their packs, and with his firearms arranged by her side, so as to make the Shadow think they were both there.

"You must not be afraid," Jed had told her. "And if you see or hear the Shadow coming, you must be still and pretend you are asleep in my arms. I will be somewhere in the darkness, watching over you. I will kill the Shadow before he reaches you."

Jed waited and watched in such a manner for three more nights. He prayed that the Shadow would soon come, for he had been sleeping for only a few hours every morning, while Sunblossom kept watch. His strategy depended on this last Ree seeing how poorly the previous Shadows' daytime attacks had fared, and waiting for nightfall.

When the third Shadow finally came it was almost an anticlimax. This Ree did not have the courage of the first two. The deaths of his fellows had indeed unnerved him. Whatever magic it was that served these devils had deserted this last, unlucky brave. He was just an anxious soul, far from his tribe, and acutely feeling that separation.

The Ree made so much noise as he approached the camp that Jed thought Sunblossom herself might shoot him. Not wanting his woman frightened, Jed never let the brave get that far. He quickly came up behind him, rammed his heel into the small of the man's back, while at the same time, locking his hands about the Ree's neck. The massive leverage Jed applied snapped the brave's spine. Jed drove his knife through the Ree's heart, and it was all over. The Shadows were dead.

Jed returned to Sunblossom, and fell instantly asleep in her warm embrace. The next morning, light of heart, they pushed on toward Fort Henry.

The fort itself had been built on high, level ground a few miles above where the Missouri joined the Yellowstone. It was nothing but a large, square enclosure. Its walls, formed of vertically placed logs, gave the impression of an oversized picket fence. Shacks had been thrown up inside the stockade. In all, it was a rough place of scant shelter, but it was all the hardened men needed to protect themselves against the winter snows.

The fort was a bustling place. Men hung slices of meat on drying racks placed over large, smoldering fires. Come the snows, and along with it drifts ten feet deep, hunting would be impossible. Dried meat would be the mainstay of the trappers' winter diet. Others were busy building bullboats. These one- and two-man crafts were light enough to be carried by a single trapper, and required less skill to construct than a canoe. Each bullboat was nothing but a sturdy basket woven out of slender young tree trunks and branches. Over this framework were stretched several scraped pte hides, stitched together. The big basket was then smoked over a fire to shrink the hide while the sewn-together seams were waterproofed with melted hump fat.

Sunblossom had steadfastly refused to enter the whites' place, Jed did not force her, for he understood her not wanting to subject herself to possible anguish. Although Fort Henry was a welcome sight, Jed had mixed feelings about entering himself. He needed wide-open spaces and clean, fresh air. As for people, there was only one he wanted by his side. Nevertheless, Sunblossom waited outside the fort with their equipment under the curious and watchful eyes of Major Henry's trappers, while Jed had a chat with the Major.

Major Andrew Henry had once had many of the same, gruff characteristics of his partner, General Ashley. But Henry had spent much of his recent life in the wilderness, and the wild country had smoothed away most of his rough edges. What he had long ago learned was that a man who is rash does not long survive.

Jed at once liked Ashley's partner. Although he was an average looking man, with a balding pate and a scruffy brown beard framing his wrinkled face, Major Henry was clearly worshipped by his men. At no time did Jed ever hear him raise his voice, and yet every order he quietly gave was carried out by his hundred trappers.

The Major explained to Jed that most of his men were at that moment on the trapping lines strung along the near-by portions of the two rivers.

"We're taking good pelts," the Major told Jed. "But the real beaver colonies lie farther up, along the Musselshell."

"But you need horses," Jed sighed. "Well, the Rees have got them. Reckon if enough of our company is around during the big fight, we can claim some steeds as rightful plunder."

"Give me a day to send some men out to bring back the trappers," Henry said. "I'll leave twenty men here; gives us eighty to sail down the Freedom right through the Rees' back door."

"Do you have enough bullboats?" Jed asked.

Major Henry led him outside. One whole wall of the fort was obscured from view by the stacked up hide tubs. "They happen to be our only means of transportation right now," the Major said drily. "Here's hoping we can soon store them away, and keep our feet dry straddling good old horse flesh. . . ."

"If you get to the villages soon enough, I reckon that will happen," Jed observed.

Major Henry's eyes narrowed. "What do you mean, 'you', boy? You're coming with us, aren't you?"

"Reckon not, Major," Jed replied. "My woman is Arikara. I've had my fill of killing them." He pointed to the mountains looming above the fort. "Reckon she and I will head up there."

"The snow's coming, boy—"

"I know it, Major, but we've got time to build ourselves a cabin," Jed said stubbornly. "If you'd give me the use of some traps, I'll start taking pelts for the company, the way I've always intended. I'm still a free trapper for Ashley-Henry, but I've got no stomach for joining up with a bunch of army types anxious to destroy a nation."

"I could order you to come, son," Henry said evenly, like a poker player trying to bluff.

Jed grinned at him. "You could, but I don't reckon it'ud do you much good."

Henry frowned, then nodded. "Well, you and your woman got a rough road ahead of you, boy."

"We've got each other, Major."

Jed politely but firmly refused the Major's offer of shelter during the night. "She won't come into the fort, and frankly, I've also gotten used to the quiet, and stars over my head when I sleep. Don't reckon there's much to fear that's human way up here. Those Shadows they sent are all done with."

"Damn, that's another reason I'd wish you come along," Henry said wistfully. "I'd love to see old Grey Eyes' face if you showed up, not only larger than life, but bigger than death."

"Far as I'm concerned, I'd rather he thought me and the princess dead. That gives him back his honor, and maybe that would cut down on the bloodshed."

"We could tell him it was Cabanne that stole her away," Major Henry offered.

"You could tell him," Jed sighed, "but he wouldn't believe it, most likely. Anyway, I don't want anyone stalking Cabanne. I aim to do that myself."

Henry nodded noncommittally. There were so few white men in this part of the world, it seemed a damn shame that they had to go killing each other off. But he figured if any man had a right to hold a grudge, it was Jed Smith. "I'll leave orders that anything you want in the fort is yours for the taking," he said. "Good hunting, Jed."

That night, Jed and Sunblossom made their camp several miles from the fort. They made love by the light of the moon and stars under the shelter of the mountains, which loomed up awesome and black against the velvety evening sky.

It was cold. As they lay together covered by their robes, they could see their own breath fogging in the air. Jed built the fire up until it was a roaring, orange-yellow beast.

Sunblossom nuzzled against him, and said, "I must sew us warm clothes for the winter. You must fetch me pte skins."

"I will start hunting tomorrow," Jed told her. "There are pte roaming the foothills, and elk and deer."

She was silent as she gazed into the fire. Jed looked at her beautiful profile, and wondered how much she understood. Did she realize that her nation was doomed to defeat? That her man belonged to those whites who would destroy the Arikaras?

"Do you miss your village, woman?" he asked softly.

Sunblossom smiled. "We can never go back, not as long as the Guardian lives. He would have to kill you, or you would have to kill him. Should either one of you die by the other's hand, a part of me would die as well."

Jed hugged this precious woman to his chest. "We will never go back," he said.

"But soon my nation will be gone, is that not true?" She turned to look at him.

Jed stared into her eyes. He could not lie to her. "Many of my kind are approaching your nation. They come from downriver and upriver. Your nation will be defeated by mine."

The princess pondered this. "Your nation," she slowly said. The very idea of a nation of whites was too much to accept. Fate had taken her far from her nation, had brought her to these mountains which she had never before seen, with this man, who had given up his nation for her.

The princess pressed her hand against Jed's bearded cheek. "Your nation and my nation will war," she whispered. "We shall no longer belong to either. We will be our own nation."

"I will be your husband, woman. And you will be my wife," Jed swore, kissing her. "Let the stars and the moon and the mountains witness our marriage."

They would answer to no laws except the natural ones. They were of the wilderness.

*　　*　　*

Sometime during the small hours before dawn, Jed awoke. He'd heard no noise, but his sixth sense told him that something was wrong. He stared out into the blackness surrounding them. He could feel the hairs on the back of his neck start to rise. He sniffed the air but he could detect no scent of man or beast except for themselves. And there was nothing to be seen. Still something was dreadfully wrong.

As Jed reached for his knife, Sunblossom started awake. Jed's fingers pressed to her lips warned her to keep silent. She placed her hands on her weapons, and watched him slip out of his robe and off into the brush.

Jed followed the trail through the black woods for a quarter of a mile. There was the scent of Ree in the air, but Jed discounted that as impossible. The Shadows were dead. They were well over a hundred miles from the Arikara nation.

But he knew it wasn't Sunblossom.

The trail ended at a stream softly bubbling out of the ground, Jed peered about him, wondering why he had been led here. . . .

To leave Sunblossom unprotected, came the sickening realization. He had been fooled.

Jed began to run back in a blind panic, not caring how much noise he made, not caring if this adversary was waiting behind some tree along the way to ambush him. One thing was quite clear to him—*whoever this foe was, he is more skillful, better than I*—

Her scream came when he was just a few yards from the camp. It was odd, considering the terror in her scream, that she didn't fire her gun.

Jed burst through the brush to come upon a shocking sight. Sunblossom sitting in the pile of robes with her rifle lying across her lap, stared blankly at the intruder standing still on the other side of the dying fire. It was Grey Eyes, Guardian of the Arikaras—

An awful fear drained Jed's strength as by the light of the fire's embers he made out the two horizontal markings on the motionless Ree's chest.

Grey Eyes was Shadow. He was Death come for Jed and his woman.

Slowly he turned to Jed. His face was set hard like cold stone. He drew his long, curved, skinning blade, and with seemingly little effort, flung himself upon Jed.

With a snarl rising from his throat, Jed brought his knife up to meet the attack. The two men slammed together like bull elks. Each locked his hand about the other's wrist in an attempt to block the slash of the other's blade.

Jed at once felt his wrist go numb under the pressure of Grey Eyes' fingers. It was not possible, Jed thought in horror. His knife fell from his grasp. The man could not have such strength!

Jed kicked hard into the Ree's groin. Grey Eyes didn't flinch. Jed kicked again, a third time, his breath rushing out of him with the effort. The Ree twisted Jed around and cart-wheeled him into the air, to land with a loud thud onto the ground.

Jed's fingers closed on the cold metal of his rifle's barrel. The Ree was coming at him fast. He had no time to reverse the weapon, but rose to his knees, swinging the heavy rifle up from the ground like a club. The solid wooden stock caught the Ree across the side of his head. The wood splintered with the force of the blow. Grey Eyes went down, the knife spinning from his grasp. But before Jed could press the advantage, the Ree bounced to his feet. No wound appeared on his face or at his temple. Grey Eyes simply grinned hideously, and advanced upon Jed.

Surely I've shattered his cheek bone, thought Jed. *What was keeping the man on his feet?*

Grey Eyes hands were now empty of weapons. He needed none. He could kill this white with his hands. *Death's song is strong,* chanted within him.

Jed, still on his knees, watched mesmerized as the Ree approached. The man's breathing was quiet and steady, in contrast to his own labored huffing and puffing. He swung the ruined Hawkens rifle around, and holding the jagged butt clear of his body, snapped back the hammer and pulled the trigger.

The blast pulled the awkwardly held gun out of Jed's hands. The ball hit the Ree low on his right side, just below the rib cage. It slammed him down flat on his back. Jed heard himself emit a groan born of blessed relief. It was short lived.

Grey Eyes got up. He stood on rock-steady legs, the horror-grin still on his broken face. There were ragged strips of flesh surrounding the jagged hole blown in his side. The wound did not bleed.

He again advanced toward Jed, in no hurry whatsoever.

Jed let loose a maddening scream, and hurled himself against his knees. Grey Eyes fell to the ground and Jed quickly scrambled on top of him. He joined both fists together and slammed them in left and right arcs, across the Ree's face. Grey Eyes' head rolled with the solidly placed blows but not once did he cry out. There was only the sound of Jed's grunts and the loud slaps of his fists against the Ree's flesh.

Grey Eyes' right hand shot up to lock itself about Jed's throat. Immediately Jed shifted his knee to wedge the Ree's left hand against the ground. Both of his own went up to the fingers digging into his throat. It was the strength of both of Jed's hands against Grey Eyes' five fingers, and Jed just managed to break the hold. As he did, Grey Eyes bucked his body up to throw Jed off.

Before Jed could regain his feet, Grey Eyes shot around to pin him flat against the ground. Now it was the Ree who straddled Jed. He placed both hands around the trapper's throat and began to squeeze.

Jed hammered his fists into the Ree's sides. His fingers dug and tore at the Ree's horridly open, pale grey gunshot wound. It did not matter. He slid his forearms underneath the Ree's outstretched arms and clubbed away at the man's elbows, his wrists, his upper arms. It was like hitting oak. Jed bucked and threw his body until he thought his own spine would snap from the effort, but the Ree seemed rooted to the earth.

Where was Sunblossom? his mind screamed as his vision darkened. But Jed knew that she would not, could not help. She was locked in superstition, panic, shock. She was frozen in Arikara legend. This man was Shadow. *What lived that could defeat Death?*

Love—The answer blazed in Jed's mind. He was a dead man, but Sunblossom—Please, let his beloved live. . . .

"Grey Eyes," he rasped, using the last drops of air in his suffocating lungs. "Our woman. Do not kill her!"

The Shadow squeezed the white's throat, choking the life out of him. Jed's blue eyes began to dim.

I am not Grey Eyes, I am Shadow! Death's song is strong! roared the Shadow.

But the man in whom Death now lived remembered back to those whites he had killed long ago, when he was only Ranking Brave of his nation. The third white had indeed stared up at him with the same human eyes. *The Law is wrong! They are human. This white is a man.*

Grey Eyes' fingers slid from Jed's neck. He threw back his head and roared his agony to the stars. His eyes filled with tears, and through his liquid vision the night sky seemed filled with flames.

Suddenly, blood welled and gushed from his side. Blood trickled from his mouth, nose and ears. Pain seared through him, for he was no longer Shadow. He was again a man. But the greatest pain of all came from his broken heart.

Sunblossom, still on the pte robes, came out of shock. As the situation became evident, she decided that she would not let Death keep her from her man. No Shadow would tear them apart. She would die with him.

She hurled herself upon the Shadow, plunging her knife to the hilt into his back. Grey Eyes' elbows shot back in a reflex action. The blow lifted Sunblossom off her feet and she collapsed upon the ground to lay still in the dirt.

Grey Eyes was at her side in a moment. As real Death shadowed him, his only anguished thought was that he had killed her. Carefully Grey Eyes lifted her head from the ground, cradling it in his large hand.

She began to move, and even as the relief flowed through him, he began to choke on the blood flowing into his lungs.

Jed came to. When he saw the Ree bending over Sunblossom's prostrate form, Jed screamed "No!"

Before Jed could clear his head of his stupor and right himself for another assault, Grey Eyes gently released Sunblossom and stumbled clear of her. He tried to stand to meet Jed Smith, but before either man could deliver another blow, Grey Eyes tumbled awkwardly to his side and rolled over onto his back. He felt Sunblossom's knife slide deeper into him, and all at once all feeling fled.

He felt nothing now, no pain, no anger, no hatred. He turned to look at the barely glowing embers of the dying camp fire. The flames had always been his friends. But the flames had died. And Grey Eyes' spirit left him as the embers lost their glow and turned to cold dark ashes.

Jed crawled over to the man's still form. He stared down into his face, down into eyes now blank. Jed picked up the man's hand, and let it fall. It landed limp against the earth. The man was dead. As he started to drag the body off, Sunblossom snarled, "No!" With her fists she beat him away.

He watched as she slowly dragged away Grey Eyes' body herself. She strained and tugged at the weight, and when Jed tried to help, she cursed and kicked him away, like a fury out of hell.

All the rest of that night, Jed sat by himself. He'd built up a huge fire. He needed lots of warmth and light just then.

He could just make out Sunblossom's silhouette off in the distance, out of the circle of light. She rocked to and fro over the body of Grey Eyes.

All the rest of that night, Jed sat alone, shivering, while the princess keened and sobbed the death song reserved for the passing of the Guardian of the Nation.

Chapter 32

The next morning Sunblossom came to Jed's side, and took hold of his hand.

"We must return downriver," she told him sadly.

Jed shook his head, angrily. "That will just get us killed, woman."

"It is not what I want," she said patiently. "It is not what you want, but we must return downriver, nevertheless."

"We do not belong with other people," Jed pleaded. "Just us, together. If we go up into the mountains—"

She pressed her fingers to his lips to silence him. "If we go up into the mountains many people of both our nations could die, all on our account. Grey Eyes is dead. It is he who wanted war, and we know why he did."

"He is dead, all right," Jed said gruffly. "And you surely mourned for him, long and hot. Are you still my woman?"

"Always. I swore it," she smiled, but then her lovely face grew serious. "But I am also Arikara princess. If we were to return to the villages, and formalize our union according to my nation's Laws, my people would be calmed. They would not fight the whites if our two nations were joined in us."

"You are forgetting something," Jed laughed. "It is my nation bringing the fight to the Arikaras. They have been waiting for such a chance a long time. They will not hesitate to destroy your nation—"

"Then you must stop them, Jed. You must tame your people, as I must tame mine." She said the next slowly, to be sure he understood. "Our union cannot prosper based on the deaths of so many. I cannot live haunted by funeral pyres."

Jed nodded, fully understanding his precious Sunblossom. "You are indeed Arikara princess," he smiled. "You so all-fired ready to go traipsin' back, how come you're cryin'?" He reached out to catch one of her tears on his fingertip.

"Dreams," she murmured. She fought back the great sadness washing over her, the sadness one felt when spring and summer faded to fall, and cold, barren winter. "I am crying over the beauty of sweet dreams."

He took her in his arms, and kissed her hair, whispering what she had taught him once, on a day after their love had come into bloom. "We live the dream we are given. . . ."

She gently broke free of his embrace. "I will pack for us, husband," she said too brightly.

Jed nodded, the awful ache building up inside of him. He said nothing, hoping against hope, but his sixth sense told him that this sweet dream was coming to an end.

Colonel Leavenworth sipped at his cognac, and stretched his sore legs out in front of Brazeau's fireplace. What blessed relief! He had never been so relieved as when his forces had tied up their keelboats at

Fort Kiowa's docks. His military expedition—thin and sickly, cold and chastened—had already lost one fifth of its strength, and without one Ree being spotted, or one shot being fired.

Leavenworth had been spending most of his days and nights in awful pain. It seemed the bones of his body had been set on fire by the Freedom's damp climate. He got his only relief late at night after drinking deep of the vile skull varnish he had once sworn to himself he would never touch. Such drink was for trappers perhaps, but not for military officers, not for gentlemen.

What he wouldn't have given for a second chance to reconsider this ill-fated mission! What if during the confrontation with the Rees, legendary as fierce fighters, his sick men were to lose?

Leavenworth flushed hot and humiliated just by the contemplation of such a defeat. How much worse would it be should such an ignomity actually blight his record, and now, in the very twilight of his career!

Josh Pilcher stomped into the big sitting room. He dragged a bench over from its place against the wall, and plopped down next to the Colonel, snapping him out of his dismal reveries. "Reckon we're right and ready to move on the Rees," he said.

"Yes," Leavenworth reluctantly agreed. He chewed on the ends of his moustache. How he hated the thought of leaving the warmth and shelter of Fort Kiowa!

"Brazeau's got enough horses for all of his engagés to ride, and some of our own boys as well," Pilcher said enviously. "Here's how it'll go. We'll float yer big guns upriver, until we reach Ashley and his survivors. Then we'll march overland, comin' around on the Rees from behind, right through their growin'

fields. The terrain is level, there. You won't have no
further mishaps concernin' yer artillery. And the Rees
will be wide open to yer firepower." Pilcher paused.
"Seein' as how you ain't never been there, and all, I
sorta gave orders to that effect, under yer name. . . ."

"Yes," Leavenworth sighed. He brightened a bit.
"That might work. . . ."

Pilcher scrutinized the Colonel. "You ain't getten
cold feet, is you?" he asked, grinning wolfishly. "Too
late to stop now, Colonel."

Leavenworth nodded. "Yes, Josh. It is too late,
isn't it?"

Little Soldier, Guardian, sat next to aged Bear in
front of his lodge. The calumet between them wafted
blue smoke into the crisp, fall air.

"I had a dream," Little Soldier told the old man.
"Thunder and lightning rained down upon our villages.
The nation was no more. Grey Eyes had a smiliar
vision. In his, fire ate up our nation."

"These are visions of war," Bear observed in his
frail voice. "Sad visions."

Little Soldier smiled. "You do not believe we can
defeat the whites this time?" The tone of his voice revealed that he too shared that opinion.

Bear shrugged. He had held on to his young
man's thoughts for a long time, but on the morning he
had been told of the theft of his daughter, he had become an old man. "Guardian, squaws and old men always hate war."

"Not just squaws and old men, honored Bear,"
Little Soldier sighed.

"Do you think he will bring her back?" Bear
whispered, on the verge of disgracing himself by sobbing. All he did these days was weep like a woman.
"Though he is Shadow. Do you think?"

"Grey Eyes is dead," Little Soldier said tiredly. "I feel it."

Bear nodded. "Perhaps the whites will not come." Again Little Soldier smiled. "They will come."

Chapter 33

The journey downriver from Fort Henry took ten days, and went without incident. The fleet of bullboats flew with the Freedom's current. Each night, Major Henry's trappers would make their camp. Each night, Jed and Sunblossom would wander off to make theirs.

They spent their daylight hours touching. They spent their private, night hours making love, memorizing each other's bodies by the flicker of their campfire, orchestrating their passion to the eternal rustling of the river.

"Sunblossom?" Jed had begun during their first night. "What if we fail?"

"We must not," she answered. "Our lives depend on it. You must know that I will stand with my people at the barricade. You must keep in mind that your nation's bullets will fall where I stand, just as I must keep in mind that my people will be shooting at you. So we must not fail."

On their last night together, Jed said, "Sunblossom, I am your man."

"I am your woman," she told him.

When she slipped from their robes early that morning, Jed awoke, but he pretended to be asleep. He listened to her gather her weapons and go off to their small boat. He heard the sound of the light craft sliding into the water.

At dawn she would be back with her nation. At dawn he would be back with his.

General Ashley and Major Henry did not pause to celebrate their reunion. Such celebration could wait until they knew just how many of their fledgling fur company would survive the coming battle.

All around was the confusion of Leavenworth's soldiers rolling their cannons and howitzers into place in the muddy growing fields to point the awesome weapons at the Ree villages. At times it seemed like every officer was shouting commands at once, and every bugler trumpeting a call. The soldiers got themselves into position, feeling like fools.

During the taking up of their lines, large groups of unarmed Rees had timidly approached as close as fifty yards. Some of the more brazen soldiers had waved at the Indians. The Indians had waved back.

For their part, the Arikaras—who had confidence born of ingenuousness concerning their ability to defeat any enemy—could not get over the sight of so many whites, and all dressed in blue! To the Arikaras, the spectacle was marvelously beautiful, and they were consumed with curiosity over its origins. Were these whites of the same nation as the trappers who wore animal skins? It didn't seem so. The whites in blue were clearly not as at ease in the wilderness as the trappers!

Colonel Leavenworth had not recognized Jed until the two were reintroduced by General Ashley. Leavenworth could not believe that the young man he'd originally met in his Atkinson office had become this bearded, hardened wilderness man.

Jed demanded that he be allowed a chance to

speak to all in charge before a shot was fired by any soldier or trapper. Both Pilcher and Brazeau, on the same side for once, tried to block this meeting, urging Colonel Leavenworth to begin the attack on the villages before the Rees could get over their surprise and organize themselves.

But Ashley and Henry sided with Jed, and Colonel Leavenworth decided in their favor, being hesitant to issue that first, fateful order which would irrevocably plunge the United States into war. The meeting took place in the command tent set up along the forest line which bordered the fields.

Pilcher and the Frenchman, both sulking, flanked Ashley, Henry and Leavenworth who was in the center. Jed explained to all the plan he and the princess had come up with. He also told them the grisly story of rescuing her from Cabanne, all the while staring hard at Brazeau, who shrugged off the story as if bored, saying that he could not be responsible for any of his men who decided to take their pleasures from squaws.

"Call her a squaw again, Brazeau, and I'll kill you here and now," Jed said quietly.

"Colonel Leavenworth?" Brazeau chuckled.

"Here now, Mr. Smith," Leavenworth reprimanded Jed. "We're all of us on the same side today. If you kill anyone, see to it that it's the enemy."

"But they're no longer our enemies," Jed argued. He told of the attacks by the Shadows, and of the final, awesome attack by Grey Eyes. "I know for a fact that Little Soldier, the new Arikara Guvner, wants peace. The princess has assured me of this."

"But Jed," General Ashley objected, "I mean no disrespect, son, but how can you be sure she's telling the truth? Or maybe, she's just plain wrong. . . ." Both Ashley and Henry looked up at their man hopefully, willing him to come up with a reassurance to their doubts. Jed's plan suited them quite well: Sunblossom would use her influence on Little Soldier to convince him that an honorable settlement for the Rees' attack on Ashley's beach camp would be fifty horses, given free and clear. With those horses, the Ashley-Henry expedition could get back to their original purpose of taking furs.

"You can't be sure, is the truth of it," Pilcher banged his fist against the table. "I say we fight 'em, we beat 'em, and then we take all the horses and furs they got. Lord knows, that's what they did to me."

"But what if that attack wasn't their fault, Josh?" Jed countered. "It's Brazeau's fault, I say. He sent his man Cabanne to get those young Rees riled up with skull varnish. Cabanne led the attack on your outpost, Josh. It's Brazeau you oughta skin to settle the score."

"You have proof of this?" Leavenworth asked.

"Of course, he doesn't," Brazeau snarled.

Jed gripped the arms of his chair in frustration. "The Arikaras know. . . ."

"But they are savages. No man here would take their word," Brazeau scoffed.

"Charbonneau was aware of it—"

"So you say," Brazeau shrugged. "But sadly, my old friend Charbonneau is dead."

"Killed by one of your own engagés," Jed spat.

"So you say," Brazeau repeated.

"And where is Cabanne?"

"Jed, I do not know," the Frenchman loudly declared. "I have not seen him since—" He stopped, abruptly.

Jed leaned back in his chair, smiling. "Since when, Cayewa?" he coaxed.

Brazeau scowled. "I am not responsible for the actions of men who happen to work for me," he insisted.

"This bickering is getting us nowhere," Leavenworth broke in. "Mr. Smith, make your proposal. Then the men here will vote on it."

As the Colonel spoke, Josh Pilcher leaned across the table, and brought his strong fingers down on Brazeau's like the steel jaws of a trap. "Cayewa," he hissed. "Iffen I ever find out that Jed here is tellin' the truth, you is gonna be my meat. . . ."

"This is what I propose," Jed began, his clear, steady gaze settling in turn on each man present. "General Ashley and I will parley with Little Soldier and the princess. In exchange for leaving them in peace, the Arikaras will agree to pay the following tribute: fifty horses to the Ashley-Henry expedition, and twenty packs of beaver pelts, or a number of packs of lesser furs to make equal amount, to Pilcher, for the damage done to his company. This peaceful settlement, combined with the living treaty forged out of my marriage to the princess, will promise future, honorable harmony between Americans and Arikaras. What'll it be, men? Bloodshed, and a loss of the trapping season, or the opportunity to trap the Freedom and beyond in peace?"

"Gentlemen?" Colonel Leavenworth asked.

General Ashley said, "Let's give Jed's plan a try."

"I agree," Major Henry said.

"I vote we fight," Brazeau demanded. "You will look like a fool to your superiors, Colonel Leavenworth. Bringing your men all this way, and then turning tail."

"Josh?" Leavenworth asked tiredly.

Pilcher locked eyes with Jed. "All right," he grudgingly said. "Let's give Jed and his woman a chance. . . ."

"And I for one would also like to settle this peacefully," Leavenworth told them all. "I've lost too many men as it is. I think Washington would be quite pleased if it turned out that I—or my agents in this matter," he grinned, nodding at Jed, "—could successfully hammer out a treaty to keep the peace." He motioned to one of his junior officers, who quickly approached to help him out of his chair. "Damn my bones," Leavenworth groaned. "Meeting is adjourned."

As the men got up Brazeau suddenly said, "I will not be bound by this treaty, I represent the interests of the French government—"

Before anyone could stop him, Jed moved around the table to grab Brazeau. The Frenchman was strong, but he was only of average size, and Jed easily manhandled him.

Brazeau's hand flew to his belt and came up with his pistol, but Jed swatted it out of his grip. As the others tried to hold him back, Jed put his hands around Brazeau's throat. "You listen good, Cayewa. I represent my own interests. If you or any of your boys fire one shot, it'll be your death." He threw him to the floor of the tent, and strode out.

None of the others looked at Brazeau as he lay sprawled, his fingers rubbing at the marks on his neck.

Brazeau stomped his way into the forest, his face distorted with rage. He walked two miles through the trees. All the while, his fingers gingerly soothed the painful bruises Jed Smith had squeezed into his throat.

When he came to a small brook, he followed it for several hundred feet, until he came to a hollow. He made his way down the incline, to come to a lean-to made out of leafy boughs.

It was dark here. The sunlight could not penetrate the roof formed by the trees. From out of the shadows there came a low, animal growl.

"Hold, Tooth," Cabanne said. He crawled out of

the lean-to, holding his cocked fusil out in front of him. "What takes place, Cayewa?"

"The Americans will make a treaty with the Rees. They will become allies with the savages." Brazeau shook his head. "We cannot allow that to happen, Cabanne. The Rees will furnish the Americans with horses. They will control the fur grounds."

Tooth suddenly burst out of the brush. Head down, and tail thumping, he nosed his way in between Cabanne's legs.

The bearded Frenchman began to gather together his gear. "*Non*, Cayewa. We cannot allow that to happen," he said.

Chapter 34

Jed and General Ashley walked across the wide, barren growing field. They could see the Ree Guvner and the princess approaching from their side. The four met for their parley precisely in the middle of that open place, precisely in the middle between the line of blue-coated soldiers on one side, and the massed army of Ree warrior braves on the other.

Jed had his pistols in his belt, but carried no rifle. Little Soldier carried a fusil. Neither General Ashley nor Sunblossom was armed.

"Greetings, Guardian," Jed began. "Fifty horses and twenty beaver packs are the seeds of peace you can sow today. Those seeds will grow into fruitful harmony between our nations."

The diminutive Arikara Guardian looked up at Jed. "There is more honor in forging peace than waging war," he agreed. "Both our nations have suffered. . . ."

"Both our nations have indeed suffered. But now we will heal. Let there be a marriage celebration announced today." Jed smiled at the princess, who blushed and looked down at her feet.

"Better a marriage than a funeral," Little Soldier observed. "Then this trouble is done?"

"This trouble is done," Jed echoed.

"Then as Guardian, I bless this marriage."

Little Soldier looked at Jed, and then to Sunblossom. "You and the princess. Your nation and ours. This marriage is a good thing." He turned, and taking the princess's arm, led her back toward the village. As they walked, she looked over her shoulder to gaze at Jed, and her face was filled with joy.

"What the hell is going on?" Ashley demanded as the Arikaras strode away. "We get what we want?"

"Yes, sir," Jed nodded beaming. "We get what we want."

Because the potential state of war still existed, everyone in the American camp, especially Jed, seemed to tip-toe around and hold his breath. No one wanted to upset the delicate balance of peace that had just been negotiated.

At dusk, Jed went to the lower village to participate in the celebration. The marriage itself would take place at dawn, as was Arikara custom. Until that time, as was also Arikara custom, the princess would be sequestered with her servants.

Colonel Leavenworth had wisely ordered that no whites attend either the festivities or the actual ceremony. The Arikaras would not pay the tribute of horses and furs until the marriage was formally concluded. Tomorrow morning, if all had gone well, Ashley would receive his horses, Pilcher his furs, and he himself could begin the journey back to Fort Atkinson and comfort.

Jed sat between Little Soldier and Bear, doing his best not to choke on the calumet they kept shoving into his face. The two Arikaras were chattering on and on to him, but he couldn't pay attention. His mind was on Sunblossom.

By this time tomorrow, the two of them would be on their way back to the mountains. Jed thanked Grandfather above for giving the Rees the Law that stated that a woman who married a white could no longer live in the nation.

The calumet came his way again, and again he pretended to puff on it. What a fine life he and his Sunblossom were going to have!

The volley of shots echoed through the village as Jed was handing the pipe to his future father-in-law. "Those are fusils!" Jed gasped. "Who are your braves shooting at?"

Little Soldier was on his feet and running toward the source of the shots. Jed was at his heels, thinking hard. He had carried no weapons into the village. What man wore weapons to his marriage? He wondered what had gone wrong, and if he was going to get out of this with his scalp.

A breathless, Arikara sentry met them. "A white!" he spat, glowering at Jed. "Guardian, a white has killed two of our braves! One was torn by his dog!"

"Cabanne!" Jed roared.

Several more fusil blasts sounded. There was pandemonium as braves ran through the darkness, fumbling with their weapons.

"What do you say to this?" Little Soldier snarled at Jed.

Before Jed could even think of an answer, the distant booms of the cannons across the fields came rolling to his ears. He heard the harsh whistling of the cannon balls arcing across the night sky.

"Oh God!" Jed cried. The first explosions came, and he was thrown off his feet to the ground.

To a man, every trapper and soldier bivouacked along the expedition's line craned his neck in the direction of the Ree villages as the first fusil blasts were heard. Colonel Leavenworth had been sleeping in his tent. When his junior officers rushed in to inform him, they found him already awake, and struggling with his boots.

Both Ashley and Henry were sitting about a fire, drinking coffee, when they heard the shots.

"Good God," Ashley paled. "Do you think they've killed Jed?"

It was Josh Pilcher who, by chance, was already at the front lines, and who gave the cannoneers the actual orders. "Damned heathens!" he swore at the shots. "They've murdered Jed! Just as they murdered my boys!"

Pilcher strode down the line, screaming the order to fire. The cannoneers looked at each other in quandary, but in the end they obeyed. There had been shots already fired, after all, and Pilcher—all during the expedition—had been issuing orders in Colonel Leavenworth's name.

The call to fire went down the line. By the time Leavenworth himself had managed to get out of his tent, and to the guns, to order a cease-fire, the three five-pounders, and two howitzers, had blasted away twice at their pre-calibrated targets in both the upper and lower villages, and were letting loose with their third volley.

Cabanne had been on his way into the village equipped with flint and fuse. His target was the hut in which the Rees stored their gunpowder. He and Tooth had managed to reach it before they were discovered by the two Ree sentries.

Tooth tore out the throat of the first, and Cabanne used that Ree's fusil to shoot and kill the second sentry.

He had no time to set the fuse, he realized. He ran into the darkness as other Rees arriving on the scene fired at him.

Hiding in the shelter of an empty lodge, Cabanne pondered his situation. Brazeau's plan had been for him to set the fuse, and then steal away. The resulting explosion was intended to have been ample evidence to the Rees of the Americans' treachery, and the war between the Arikara nation and the United States would have been resumed.

At the sound of the cannons, and the scream of the rounds flying through the air, Cabanne huddled in a corner of the lodge, Tooth pressed tightly against his side. The war it seemed, was starting a little too soon!

Man and dog tore from their hiding place as the first balls screamed down. A Ree ran smack into him, but Cabanne clubbed the brave down with the butt of his fusil. Another brave rushed at him, but Cabanne pointed the shotgun and fired. The range was point-blank. The Ree's chest blew apart.

Then, as the shells landed, the panicked Rees took no further notice of him. The awesome explosions tossed great clumps of dirt into the air, and metal shards hummed into unlucky Rees like arrows, but much faster and much more deadly.

A ball landed amidst the horses crowded in the corral. Those that survived smashed through the gate. They stampeded, crazed with fear at the noise and confusion around them. Those Rees, both men and women, who did not get out of the herd's way, were trampled.

A cannonball hit the Ree magazine, Cabanne's original target. The powderkegs erupted in a deafening blast, sending a huge gout of blue flame into the sky. Flaming bits of the building fell upon the wattle roofs of the surrounding lodges, which smoldered and then burst into flame.

From his vantage point on the other side of the growing fields, Colonel Leavenworth stood silently, Pilcher and the others around him. They all watched as flames danced from structure to structure, in both the upper and lower villages of the Rees. Now that the firing had stopped, there was no sound but the crackling of flames and the nightmarish howls of wounded, crying Arikaras as their nation burned.

Jed stumbled from one burning lodge to the next. He was dazed, in shock. All around him came the moans and cries of the wounded.

Where was Sunblossom? Still in the upper village, Jed hoped. From where he stood, he could see the flames eating up that town as well, although it was not quite as devastated by the artillery barrage as the lower village.

While he stood peering into the night turned to eerie day by the flames, he saw Cabanne, followed by his dog, running off toward the growing fields.

Jed scooped up a fusil lying next to the body of a legless brave and set off after him.

At the last Arikara lodges at the outskirts of the lower village, Jed caught up with them. "Cabanne!" he roared, wanting the brute to know who it was sending him off to hell.

Cabanne whirled about. As Jed raised his fusil, the Frenchman threw himself to one side, out of the line of fire, behind the flaming skeleton of a lodge.

Jed cursed, lowering his weapon. Slowly he approached the burning structure. The wails and shouts of the Rees, in combination with the loud crackling of the surrounding fires, filled his ears. Jed did not hear the sound of Tooth coming up behind until the animal launched itself at him.

Jed spun to meet the attack. There was no time to bring the barrel of the shotgun to bear on the hound. He slammed the side of it against the dog's head as it sunk its fangs into his forearm. The blow had no effect.

Tooth's weight dragged Jed to his knees. The dog worked its head from side to side trying to tear off his arm. Finally he slammed the butt of the gun into the animal's teeth, cracking through the fangs embedded in his flesh. Howling in pain, the dog backed off.

At that instant, Cabanne stepped out into the open and fired his own fusil.

Jed felt the sting of several pellets, but the main charge had missed him. Still, he threw himself down on his stomach, his fusil beneath him, pointed in Cabanne's direction but out of his sight.

In an instant the bloody-mouthed dog was again upon him.

"Hold Tooth!" Cabanne shouted.

The hound stood above Jed, its face inches from his own. The dog sniffed suspiciously at Jed's still form, its yellow eyes made more evil by the darkness.

"Wait, my pet!" Cabanne laughed with relief as he viewed Jed's still form. "I want his scalp. Then shall I feed you his heart." Pulling his knife, the Frenchman strode toward Jed's body.

Jed watched Tooth. At the moment the hound shifted its gaze from his face to look up, and then slink back to Cabanne, Jed flung himself up on his right side.

Cabanne stared down in shock. All he could see was the black snout of the shot gun.

Jed fired the fusil. Cabanne never uttered a sound as the full force of pellets tore into his face and neck, nearly severing his head from his body as he hit the ground.

Jed flipped all the way over onto his back, flinging away the spent fusil, to catch hold of the hound's slavering jaws. He got a grip on the Tooth's snout and jutting lower jaw, and as the dog's paws scrabbled for purchase in the dirt, Jed slowly began to pry the hound's jaw wider and wider apart.

The steady, constant, growl spilling from Tooth's throat changed to an ever-rising, ever-louder keen of pain as Jed levered the animal's jaws past the natural arc of their hinges. Now all thoughts of attack were forgotten as Tooth twisted wildly about, trying to get away from this thing which was causing it such anguish.

Jed rose to his knees. His hands were bleeding from the sharp points of the broken fangs as he stretched the dog's jaw wider and wider. Suddenly there came the loud snap of the bones breaking, and the dog's jaw went slack in Jed's grip.

Blood poured from Tooth's mouth. He howled in agony. Tail between his legs, the hound tried to slink away, but before he could, Jed reached down to grab the animal's right paws, front and rear.

Jed dragged the hurt beast to the nearest burning lodge and flung the howling, craven thing into the midst of the fiery wreckage.

As Jed watched the roof of the lodge cave in, he thought about Sunblossom. *Where was Sunblossom?* His own mangled hands hanging useless, he stood with the dead and the dying under the night sky, red with fire and smoke, certain that he would never see his woman again.

Chapter 35

The dawn light revealed such misery and destruction that Sunblossom could do nothing but hang her head and weep for her people.

The princess walked the streets of the upper village. Not a lodge had escaped unscathed. Not a family existed that was not mournfully singing the song of death for at least one of its own.

She had escaped with others to the relative safety of the dark, open growing fields when the whites' thunder and lightning had begun to rain down upon her nation. Why this had happened she did not know.

On her walk to the lower village, she met Little Soldier.

"How many have died, Guardian?" she asked. She had begun again to sob.

"Many," he said. Her eyes were red and raw from his own tears. "His vision was a true one," he murmured. "The nation has gone up in flames."

"His vision was indeed a true one," she replied. After a moment she asked, "What is left for us, Guardian?"

Little Soldier looked up at the sky. The sun was all but obscured by the ugly smears of grey smoke rising from the charred remains of the two villages. "We must go away from here. Here there are now too many ghosts for the . . . remains of the nation to ever again prosper."

The princess pondered his pronouncement. "The nation will wander," she said sadly. "Without the villages, without the river, what chance have the pitiful few against the Sioux and our other enemies?"

"The chance we make for ourselves," the Guardian answered. "The few must focus on the sound of *now*. The few must remain right thinking. The few must keep the precious little they have left."

"But Guardian, what is the use——"

"Silence, woman!" Little Soldier thundered. "Do not speak in such a manner. Are you not Arikara royalty? Think right, woman! Are you not Arikara princess?"

"I am Arikara princess," she said. Her proud smile, or at least the ghost of it, flitted across her face.

Little Soldier nodded silently in approval. He turned to continue on to the upper village.

"Where do you journey, Guardian?" she asked.

"To take council with your father, princess."

"Guardian, my father, Bear, is dead."

While Little Soldier absorbed this, several braves wandered by. As they passed, each paid his respects to the Guardian, and each bowed to their princess. She could see the joy in their eyes to know she was unharmed. Their decent loyalty to her, or at least to her station, both warmed her, and threatened to again make her cry, for what had been destroyed during the night.

But she didn't cry. Instead, she said to the braves, "Be strong Arikara warriors! The nation needs you!" And when they had gone, she looked at Little Soldier and said, "Guardian, Bear is dead, but I am Arikara princess. Take council with me."

"The trial will now come to order!" Jed announced from his place at the head of the long table in Colonel Leavenworth's command tent. On either side of the table sat the jury: Ashley and Henry, Josh Pilcher, Bill Sublette, John Clyman, and as many other trappers from the expedition as could squeeze themselves a place.

At the foot of the table sat a glowering, sweating, Joseph Brazeau. "I do not recognize this court!" he began. "Colonel Leavenworth!"

Off in one corner of the tent, the old soldier looked up from his chair. "What is it, Cayewa?"

"The United States has no right to put me on trial," Brazeau sputtered. Before he could go on, Jed cut him off.

"The United States ain't putting you on trial, Cayewa," Jed said. "This here's a trappers' court. You're being judged by your peers, Cayewa. The United States ain't got nothing to do with this."

"Damn right," Pilcher growled. "What be the charges, Jed?"

"That Cayewa, through his agent—pardon me through his late agent, Cabanne, did supply the Rees with skull varnish, that he did cause them to go on the war path, costing Josh Pilcher his company."

"And cause of that, costin' me my arm," John Clyman growled.

"And costing the lives of many other good men," Jed stated. "Men like Hiram Angus, Jimmy Beck, Eddie Rose—"

"This is all your idea!" Brazeau shouted, pointing his finger at Jed. "Admit it!" He tried to stand up, but the strong hands of several nearby trappers forced him back into his seat.

It had been his idea, born of his fury of the previous night. Jed had intended to kill Brazeau for his evil-doing, but once the younger trapper had found out that Sunblossom was alive and well, he'd calmed down. He still hadn't gotten the chance to speak to her. But all in good time. First he would deal with this villain, right and proper.

At first General Ashley and Major Henry didn't cotton to the idea, but that was only because they were so dejected over once again losing the horses so essential to their endeavor. But when Jed fully explained his plan, they'd been quite anxious to go along.

"What do you hope to accomplish?" Brazeau demanded. "All of you? I cannot be executed——"

"That is true," Leavenworth interjected. "You cannot be executed. . . ." He sounded sorry.

"But you can be shot down like a dog," Pilcher laughed. "We're talkin' a trappers' war, Frenchie. Us against you."

Brazeau paled. "Colonel . . . ," he stuttered.

"I would do my best to protect you," Leavenworth offered. "But that would of course mean that you'd have to remain at Fort Atkinson. Otherwise . . ." he shrugged.

"But I cannot. . . . My trap lines, my company," Brazeau pleaded. Suddenly his expression grew fierce. "I have one hundred engagés," he boasted. "If you wish a trappers' war you shall have one . . ."

"You're bluffin' Cayewa," Jed snorted. "How long do you think those boys will work for you iffen they know it makes them fair game for every other trapper in the territory all up and down the Freedom? They'd desert you in a minute if it came down to it. Now isn't that right?"

Brazeau did not answer, but he knew that it was true.

"Ain'tcha gonna write to the President, or the

king, or somebody?" Pilcher asked sarcastically, to the general amusement of the others.

"Sure he might," Jed said. "Of course that would take some months, and he'd be pushing up wildflowers by then."

"What do you wish of me?" Brazeau quietly asked.

"Hold on now," Jed chuckled. "We ain't found you guilty as of yet. This here's America. We don't allow no Star Chambers."

Brazeau winced.

"What say everybody?" Jed called out. "Is he guilty or what?"

"Guilty!" came the cry.

Brazeau swiveled around. He looked like a cornered rat. "What will be done with me?" he asked fearfully.

"You're gonna pay a fine," Jed said. "Here it is. To Ashley-Henry, one hundred horses. To Pilcher, twenty-five packs of beaver pelts."

"That is robbery!" Brazeau fairly screamed.

Jed nodded. "Will you pay it?"

"He'd better," came a growled remark from John Clyman. He glanced meaningfully at the place where his arm used to be.

Brazeau hung his head in defeat. "I will pay it. . . ."

No one mentioned the enormity of the virtual genocide inflicted on the Arikara nation, especially to Pilcher. But then, truth to tell, the Rees were Indians, and they were white men, free trappers, men of the wilderness. Jed was just happy that Sunblossom was alive. For any wilderness man to concern himself with an entire Indian nation was folly.

Jed found Sunblossom by the tributary where their

love was first born. The devastated sites of the two villages was no place for a white man. Jed instinctively knew she would probably be by the stream. She was standing with her back to him as he approached.

"Sunblossom!" Jed called to her. "Come to me, woman!" He ran toward her.

She did not move but only turned to face him. Jed looked at her eyes, at what was in them, and all at once his heart broke in two. He'd lost her, he realized.

"You blame me, woman?" he asked, all the joy gone from him. "For what happened to your nation, you blame me?"

"I do not blame you," she said. "We live the dream we are given, Jed."

"Will you come with me? To the mountains?"

"I cannot."

"Then you do blame me!" Jed cried. He swept her up into his arms and kissed her. And, to his consternation, her kiss was as passionate and deep as it had been during their time of happiness together.

He held her away from him, staring at her, wordlessly asking her why.

"My people have little. I represent what they used to have, what they might dream they could again have. I cannot desert them now. I am Arikara princess."

"Then I will stay here with you," Jed pleaded. "Trap the waters down by Pilcher's fort. He needs men. I'll work for him."

"You cannot toil as another's servant," she scolded. She broke free of his embrace, but as she spoke she fingered the cross around her neck. "In my heart I took you for my husband. And in my heart you remain my husband. There will be no other. But though this is so, we must remain apart. We are like a piece of cloth. We are one. But that piece of cloth has been torn in two by what has been done to my nation. Someday, perhaps, we might be mended together. But the tear will always remain. The jagged stitch will always be there. . . ." She could not hold back the tears that welled in her eyes. Jed knew that she felt only affection and no hatred toward him. "You are my man," she said with pride.

"And you are my woman," Jed nodded, unable to keep the tears out of his own eyes.

Sunblossom placed her hand against his cheek and wiped away a tear. Then she raised her hand in a gesture of farewell.

Jed turned his back on Sunblossom and walked back the way he had come through the woods.

As she watched him disappear into the forest, she wondered how she could live with this ache in her heart. "Lo-ve," she stammered in English, for there was no word in the Arikara tongue for what she felt.

Epilogue

Winter in the Wind River Mountains—The lone figure strode across the barren, dazzling white snowscape. Bitter winds which could bring the temperature down to forty below tugged at the woolly, double-thick pte robes belted about his body. The winds pulled at the Hawkens rifle clasped in the crook of his arm, seized the cloth wound about the lower half of his face and the slitted strip of fabric protecting his clear, blue eyes from snow blindness.

He walked his domain, his empire of ice, his world of solitude. In this silent place there was no sound but the wind's whine, and on occasional crack! as ice split the trees open.

He had trapped during the first part of the winter,

but now trapping was done until the spring thaw. He contented himself with the wandering and the hunting for food. The scraping of the pelts he'd already taken. He had gathered plenty of firewood, and chinked the holes in the small cabin he'd built.

All the others had gone downcountry for the winter, but he had refused to go with them. They'd pleaded, saying that the loneliness could make a man insane, but he'd just laughed.

He was never lonely. He had the entire wilderness for company.

They'd shaken their heads, Bill Sublette and Josh Pilcher, and had gone down. He could imagine them telling the tale to old John Clyman, sitting there warm and cozy at the Fort Henry outpost, clucking over the ledge accounts of the free trappers. "Jed is plumb loco, for sure," they'd complain. "Why, nobody for company, nothin' to do. . . ."

"He's that kind, is all," John would mutter. Good old John!

A better man with just one arm than most with two.

Jed was glad he'd hired him. And Sublette and Pilcher, and all the rest. They were all good men who worked for him now. When old General Ashley had retired two years ago, he sold Jed his share of the company. Soon Major Henry went the same way.

So Jed Smith was a rich man now. And not only in coin. He was rich every way it was possible to be wealthy.

Jed paused, squinting through the cloth protecting his eyes. Looked like pte tracks up ahead. Rare for one to be up this high, he thought, but maybe the old bull liked solitude as much as he did. . . .

He primed his rifle and began to stalk the buffalo. It didn't take him long to catch up. It was a bull, big and brawny. The breath huffed out of the brute's snout in twin clouds of vapor.

The Hawkens gun boomed away, and the bull fell over hard. He shook once, and then was still. This one pte would give him meat aplenty for some time to come.

Before he cut into the animal, he gazed out toward the peaks all around him, sparkling like gems in the eggshell-blue sky.

He shoved the butt of his rifle into the snow, cupped his mittened hands to his mouth, and gave a call born of the joy of being alive, *"Yippie-Yay! Hallo!"*

Yippie-Yay! Hallo! the mountains shouted back, polite as you please.

"Lonely," Jed snorted. "Hell. How can a man be lonely with the mountains to talk to?"

With the first cut into the pte, steam rose from the split carcass like meat just pulled from boiling water. Tucking his rifle through his belt, he hoisted a quarter of the beast up onto his shoulders and began to trudge with it home toward his cabin. He'd return tomorrow for the rest.

After the fine roast dinner with dumplings, he made himself a big pot of black coffee, and resumed work on his journal. He had a lot of work left to do. He had to get that story that Hiram had once told him down right and proper. And the lore Charbonneau had given him, and the things he had learned and seen for himself—there was all that to write. It seemed that every time he filled a page, he remembered enough to fill two more. He had already filled quite a few pages about a beautiful fair-haired Ree princess, who was somewhere on the other side of the mountains tending to her people. Hell, she was more a queen than a princess these days, he reckoned.

"Sunblossom! Yer Jed loves you! My woman, my wife!"

The mountains always told him the same thing, but he didn't need their confirmation. Not a night went by in his dreams where he didn't kiss her 'til they both fell asleep. He reckoned she did the same. He'd always had sixth sense about her. . . . Perhaps this spring. . . .

Ah, but old Bill Sublette and Pilcher would be damned surprised come the spring, when he told them what he'd discovered in his ramblings.

It was a pass. The South pass, now locked with snow. It had been discovered and lost and discovered again by men down through time, Jed reckoned. But now he, Jedediah Strong Smith, had found it. It thrilled him to contemplate it.

Old Bill and Josh 'ud come trudgin' up, and he'd say, "*Boys, I found us a way through to the Pacific. What say we git ourselves the best horses we own, and take a little ride, to see what we see. . . .*"

And they'd all go. To see what they'd see. To savor the joys of the open country. To feast on the pleasures of being a wilderness man.